"*Dreams in the Distance* is a big juicy epic n
The Choice series and connects believable cha
and admire as they navigated difficult choices.
bravery, depth—even faith—as they struggle through war, endure death, experience romance, and deal with other life circumstances which drive this intriguing plot. As a follower of C. S. Lewis and J. R. R. Tolkien, I found the ties to these great authors as background characters to be fun and satisfying. This book is full of heart. I look forward to more from this author."

Carolyn Curtis
Award-winning journalist and author, whose latest book is
Women and C.S. Lewis: What his life and literature reveal for today's culture
(Lion Hudson plc, Oxford, England)

"Nan Rinella's great love for C. S. Lewis and for modern British culture come together beautifully in the first of her historical novels, *Dreams in the Distance*, Book 1 of *The Choice* series. She takes you to Oxford in the early 20th century, where her characters rub shoulders with the likes of C. S. Lewis and J. R. R. Tolkien while dealing with the challenges from the war, the challenges to their faith, and the challenges of finding a lasting love. This story is entertaining, inspiring, and thought-provoking."

Terry Glaspey
Editor and author of a dozen books including
C.S. Lewis: His Life & Thought;
Not a Tame Lion: The Spiritual Legacy of C.S. Lewis and the Chronicles of Narnia;
and *75 Masterpieces Every Christian Should Know: The Fascinating Stories behind Great Works of Art, Literature, Music, and Film*

"*Dreams in the Distance* is a novel of love and war, faith and doubt, intellect and insight. Fans of J.R.R. Tolkien and C.S. Lewis will be charmed by the interweaving of familiar Oxfordshire settings and by the appearance of these literary giants as secondary characters. Throughout, author Nan Rinella displays her passion for history and literature, and for the research that brings it together."

Joy Jordan-Lake
Part-time professor and the author of the bestselling novel
A Tangled Mercy, as well as the award-winning
Blue Hole Back Home and other books

"It was a pleasure to see the fruition of Nan Rinella's study of C.S. Lewis and J.R.R. Tolkien and their works. She has breathed life into the memory of these spiritual giants. It was a joy to experience their company again as they acted as spiritual mentors to her characters. *Dreams in the Distance* should appeal to Lewis/Tolkien devotees and draw readers to further explore their lives and works."

Steven Elmore
Vice President of Events & Communications,
C.S. Lewis Foundation

Make your choice, adventurous Stranger,
Strike the bell and bide the danger,
Or wonder, till it drives you mad,
What would have followed if you had?

The Magician's Nephew,
C. S. Lewis (1898–1963)

THE CHOICE

THE SERIES

NAN RINELLA

Two roads diverged in a yellow wood,
And sorry I could not travel both
And be one traveler, long I stood
And looked down one as far as I could
To where it bent in the undergrowth . . .

The Road Not Taken,
Robert Frost (1874–1963)

DREAMS IN THE DISTANCE

BOOK ONE

NAN RINELLA

DREAMS in the DISTANCE
© Copyright 2019 by Nancy D. Rinella. All rights reserved.

All rights reserved. No part of this publication may be reproduced or transmitted by any means or in any form including but not limited to electronic, photocopy, or recording without the prior written permission from the author. Brief quotations in printed reviews are considered an exception and permissible.

This volume is a work of fiction. Characters and incidents are a product of my imagination. Historical characters and events are used fictitiously. Any resemblance to actual persons (living or dead), events, or locales is entirely coincidental. Except for certain beloved dogs and cats who have granted their permission.

DUBLIN Press

Cover design by Paul Trif of TwinArtDesign
Interior design by Jonathan Price Design

Printed in the United States of America

ISBN 978-1-7337141-0-5

*I dedicate THE CHOICE series
to the British and American veterans of WWII
who had to remake their lives anew after the war.
Thank you for your service.*

*Bless you Uncle John Stewart Donnelly (96 at this printing),
who flew a P-26 Marauder, a light bomber,
for the US Army Air Forces.*

*I dedicate this book to my husband, Joseph Rinella,
for his enduring patience.*

*And to my parents, Mary Helen and Buzz Dublin,
for making it possible for me to embark
on my second career of writing.*

TABLE OF CONTENTS

Introduction 1
Prologue: The War 3

   i.   A Noble Brother 5
  ii.   A Scottish Lad 13
 iii.   A California Yankee 23
 iv.   Two Daughters 33

  1.   The Vicar's Daughter 35
  2.   The Challenge of Job 39
  3.   The Earl's Daughter 45
  4.   A Decision 53
  5.   The Chauvinist and the Feminist 57
  6.   Worldly Lures Versus Heavenly Tenets 63
  7.   Not Always Black and White 69
  8.   Beauty and the Brain 75
  9.   Unwelcome Visitors 79
10.   The Weight of Love 85
11.   Dreams 91
12.   Cinderella Hopes 95
13.   Expectations 101
14.   The Bomb and Best Wishes 105
15.   The Ball 113
16.   Meow 119
17.   In Fate's Footsteps 125

18.	A Day Like No Other	129
19.	Crushed	137
20.	Gone	141
21.	The Uncle	149
22.	Dark Dreams	153
23.	Ruth	159
24.	Treasure Chest	163
25.	Lilies and Laid to Rest	167
26.	Between Sorrow and Sadness	173
27.	The Memorial	183
28.	International Incident	187
29.	Whisperers	199
30.	Dark Night of the Soul	207
31.	A Fire Within	217
32.	The Brother	225
33.	Tea and Talk of Cold War	237
34.	Lily in Wonderland	245
35.	The Interview	253
36.	Celebration	259
37.	Separate Paths	263
38.	Voices of Fear	271
39.	Goodbyes	277

Discussion Questions	283
Acknowledgments	285
About the Author	287

INTRODUCTION
TO
THE CHOICE
THE SERIES

Choices make or break us.
What voices are influencing our choices?
Why do we take one path over another at the fork in the road?

> Literature is a luxury; fiction is a necessity.
> *Laughter and Humility,* G. K. Chesterton (1874–1936)

In my opinion, there's no better way to appreciate history than reading authentic historical fiction. They say that *experience* is the best teacher, *but it doesn't have to be your own.* Human nature hasn't changed since Adam and Eve. History *does repeat itself* and offers much we can learn and benefit from, whether from our own experience or while perusing the lives of those who lived it—both real and imagined.

> History often resembles myth, because they are both
> ultimately of the same stuff.
> *On Fairy-stories,* J. R. R. Tolkien (1892–1973)

I've always relished digesting history in a feast of delectable fiction. Exceedingly scrumptious are the thick tomes of James Michener, Herman Wouk, Leon Uris, Michael Phillips, Edward Rutherfurd, and, of course, Tolkien.
The Lord of the Rings was not historical, you say? Oh, but it was, just not of our world—exactly.

Michael Phillips dedicated his 1999/2000 Caledonia series to the memory of Michener. In his Introduction, Phillips quoted the master of the historical novel from his autobiography, *The World Is My Home*:

> When people tire of the forty-eight-minute television novel, they will yearn for a substantial book within whose covers they can live imaginatively for weeks. The eighteenth-century, discursive-type novel will enjoy a vigorous rebirth, because readers demand it.
>
> James A. Michener (1907–1997)

Michener thought this true in the 1950s and gambled his professional life on it. The rest is history. Beginning with Book One of THE CHOICE series, I'm banking on the pendulum effect and a resurgence of the fluent and expansive-type novel again. I hope you enjoy the journey.

Caledonia touched my Scottish soul. My Irish heart grieved at Ireland's melancholy history in Uris's *Trinity* and Rutherfurd's *The Dublin Saga* (Dublin is my family surname). Michener's *Texas* functioned as my tutor when I migrated from Los Angeles to Amarillo in 1991. Wouk's World War II novels brought that era alive.

I especially owe so much to J. R. R. Tolkien and C. S. Lewis, whose lives and works have influenced my life and writing. Through them, God illuminated the way of this "hobbit in Narnia."

> To construct plausible and moving 'other worlds' you must draw on the only real 'other world' we know, that of the Spirit.
>
> *Of Other Worlds,* C. S. Lewis

Frank E. Peretti and Randy Alcorn introduced me to the angelic beings who accompany us in this life, influencing our choices—toward the light or the darkness. Ted Dekker is today's prophet with his fantastical, speculative, otherworldly novels. They helped me recognize those competing voices that whisper in the ears of our hearts and minds—*the voices*. And, I wonder dear reader, *who has your ear?*

Join me at NanRinella.org for ongoing discussions of the relevancy of those voices in our lives today as they influence our choices.

PROLOGUE:

THE WAR

World War Two (WWII) began on the European front when German troops invaded Poland on 1 September 1939. Then on 3 September, Britain and France declared war on Germany.

When the Reverend Jonathan Whitely tried to explain war to his young daughter, Lily, she couldn't understand. But as the bombs began to fall, she and her best friend, Philomena Claiborne, became convinced that dragons were real, breathing fire from the sky.

For Phila's father, Rear Admiral Henry Claiborne, this meant another separation from his family when his destroyer deployed to the Atlantic. As she had during WWI, his wife, Beatrice, waited and prayed for his safe return.

After France fell to Germany on 22 June 1940, the soldiers of the 51st Highland Division were taken captive. Master Sergeant Duncan MacWhirter of the Seaforth Highlanders managed, along with a few others, to escape and help rebuild the new 51st Division. Training raw recruits proved challenging given hotheads like 6'6" tall O. C. Ogilvie, who had enlisted with his cousin, Sandy. As the invasion of Great Britain appeared imminent, the Seaforth Highlanders trained and remained in Scotland for a year to defend the northeast coast against the potential German invasion that never came.

Rather, in an effort to destroy British air power, the German Luftwaffe conducted unrelenting air raids from July through September 1940, beginning with the ports and air bases. On June 4, 1940, Prime Minister Winston Churchill said:

> The Battle of Britain is about to begin—We shall fight with growing confidence and growing strength in the air, we shall defend our Island, whatever the cost may be. We shall fight on the beaches, we shall fight on the landing grounds,

we shall fight in the fields and in the streets, we shall fight in the hills; we shall never surrender!

Burning with a desire to be a pilot Lily's brother, Flying Officer Benjamin Whitely, joined the Royal Air Force. The RAF's resounding victory over the Luftwaffe, despite the loss of many of its pilots in The Battle of Britain, forced Germany to shift night raid targets to London, other cities, and industrial centers. The Blitz lasted from September 1940 to May 1941. The first day of bombing, 7 September, caught Admiral Claiborne's eighteen-year-old son, Hugh, and eight-year-olds Phila and Lily returning from the Tower of London. Soon after, like many children in London, they were sent to the country to keep them safe, while Hugh returned to Cambridge University before joining the Royal Navy a couple years later.

By the time the United States entered the war, most of Europe had been occupied by Germany. O. C. (Ollie) finally got his chance to fight and demonstrate a courageous disregard for his own life in North Africa.

On 7 December 1941, the Japanese bombed the American fleet at Pearl Harbor, Hawaii, which launched the fight in the Pacific and brought America into the European theater. The US Army's Eighth Air Forces bombers and fighters flew missions from England over the Continent. California hotshot Lieutenant Daniel McCauley achieved his childhood dream, promoted to team leader of a fighter squadron.

WWII ended in the European theater on 7 May 1945 when Germany surrendered.

After the battles and bombs had ceased, the scars of war cut deep across the land and souls. Post-Traumatic Stress Disorder, PTSD, was yet to be diagnosed, however, both Ollie and Dan contended with the symptoms of what was then known as "battle fatigue." Regardless, Hugh envied the heroes and their honors.

Change was in the air as Brits tried to put the war behind them looking ahead to prosperity and peace. As society became less rigid and more reverential—Phila and Lily, Ollie, Dan, and Hugh began to wonder, might their dreams be possible?

i
A NOBLE BROTHER

> My armor is like tenfold shields, my teeth are swords, my claws spears, the shock of my tail a thunderbolt, my wings a hurricane, and my breath death!
>
> Smaug, the dragon
> *The Hobbit*, J. R. R. Tolkien

1940
7 September, 4:30 p.m.
Tower Bridge spanning the River Thames, London
A loud wail split the air.

Suddenly, Lily's delight in seeing the Crown Jewels and the Tower of London turned to fright. She glanced up at Phila's brother.

"Air raid siren." Hugh Claiborne scanned the sky. "That's just ace! I'm playing nanny to two little girls and the Luftwaffe is bombing the docks again. Why couldn't I have been back at university?" He looked down at the eight-year-olds, then smiled sheepishly. "Sorry. Let's make a dash for the Tube station, just to play it safe." He grasped their hands.

Blood-curdling shrieks whistled around them.

"Hughie!" Phila screamed. *"Dragons!"*

Thunder boomed behind them, again and again, seizing Lily with panic. Hugh howled. "The docks my eye; the target is us!" He yanked her arm. Phila screeched. "Hughie, I can't keep up!"

He picked up his sister with one arm, dragging Lily with the other.

A huge boom burst around them sending hot pebbles raining down. An ear-piercing whine shot terror through her.

"The dragons are coming to eat you, little girl!"

Hugh shoved Lily and Phila down and dived on top of them as a dragon roared by shaking the sidewalk, stinging their ears. Lily's hands and knees hurt; Hugh's body pressed her into the cement, so she could hardly breathe. The dragon's hot breath burned.

After what seemed forever a small hand gripped hers, pulling her out from under Hugh. Phila hugged her. Shaking in the still darkness, they fretted: Will the dragons come back?

Lily couldn't see anything for the thick, pinkish smoke. It was hot and hard to breathe. Her eyes burned. Both children coughed and sneezed. Together they turned Hugh over. He didn't move. They felt his face. His eyes were closed, and his forehead and hair gooey wet. She froze with fear.

"He's dead. You're all alone."

Strangers bumped into them. "Help!" Lily yelled, but she couldn't hear herself. "Dear Jesus, help us please!"

The earth shook again and again, but she couldn't hear anything. Thick smoke swirled around them, showering them with hot dust. She clung to Phila as they huddled over Hugh.

A big hand gripped Lily's shoulder. "I'll help you." The voice comforted her.

The huge shadow man lifted Hugh, telling the girls to hold onto his jacket and follow close.

Just as his coattails led them to the station entrance, everything went whoosh like being caught in a crashing wave at the seaside. Only instead of rushing water, the burning breath of the dragon pushed Lily down the stairs. She bumped into the big man. Arms thrust her down as something flew in from above.

Panting and shivering, Lily gaped at ghostlike creatures squeezed together against the walls of the tunnel. Two white ghosts made room for them. The man carried Phila over and set her down, then went back for Hugh.

Wide-eyed, Phil babbled swinging her hand back and forth and making motions like when they played charades. Her hand flew back and—*flew!* "It was *you* who flew in." She pointed to Phila, who nodded. Oh, my goodness! They couldn't hear each other.

The girls huddled together in the eerie silence. Lily felt the floor shake over and over, but still no sound. The man began singing hymns. Comforted, she relaxed some.

After ever so long, the shaking stopped, and the trains started running again. The man, toting Hugh, helped them on and off cars all the way to Victoria Station.

Coming up from the Tube, they took deep breaths of fresh air. Lily saw a red glow far away and billowing pink smoke. Her eyes smarted. The white stuff covered everyone except the big man. He carried Hugh to the Claiborne's flat. At their knock, the door opened.

"Mummy!" Lily ran into her arms, then Father's. Poor Phila, her father was at sea. But her Uncle Rayner carried Hugh inside. Phila's mum hugged her daughter.

Even in front of the roaring fire and after cups of honeyed tea, both girls still shivered. Mum had just finished tending to their cuts and bruises when her head jerked up. Her lips mouthed "air raid siren" as she pointed to the ceiling. Fear knifed through Lily.

The dragons are coming back to get you.

Grabbing their hands, Mum hurried them downstairs where they joined others dashing for the shelters. Lily and Phila clung to their mums through the long night, huddled together with Lily's little brother, Stevie, and a couple of servants. Father had gone with Phila's uncle and his chauffeur to take Hugh to hospital.

A year earlier, when Father explained that England had declared war on Germany, Lily couldn't understand what that meant. Now she knew. Dragons are real.

Sirens. Big booms. Hot rain falling. Fires. Every night. Frightened all the time, she wouldn't leave her mum's side at home or in the shelters. When she slept, she often woke crying from wretched dreams of fire-breathing dragons.

Phila's Uncle Ray was an earl with a country house in Oxfordshire. After a week of bombing, he had sent his chauffeur to collect Lily, her mum, and little Stevie to drive them to Rivenwood, along with the Countess, Phila, and her mum. The Earl, Father, and Phila's young Aunt Audrey remained in London. An ambulance delivered Hugh along with a nursing sister to care for him. He hadn't woken since being hurt.

19 October
Rivenwood on Thame, Oxfordshire

Lily sat with Hugh. Phila was in the toilet.

Lily closed her eyes. "Please, Jesus, bring Hugh back to us."

"Lily?"

"Yes, Lord? Here I am." Just like Samuel in the Bible. God's talking to me. She got all tingly.

"Lily?" But wouldn't God's voice be stronger? She peeked.

"Lily." Hugh's eyes were open.

"Hughie."

He looked around. "Phila?"

"We're fine. You saved our lives. You're a hero, Hughie."

"I am?" He grinned.

"Thank heaven, you've come back."

"From where?"

"Oh, Hughie, you've been un-con-scious." She pronounced the last word carefully. "We've been so worried."

"Where are we?"

"At Rivenwood. The Germans are bombing London . . . every night."

"What day is it?" Hugh raised up. Turning pale, he fell back on the pillow.

"The nineteenth of October."

"That's got to be—"

"Six whole weeks."

He blinked and looked like he would be ill.

Phila burst into the room. "Who are you talking to?"

"Hugh."

"Hughie!"

The nursing sister rushed in and hustled the girls off.

20 October

Phila knocked on Hugh's door, then peeked in. "Can we see Hughie now?"

Mum pushed a lock of hair off his forehead.

"Mum, I'm not a little boy anymore. Please, I'm eighteen!" Hugh sat in an overstuffed chair, looking pasty and ever so thin, with his long legs stretched out on an ottoman.

"Sorry, darling, but you'll always be my boy." Her eyes glistened. "Your father is going to be so proud. Although, he will be upset with me for allowing you three to go to the Tower. But then, how were we to know that was the very moment the Germans would begin this ghastly bombing?"

Mum stepped away as the two girls drew up chairs on either side of Hugh.

"OK, ladies, tell me what happened."

"Flying dragons." Lily shuddered. "Breathing fire and brimstone. We couldn't see or hear anything."

Phila shrunk back as Guilt lashed out at her again. *"It's all your fault Hugh was hurt."*

Tears crowded her eyes. "I thought I'd killed you."

He opened his arms and she fell into them.

"Now, now, lovey, it's OK. Here I am alive in the flesh." He held her tight as she pulled herself together, sniffing.

Phila gazed up into his face. "I insisted on taking Lily to see the Crown Jewels and Mum made you take us. And then, I had to stop for lemon squashes by the Tower Bridge." She had cried herself to sleep nearly every night since, trying to stuff her fists in her ears to stop the frightful voices yammering at her.

"Water under the bridge." He ruffled her hair. "Did you hear that? I made a pun."

Phila managed a weak smile.

"Yes, darling," Mum peeled her from Hugh, hugging her, "you must stop berating yourself. Let's just thank God you all are fine."

"Your face was a gooey mess," said Lily.

"Do I look bad?"

Lily shook her head. "Not anymore. You're as pretty as ever, Hughie."

He felt the scar on his forehead and grinned.

Hugh's not upset?

Lily tittered. "I asked Jesus to help us, and he sent an angel — He carried you and took us home. And then he —"

"Just disappeared. Poof!"

"Dragons and an angel, really Petunia?" He'd given her that nickname at her birth because of her red and wrinkly appearance — like the flower. Later their mum shortened it to Pet.

"Honest!" Lily bobbed her head. "And he caught Phil when she flew down into the station."

"Really Mum, you shouldn't let the girls take pretending this far."

"No Hugh, it's true. Apparently, the blast blew Pet in. The doctor at hospital said it was possible."

"See Hughie, I did fly. So there."

"What did this man look like?"

Phila beamed. "A giant!"

"And he sang hymns to us." Lily's eyes danced. "We had to sit on the floor in the Underground for—"

"Hours and hours waiting for the trains to run again."

"So many people. We were all stuffed together like sardines and—"

"It was so still, really eerie."

"But you could hear the man singing?" He cocked an eyebrow.

"Because he was an angel, Hughie Louie!" Phila glared at him. "*And*, for your information, all of us were covered in this horrid ash, but he wasn't."

"Clean as a whistle." Lily folded her arms.

Hugh raised both eyebrows in disbelief as the sister entered, to shoo the girls away, again.

Later that evening
Hugh returned the hand mirror to Mum, grinning. He could hardly wait to get back to Cambridge. His mates would be so impressed with his scar.

After a quick knock, Phila tripped ahead of Lily, waving a book at Hugh. "Will you read *The Hobbit* now that you have time?"

"I won't be bored enough to read a children's story."

"Darling, I think you would find Dr. Tolkien's story has merit for adults." Mum gave him *the look*.

Hugh groused. "Fantasy. Dragons and angels?"

"There aren't angels in the book." Phila glowered.

"Dragons?"

"Of course."

Mum narrowed her eyes, frowning. She had explained how the girls were so terrified of the bombing that the only way they could fathom it was to liken it to being attacked by dragons.

A wave of guilt washed over him, but only for a moment.

OK, the girls were traumatized and not recalling correctly. "Surely, Mum, the man was only a good Samaritan."

She shrugged her shoulders, a cockeyed expression on her face. "Darling, what can I say? Rayner opened the door, you fell into his arms, and Pet and Lily rushed in. Neither your uncle, Lily's mother and father, nor I saw a man or an angel. I accept their story."

"You're not buying this, are you?"

Hugh stared at her.

Skepticism jeered. *"Of course, your mum would believe it was an angel."*

He must have a quizzical expression on his face. "Hugh, we do entertain angels unaware. The girls couldn't hear us, and the next day at hospital the doctor said they were suffering from blast-induced hearing loss. It was days before they could hear normally."

Phila and Lily bobbed their heads, grinning.

"You're not going to win the argument against this lot."

"What about me?"

"That is another curious tale and miraculous, as well." Mum's eyes sparkled. "The next morning Jignesh related what a frightening time they had driving you to hospital. The streets were chaotic with the blackout and all the emergency vehicles screaming past. He said a policeman hopped on the car's fender, making sure they arrived safe."

Hugh chuckled, picturing his uncle's old Indian chauffeur telling the story.

"But, was it a *real* bobby?" Phila's expression dared him, "or another angel?"

Lily's face paled. "We were so scared you would die."

Close call, huh? "Didn't Uncle Ray tell the doctor he was the Earl of Wembley, and his nephew could not die before getting the chance to join the Navy and fight *and* that his father was commanding a destroyer defending the merchant ships in the Atlantic?"

"Oh, darling. Ray was splendid. It gives your father such peace to know he's looking after us. When I heard on the wireless about the bombing, I rang him, and he came straight away. We had no idea where you were, but I knew you would bring the girls home."

"Apparently, *they* brought *me* home with the help of an angel." He winked. "Now what about this bombing, Mum?"

Phila burst forth. "They're calling the seventh of September 'Black Saturday,' and the bombing in London 'the Blitz.'" She jutted out her chin.

"That's for the German *blitzkrieg*, which means 'lightning war.'"

"Yes, Londoners are sending their children to the country."

Phila wrinkled her nose. "It's been *forty-seven* straight nights."

Hugh frowned. "Will the Navy have told the men at sea?" Dad would be concerned.

"I imagine so, darling."

"You haven't sent word of our . . . misadventure, have you?"

"No, I saw no reason to add to his burdens."

"Good." Phewww.

21 October

Hugh sat staring out the window, trying to make sense of the sketchy impressions teasing his memory. Dreams? Had he imagined Dad giving him a scrubbing for deserting his command of watching after the girls. What about seeing Zeus again?

He dropped his arm to scratch behind Neptune's ears. The black lab licked his hand. "I think I got to say goodbye to your sire, boy." Zeus had died while he'd been at university.

The girls trooped in.

"Now that I've saved your lives for some grand future, ladies, what are you going to do with them?"

Lily beamed. "I'm going to make gorgeous gowns for noble ladies."

"And I'm going to write books and go to Oxford."

"To *the other place*, Petunia? Why?"

"Because *you're* going to Cambridge."

ii
A SCOTTISH LAD

> Be sure it is not for nothing that the Landlord has knit our hearts so closely to time and place—to one friend rather than another and one shire more than all the land.
>
> *The Pilgrim's Regress*, C. S. Lewis

1942
23 October
North Africa, northwest of Cairo
Egyptian railway halt of El Alamein
"Ye know the trouble with you, Private Ogilvie, is that ye make such a conspicuous target." Master Sergeant MacWhirter looked up at the six-foot, six-inch recruit. "Laddie, keep your head down and your helmet on covering that red thatch of yours. Ye're only eighteen, and I'd really hate to lose ye in your first battle."

The soldiers standing around Ogilvie guffawed. "Leuk, his lugs are red."

Blast me big ears. Ollie could never hide embarrassment, which in turn would launch a tirade from Ridicule.

"But, that's the plan, dochtless daenaguid. *Charge bravely forward. Die heroically. Make your father proud after all your rebellion. Make your life count for something."*

More often than he could recall, Fergus had called him a worthless ne'er-do-well. Would his brither regret how badly he had treated him? Mam would miss him and Da. Too late to think of that now.

When Ollie couldn't stomach his brother's verbal abuse any longer, while Da was in London, he abandoned Arbroath and headed for the Highlands and his mother's clan. He and his cousin, Sandy, also seventeen, joined the Seaforth Highlanders to fight the Germans. They trained and remained in Scotland for a year on the northeast coast as defense for a potential German invasion that thankfully never came.

Whenever Ollie got bored, trouble beckoned, pestering his brain. But the sarge kept a tight rope on his new charges. They respected him and held him in awe.

The recruits had heard of the devastating defeat and subsequent surrender the 152nd Brigade in France in June 1940; how over 10,000 soldiers were taken prisoner by the Germans and marched through Belgium to Poland, sometimes loaded into canal barges or in cattle wagons on trains; how there were some remarkable escapes early on; and how, of the 290 who made it back to Britain by summer 1941, 134 were infantrymen of the 51st Highland Division—one of which was Sergeant Duncan MacWhirter.

※ ※ ※

The first battle of El Alamein in July 1942 had been considered a draw. Field Marshall Bernard Montgomery intended to be victorious in the second battle over the Germans and Italians.

"You have the honor to be part of the new 51st." Sarge had looked each man in the eyes. "I did not escape to ever surrender again to the Germans. We will avenge our lads, then bring them home." They had landed in North Africa in August just in time to join the battle.

※ ※ ※

For five and a half hours, British guns shelled the German and Italian lines. Then the infantry advanced, picking their way through the anti-tank minefields. Sarge had told them that men were too light to set off the mines.

"Maybe for these smaller lads, but a giant like you?"

The taunt threatened to invade Ollie's bravado.

Then when the tanks advanced, they stirred up so much sand and dirt the infantrymen couldn't see at all. Why did he expect there would be order like in training? Instead chaos. Tanks bogging down and running into each other. Ollie lost track of his mates.

Just after dawn, huge explosions erupted all around him, shooting sand spiraling like geysers. He hit the ground, his heart threatening to jump out of his chest. Smoke swirled around him. His eyes burned. He rubbed them, peering ahead at vague shapes. Panzers. He froze; fear tearing at his gut.

"Afraid to die, coward?"

"Scairt?"

Aye. He glanced around to see who said that. But only a wee chap in a kilt and bonnet stood there.

"I reckon ye'll finally be tastin' fear. Gude."

Ollie blinked. "Ye better git doon. Noo, ye'll be tellin' me who ye are?"

"A messenger."

"From whom?"

"The Awmichtie."

"Almighty God?"

"Aye."

"You're seeing things. Ignore him."

More artillery exploded around them, raining down sand. "Ye better git doon, anyway."

"Na need, laddie. You, on the t'ither hand, are in grave danger."

"Tell me somethun I dinna ken."

"Ye need to ken ye're in danger of losin' your immortal soul, laddie."

"Ye'll be tellin' me I'm gaun to be dyin', noo?"

"Let's juist say if ye du, ye'll be lost."

"Dinna go throwin' me brither's God-talk at me."

"Nay, your brither is no a gude example of a godly mon. But ye'll be considerin' your fither to be one, aye?"

"Aye, he be that."

"Weel then, will ye be thinkin' he wants his mac destined tae perdition?"

"Nay. Da wadna."

"Nay, he most certainly doesna! He'll be on his knees a prayin' at this verra moment frae you, laddie."

"An' how du ye ken?"

"I've always thocht you to be a bricht lad, but . . . the Awmichtie sent me to tell ye to make your choice."

"What choice?"

Doubt niggled. *"You've been hit in the head and are imagining this."*

"To be choosin' right noo to be a child of our heivenly Fither instead of the child of the devil ye hae been."

More explosions, kicking up sand. Ollie saw a soldier thrown in the air, dropping right in front of him.

"Ogilvie, what's wrong wi' ye? Git movin'!" His mates moved on ahead. "Weel, laddie?"

I'm gaun to die. "OK. I choose God." He grabbed his rifle and followed the others.

"Och, laddie! This glorious death wish of yours? It's a lie frae the enemy. Ye really want to be stabbin' your fither through his heart?"

First week in November
Much to his surprise, Ollie was still alive, a seasoned warrior, and the casualties had been enormous. They continued to clash with Panzer units.

8 November
51st Division Medical Operations, Marina El Alamein
Ollie came to in pain. *If I'm hurting, I'm no dead.*

"Private Ogilvie?" A gentle voice broke through the fog. Ollie opened his eyes to soft brown hair framing a smiling face and deep brown eyes that bathed him in comfort.

"You're awake. Welcome back, Private."

Ollie pushed his arms down to raise up, but stabs of pain shot through his chest, shoulder, and hand, forcing him back down.

"No, don't try to move, Private, you'll start bleeding again. You were hit in the chest and arm. It's a blessing that the shrapnel didn't hit organs, but only lacerated muscle and bruised bones. Still, it will take time to heal, so just rest."

"Who?" She wore desert gear, second lieutenant bars on her shoulders.

"I'm your nursing sister, Glenda Goodfellow."

English. "Lieutenant." *And pretty.*

"I'm a nurse before an officer. What is your Christian name, Private?"

"Och na, Ma'am. I dinna tell."

She squinted at him. "Really? That bad?"

"Aye, Ma'am, 'tis." She had a pretty smile.

"What do people call you?"

"Ogilvie, Ma'am."

"Not the Army, soldier, your friends and family."

"O.C. or Ollie."

"That's better, Ollie." She said it nice.

"Whaur's the latrine, Ma'am?"

"You can't get up just yet. I'll bring it to you."

That unwelcome rush of heat invaded his chest, face, and ears.

She smiled kindly. "Don't be embarrassed, Ollie."

"Humiliating, isn't it?"

He swore he could hear cackling.

A couple of soldiers in the next cots guffawed. "Better be gittin' used to it, laddie," jibed one. "Wait'll she gies ye a bath."

"Ogilvie, ye blush like a wumman," jeered another.

By now his whole body burned. He cussed at them.

After he'd relieved himself and the lieutenant took the receptacle away, she returned to change his dressings.

"You're awfully warm, Ollie." She took his temperature. "Seven degrees above normal." He heard snickers.

"Lieutenant!" A familiar voice blasted the quiet.

"Yes Sir."

"Where's Ogilvie?"

"Over here, Sir." She pushed on his good shoulder to keep him down.

Captain Dunbar stomped up to Ollie's cot. "Damn, Ogilvie, don't you ever think before you act?"

"Naw, Sir, I'd git scairt."

"You won't make it to twenty-one, Private."

"Och, Captain, 'twas only twa tanks, an' I'm too big an' ugly tae kill."

"Keep thinking that way, and you will be." His bark softened. "How is he, Lieutenant?"

"If he follows orders, Sir, we'll have him right as rain."

"He will!" The captain glared at him. "You accommodated yourself bravely saving your mates and leading the charge. Grenades wouldn't have taken tanks out, so using satchel charges was smart thinking. But running up and attaching them to the tanks was barking mad. I have battles to win and don't have time to write up commendations, so no more heroics, *Corporal* Ogilvie. Walk with me, Lieutenant."

Ollie twisted his head watching them go. She was taller than Dunbar. Promoted!

When she returned, she smiled, her eyes shining.

"Ma'am am I really OK?"

"Absolutely, Ollie."

"Then whae was that aboot? Ma'am?"

"He asked exactly what your wounds were, then told me what you did." He flushed again. "But he sure was angry."

"You know why, don't you?"

"Officers hate losing their men."

"He cares."

"Dinna make me laugh, it hurts."

A week later
"When are you going to call me by my name, Ollie?"

"Are ye a Christian, Lieutenant?"

"Yes. Are you?"

"I dinna actually ken wither I was or no, but there was a moment oot there when the question cum oop."

"That's not uncommon." She pulled up a stool.

"Me fither is a godly mon, however, me brither goes to kirk but acts like the devil t'itherwise. I kinda reckoned it wasna frae me."

"I'm sorry."

"Thenk ye."

"Ironic, isn't it. Jesus said people would know we are his followers by the love we have for one another." Her eyes shone. "The Germans are Christians. They go to church but look what they are doing. We are Christians too, but we are killing each other. We go to church and pray for victory."

"That's no new, Protestants and Catholics, Scots and English, hae been killin' each other frae centuries, no to mention the Jews."

"Yes, the rumors coming out of Poland—it's inconceivable that humans can do such things to each other. When are we ever going to stop killing?"

"Lieutenant, that's the thing, ye see. Why wud God permit this if He *is* God?"

"Glenda, my name is Glenda, Ollie."

A hoot rang out. "Hey, Lieutenant, how cum ye be gien' Ogilvie so mooch attention?" The guffaws moved through the tent. Heat rushed to Ollie's face and ears. "It's no like he's sum lady killer."

The lieutenant stood up and faced the other cots. "You listen up, jocks!" Ollie glanced around at their wide eyes and dropped jaws.

She strode around the tent peering into their faces. "Do you men believe in God? If you don't, you should. You're alive when others aren't. Corporal Ogilvie and I are discussing the Almighty. Would you care to join us?"

Silence.

She returned to his cot. "Do you read, Ollie?"

"Aye, Ma'am."

"I've a book you might like."

The next day she brought it to him. "It's by another man who goes by his initials — C. S. Lewis. *The Pilgrim's Regress* might interest you. It's akin to Mr. Lewis's fantastical rendition of his search for meaning and spiritual fulfillment."

As Ollie recovered, they enjoyed discussing that book, as well as the writings of George MacDonald, G. K. Chesterton, and others. The strength of her faith made an impact on him.

On a break Glenda joined him in the sitting area. "Ollie, you are educated, well read, and I suspect genteel born. Why aren't you an officer?"

He blanched. "Och, I'm juist a regular jock."

"No, you're not. I suspect you're a chameleon like that gecko that just ran under your foot, changing color with different backgrounds."

"Ye're callin' me a lizard, are ye?" He winced like he was hurt.

She giggled. "Ollie, you speak with a broad Scottish burr when you're talking with your mates, but the longer you spend with me the more you use proper English. That says you're not a regular jock."

"Oh, that? It's just I'm double-tongued. I speak English wi' the English, Scots wi' the jocks, and Gáidhlig — Gaelic — in the Hielands."

"No, it's not just that. You are masquerading. Why?" Her eyes penetrated him like his mam did when she suspected him of trying to hoodwink her.

"I've got me reasons." Should I trust her? "Can ye accept that . . . for noo?"

"Yes, Ollie I can — *for now.*" She smiled, patting his good hand.

Whenever she touched him, the strangest sensation stirred up his insides. Glenda had touched his soul as well. He could actually believe in her God.

A month later
Ollie paced outside the medic tent waiting for Glenda to finish her duties.

Doubt assailed him. *"Do you actually think she cares that you're leaving?"*

When he saw her, the sun came out and warmed him all through.

"I came to say thenk ye an' gude bye." The idea of not seeing her again had kept him awake for nights. He'd hardly been able to think of anything else but her. Is this love?

"Idiot! An officer love a regular jock? Ha!"

They walked out of the compound by the marina. Tall for a woman, the top of her head almost reached his shoulders. The sun sank into the Mediterranean Sea. Twilight, the time of the gloaming, a magical time in Scotland, woke sensations of expectation in him.

"No woman could ever love your ugly mug."

Git ootta me head, Fergus.

But when Glenda had told him he was ruggedly handsome, and his red hair became him, Ollie felt worthwhile for the first time in his life. He had smiled from protruding ear to protruding ear.

Early on while she was changing the dressing on his wound, she'd asked about the large tattoo on his chest.

"My mates an' I had them doon on a lark a few years ago. I'm a Lowlander. Our ancestors in ancient times were the Picts, the 'Painted People.' They tattooed their clan crests on their chests an' painted their faces when they went into battle." It seemed so juvenile now, and he had wanted to appear mature for this grown woman.

He looked down at Glenda attempting to memorize everything about her. Her smile sent sparks through his body.

She gazed up at him. "I don't want to say goodbye."

His neck, face, and ears burned. "But I have to return to me unit."

"I know. I don't want to say goodbye *forever*. I want you to come back to me."

"Ye want me to cum back wounded again?"

"Absolutely not! Don't you dare get hurt again!" Glenda was the same age as his older sister and sounded just like her for a moment. The last thing he wanted would be her mothering him like Maegan?

"Will you come visit, if you can?"

He didn't know what to say. His heart stuck in his throat. His gut twisted.

His ears rang. He studied her pretty face.

Her smile twitched, and her eyes glistened. "Ollie, I've never known anyone like you."

"This muckle, ye mean?"

"You are a big man, but I don't mean in size."

He wrinkled his brow. "I dinna—"

"Do you really not know?"

He shook his head.

"Ollie, have you never been in love?"

"Naw, dinna think so."

"How about now?"

He gulped. "Is this love?"

"Oh, yes, dear boy, it is. I love you, Ollie. Do you feel the same way?"

"But ye're an officer an' I'm juist a wee corporal. It's against regulations."

"Love knows no rank. After the war I will be a nurse, and you will be whatever you make up your mind to be. Have you thought more about that?"

"Da wants me to go to Oxford like he did."

"You gecko, you." She'd found him out. "Then, that's what you should do." She reached up her arms pulling his head down to hers and waited, her eyes inviting. He kissed her.

"That wasn't so difficult, was it?"

He wrapped his arms around her and couldn't get enough of kissing her.

"Write me, and come back to me, Ollie."

"I will, Glenda." For the first time since joining the Army, Ollie wanted to live.

iii
A CALIFORNIA YANKEE

> Men are not angered by mere misfortune but by misfortune conceived as injury. And the sense of injury depends on the feeling that a legitimate claim has been denied.
> *The Screwtape Letters,* C. S. Lewis

1945
Sunday, 18 March
Over the English Channel
US Eighth Air Force raids Berlin

"This is big!" Pride gushed.

"Your Mom's 'Danny Boy' is right in the middle of the big show, starring as the brave newly promoted squadron commander flying the racehorse of the fighter fleet."

Hot dog! Hollywood would make a movie of it after the war. Born in "Tinsel Town," after all, and the son of an actress, that was the way Dan's mind played.

Dan had flown his former "Jug," the P-47 Thunderbolt on bomber escort duty since deploying to England in '42. However, the plane lacked the range needed to protect sustainable bombing deep into Germany. B-17 losses were horrendous. But the Mustang P-51s with their upgraded Rolls-Royce Merlin engines had the range to make the full 550-mile round-trip from Britain to Berlin and back, providing defense for the entire mission. He'd been flying the P-51 for nearly a year, a cowboy riding a mustang roping a Messerschmitt Bf 109, painted on the nose with the caption: "Ride 'em Cowboy."

To be one of 670 long range fighters escorting 1,250 bombers in the heaviest daylight raid on Berlin to date was a heady sensation. Two bombers per fighter. In the briefing, the intel officer had warned them to keep their eyes peeled for the Luftwaffe's jets. "You should see those Messerschmitt 262s any day now. Kentucky Derby is the code name if you encounter them."

Then in an aside, Colonel Barker, the group leader, had muttered, "You're lead squadron for Range Rider Group, but don't get cocky, McCauley."

Major Daniel McCauley—call sign this mission, Ramrod Lead—polished his new brass oak leaf insignias on the shoulders of his flight jacket.

"Pride goes before a fall, Danny."

Thanks Uncle Mike. With a priest for an uncle, who needs a conscience?

Their armament officer pulled their chains regularly, interjecting levity into their stress with his ubiquitous wisecrack, "Without ordnance, it's just another flying club."

As an ace with thirteen kills, how could Dan not feel proud? He'd been awarded the Distinguished Flying Cross and a Purple Heart to prove it. But performance alone didn't move you up in rank; vacancies due to killed or missing in action did. And he had survived three years of missions. His wheel hat long supported the "50-mission crush."

Promotion had been exhilarating. Accountable for four flights, four fighters a piece—sixteen aircraft, sixteen *men*—a daunting responsibility.

With anticipation of the mission came the usual jitters. Nerves of steel, though, when the battle starts. So, jettison Fear.

"Yeah right, Danny boy!"

Over Eastern Germany

General "Jimmy" Doolittle ordered the fighter squadrons to hunt the enemy interceptors instead of flying close formations with the bombers they escorted. As a former high school and college quarterback, Dan preferred offense to defense any day.

"Ramrod Squadron, Ramrod Lead," he alerted his four flights, "approaching target area. Expect Jerrys will bounce us shortly."

"Roger," squawked Ramrod, Wrangler, Cowboy, and Drover flights.

The B-17 Fortresses threaded their way through pyrotechnics of antiaircraft flak, so thick you could walk on it, to make their bombing run. Dan spotted small moving specks in the eastern sky. "Ramrod Squadron, Ramrod Lead, it looks like we've got company. A couple dozen."

He had been elated when the mission frag shop assigned his squadron the call sign Ramrod, part of Cattle Drive Wing. Raised on a ranch, Dan had shared cattle terms they could use on the radio to fool the German pilots. Uncle Mike often teased him for never outgrowing his passion for being a cowboy. Flying a fighter was just another way of riding a bronco.

The P-51 cockpit windshield gave its pilot a panoramic view of the skies. Silver specks appeared out of the clouds. "Ramrod, Wrangler, Dan; bandits at three o'clock high. Cowboy, Drover, more at five o'clock high." A chorus of "rogers" acknowledged, and Dan led the charge after the gaggle of 109s headed for the bombers.

The dogfight was on.

Dan had learned early on you couldn't fight the entire melee of tumbling, turning, twisting crafts like mad dogs in a chaotic brawl. Focus on one bogie at a time.

"Dan, break hard now! Jerry at six low, gun range!" shouted his wing man.

Dan broke sharply right in a hail of bullets, turning so tight he blacked out for a second. Recovering, he reversed hard, while avoiding a high-speed stall. The 109 overshot. Sucking in air again, he bore full throttle chasing the Jerry, closing in on him. Dan pressed the trigger. The 109 caught fire, spiraling down trailing smoke and flames.

"Dan, Tommy. Good shooting, you got 'em!"

Number fourteen. Dan owed the kid. His mouth was dry and his body damp with sweat. But with the sky so busy, no time to take a bow. Then in the distance . . . he saw it. A line of faint contrails. In seconds tiny silver flecks burgeoned. "Ramrod Flight, Lead, twelve o'clock high bandits coming in fast."

A glut of crude expletives burst over the radio as the silver jets streaked overhead racing toward the B-17s.

"Whoa!" Dan's jaw dropped, and his stomach lurched.

"Dan are those —?"

"Affirmative, Tommy. Ramrods, form posse; head 'em off at the pass." So, these are the Me 262s. A jolt of electricity fired through his body. Intercept and destroy. If they can catch them. "Range Rider Lead, Ramrod Lead, Ramrod off to the Derby."

Colonel Barker responded, "Range Rider Lead, roger Dan. Circle the wagons, Range Riders." The rest of the group would back them up.

Full throttle, climbing, Dan led the pack. They were chasing racecars on foot with pesky mosquitos diving at them, trying to avoid the 109's bite. The 262s took out two of the lead B-17s but did not engage in dogfights with the P-51s, leaving that to the 109s. Though fast the jets obviously couldn't turn on a dime.

After Range Rider's B-17s dropped their loads, the entire group turned toward home.

"Ramrod Flights, Ramrod Lead. Let's skedaddle."

But the enemy didn't intend to let them fly off into the sunset. "Ramrod Flights, Ramrod Lead; bandits, nine o'clock level, at least a dozen."

"Roger, Dan, engaging," came a bevy of responses. The flights of P-51s split into separate fights with Dan closing in on a Jerry. He had his fangs out, going for the kill.

"Dan, *break! Hard left!*" Bogie closing to your six!"

As Dan turned, tracers shot by him. He felt impacts of multiple hits. Heart palpitating, he quickly cut throttle, yanking hard on the stick, and causing the 109 to hurtle past. The attacking Jerry broke off and left the fight, leaving Dan berating himself for breaking the cardinal rule of air combat—don't get your fangs out and forget your six.

"Watch your six at all times, Major Super Ace Fighter Jock!"

Brilliant example of showing his green wingman how it's done.

Meanwhile, Wrangler, Cowboy, and Drover gave chase to the Jerrys.

"Much obliged, Tommy. Look me over. I felt some hits."

"Roger Dan." The lieutenant moved his craft in close. "Affirmative, you have some holes in your fuselage just under the cockpit, and some other damage on the wing." A pause. "Are you OK?"

"Tommy, I've taken a hit in my left side, feels like some blood maybe. Let's head out."

"Roger, Dan. Will cover your six. Let me know any control problems."

The tenderfoot is coming along nicely.

His side ached. Was it a graze or a bullet? He reached over below his ribcage, his gloved hand came back wet and red. He cussed out the Jerry for ripping his flight jacket. Grabbing his scarf, Dan staunched the wound.

A fresh squadron flew overhead toward the fight. "Ramrod Flights, Ramrod Lead, here comes the cavalry. Let's hightail it to the bunkhouse." His flight leaders acknowledged.

By the time Ramrod Flight had made it across Germany, and closed in on Belgium; Wrangler, Cowboy, and Drover had joined up. Dan flew the plane at reduced speed to maintain control.

"Wrangler Lead, Dan. Take lead of the flights, Harve."

"Dan, Harve, what's your stat?"

"Bit woozy, but I'll tough it out. Harve, take Ramrod Three and Four with you. Tommy will stick with me." And hopefully won't see me go into the drink. His scarf was soaked and the pain downright annoying.

"Roger Dan. Meet up with you at the bar." Ramrods Three and Four chimed in to acknowledge.

"Tommy. Dan. Just us now, kid. Wake me up if I start snoring."

"Dan, Tommy. Roger."

The coast greeted Dan just as the sheep were lining up to get counted. Only one more lap. The English Channel measured a little over thirty miles wide, and Dan had sweated the entire way.

He sang "Comin' in on a Wing and a Prayer," to distract himself from the pain and anxiety. But could he pray to a God he wasn't sure he believed in anymore?

Scorn shouted—*"Hypocrite! So, what now? The ace pilot is finally in a fix he can't get out of alone?"*

"Worth a try."

"You really think there's a loving God who allows war? And would help a killer?"

"I honestly don't know. I was doing a job."

"Come now, Ace. You didn't get to be an ace just doing a job. There was a man in each of those planes you shot down."

For three years, Dan had forced those thoughts from his mind.

"How about those bombers you escorted who dropped bombs on Berlin today probably killing thousands of civilians—women and children, too?"

Dan had built a wall barring Guilt. Now a crack. Condemnation rushed in. He was getting light-headed and dizzy. Blood loss? He looked down at the gray ocean.

"You won't make it. Go ahead, killer, dive. It will all be over in a minute. Killers deserve death."

Dan inhaled. What's that foul stench? Sweat? Blood? Fear?

He puked.

A heavy gloom descended on him as consciousness faded in and out. Dan leaned forward on the stick, diving toward oblivion.

"Pull out, Dan! You're in a dive. Can you read?"

Dan's eyes flew open. Urgent messages fired in his brain.

"Danny, stop! Don't do this."

"Dad?"

"Pull up, son. Now!"

Dan yanked the stick back, gaining altitude again. He was breathing hard and sweating profusely, fighting the sticky fog trying to overtake his brain. Whatever got into him, hearing voices? First Guilt, then Dad. His father had been gone only a few months, and Dan had thrust that grief behind the wall, too.

Tears washed down his cheeks. He swiped them away with his fists as a memory emerged. He was back on the ranch.

❋ ❋ ❋

The seven-year-old boy sat on the ground bawling after being thrown from his horse.

Dad dismounted and stretched out his hand. "Come, Danny. You gotta get right back on."

"No-o-o, Daddy, I can't!"

"Yes, you *can*."

"*Can't*."

"Do you remember the little engine that could?"

"But he didn't fall off a horse."

"No, but he had an enormous hill to climb. Remember—The little engine chanted: 'I think I can, I think I can, I think I can.'"

Dad lifted him back on the mustang, and Danny rode again.

❋ ❋ ❋

"Son let's get this mustang back to the coral."

"Dan. Tommy. What was that?"

"Lost consciousness for a sec, OK now."

Spots danced in front of his eyes when the green coastline of Essex materialized out of the sea like a beautiful sign flashing, *Welcome back, Danny*!

He would be lucky to make it there. "Going in at Colchester. Catch you back at the bar in Debden."

"Roger, Dan. You're wobbling all over the place."

"Pay attention, Danny." He cut back on the throttle maintaining a minimum controllable speed as he struggled to set up a long straight approach. He strained to maintain consciousness. "I think I can, I think I can, I think I can."

The landing strip emerged in front of him. It took all his remaining strength to bring the craft down. Too slow! Just about to touch down, he lost control. The craft bounced, jolting Dan as the plane did a ground loop, violently rotating the craft. So, this is it! Something sharp knifed into his back before he blacked out.

Colchester Military Hospital, Colchester Garrison
Pain, nausea, delirium.

Dan pulls back on the stick, climbing, but he can't get over the thick fog. "Tommy, do you read me?" Silence.

"Major McCauley?"

"Tommy?"

"No, Major, you're back on the ground. It's Dr. Preston-Doyle, your surgeon."

Dan didn't like the expression on the face of the white-coated man. He'd seen it before. When Sister Brigit had had enough of his tomfoolery, she sent him to the principal's office. Father McLaughlin wore a deathly mask that struck dread in the heart of a young boy.

I'm going to die.

"You're lucky to be alive, Major. Your injuries are severe, but you'll live. I had to remove one of your kidneys, it was so badly damaged. The liver was impaired, but if you treat it well, not too much alcohol, it will last. One good thing, you're out of the fight now. You can go home."

No!

The surgeon started out the door as Colonel Barker entered. Dan's CO turned and walked out with the doctor. When the colonel returned, his face was grave. "Well, McCauley, good job over Berlin. The mission was successful. We dropped 3,000 tons of explosives. Lost six 51s and thirteen 17s."

"Sir, we have to come up with a strategy against those 262s."

"We will. You took out one of two downed 109s. You are the only casualty in your squadron. Nothing like going out in glory."

What? *Out?*

"Oh, all the boys send their best wishes. They sang a few rounds of "Danny Boy" in your honor at the officer's mess."

"Yes, Sir, they did it here too." Will I ever ditch that juvenile nickname?

The colonel raised a bushy eyebrow. "Rotten luck on that landing. You're one of my best. I hate to lose you."

"Colonel, I'll be up and at 'em in no time, just like last time."

"No, Major. You won't. Not without a kidney and part of your liver. I'm sending you home."

"You're grounding me, Sir?"

"Afraid so. Son, I couldn't be prouder of you if you were one of my own, but you've given your all for God and country. Now go home and live your life. You owe it to the guys who won't go home."

A dark cloud descended on Dan.

Two weeks later

The nurse pushed Dan's wheelchair back into his section past the other two beds. A tall, hefty man in a black cassock stood talking to Dan's two cot mates. The priest turned, a big smile breaking across his face.

"Danny!" That familiar voice the first ray of sunshine since regaining consciousness.

"Uncle Mike? What are you doing here?"

"I've come to take you home." His broad Irish face grinned, framed with black hair and dark eyes sparkling.

"I don't want to go home."

"As I understand it, you don't have an option."

Another wave of despair washed over Dan.

"So, what did the colonel do, cable Stella to come pick up her boy?"

"Not quite. When the cable arrived, your mom went to pieces. So, I made the sacrifice—an Irishman setting foot on English soil."

"Can you pray me better, lay hands on me and make me a new kidney?" His lower back hurt and his gut ached as the nurse helped him back onto his cot.

"Or exorcise the demon of self-pity, Danny? Where's my happy-go-lucky nephew? You still have your pretty face and, as I understand it, your manhood is intact. You've a chance for a wife and family. So many men have lost that possibility."

"A priest, thinking about women?"

"Not for me, laddie. You."

"You can't possibly think any woman could ever make up for my being grounded?"

"Just bringing up what you can be thankful for. Daniel, you are only twenty-three and have your whole life ahead of you."

"Without flying?" Bile rose in his throat, tasting bitter.

"I imagine you can still fly, just not for the Army Air Forces."

"But that's all I've wanted to do since I flew my first fighter. I won't be able to fly our jets when we get them."

"I understand how in love with flying you've been ever since you saw your very first plane as a small lad, but the Lord has other plans for you now."

"What kind of a God takes away the thing I love most in this world?"

"Our blessed Lord," Mike's eyes drilled his nephew's, "who has something better in mind for you."

"Don't preach, *Father* Mike. I'm not too happy with your God right now."

But the priest didn't need to use any hocus pocus to exorcise Dan's feeling sorry for himself. All it took was a reminder that one of his cot mates had lost both legs and the other could never make love to his wife again quashed his pity party for the moment. However, Dan could never love anything as much as he did flying.

Southampton, The RMS Queen Mary

Dan's uncle pushed him down the dock toward the ship. "Here we are, Danny."

How humiliating, confined to a wheelchair. Glancing around he was not the only one. "Tell me again," Mike, "why are we not flying home?"

"Doctor's orders. You're to rest."

"How exciting." Dan glowered at his uncle. "We are *not* taking the train to the West Coast."

"OK, we'll fly."

They boarded the great ocean liner with other American soldiers going home on stretchers, in wheelchairs, on crutches, bandaged and limping.

"Enjoy the luxury, Danny boy. The Cunard Line loaned this ship to the US to carry troops between Britain and home."

"Four days, Mike? What will we do?"

"I know, you get bored so easily. I have a book for you, and it's devilishly clever. It's by a man who teaches at Oxford, a C. S. Lewis." Father Mike handed Dan *The Screwtape Letters*.

"Your uncle has an agenda, you know."

When doesn't he?

"Speaking of Oxford, Mike, you should see it and Cambridge sometime when you're not taking your nephew home to mommy. They're nothing like our colleges and universities. When this war is over, I want to return and really see them."

Dan leafed through the volume. "Devilish, did you say? You were serious."

iv
DAUGHTERS

> Where there's life there's hope.
> *The Hobbit*, J. R. R. Tolkien

1945
Sunday, 13 May
St Peter's, Eaton Square, London
Phila loved the stately white church with its six tall columns, square steeple, and gold cross pointing the way to God. Inside, the rich dark wood paneling, side balcony railings, and pews emanated such opulence. The circular ceiling and carved stone pillars drew her gaze upward. A waterfall of colored lights shimmered through the stained-glass windows above the altar.

People filled the church to brimming. Phila followed her mother and brother up the aisle. Royal Navy Lieutenant Hugh Claiborne was twenty-three and dashing in his uniform. Every young girl turned her head to look as they passed up the aisle to a front pew.

Self-pity consumed Phila. *"He certainly never wants for attention. Obviously, he received all the good looks. Too bad God didn't save just a little for you."*

She slipped into the pew next to Lily. Their mothers greeted each other. Seven-year-old Stevie stared at Hugh in adoration. Lily's baby sister, Kit, remained in the nursery.

Pretty Lily had shiny dark hair, deep pewter eyes, porcelain skin—not one freckle. I'm plump. She's willowy. I'm a brain, and she's a beauty. What a pair.

Father Whitely stepped up to the pulpit. "On Monday last, the eighth of May, we celebrated Victory in Europe Day. Peace, at last." He paused. "What can be more appropriate than hearing the 'Hallelujah Chorus' from Handel's *Messiah*?"

The congregants joined the choir singing:

King of kings, and Lord of lords
And he shall reign forever and ever . . .
Hallelujah! Hallelujah!

Joy bubbled up overflowing, propelling gratefulness heavenward.

"Welcome all, on this glorious Sunday to worship our almighty Lord and thank Him for this cease-fire and German surrender. Our soldiers and sailors will be coming home. And our prisoners of war have been released and are on their way back. We have much to celebrate."

Papa will be coming home. Two whole years since they last saw him. Phila smiled and squeezed Lily's hand.

※ ※ ※

Whenever Lily listened to her father speaking from the pulpit, it was like hearing God's voice.

"Of course, not all our loved ones will be coming back to us. Some have gone home to our Lord. 'The LORD gave, and the LORD hath taken away; blessed be the name of the LORD.'" His voice was husky.

Lily swallowed hard. A cold hand squeezed her heart. She couldn't look at Mum.

"Next Sunday evening we will have a memorial service for our fallen heroes. Let us pray now for them."

Silence hung heavily in the colossal church.

"But this morning is a time of celebration. Let us rise and worship." He lifted his arms.

Powerful hymns infused Father's homily with hope.

※ ※ ※

That night Phila wrote in her journal.

Lily's twelve; I'm thirteen. The war is over. We don't need to be frightened any more. It is time again to dream dreams.

CHAPTER 1

THE VICAR'S DAUGHTER

My dreams were all my own; I accounted for them to nobody.
Frankenstein, Mary Shelley (1797–1851)

1952
Wednesday, 24 September
St Peter's Vicarage, Eaton Square, London
Lily's eyes opened to sunlight streaming in through the window. Life was unfolding perfectly. In exactly fourteen days, she would win the grand fashion prize for designing the most original gown for Queen Elizabeth's Coronation, and her destiny would be assured. Pride swelled.

"When, not if. Of course, you will win the St Martin's School of Art's contest."

To lose would be the worst disaster in her whole life. "So, I simply shan't consider it."

The Norman Hartnell—who was designing the Queen's Coronation gown, and who had created the royal wedding dress, would judge the finalists.

"I will meet Mr. Hartnell, and my gown will be displayed in his fashion house for all to see."

"Who says a vicar's daughter can't pursue a career in couture?"

Madam Gianna had told her she had the talent.

"You are her favorite student. You can't lose."

Delicious anticipation grew for that moment when the fashion mistress would announce the winner—Lillian Grace Whitely.

She sat up in bed, threw off the quilt, stretched her fingers to touch her toes, and got up quietly so as not to disturb Kit. Her little sister lay curled up in her covers, the woolly ball of fur she named Snowy nestled against her legs. In all Kit's seven years, she had been nothing but a delight to soften her sibling's more serious nature.

Stevie hadn't grabbed the lavatory yet, so Lily seized it before he woke and made a mess. She washed up, rubbing her ivory skin with the towel till her cheeks shone rosy.

"Too pretty for a vicar's daughter," she sniped at the looking glass in a gossipy tone, parroting the ladies of the parish. She brushed her shoulder-length hair, admiring its glossy blackness, and gathered it in a ponytail. Dark eyes sparkled back at her.

"Eat your hearts out, you old biddies." She made a face at her reflection. "Life is beautiful. I am beautiful."

"Vanity, thy name is woman."

The adolescent voice startled her, and she spun toward the door. "Stevie, you cad!"

"Actually, that's a misquote of Shakespeare's. It was *frailty*, not vanity, but you are hardly frail. You're so absorbed in yourself, sis, just like the subject of *Lady Lilith*, Rossetti's painting that led to the misquote." Her brother stood there, a smirk on his face.

"Show off." She returned to her room to preen more before the looking glass on the wardrobe door. Stevie could be as annoying as Phila and her brother when they spouted their superior knowledge. *I'm surrounded by human encyclopedias.*

The small room glowed golden in the bright autumn sunshine. Outside, a robin boldly sang his joyful song. The flowers on the curtains and quilts appeared to bloom before her eyes. Mum must have crept in earlier and started the fire; her lavender scent lingered.

"You are on the dawn of achieving the first objective of the Grand Plan."

Lily took a deep breath, hugged herself, and twirled. Opening the wardrobe, she gazed at the three sketches of her gown on the inside of the door, each sketch with swatches of fabric tacked to it. The slender design that accentuated her willowy frame actually used less fabric, a thrifty move. A gathered bodice gave way to a straight line in front, gathering to a slight bustle at the lower hipline. She'd designed an off-the-shoulder neckline with flared sleeves.

"Ten days from today you will wear your very own creation to a real ball."

"And I will belong—a mere commoner amongst all those young

progenies of nobility." Progenies. Oh, the lofty words she learned from Phila. They even impressed Stevie.

He never let her forget how smart he was. Probably not as gifted as Benjie had been and by no means as humble. Grief briefly grazed her happiness. Her older brother should have been the one to escort her down the stairway into the ballroom.

Lily walked to her dresser and picked up the invitation. Her closest friend was now the daughter of an earl. When Phila's Uncle Rayner died, her father assumed the title.

His Lordship, Sir Henry, Earl of Wembley

Rear-Admiral Royal Navy

&

Her Ladyship, Beatrice, Countess of Wembley

Request Your Presence

On the Fourth of October Nineteen Hundred and Fifty-Two

Eight O'Clock

Rivenwood on Thame

Celebrating

The Twenty-First Birthday of Their Daughter

Philomena Justine Claiborne

Lily willed back her daydreaming of Phila's ball, twirling around the glittering ballroom in her stunning lapis-blue gown with one handsome young man after another.

"All those snooty blue-blooded girls will be seething with envy."

A smile blossomed across Lily's face.

"They will think your exquisite gown is from Paris."

She sniggered.

"Then when London's most eligible bachelor, and the handsomest man at the ball, escorts you down into the ballroom, won't they just die of jealousy? Revenge is sweet."

CHAPTER 2
THE CHALLENGE OF JOB

> Shall we receive good at the hand of God, and shall we not receive evil?
>
> Job 2:10, KJV

"Lily?" The small voice broke into her reverie. Kit sat up blinking her eyes.

"Good morning, Kitten."

She bounded out of bed, pitching the cat onto the floor. "Sorry, Snowy." Kit scooped up the white bundle of fur and put her outside the room. "Run along. Mummy will give you a saucer of milk and let you out." She turned back around. "Your beeeeautiful ball gown—when will we get to see it?"

"After the ball, Kitten."

"Do I *have* to wait?" She fixed her wide hazel eyes on Lily. A ploy the little minx knew worked all too well.

"Maybe I can take you and Mum to see it Saturday." Lily tweaked her sister's nose. "Would you like that?"

"Oh, yes please, Lily, do. And we'll see Phila too?"

"Of course." How could she say no to that smiling face framed in golden brown curls?

"I love Phila." She twirled a curl around her finger. "She gave me the lovely Narnia books about Aslan, and she still loves to make believe."

"I know. Let's get you dressed. Father will be waiting."

Lily took Kit's hand as they hurried downstairs and into the dining room. Sunlight streamed through the windows onto the table and glinted on the aluminum Festival-of-Britain teapot, giving a warm hue to the embossed pictures of the Houses of Parliament and the Tower Bridge. Steam rose from the spout.

Lily inhaled the yeasty fragrance of fresh-baked rolls.

Father was seated, as usual, with his Bible open. "A wee bit tardy, girls?" His warm chocolate eyes flashed at them, but his mouth smiled.

"Sorry, Father." Lily glided into her chair.

Kit plopped on hers.

"Mummy, Lily's going to take me to see her gown Saturday."

Mum pulled Kit closer to the table. "Settle down, Little Miss Muffet." She patted her on the shoulder, then glanced at Lily. "That's thoughtful of you. Kit's been so keen on seeing it."

"Would you like to go, too?"

"I would indeed." Her face lit up just like Kit's had done. How alike they were. The same short honey-brown curly hair, though Mum's was struck through with silver. Round faces with widow's peaks. Kit would grow up resembling her.

Stevie rushed in, plunking his books on the table. Even at fourteen he represented a spitting image of Father, so lean and serious. He verged on being as tall and handsome with the black curly hair, but his dark coffee eyes reminded Lily of the Claiborne's Labradors.

"May we begin now, Steven?" Father tapped his Bible with his long fingers.

"Mrs. Terrill, you may serve in fifteen minutes." Mum smiled at the plump middle-aged housekeeper with startling red-dyed hair as she walked into the kitchen.

"What have we learned from our study of the book of Job?"

Stevie jumped in. "No matter what happened to Job, he never turned from God."

"Not even when his wife told him to curse God and die." Lily grimaced.

Father's forehead creased. "Was that good advice?"

"No, but I certainly understand it."

"Lillian Grace Whitely!"

She jumped at his stern tone.

"No, Jon, I do too." Mum patted Lily's arm. "She was a mother who bore ten children, and they all died at one time. That would crush any mother's spirit."

"I wouldn't blame her for being angry with God." Lily shrugged.

Stevie and Kit exchanged a concerned look.

"Do you believe it's justified to be angry with *God*, Lillian?" Father raised an eyebrow.

"Why can't we be angry with God when He allows a horrid tragedy in our lives, like when Benjie was killed?" The anger from twelve years before rekindled deep in her heart.

Sadness crept across her father's face. "I confess; you have a point there. I grappled with it myself."

"Father, *you* were angry with God?"

Sorrow clouded her mother's expression.

Father closed his eyes for several seconds. "At first, yes, but we can't let ire eat away at us the way Job's wife did until it becomes bitterness. Ask the Lord and He will give you the grace to let it go." He cleared his throat. "Katherine, read your verse, please."

"'The Lord gave, and the Lord hath taken away. Blessed be the name of the Lord.'" Kit beamed.

"There's your answer, Lillian, as difficult as it is to accept." Resolve returned to his face.

Could it be that she'd not seen through her tough father's stern facade?

"From the mouths of babes," said Stevie.

"Don't call me a baby!" Red-faced, Kit glowered at him.

"Perhaps the wife repented of her anger later on." Mum topped off Father's tea.

"I'd say God punished her for suggesting Job curse him." Lily locked her eyes on her father's. "She had ten more children."

Father's eyes widened. "What a thing to say! Children are a blessing from God."

"Yes, Father, to Job, maybe. But he didn't have to give birth to *ten more* babies."

"Lillian, I do believe you're being seduced by this new feminist movement."

Did he know that she and Phila had sneaked out to hear Baroness Summerskill speak? The talk on women in the workplace and women's health by the young female member of Parliament had been eye-opening.

"Have you been seeing films I wouldn't approve of and reading women's magazines with your friend?"

"Yes, Father, but they all favor old-fashioned values."

"Old-fashioned?" His face screwed up in astonishment. "The values the Bible teaches are always relevant."

"Actually, Jon, from a woman's perspective—a woman of any age—

bearing *twenty* babies is certainly more than I can perceive of."

"All right, ladies," raising his hands in surrender, "childbearing is out of my purview."

Whew. Lily had overstepped her boundaries, but sometimes it was so hard to keep quiet. After watching Kit's birth, she wasn't sure she wanted any children at all.

"Your Scripture, Lillian?"

"'Shall we receive good at the hand of God, and shall we not receive evil?' But how are we supposed to accept something horrible and still love God?"

Father winced. "Steven?"

"'Though he slay me, yet will I trust in him.'"

"Trust, Lillian. Trust that the Lord loves us no matter what."

Kit lit up. "I know, after God tries us, we will be gold."

"'And a little child shall lead them.'" Father nodded to Lily.

Well, of course, Kit was too young to have a skeptical thought in her head. Lily looked down at the little girl. You don't know doubt yet, do you, Kitten? Lily reached over and smoothed her curls. You're too good for this earth, little one.

"What did God teach Job, Steven?"

"That God was God, and Job was not."

Father beamed at him. "Well done, son. That's certainly the short of it."

"Ruth, your verse?"

"'Who is he that hideth counsel without knowledge? Therefore, have I uttered what I understood not; things too wonderful for me, which I knew not.'"

"I don't understand that." Stevie blinked.

"Well, son, Job realized that he had been arrogant with God. He wasn't as righteous as he had thought after all. He spoke without knowledge and wisdom and made a fool of himself. He had been humbled, and like you most aptly said, he was not God, and maybe next time he should be silent."

Both siblings' eyebrows shot up as they turned to look at Lily.

"I'll never understand Job, not to mention God. Really, Father? Is God sitting up there in heaven waiting for the devil to ask if he can throw more suffering at us?" Did I say that?

Stevie rolled his eyes, and Kit covered her mouth. Neither of them would ever have tested their father that way.

"Lillian, the Lord allows—"

"He *allows*? Then we are supposed to just silently accept whatever comes our way, and be thankful? If he's such a loving God, why did he let Benjie die? Why?"

"Lillian . . ." Father seemed to choke back further words.

Mrs. Terrill popped her head in the doorway. "Father Whitely, it's the bishop ringing. He says it's very important."

"My, he's never rung so early." Mum frowned. "What could have happened?"

Father rose, then stopped behind Lily's chair, laying his hands on her shoulders for a moment. "We need to talk."

As he left the room, Kit squealed. "Oh, are you in trouble."

CHAPTER 3

THE EARL'S DAUGHTER

Books — oh! no. I am sure we never read the same, or not with the same feelings.
Pride and Prejudice, Jane Austen (1775–1817)

The Green Park, Belgravia, London
Phila skipped ahead of Hugh, following the two sleek black Labradors. "So, have you a girlfriend in Washington?" She turned to see her brother's face as the year-old pup dashed ahead to find a tree.

"I might." He turned away.

Triton's sire trotted alongside his master, then joined his pup marking the tree.

"Why do you have to be so taciturn?" Phila glared. "Is dating an American girl a surreptitious affair? Or do you think there are spies behind all these trees?"

"I don't think my social life is of interest to anyone other than my overly inquisitive sister. Can we not merely enjoy this beautiful London afternoon, walking the lads together? Neptune, heel." The older lab was at his side in a flash.

"What's she like? Triton, heel!" The pup frolicked ahead. "She's probably enamored with the idea of being a countess."

"Who?"

"Hughie!"

"Need-to-know only." He snickered. "Triton, heel." The pup joined his sire at his master's side.

"You're as bad as Papa," she huffed. "Is everything in the Navy confidential?"

"Pet, I haven't been home in nearly six months. Right, lads?" He knelt on one knee, stroking the dogs' wiggling bodies and receiving a face washing. His eyes took on a sad mien. "Devin was supposed to be Earl. But he was the hero, and now I'm to be the stuffed shirt."

Phila missed their cousin, too, slain on the fields of Normandy, the D-Day invasion. "We shall never hear Devin laugh again." She moved over to Hugh as he stood and gave her a hug.

He mussed her curls. "So sad for Aunt Gertrude, losing her son then Uncle Rayner. Hopefully, she's found solace in her new marriage."

They walked in silence for a while. However, Phila never could bear quiet too long. "So, why are you home?"

"For some leave." He straightened and started for home, then tossed a final remark over his shoulder. "Oh, and a top-secret assignment for the ambassador."

The Havens, Eaton Square

Phila trooped after Hugh into the parlor, the labs prancing in her wake. "You're all head and no soul, Hughie. Can't you just enjoy cinema simply for its artistic value?" She plopped into the green-and-blue plaid chair by the fireplace, across from the tartan-green brocade Queen Anne chairs where their parents sat.

Had God given her the choice of selecting her parents, Phila couldn't have done better. Papa had a demeanor that demanded respect, which matched his position of Naval Secretary and Earl of Wembley. He cut a stately figure with wavy gray hair, hawk-like features, and a tall stature.

Though much shorter with a slender build, her mother's carriage made her seem much taller. Phila envied Mum's wavy ginger hair that actually obeyed her wishes. The word "gracious" was coined for her soft-spoken mum.

Why then, couldn't she have inherited their good looks? *If Mum had birthed a litter, I would have been the runt. If her infant brother had survived, and the two miscarried babies, would they have been as handsome as Hugh?*

As for her brother? Words such as arrogant, annoying, and . . . what's an "A" word for secretive? I know—arcane.

Papa snapped his fingers. Neptune and Triton settled at his feet.

Phila's mother reached down and stroked the dogs' muzzles. They licked back vigorously.

"Beatrice."

"Yes, Henry. But they do so enjoy attention." Her greenish-blue eyes looked lovingly at Papa, but a mischievous twinkle sparkled.

"Hunting dogs, my dear, they're hunting dogs—not people."

Phila adored Papa's commanding bass voice. He flashed a hawkish glance at Mum, but his mouth twitched as he fought a smile.

Mum winked at Phila, then glanced up. "Oh, Giselle, how nice."

The handsome middle-aged brunette maid, who had been with the family as long as Phila could remember, set down the tray with tea and crumpets.

Two black noses perked up and sniffed. Two sets of liquid coffee-colored eyes fastened on the cakes.

While Mum poured tea, Phila pilfered one of the cakes, broke it in half behind her back, and dropped her hands to the waiting mouths.

Mum pretended not to notice. Papa frowned, shaking his head. Hugh chuckled, then looked away. Two black heads rested on Phila's knees.

How wonderful to be together again for afternoon tea in the small comfy sitting room just off the dining room. Hugh was home and she between terms at Oxford.

"I was telling Petunia that there are other values more important than artistic ones." Hugh lifted his chin and squared his broad shoulders in a royal stance.

At times his dreamy baritone sounded absolutely plummy. There he goes again, putting on airs. "Don't call me that. I'm grown up now." She scowled at him.

"Should I say *children*, my dears?" Mum gave them *the look*. "You are adults, and this bickering is quite juvenile. I would expect the Assistant Military Attaché to Her Majesty's Ambassador to the United States—and a man of thirty—to display more decorum."

"*Children*, Mum?" Hugh bristled.

"*Look at him*—Lieutenant Commander Hugh Claiborne, Royal Navy. The last thing your pompous sibling can tolerate is being called a child." Jealousy nettled.

Irritatingly handsome, whether in uniform or civvies—today her brother wore gray tweed trousers, a white shirt, and blue jumper. In the States, Hugh said, they call it a sweater.

"Well perhaps if I had grandchildren, I could think of my offspring as grown-ups." Mum handed him a cup and saucer, a coy twinkle in her eyes.

Hugh glowered.

"O-o-oh, here comes Papa's spiel." Phila dropped her voice a few octaves. "'At your age, I was married for eight years and had produced an heir, son.'" She snickered.

Her brother flashed her his *I'll-get-even* look.

"You have touched a nerve." Satisfaction simmered.

"That's enough, Philomena." Papa shot her a stern look.

"Aye, aye, Sir, but he's still Hughie Louie. And all I was saying when we came in was that *Limelight* sounds like an interesting film even though Charlie Chaplin's politics are suspect." Will Hugh take the bait?

"A film written, produced, directed, and starring an avowed Communist." Her brother's eyes glinted.

He did.

"I don't believe it's been proven that Chaplin is a Communist sympathizer." Papa took his tea. "I understand the Americans suspected him of Communist ties because he supported the Russians during the First World War. And his popularity declined after his personal diatribe against war and fascism at the conclusion of his 1940 film, *The Great Dictator*."

Ramp up the discussion. "He is considered to be one of the greatest filmmakers in the history of American cinema. A child star and silent film actor, for Pete's sake. Don't you think his Little Tramp in so many films was absolutely brilliant?"

Mum patted Phila's hand. "I agree, darling. How can one not be delighted with his penguin-like walk, toothbrush mustache, bowler hat, and bamboo cane? They're legendary."

"Well, the chap *is* being investigated by the U.S. Citizenship and Immigration Service." Hugh wrapped his long fingers around his cup and drank. "And he's being refused reentry into the States after sailing here to attend London's premiere of the film next month."

"Here you go. You've snared him."

"Such a shame, all this Communist name-calling in America." Mum passed the plate of crumpets. "It seems to be escalating into quite a witch hunt."

Papa took a cake. "These accusations their Senator McCarthy is fostering about subversion in their government seem rather demagogic."

Her brother nodded. "He certainly is appealing to American popular desires and prejudices."

"It's not like we don't have our own Communists right here." At last, the opening Phila had been striving for.

Hugh gave her a patronizing glance. "Do you even know what Communism is Petunia?"

"Of course. Sounds frightfully dull. A classless society? Everybody shares in the labor and profits, and the state owns and operates industry on behalf of the people. Might as well go back to people being serfs. A form of socialism, actually. Karl Marx wrote it all depends on a person's ability and need." *So there*, she lifted her chin. "But isn't it rather a dichotomy that Russia would embrace a German philosopher's ideal after the two countries being such fierce enemies in two wars?"

"Quite so. You never cease to surprise me." Hugh inclined his head in approval. "I suppose there is hope for you yet."

"I *am* attending Oxford, if you please." What an offhanded compliment. But then she had trespassed on a touchy subject for him.

"That's the whole problem, sister dear, going to *the other place*."

Mum gave an exasperated sigh. "Darlings, it is utterly beyond me how intense this rivalry is between Oxford and Cambridge."

"It's been that way from the beginning of the thirteenth century, my dear. And I suppose with our progeny's propensity for competition, it was predetermined that they would attend different universities." Papa raised an eyebrow. "However, let's not get into a battle of the books. You two parry author quotes as if they were sabers."

"But, Henry, that's when their education and intellects shine forth. Imagine, both with photographic memories. I thought their match of parrying quotes from Alexandre Dumas's *The Count of Monte Cristo* versus Jane Austen's *Pride and Prejudice* was so entertaining and absolutely brilliant." Mum beamed. "They continue to amaze me. If I hadn't given birth to them, I'd wonder where they came from."

"My dear, their intelligence came from my father, their personalities from your side of the family. And their big heads from us giving compliments in their presence."

Hugh scowled.

Phila smirked but turned back to her brother. At last, she could ask him about the two diplomats gone missing last year. Both had been stationed at the Washington embassy. Obviously, she couldn't ask on the telephone or in a letter since all communications were censored. "So, has the Secret Intelligence Service found out if those chaps were spies and did indeed defect to Russia?"

As her father and brother exchanged a wary look, Phila continued: "We-e-e-e-ll, do you officials of the Crown know anything?"

"About?" Her brother munched on the cake, his face deadpan.

"About *Donald Maclean* and *Guy Burgess*, who disappeared a year ago last May. I think I read they both attended Trinity College, like you."

"About ten years before me. Hardly mates."

"They *did* work with you in Washington, didn't they?"

"Yes, but I can't say I was upset to see either leave when they were recalled to London. As to what happened to them, that's the purview of the SIS."

"And that about says it all—*secret* and *intelligence*." She chortled.

"Why would I know? I'm Navy, not MI6." He shrugged.

"And MI6 is not Military Intelligence, Section Six?"

Hugh donned his lecture face. "For your information, although MI5 and MI6 have kept the original Military Intelligence designations, they are civil service now. MI5 is domestic, and MI6 is the SIS, international. The States have the same thing, their Federal Bureau of Investigation—FBI—is like MI5 and the Central Intelligence Agency—CIA—is similar to our MI6. Got it? Not military. I'm just Navy."

Would he *ever* answer her directly? "OK. But back to the spies. Wasn't someone watching them in London?"

"I would have thought so. Dad, do you suppose we have the makings of an English Mata Hari?"

"Who knew too much for her own good and was executed as a German spy in the Great War." He gave Phila his pay-attention stare.

"Why don't you interest yourself in more female pursuits, like . . . Lily?"

Phila nearly burst from her chair. "Hughie, you're a blooming chauvinist!"

Mum gave her a blank look. "A what, darling? And watch your language."

"I'm a belligerent male who believes in the superiority of men over women."

"Surely you *don't*, darling?"

Even her mother sounded piqued. But if *any* man acted superior, it was her brother. "Nicolas *Chauvin*, Mum, was a French soldier and fanatical

Bonapartist even after Napoleon abdicated. So, the word has come to mean a fanatical devotion to a cause."

"My sister apparently thinks I'm a chauvinist. What can I say? Feminine ladies are much more appealing."

"Then what? Then intelligent females? It doesn't help that Lily's so beautiful, not that you've seen her in ever so long. Which is why *I* need a brain."

"Darling," Mum gave him *the look*. "If you're trying to win over your sister, you're failing."

"Then I shall inquire of her intelligence. And what did you think of Richard Nixon on the telly last night?"

Now, he wants my opinion? "I thought he was superb."

"I doubt General Eisenhower will drop him now as a vice-presidential candidate." Papa handed his cup and saucer to Mum.

She settled the china on the tray. "What exactly was the fuss about, Hugh?"

"Mr. Nixon was accused of accepting a gift of $18,000 from some Californian businessmen for his political fund and misusing it. There was talk of him spending it on a mink coat for his wife. And he apparently accepted the gift of a cocker spaniel, too."

"Do tell." Mum's eyes sparkled.

"So, what did he say so superbly last evening when your mum and I were out?"

Phila beat Hugh to it. "He said that he spent the funds on legitimate political expenses, and that his wife, Pat, doesn't own a mink but wears 'a respectable Republican cloth coat.' And he would never return Checkers, who was now his daughter's."

"Apparently, General Eisenhower believes that his running mate has been completely vindicated as a man of honor and stands higher than before," said Hugh. "It appears to be plain sailing now for the pair."

OK, Mr. Know-it-all. "And just Mr. Nixon's saying so changed people's minds? Though he did sound genuine."

"I think not so much *what* he said as *how* he said it." He stretched his long legs. "His performance was stellar and quite emotional, especially when he talked about not returning the dog. Right, lads?" Four black ears perked up. "That's two Brit canine votes for Nixon."

Two black tails attacked the tray of goodies and china as the labs vied for Hugh's attention.

Phila dove for the table, swooping up the tray rescuing it from disaster. She straightened the china.

"There is quite an advantage to seeing people in person instead of just hearing them on the wireless," said Mum. "This television is bound to influence history in the future."

Father gave her his arm and escorted her out. "My dear, I fear you are right, and perhaps not all for the good."

CHAPTER 4
A DECISION

> Life's business being just the terrible choice.
> *The Ring and the Book: The Pope,*
> Robert Browning (1812–1889)

St Peter's Vicarage

The famine of conversation at dinner that evening unnerved Lily, as did Father's brief grace.

Kit's eyes widened. "Father, that—"

Mum grasped her hand, shooting the little girl a silencing look.

A fog of apprehension engulfed Lily. She and Stevie swapped wary glances. He suspected something, too. But they knew better than to rush in "where angels feared to tread," though she had trodden not so softly that morning.

Mum made a production of stirring and ladling out the mutton stew. Stevie dug in like a starved man. Father concentrated on his meal. Mum coached Kit. Lily toyed with her food.

When they finished eating Father broke the silence. "Let us go into the parlor. I have something important to tell you."

Lily glanced at her mother, but she was hustling Kit from the room.

It took so long to get settled; Lily wanted to scream. When they were all seated, Father began. "Bishop Osred rang up this morning. Father Herring's mother has been taken seriously ill."

Why is this important? Lily looked over at her mother, who again avoided her glance. Oh, dear. She stared at Kit stroking Snowy.

"He won't be able to go on his mission trip to Scotland next week. The bishop doesn't want to cancel the tour. He's requested that I assume the assignment." His face reflected Stevie's usual exuberance. The last time she'd

53

seen her father so excited was at Kit's birth.

Mum beamed at him. "This is quite an honor for your father."

"I say, good show, Father." Stevie slapped the table.

Father's eyes shone. "This will be an excellent opportunity for the family to take a trip together. The bishop has offered to cover the expenses."

"A real holiday!" Stevie nearly bounced out of his chair. "For how long?"

"Eleven days."

A niggling tickle crawled up Lily's throat. "When?"

"We need to leave for Edinburgh on Monday."

Kit squealed. "Oh, how luverly!"

"*This* Monday, the twenty-ninth?" Lily gaped at her father, counting the dates on her fingers under the table.

Mum stared at her hands. "Not much time to plan, of course."

"Where, Father?" Stevie jounced about.

"Edinburgh, Glasgow, Sterling, Inverness, and Perth. I thought we'd visit the Isle of Skye for a wee holiday." He winked at Kit.

"I say, Father, how absolutely splendid." Stevie popped up. "Loch Ness too? We can look for the monster. I'll start packing."

Kit jumped up from her seat. "I can hardly wait! Lily, we shall have such fun."

Lily sat frozen to her chair. "But Phila's ball is a week from Saturday—the fourth, Father. And the announcement on the eighth. We wouldn't return in time."

"Yes, Lillian, but is not a call from God more important than a dance and a frock?" His tone was gentle and his eyes entreating.

Lily gulped in air. How did one argue against God? "But it's my first ball, Father. And winning the contest is my big opportunity."

"This opportunity is very important to me."

The passion in his tone struck her. "The ball and contest are very important to me, Father."

His eyebrows shot up, Mum winced, and Stevie and Kit gasped.

"More important than God?" Lily wilted under his gaze.

Three sets of eyes glanced from father to daughter.

"Fa–ther, that's so unfair." Lily wracked her brain for some defense against the Almighty. "I appreciate that you want me there, but it's *you* who will be preaching and gathering souls. Not me."

"Do you not want to be part of the Great Commission, daughter?" His look of disappointment cut her to the quick. "And, an actual holiday for our whole family?"

"Of course, Father, but not next week, *please.*"

Silence permeated the room. No one moved. Even Snowy's loud purring ceased. Lily held her breath.

"I want you to come, Lillian." His dark eyes penetrated her heart, pleading.

"And I want"—her voice quivered—"to go to the ball and be here for the announcement. Please, Father? You don't need me there."

"Of course, I don't need you, but I value your presence and want you with us, dear one."

"Lily, darling, your Father—"

"Mum, I'm not a child. I'm twenty. It's my first ball and winning the contest is my future."

"Yes." Her father sighed. "You are of an age to make your own choices. Did I not allow you to choose not to marry three worthy young men who asked for your hand?"

"Father, I didn't love them, and I didn't want to go off to Africa or China or India. I *want* a career!"

"Oh, child, there is a way that is broad and a way that is narrow—"

"Oh Father, do stop preach—" Lily's hand shot to her mouth. She'd never spoken to him like that.

He stood up, still as a statue, a stricken expression on his face.

Mum took a deep breath. "Upstairs with you two." She herded Kit and Stevie out of the room.

Lily rose slowly. Her mother turned back taking her daughter's hands in hers. "Dear heart, this is not a decision to be made lightly."

Why did it have to be either/or? She had to go to the ball and be there for the announcement, didn't she?

Of course, Guilt objected: *"Selfish girl! A party—a contest—is more important than your family?"*

She flinched. "Father, I didn't mean—"

"I know, child." He looked pained and weary—and old.

"Why didn't you just stab your father through the heart? Happy with yourself? He's not excited anymore. What a loving daughter you are."

He laid his hands on her shoulders. "Please pray about this, Lily, and meditate on Proverbs chapter eight, especially verses ten and eleven." He kissed the top of her head. "After Benjie died, you became our next hope. It will mean so much to have you there. Will you not choose wisdom over gold and rubies?"

CHAPTER 5

THE CHAUVINIST AND THE FEMINIST

What strange creatures brothers are!
Mansfield Park, Jane Austen

The Havens
Hugh rose from the table, the rest following. "No one can beat Flora's steak and kidney pie. That was one fine dinner." He had consumed too much.

"Darling, doesn't the embassy have a decent chef? You're looking way too thin." Mum turned to the butler. "Duncan, please tell Flora to prepare all Hugh's favorite foods while he's home."

The labs stood at attention by Duncan's side in the foyer. "All hands on deck, Commander. You've got the con now, Sir."

Hugh inclined his head. "Thank you, Sergeant Major. I'll take the lads out tonight." Who'd have thought when the retired Scottish Army sergeant major came onboard six years ago, the Navy and Army would have forged such a partnership of mutual respect?

The sergeant major had commandeered Neptune into his company and initiated Triton's recruit training as soon as he was weaned.

"Excellent progress with the new hand, Sergeant Major." Hugh scratched Triton's nose.

The stocky balding butler saluted. "Thank you, Commander."

They were still his dogs, but their loyalties were now divided. He didn't really mind.

Phila and Mum started up the grand staircase. "Off to read, ladies?"

They turned around. Mum's gentle smile warmed him. "Yes, darling, I've just purchased Mr. Lewis's *Mere Christianity*. He's collected his BBC talks from the war and put them into a book. I did so love those talks. What an encouragement they were to us all."

Phila smirked at Hugh. "His lectures are brilliant. Fortunately, anyone—even females—can attend. Not that we women are allowed to read with tutors like him in the men's colleges. What I'd give to be able to read with him and Professor Tolkien."

"Here we go again, more feminist drivel about men's colleges admitting women. Not for decades, Pet."

"It *is* 1952, brother dear, high-time women were given equal rights!"

"And you, sister dear, are a feminist!"

"I'm not the only one. For your information, so is Lily. She wants a career, not a husband like all the silly girls throwing themselves at you."

"And you're not dreaming of some prince?" He sniggered.

Duncan retreated, an amused expression on his otherwise phlegmatic face.

Phila glowered at Hugh. "By the way, Mum, I just acquired *The Voyage of the Dawn Treader*, Mr. Lewis's new Narnia book."

He snickered. "A book for children?"

"A lot more fun reading than *The Old Man and the Sea*. Your book, I presume, on the Chinese table in the library?"

"OK, Pet, what novel is this from? 'I can't stand it to think my life is going so fast and I'm not really living it.'"

"*The Sun Also Rises*. Interesting line, Hughie, does it mean something personal?"

Does it? "How about, 'The world breaks everyone and afterward many are strong at the broken places?'"

She screwed up her nose. "*A Farewell to Arms?*"

"Righto. Ernest Hemingway is going to be one of the most important writers of our century, even if he is a Yank."

"You're being rather foreboding with those quotes. Are you having premonitions?" She simpered, then threw her hands in the air. "My turn. 'I believe a strong woman may be stronger than a man, particularly if she happens to have love in her heart. I guess a loving woman is indestructible.'"

"*East of Eden*. Really, ole girl? John Steinbeck. I'm impressed."

"Darling, I do believe your sister won this round." Mum gave them both a kiss and proceeded up the stairs.

"You should be impressed, Hughie. *The Grapes of Wrath* may have been awarded the Pulitzer Prize, but a story of the depression in the States was so—depressing. *East of Eden* seemed more uplifting. Good night, and don't get shipwrecked."

She gave him a good-natured wave and climbed the winding stairs to her rooms.

So, his little sister is finally growing up. The excitement of Washington aside, he enjoyed being home. He went to join his father. Should he mention Darlene? Would his father approve of marriage to an American?

✻ ✻ ✻

Phila shut her door and lit the fire. Molly had been there and turned down her bed. When would Hugh begin to take her seriously?

Pride insisted, *"Your intellect is equal to his."*

"Not that he'll ever admit it. And, if I tell anyone else, I'll be accused of arrogance." Of course, with firsts in Russian, German, and political science, along with his being assigned to Naval Intelligence and serving as information officer to Admiral of the Fleet during the latter years of the war, he had a pretty superior mind.

She snickered. His mates at Trinity College had nicknamed him Genius. It stuck and followed him into the Navy, much to his chagrin.

"Think of the opportunities you would have if you were a male."

Undoubtedly, her sexist sibling would be concerned if he knew she had read Simone de Beauvoir's *The Second Sex*—in French, mind you—since it had yet to be translated into English. De Beauvoir's 1949 treatise on the treatment of women throughout history could issue in a new wave of feminism.

Hugh would worry she was falling under the influence of the existentialist philosopher and feminist theorist, especially in light of the rumors that she was carrying on with Jean-Paul Sartre, a leading figure on French philosophy and Marxism.

Hugh is such a Tory.

Her favorite quote from de Beauvoir's book was: "Her wings are cut and then she is blamed for not knowing how to fly." Now that's a call to arms for today's emerging womanhood. She would have to toss that quote at her ultra-conservative brother. Will he have a comeback for that?

"I know a quote to torpedo him!" She squealed. "'What would Prince Charming have for an occupation if he had not to awaken Sleeping Beauty?'"

Speaking of a charming prince, Hugh was gifted with all the good looks—the height, silky thick honey-colored hair, and a *girls'-mooning-over* face like a cinema star. Even the scar that sliced across one side of his forehead didn't mar his looks. He insisted it gave him character and a rite of passage into manhood. Of course, he *had* saved their lives that day.

Phila undressed, drew her dressing gown around her, plunked down on the padded chair in front of her dressing table, and grabbed her hairbrush. Why bother? She grimaced at her reflection. Her round pale face glowered back flushed with light freckles. Hughie didn't have a single freckle. Her nose turned up. Her brother's stately nose was hawkish like Papa's. Her eyes were pale blue. Hugh's, startling lapis like Lily's gown. He had long brown eyelashes. Hers were so pale they might as well not even be there. Lips, too thin. His full. His hair so thick, it even covered part of the scar that cut into his scalp. Hers, unruly and that awful carrot color. At six feet two inches he dwarfed her five feet four.

Mum insisted that God looked at the heart, not the outward appearance. But young men certainly didn't. Obviously, Mum had forgotten what it was like.

"How fair is it that Lily is so gorgeous and you're not?"

Where did that envious thought come from? She shuddered.

"Lil, I'm so sorry." Her friend was exceptionally talented. The gowns she had made for Phila and herself were as good as any from Paris.

Phila walked through her sitting room to the closet Lily used as a workroom. But no gown graced the mannequin. Of course, Molly had taken it to press. Phila's gown still hung in the corner. Maybe when she put it on she'd become Cinderella with a fairy godmother waving her wand to make her beautiful. Mum would pray, and her big evening would bring a Prince Charming.

Oh well, a girl can dream.

Doubtless Lily would attract a whole ballroom of charming princes. Why not? Why didn't Lily deserve to make an advantageous marriage?

Phila recalled the day they met. She had been at All Saints Church in Poplar Parish helping Mum pass out clothing and shoes to the impoverished people of East London. She noticed this beautiful girl, who looked like one of the china dolls in her collection except the girl's frock was plain, pouring tea at the victuals table. Phila excused herself, went over, and asked for a cup.

"Of course, milady." China Doll handed her a cup.

"Oh, I'm not a lady—yet. I'm just Philomena Claiborne."

"Hello, Philomena Claiborne. I'm Lillian Whitely, and my father is the new vicar at St Peter's. Your frock is lovely."

"Thank you. Your hair is so shiny black."

"Thank you. I brush it at least one hundred times every night."

"If I did that, mine would fall out."

"Surely not."

They both giggled. Phila had liked this beautiful creature from that very first moment. They were destined to be friends.

Weeks later, Phila's mother invited the new vicar and his family to Sunday dinner at their Belgrave Mews flat. It had amused Phila to watch Lily stare wide-eyed at all their fine things.

Sometimes Phila fantasized about Hugh and Lily getting married so they would be genuine sisters. She smiled. Papa and Mum wouldn't mind that Lily wasn't nobility. Mum wasn't high-born either, but she certainly lived more nobly than many of the aristocracy. Like Lady Napier-Jones. Phila huffed. That haughty woman carried on like royalty. Always polite, but even Mum struggled to tolerate the woman—and her spoiled daughter, Jacqueline, who used every opportunity to humiliate Lily.

"Wouldn't putting that shrew in her place be delicious? Is not the idea of spite sweet?"

Phila rubbed her hands together. No, I'm certainly not my saintly mother.

Jacquie had fawned after Hugh his last two visits home. But her savvy brother saw through her ostentatious act. Then there was Todd Thorndike. Phila swooned. Why couldn't he see through that horrid girl? Todd had danced with Jacquie half the evening at the last ball.

He didn't even look my way—not even once. Life wasn't fair.

She changed into her nightgown, crawled into bed, and picked up *East of Eden*. "Here I am in bed with a book—but not a child's book, if you please." She sighed then began singing the song from *Cinderella*. "Someday my prince will come . . ."

Papa says so.

But not Self-Pity. *"But he'll be enchanted with your father's wealth and position, not you."*

She pouted. "Dear God, make Papa right, that there's a man who can love me for myself. Please make next Saturday a night I'll never forget."

Phila tossed *East of Eden* onto her nightstand and went over to her shelves and selected *Pride and Prejudice* instead.

CHAPTER 6

WORLDLY LURES VERSUS HEAVENLY TENETS

Receive my instruction, and not silver; and knowledge rather than choice gold. For wisdom is better than rubies; and all the things that may be desired are not to be compared to it.

Proverbs 8:10–11, KJV

St Peter's Vicarage
Lily dragged herself upstairs, Guilt weighing heavily on her shoulders.

Sitting in bed reading Proverbs only increased the pressure on her soul. "Am I chasing after gold and rubies instead of wisdom and knowledge? Is it evil?"

"No!" Shouted Rebellion. *"You're not after gold and rubies."*

"Of course, gold lamé and ruby red silk is stunning—and together, ooh la la."

"What's wrong with creating exquisite clothing to make women more beautiful? Did God not create beauty?"

She had to make a choice between beauty and Father.

Life was so unfair.

Thursday, 25 September
Lily woke, still perturbed.

She didn't care to hear more of her father's preaching—warnings of the earth's demise, that the times were evil, that Christians were to live in the world but not be a part of it, and that they must always be aware that death could come at any time. What, pray tell, was wrong with being worldly.

Rebellion concurred. *"Didn't God give us the world?"*

Why couldn't she enjoy life?

Church life was so restricting, full of rules and regulations, old-fashioned and solemn. There were so many other attractions vying for attention.

"People think you're beautiful. Shouldn't you make the most of that?"

She loved her father dearly, but he was wrong.

"You have plenty of time to think of eternity when you're older. You can, too, experience heaven on earth."

It must be his age. He'd been so serious lately, like the world would end next week. Even Mum seemed outside herself, almost.

She reread the verses. "I am following your instruction, Father, but verse nine?"

"For they shall be an ornament of grace unto thy head, and chains about thy neck."

What a reminder that all the Bible reading and memorizing and hypocritical carrying on within the church were chains around her neck.

"But how do you break chains without hurting people?"

She left Kit and Snowy sleeping soundly, purring in soft unison. Half six. Father and Mum would be in the parlor praying and talking, as they did every morning. Barefoot, Lily crept down the stairs on the outermost side of the steps, careful not to make them creak. She tiptoed past the dining room, halting just outside the parlor door.

"I've so wanted to turn the girl's interest back to spiritual things. Oh, Ruthie, she received such an awakening in the spirit. Has it really been twelve years already? And now she seems to be slipping away." His tone so sad.

"Our Lord certainly shielded her, Phila, and Hugh that day. It was a miracle they were not killed. And Jon, Lily prayed to Jesus and he sent an angel."

The dragons' roar, their scorching breath, the fiery hail storm, the horror of that day returned, frightening Lily anew.

"She was so excited that Jesus answered her prayer, I didn't think she'd ever forget or that her faith would fade. But then we lost Benjie so soon after."

"That shook her faith considerably, not to mention ours." Mum stifled a sob. "Oh, Jon. On the last day of the Battle of Britain. Only one more day and he'd still be alive."

"Don't, Ruthie."

"I know."

Benjie had flown his Spitfire in the RAF's successful defense against the unremitting and destructive air raids by the Luftwaffe from July through September 1940. Failure would have exposed Great Britain to invasion by the Germans. That had been Benjie's sacrifice.

Pain knifed through Lily. "Why did God save Phila's brother but not mine?"

"Ruthie, she was right about being angry at the Lord. After Benjie's plane was shot down and they brought him home so crushed and burned..." Father broke into sobs.

She should go back upstairs, but stood rooted to the floor, her heart aching. After a few minutes he quieted, then blew his nose.

"You remember; I couldn't preach for weeks." His voice sounded strangled. "How could God take my son? He was truly a man after God's heart with such a future. I argued with the Lord for so long before I was finally able to surrender to His will."

The finger of Guilt prodded her heart. *"What a selfish wimp you were, Lily, so intent on your pain you never considered theirs."*

"Yes, my darling."

"I'm not certain I've completely forgiven the Germans." He groaned.

How could she have judged her father so harshly? What a wicked girl she'd been. Love for him flooded her heart.

But even that didn't change the fact that her faith had been devastated by her brother's death.

"Losing a child to death is agony, even though I know Benjie is with our Lord. But to lose a child to the world and not be with her in heaven, that would be inconceivable anguish."

"Oh, Jon, surely the Lord will honor our prayers for our children's salvation."

"So much attention for a mere dress—hours and every penny spent. 'Man looketh on the outward appearance, but the Lord looketh on the heart.'"

"That *mere* dress represents a good half year of diligent labor." The pride in her mum's voice thrilled Lily. "Winning that prize is her dream and a chance for the future."

"Mummy, you understand," she whispered.

"But, has it become an idol for her? Has she set her heart on a dream that will only disappoint—so much effort on an earthly desire. What kind of a realistic future has she really?"

"I don't know, my darling; 'nothing is impossible with God.'" The mischief in her mum's voice, charming her father, brought relief.

"Ruthie, shame. Using the Lord's words to work on me."

"Isn't that what you do?"

"*Woman* did the Lord ever know my heart when he put you in my life—to keep me from giving in to those tempting voices of pride and intolerance?"

She could almost see her father nod to her Mum and her beaming in response.

"Ruthie am I wanting Lily with us out of pride or love?"

"Jonny, I'm not the one to ask."

"God knew how much I needed you."

"Is that the only reason?"

"Darling, you know it isn't."

The silence that followed went on so long, Lily's cheeks grew warm.

"Jon, you put a lot of study and prayer and time into your sermons. You have a dream and a future."

"That's different."

"Is it? It's just as important to her. And, Jon, she has real talent."

"Surely that talent could be directed into a less worldly pursuit."

"Perhaps in time, my dear, but for now she's at that stage in life when her mind is taken up with more trivial things."

Mummy, what would I do without you?

"We allow her to be seduced by the world? You were never like that."

"Wasn't I?"

Mum's tone sounded coquettish. What's that about?

"No, you weren't."

"Not with clothing, my dear. But did I ever fritter away the hours reading Shelley, Browning, and Lord Byron—and writing love poems. And, to whom?"

There it is again. Is Mum flirting?

"But Ruthie, that was different."

"My misspent youth? I believe you still have the poems, Jonny?" She giggled, and he suppressed a cough.

Lily's face burned now. She had intruded on their privacy. She turned to go.

"You think I should allow her to stay?"

"I think you mustn't make her go."

"I'm thinking of her spirit."

"And I'm thinking of her heart—for now."

"But isn't it my duty to see to the fate of her soul?"

"Not any longer. You've realized your obligation as a father and her spiritual head. It's now her responsibility. The choice is hers alone."

Dearest Mum, reasoning with Father as only she can. How wonderful, her mother's gift of gentle persuasion—especially when it worked in Lily's favor. Would Father recant his objection?

CHAPTER 7

NOT ALWAYS BLACK AND WHITE

> If you reveal your secrets to the wind, you should not blame the wind for revealing them to the trees.
> Khalil Gibran (1883–1931)

Lily stole back up to her room. After dressing, she tripped cheerfully down stairs, knocked on the dining room door and entered.

"Good. I'm pleased you came down before the others." Father had a glow about his face and a twinkle in his eyes. "Your mother has presented a convincing case for your position. She would have made a compelling lawyer."

Lily pressed her lips together to prevent a grin from breaking out.

Mum sat with her hand covering Father's, a flush on her cheeks. His fingers curled around hers. Little sparks danced in her eyes as she smiled at Lily.

The intimacy her parents shared was embarrassing—and enchanting. She blushed.

"You are of age and able, as your mother so aptly makes the case, to make your own decisions." Father slumped a bit in his chair. "I disagree with your choice, but I will not quench your spirit."

"Father, thank you!" She ran over and gave him a big hug and kiss. Guilt edged in on her conscience. Yet again she had judged him too severely. "And I do ask your forgiveness for my impudence. I was disrespectful. I am so s—"

Stevie and Kit burst into the room.

"I didn't hear a knock." Father narrowed his eyes.

They dropped into their chairs and bowed their heads for the grace.

"Steven, please recite the Scripture for today." He gazed straight at Lily.

Stevie looked at the ceiling. "'In everything give thanks: for this is the will of God in Christ Jesus concerning you. Quench not the spirit.'"

Mum patted Father's hand.

So, it wasn't only Mum, after all. Fancy that. Father's great Almighty was on her side for a change. The Lord had spoken, and Father would comply. Maybe miracles did still happen. Lily smiled at her mother then caught her father's eyes full of love.

Room 39: Admiralty Building, Whitehall

"Lieutenant Commander Claiborne, the captain will see you now." The lieutenant opened the door for Hugh.

"Captain Conner." Hugh stood at attention locking on his superior's eyes.

The man reminded him of his Uncle Ray, with his thin face and deceptive smile. The captain had been Hugh's commanding officer since he deployed to Washington in 1948 as Naval Attaché with a top-secret undercover mission to identify possible Soviet agents suspected of leaking secrets from within the embassy. Hugh's involvement was need-to-know only.

"Have a seat, Commander. You recall Mr. White and Mr. Black from your other briefings."

"Aye, Sir. Gentlemen." He dipped his head to the two MI5 agents whose names were not, in fact, Black and White. They nodded back.

The captain sat behind his desk. "First, Commander, on behalf of Her Majesty, I want to thank you for your excellent work on this mission. You were in good part responsible for providing the intelligence that identified Burgess and Maclean as the probable leaks to the Soviets."

"Of course," Black lit the cigarette in his left hand, then rubbed the two moles on his middle finger with the ring finger. "You were selected for the assignment because of your expertise in intelligence during the war and your attending the same college as Maclean and Burgess, and interestingly, Kim Philby."

How the devil does the chap do that with his fingers? Hugh tried and couldn't. "Philby put up Burgess in his basement. Have you confirmed any of the suspicions of the former MI6 chief?" Personally, he had no doubts. Something about Philby had always nagged at him.

"Let's just say that his association with the other two is suspect." White's expression gave away nothing.

"Do we have any solid proof of their defection to Russia?" Hugh studied the men's faces.

"Only speculation, so far."

"Quite," said the captain, "considering that as the newly appointed First Secretary to the embassy in '49, and the chief British Intelligence representative in Washington, Philby was instructed to discover the identity of the Soviet mole and was also responsible for liaising with the new American CIA."

Black sneered. "Obviously, looking back, MI6 made an egregious error assigning Burgess as Second Secretary. Especially since Maclean came under suspicion in April of '50. Then they both went missing on the same day."

No loss to the Intelligence Service or their country.

Maclean hadn't seemed too objectionable, but Burgess—what a degenerate and drunken crud. Most of Hugh's mates called him Genius in jest, but Burgess threw it at him like an insult.

Stone-faced, Hugh hid elation at their departure, but how damaging to the free world their betrayal.

"After a year of investigation, we and the FBI were planning to confront Maclean on the twenty-eighth of May while he was in London," said White, "but he missed the appointment."

No one laughed.

Hugh snickered. "You chaps should have gotten him a birthday present. It was his thirty-eighth."

"Talk to MI6." White scowled.

"You chaps don't talk to each other?" Hugh already knew the answer.

"Come now, Lord Claiborne, as a future earl, you know MI6 is your kind. We're 'below the salt,' just middle-class blokes. We don't exactly go out to the pub for a pint together." Black blew cigarette smoke at him.

It didn't take intelligence experience to read resentment in the man's tone and the other's sneers.

"All right, gentlemen." His CO frowned. "Shall we get underway with the mission at hand?"

"Aye, Sir." The others nodded.

"As you know," Black said, "Philby was recalled and resigned from the SIS. MI5's interrogation of him didn't come up with anything substantive. MI6 is defending him all the way. So far he's looking for work as a journalist."

"I reckon he is guilty." Hugh fingered his wheel hat. "But what now?"

"We still believe there are more men involved," White said. "So, keep at it."

Black and White rose to leave.

Hugh rose too and offered his hand.

A look passed between them, then they shook hands. *What do you know, the self-proclaimed, below-the-salters are meeting my kind halfway? Will wonders never cease?*

Captain Conner looked on at the exchange, a sly smile on his face. "Lieutenant Commander, we'll keep you there till Sir Oliver's replacement arrives in December, then a change of assignment will appear natural."

"Sir, the new assignment?" Hugh hoped to hear today.

"All in good time." The captain rose and strode over to him, then reached up, loosened his epaulettes, and replaced them with another pair that had an additional stripe. "Congratulations, Commander Claiborne. Fine job."

"OK, Genius, in lieu of a medal, a promotion will have to do." Pride's tone had a barb to it.

He smiled.

The Havens

At nineteen hundred hours, thirty-three minutes, Duncan opened the door for Hugh. "You are late, Commander. *Commander!*"

Of course, the former sergeant major would notice the change in rank on Hugh's shoulders.

"Congratulations on your promotion, Sir." He hurried ahead of Hugh into the parlor.

"May I introduce *Commander* Claiborne." The butler stepped aside.

Hugh's father rose and came to shake his hand. "Congratulations, son. Duncan, champagne to celebrate my son's promotion."

"Oh, darling, I'm so proud." Mum embraced him.

Before he had a chance to recover, Phila was all over him with hugs. "I just knew you were on some critical mission, Hughie. Whatever did you do to get rewarded?"

"Dad! Help!"

"Son, you need to know how to fend off even the most loving assault." His father directed his mum and sister back to their chairs. Then the man of the moment caught the butler grinning at him, obviously enjoying the spectacle.

After Duncan served the champagne, Dad lifted his flute. "To my son, *Commander* Claiborne." They toasted the new commander and clapped.

Hugh stood tall and dipped his head to the acclaim. Of course, he hadn't done anything heroic like Dad, his uncles, and cousin. This would have to do, and few would even know what he'd done.

"So, Hughie, what did you do? Were you the one who exposed those traitors?"

Pride hungered to crow, but—"Petunia, curiosity killed the cat. Proceeding up the chain of command is really quite boring. You do the job, don't rock the boat, mind your P's and Q's, obey orders, and escort admirals' daughters once in a while."

"*Not bad, Genius.*"

"I say, son, you do know the ropes." Dad sent him an approving glance.

When dinner was over, they gathered in the parlor for coffee and pudding. Hugh always enjoyed this custom, especially after being away for long periods of time. His next assignment was the topic tonight with speculations as to where he might be sent.

When they rose to leave, Dad took Phila's hand. "Daughter stay a moment, please."

Hugh escorted his mother out and then collected Neptune and Triton for a walk. The labs gushed with elation. Hugh walked, head high. That Dad radiated pride for him was worth everything. He never said but, of course, he had to be aware of Hugh's assignment. Best Mum didn't know. She'd worry. And if Pet knew? She'd tell the world.

But is this the way my life is heading? That Hemingway quote he threw out at Pet? Ah yes . . . "I can't stand it to think my life is going so fast and I'm not really living it."

❋ ❋ ❋

Phila stood at attention.

Papa laid gentle hands on her shoulders. "Philomena. You need to curb your curiosity and mouth and think before you speak." His eyes cut straight to her conscience.

"Aye, aye, Sir." She wanted to explain how she just couldn't help it, but Papa didn't take excuses from his men or his children.

"Do you recall those American posters during the war that read, 'Loose Lips Sink Ships?' They were making a point that speaking of ship movements carelessly could, if overheard, allow the enemy to intercept and destroy our ships."

"But the war is over."

Papa's frigid expression indicated that nothing was over. *Why did God give me such a curious nature, then make me live with people who keep secrets?*

"Not this new conflict involving the threat of Communism. This peril could prove more insidious than the Nazis."

"Are you saying Hugh is involved in this new danger?"

"Oh, Pet," Papa exhaled an exasperated sigh, "I am not involved with what your brother is doing for the Navy."

"But you're the Naval Secretary, Papa."

Her father pulled himself up to his full height, no longer her papa but the powerful admiral heading into a squall. "Now hear this, Philomena Justine. What I am saying is—it is *none* of your business—and—you need to quell your questions and give the subject a wide berth from now on. In other words, my daughter will *not* be a loose cannon. Is that understood?"

"Aye, aye, Sir." Phila trembled, gazing up at his stormy face.

"One more thing. I know you would never cause your mother more concern than she already has for her children, but *I do not* want her to hear of *anything* that would cause her additional worry for Hugh. Do you read me loud and clear, young lady?"

"Aye, aye, Sir." *I will not cry.*

Papa surprised her then by taking her in his arms. When he released her, he kissed her forehead. "Let's do our part to support your brother. Now go and say good night to your mum."

Phila stood there for a long time. She still shook from his reprimand—from his anger with her and the realization that Hugh *was* in danger.

But surely there's a way to find out, at least for myself. She wouldn't breathe a word.

CHAPTER 8
BEAUTY AND THE BRAIN

Words are easy, like the wind; Faithful friends are hard to find.
The Passionate Pilgrim, William Shakespeare

Friday, 26 September
The Vicarage
As Lily prepared to leave for Phila's, she bent down to kiss her mother. Mum hugged her close, then backed away a step. Taking hold of her hands she looked Lily in the eye. "I know how much the ball and contest mean to you. I understand. Really, I do. But I wonder—"

"I thought I had your blessing." Lily's stomach flipped.

Mum's face shone with tenderness, "Oh, my child. I give you my blessing always, but I must also give you truth. I wonder if I was right to argue in your favor, counter to your father's position."

"You're not changing your mind?"

Father came to the door behind Mum.

Panic seized Lily's heart. "You're *not* are you?"

"No, but we have reservations." His eyes grew dark, like a shadow had passed over. "I fear this decision will endanger your faith. Oh, I do fear for you, Lillian." But he gathered her into his arms and kissed her atop her head.

She had been so excited to receive his blessing. But now? And Mum, what is she fearing?

Too confused and perplexed to go directly to The Havens, she walked to the private gardens at Belgrave Square and sat under the pergola watching the leaves of the ancient plane trees dancing in the wind.

A glimpse into her father's heart had revealed his pain. She felt like one of those big leaves being tossed about.

Father had always considered his faith unwavering, steadfast. He said God was the same yesterday, today, and tomorrow—always constant, never dithering. She believed her father's faith unshakable like the house built on the rock.

"*If you can't count on your father, how can you trust God?*" Doubt sent a shiver down her spine.

That and eavesdropping yesterday on an intimate moment between him and her mum left her baffled and embarrassed. And frightened.

The late September air had cooled promising rain. An inquisitive robin bounced across the grass, hopped onto a branch, lifted up his head, and sang his warbling trill.

Fading sunlight shone through the gracefully aging leaves of the beautiful Dutch elms. A dappled golden-green light shimmered as the leaves swayed in the autumn breeze. The trees whispered softly, peacefully. Slowly, the calming breeze began to sweep her doubts away. The robin flew away, taking her disturbing thoughts with it.

Phila had invited her to spend the night, putting the finishing touches on the gown. She'd accomplished all the work in the small room off Phila's suite—a large closet, actually. Neither vicarage nor school would have been suitable for privacy. No one had seen the gown but her friend—until yesterday, when she gave it to Molly. The young Irish maid was an artist with an iron.

Just short of miraculous, an earl's daughter befriending someone of Lily's station. Though still not generally accepted in these times of emerging equality, nobility and commoners mixing didn't often occur—not even after King Edward VIII renounced his throne for love.

She and Phila had only been four years old in 1936 when he stepped down.

She smiled, recalling her mum telling them about it on the tenth anniversary of the abdication—the twelfth of December 1946.

Phila had nearly swooned. "How romantic—relinquishing a throne for love."

"Maybe so," said Lily's mum, "but the whole affair disrupted the entire country, causing a constitutional crisis, if you will. The new king wanted to marry an American. That was upsetting in itself, but she was divorcing her second husband. No one approved of the union, not the church, government, or public. But King Edward abdicated and married Wallis Simpson anyway."

"What about his duty to England?" Lily frowned.

Phila had ended the conversation. "What's more important than love?"

Edward's younger brother, Albert, had become King George VI in 1936. He died in February and Princess Elizabeth became Queen.

Lily chuckled recalling how excited Phila had been when the former princess married Prince Phillip in 1947. "He's so-o-o handsome," she had crooned.

Nine whole months stretched ahead until the Coronation. But first, Phila's birthday ball, Lily's introduction into upper-class society. But Phila wasn't solely an entry into society.

"You can't deny that Phila is that."

She brushed aside the mercenary thought. How could she not love Phila? She's so honest, so genuine, so — really — real. Of course, Phil would use a word like unpretentious. Her friend's impressive intellect and thirst for knowledge were amazing. Words thrilled her like a new fashion stirred Lily.

If only she had Phil's incredible memory to make the daily memorizing of Scripture easier. Her friend had such a passion for reading every book she could get her hands on and debating her brother about what he read. She loved to quote famous people. She didn't do it to impress, but rather to spice up her conversation. Her imagination knew no bounds. Even in her final year at Oxford, she still loved and read fairy stories. Kit loved how Phila would sit with her little friends and tell them made-up stories. We couldn't be more different — hardly kindred spirits. "Whatever drew us together?"

Phila had an insatiable appetite for learning, whereas Lily found any kind of studying a bore, unless it had to do with fashion. Her friend admitted it outright; labeling herself "puny, pudgy, and plain." She loved using — what did she call it? Alliteration. A "writer thing" Phil said, running words together beginning with the same letter. She claimed being around one so beautiful as Lily helped make up for her homeliness.

They had both been seven-years-old when Lily's father left Holy Trinity Church in Harrow to be the vicar at St Peter's. About a month after they moved to Eaton Square, Lady Beatrice invited her family to Sunday dinner. Lily laughed as she recalled how she sat across the ornate table from Phila's teenaged brother, who seemed to be all thumbs throughout the meal.

After dinner, while the maid served coffee in the drawing room for the adults, Phila showed Lily up to her rooms. The walls were lined with shelves full of books. Magnificent dolls from far-away countries paraded across the higher shelves. A bevy of stuffed bears lounged on the huge four-poster bed hung around with yards of frothy pink fabric.

"O-o-oh . . ." Lily gazed around the fairy-tale room like the pictures in her *Cinderella* book.

"Do you think it too ostentatious?" Phila scrunched up her face.

"It's very beautiful." A four-poster bed with lace canopy topped with a crown. A soft breeze smelling like lilacs wafted in through the window.

"Sorry. I just learned that word today. *Ostentatious*. Isn't it delicious?" The girl beamed.

"What does it mean?" Oh yes, this room is delicious.

"Too showy. Do you think it's too showy?"

"Well, you are nobility. I expect this is how you live."

"Like a fairy princess?"

"Yes, I suppose." She walked slowly over to the doll collection. "What lovely gowns."

"Papa brings the international dolls back from his travels. They're quite educationally interesting, actually, especially when one learns about the customs of the dress. The others are copies of famous designer gowns. Exquisite, of course, but I prefer my books."

Lily stood admiring the dolls, studying each carefully. "I think I should like to make gowns this lovely someday."

"And I shall write books. Shall we be friends?"

"Why, yes, Philomena."

"Phila. And you?"

"Just Lily."

They had giggled, ever staunch companions after that.

That unlikely friendship — what was the word Phila used? Inconceivable. It's the best thing ever to happen in my life — so far. Mum said it was God-ordained. Or perhaps simply marvelous luck that the Countess thought Lily talented enough to attend a school of fashion and had obtained a scholarship for her.

By the time Lily walked to Eaton Square and saw the steeple and six pillars of St Peter's, her mood lightened considerably even though the wind had picked up and dark clouds were rolling in from the north.

What could possibly go wrong now?

CHAPTER 9
UNWELCOME VISITORS

My hopes were all dead . . . my cherished wishes, yesterday so blooming and glowing.
Jane Eyre, Charlotte Brontë (1816–1855)

Arbroath, County Angus, Scotland
Ollie's sitting room at home
Ollie tossed and turned on his couch, sweating profusely as his subconscious returned to North Africa.

* * *

Round after round of mortar fire burst all around Ollie launching geysers of molten sand like a thick forest of fiery trees.

A Dhia! I'm in Dante's Inferno. But I'm no dead . . . yet.

Blood-curdling screams sear his ears as comrades fall. Whaur are our tanks?

Out of the swirling red sandy haze surge two fire-breathing beasts of the Wehrmacht. Groans and yowling tell him his mates are lying wounded in the direct path of the Panzers. Stop them. How?

He feels for the grenades hanging from his belt. Grenades willna take oot tanks. Who's got the satchel charges? Campbell. Ollie looks wildly around, bellowing, *"Campbell?"* It takes several shouts before he barely catches an answering howl. He follows the wailing to the jock, grabs two satchels charges of C-4.

Sweat pouring down his face, in his eyes, and his heart pumping like a rapid-fire machine gun; he charges the tanks, dodging strafing. Gotta git right on tank.

His brither's voice taunted: *"How's your hand off, oaf? Still got it? It's not rugby."*

He mounts the first tank jamming the satchel charge between the turret and the tank's body, pulls the igniter lanyard. One down in seconds.

Another dash. Another attach. Another pull. Number two. The world explodes. He dives. Too close. Too late.

※ ※ ※

Ollie launched off the couch grabbing his chest. Lightening lit up the room. Thunder crashed. He panted, his shirt damp with sweat. The wounds didn't hurt anymore, but memory of the pain still ached. He'd fallen asleep reading. Damn. Another flashback. Would the dreams never cease, Gilt leave him be? Ten years!

"You're a killer. You don't deserve peace."

Staggering to the window he gazed out at the storm. Lightning flashes. Peels of thunder. His mind's eye revisited North Africa and the sands of hell. Only difference—no dying. He looked down at his hands seeing them still covered in blood.

"Thou shalt not kill."

His mate's screams still reverberated through his brain. How many shattered bodies had he dragged to safety?

"So, you think all your heroic actions absolved your guilt?"

More beasts hammered down on him in the red din.

"Ogilvie, they're ours, lad. Ye done weel." The sarge had grabbed him. "*Blessed St Michael*, ye're bleeding like a stuck hog."

War's over. Seven years. How—no, he knew how—why did he make it home alive? The others didn't.

Eton Square

Lily could see a storm approaching, but she felt sunny all over. What luck, the not-quenching-the-Spirit verse was part of today's devotions. Now, she had God's blessing, too.

Skimming past St Peter's down Upper Belgrave Street, she almost flew past the block of white, three-story town houses, their one-story pillars guarding the doorways with a landing atop enclosed by black wrought iron. She paused at the Claiborne's townhouse.

What a delicious sensation, this walking on air. Lily could taste success, her mind drunk with the anticipation of seeing the gown all pressed and finally ready.

"You will win the school competition, hands down."

The Havens

Lily walked past the two columns on either side and pulled the bell. "Duncan," she murmured, dashing past the butler when he answered the door. She sped through the living area, across the great kitchen, and flung wide the door to the laundry room.

But the only garment hanging on the drying line was a lacy royal-blue garment that probably belonged to the Countess. Lily whipped around and dashed upstairs into the closet workroom. The mannequin stood near the window, as bare as when she'd left it yesterday.

She raced back to the laundry. Panic seized her as she scanned the room a second time.

"Gone! Your dream to break the chains and escape from the existence of your father's confining universe."

"Gone! Your chance to enter the world of design."

"Gone! Showing those hoity-toity girls who look down on you because your father is a commoner."

"You can't attend Phila's ball now, much less win the contest."

Feet glued to the floor, she refused to listen to the voices inside her mind. My gown couldn't just disappear. She sucked in a deep breath and exhaled. I'm a goose. Of course, the maid must have it. "Surely no one would take it."

Molly tripped down the back stairs, tucking an errant coppery-red curl under her white uniform cap. "Miss L-lily?"

"My gown, do you have it?"

"Yer l-lovely dress? Sure an' I don't k-know, Miss," her Irish brogue at high pitch. "'Twas here y-yesterday afternoon. Just gittin' to c-come and press it now." She looked around the room and crossed herself. "Oh, M-miss . . ."

Alarm flashed in her pale eyes, a pinched expression on her freckled face.

Mrs. Schulz marched in, obviously ready to quell any unwelcome disturbance in her well-run domain. The housekeeper insisted on order and harmony in the household, as she did with her sturdy person, from the steely gray coronet of braids on her head to her polished brown oxfords. "Vhat's the fuss?"

It would be easy to be afraid of the German housekeeper if one forgot that she had been housekeeper at the British Embassy in Berlin and had been secreted out of Germany when the SS discovered her mother was Jewish. Even Lady Beatrice didn't wish to go up against "The Schulz."

Lily and Molly stepped back a little.

Molly wrung her hands. "M-miss Lily's gown's gone m-missing, Mizz S-schulz."

The woman took one glance at the remaining evening dress. "*Um himmels willen!* Don't tell me, *ein dummkopf* came early and took the wrong gown. That vas not the schedule we agreed upon."

"Who?" Lily stood there gaping.

"My apologies, *bitte, Fräulein.* Da messenger from Hartnell's." She frowned. "Deez people never get it right, even from the royal dressmaker—mind you—unless one is right there to supervise."

"Oh, M-miss, sure an' we can git it b-back."

Lily stood there holding back tears. They *had* to. This couldn't happen, not when she had worked so hard, pinning all her dreams on the gown.

Lady Beatrice glided into the room. "Lily, what a jolt! I'm certain we can rectify the situation. Mrs. Schulz, would you please have Giselle serve tea. Obviously, we all need a strong brew." Calm flowed from her reassuring smile and softly draped, moss-green frock.

She put her arm around Lily. "Come and sit down in the drawing room, my dear. Molly go fetch Miss Phila. I left her in the garage having some discussion about Hungary with János." Her ladyship ushered Lily to the rose-and-ivory brocaded love seat. "I'll ring Hartnell's in a moment." But first she sat beside Lily, talking quietly to her. The Countess's voice was a calming tonic.

"I'll be back directly." She smiled and exited the room, moving much like one of the swans Lily loved to watch gliding across the pond in the West Garden of the Earl's country estate.

Phila rushed in, flushed and panting, her tangerine curls bouncing.

"What's wrong? Molly said there's an emergency."

"My gown has . . . *disappeared.*" Her voice cracked, all calm dissipated.

"Oh, Lil, surely not!" Phila's round, guileless face cringed.

Giselle brought in a tray of tea things, followed by Lady Beatrice.

"I spoke with the custodian. They've closed for the day. I'm sorry, Lily, but we will have to wait till tomorrow to find out. *Merci*, Giselle, *vous êtes excusé.*"

The woman bowed and departed.

The Countess sat in the Queen Anne chair facing the tea table and began pouring tea for the three of them.

Lily listened to the tea and cream daub into the delicate china cups, the clunk of the sugar, and the clink of the spoons on the saucers as she sat frozen. How could her ladyship go on as if everything was fine?

Phila wanted details. "How ever did this happen, Mum?"

Her mother explained the horrible mistake.

"So, we can get it back and everything will be fine," said Phila. "But what a scare, Lil. You must be done in."

"I'm so very sorry, my dear." The Countess stared down at the teacups. "My, my, where is my mind?" She handed a cup and saucer to Phila, then placed one into Lily's shaking hands.

My gown. I might as well die. Or go to Scotland. Her dream was over before it began. Lily rung her hands as Defeat pressed its advantage.

"You'll remain cloistered at home until Father marries you off to some insipid missionary."

This is the worst day of my life. She leapt up and fled.

CHAPTER 10

THE WEIGHT OF LOVE

Meanwhile the cross comes before the crown and tomorrow is a Monday morning.
The Weight of Glory, C. S. Lewis

Phila jumped up to follow, "Lily!"

Mum stopped her. "Let her go. It's been a shock. She just needs time to herself. It will be OK."

"But not knowing until tomorrow morning. That's forever!"

"Yes, waiting is always difficult."

How can Mum be so calm? "It's blooming *onerous*!"

"Let's pray." She held out her hand to Phila.

But Phila balled her fists. "This was her dream for another kind of life."

"It's not easy being the child of a clergyman." Mum looked wistful.

"Was it burdensome for you?"

"Not often. Oh, and my papa had such a pastor's heart." Her eyes took on a nostalgic gleam. "He gave such inspiring sermons."

"I remember. It was like hearing bedtime stories. Lily's father gives lectures and almost shouts." She grimaced.

"Yes. Father Whitely is an evangelist and a passionate preacher. His words ring with such a force of truth that they strike straight to the soul. He definitely has the gift of exhortation. Your grandpapa spoke softly, embracing you with God's love; such a gentle shepherd."

"You mean Grandpapa was a blanket, and Lily's father is a trumpet?"

"Why, darling, what an imaginative way to put it."

"Lily thinks her father is hard and inflexible."

"Children tend to have that perception of their fathers — especially when being corrected or instructed. I can recall such memories of my papa."

"Not Grandpapa, surely?"

"It's a father's job to set a child on the right course, as your own father would say." Mum patted her hand. "My perception of Jon Whitely is one of a friend, not a parent, so I see a true man of God. He will win a multitude of souls to the Lord on this trip north."

"I never thought of it that way, and Papa does get fearsome at times."

Mum chuckled. "I reckon your father was quite intimidating on his ship and is in fleet headquarters."

Papa certainly intimidated her the other day. However, she couldn't visualize her grandfather being stern with her mum. But then she couldn't picture her mother ever needing correction. "You liked being a pastor's daughter, didn't you?"

"I did." That dreamy expression took over her face as she remembered.

"Lily doesn't." *Not certain I would either.*

"It does have its drawbacks." She frowned. "People expect more of a cleric's family. One's actions and appearance are always open for criticism. And although Christians shouldn't judge, they do, and usually more harshly than unbelievers. They expect the children to be models of perfection."

"That's what Lily says." *I'd hate that.*

Mum brought her hands together, touching her lips. "It can be a trial at times, especially for the minister's wife."

"That's the last thing you could ever be."

No kidding. "Lily only wants to be perfect when it comes to designing clothes and be famous like Balenciaga or Coco Chanel."

Mum smiled. "That's quite an ambition. But I'm certain they're not perfect. None is perfect except—"

"God. *I know*, Mum. Speaking of preaching."

"Was I? It's so easy to fall into it. Growing up in a pastor's household, one is so inundated with Scripture all the time that I felt at times almost like a parrot." She smiled.

"Lily says verses invade her brain unbidden like the refrain of a song you can't rid your mind of."

"I imagine it's a curse and a blessing at the same time, like a little voice whispering in your ear. Sometimes the rebel in you doesn't want to listen, but often it's so very welcome when the tempters woo your baser nature."

"Like the good and bad angels sitting on either shoulder pouring conflicting notions of good and evil in our ears?" Phila wrinkled her nose. "Those stories you told us when we were little?"

"Obviously, you are ready for the adult version. Those fiendish voices will continue to pummel your thoughts, which is why you need to know Scripture to combat them. What is consistently poured in will pour out. It's meant to, like a river." Mum had such a gentle way of teaching.

"I know, Mum, but I enjoy quoting all sorts of things."

"Yes, you're amazing."

"Precious little good it does me, seeing as how I can't read with Oxford's eminent philologist. Did you know Professor Tolkien actually made up languages for the elves in *The Hobbit*?"

"Oh, how you loved that book. It's surprising that he and Mr. Lewis, such distinguished men of academia, could write such delightful books for children." Mum beamed. "From the time you and Hugh learned to read, you devoured every book you could get your hands on. You loved Beatrix Potter and Edith Nesbit; your brother, Sir Arthur Conan Doyle."

"Sherlock Holmes, of course." Phila adopted an affected pose. "'It's elementary, my dear Watson.'" She giggled. "I loved *Squirrel Nutkin* best. And Nesbit's *The Railway Children*. I want to write stories like that someday."

"I'm sure you will."

"Did you know Professor Tolkien is writing a sequel to *The Hobbit*?" Excitement welled up just thinking about it. "Apparently, he's been working on it for over a decade, and it's a fairy story for *adults*. Can you imagine?"

"It's bound to be an excellent read, then." Her mother poured them fresh cups of tea from the pot Giselle had just topped up.

"I read Mr. Lewis's third Narnia book, *The Voyage of the Dawn Treader*, last night. *The Lion, the Witch, and the Wardrobe* was the best, and what a brilliant title and delicious reading. I think there's more to them than just for children."

Mum chuckled. "I'm happy you're enjoying the books from an adult perspective. It was thoughtful of you to give a copy to Lily's little sister for her birthday."

"Lily says Kit carries it with her everywhere and talks of little else. I gave her a copy of *Prince Caspian*, the second book in the Chronicles, last week."

"You're being very kind to little Katherine." Her gentle voice bathed Phila in its warmth.

"Mr. Lewis's books are usually pretty serious. I'm looking forward to his lectures this term. Their styles are quite different. Professor Tolkien mumbles, and you have to listen very carefully. Mr. Lewis's voice is so booming you can hear it down the hall. Every seat is taken."

"His voice is extraordinary. I doubt I missed a single one of his BBC broadcasts during the war. He and Mr. Churchill inspired and encouraged us all."

"I listened too."

"That you did. But hearing him preach in Oxford at the Church of St Mary the Virgin in 1942 affected me greatly. *The Weight of Glory* was the title of his sermon. I'll always remember him saying something to the effect that no one is just mortal and that every day, to some extent, we're helping and encouraging each other in our choices, either onto the path that leads to eternal rewards or damnation. I've never forgotten that."

Phila frowned. "That's an awfully formidable responsibility. It's not one I ever want to take on."

"Life is full of *weighty* choices."

"And you talk about Father Whitely saying *weighty* things." It tickled her that she'd met Mum's pun with one of her own.

Her mother began gathering up the tea things and rang for Giselle. "I'd like to read one of the Narnia books. I've just reread Mr. Lewis's *The Screwtape Letters*, and something in a lighter vein would be a pleasant change."

Phila handed Giselle the cups and saucers. "Brilliantly clever how a devil instructs a novice on how to lead his human down the path to perdition—Uncle Screwtape to his nephew Wormwood. Aren't those names absolutely diabolical? It was incredibly entertaining."

"And I hope, my dear, *enlightening?*" Mum raised an eyebrow.

"I thought it outrageously hilarious." Remembering brought on a big grin. "It does challenge the wits with the perspectives all catawampus, picturing things from an evil viewpoint. Actually, wicked characters are much more amusing and interesting than the goodie-two-shoes." How she admired Mr. Lewis's writing.

"I think you've missed the message. I believe the author meant it to be taken seriously." She lifted a forefinger. "That was only Mr. Lewis's approach, to help one recognize when the tempters are whispering in your ear."

"Yes, of course. But were you not amused when that vicar wrote to *The

Guardian to cancel his subscription because the paper was publishing such a devilish series?" Phila laughed, then gave her mother a hug. "I'll go up and see Lily now. But what do I say?"

"Just listen to begin. Then the words will come."

CHAPTER 11

DREAMS

So runs my dream, but what am I?
An infant crying in the night
An infant crying for the light
And with no language but a cry.
    "In Memoriam," Alfred Lord Tennyson (1809–1892)

Lily had fled up the grand staircase, flung open Phila's door, slammed it, then backed up against it like the furies were after her. She stood there panting. Gasping for air and sobbing, she sank to the floor.

If they don't find my gown, my life is over.

Finally, she stalked to the closet and dropped on the stool facing the stripped mannequin. Naked, like her. She fingered a piece of the lapis fabric, then crumpled it up. Was this God's punishment?

"Whose adorning let it not be that outward adorning of plaiting the hair, and of wearing gold, or of putting on apparel, but let it be the hidden man of the heart."

Oh! Would those memorized verses ever leave her alone? The intimidating voice made them sound harsh, outdated. She squeezed her eyes shut and covered her ears.

Why was it so difficult for Father to understand? When she asked him if God had given her the talent, he had acquiesced. Then why couldn't she use it to make women look beautiful? Mum understood, but then she was a woman.

"What is wrong with liking fine clothing and wanting to design lovely clothes?"

Lily threw herself on the bed and pounded the pillows. It was so unfair.

"You deserve credit for your accomplishment."

"Yes, I do."

Scripture had whispered its response: *"Let us not be desirous of vain glory."*

Saturday, 27 September

The sun had barely peeped up over London's skyline when Lily opened her eyes. She slid out of bed.

"You awake, Lil? What time is it?"

"Barely half six. Sorry, I didn't mean to wake you."

"No worries. We won't sleep till we know."

"It's Saturday. Will Hartnell's even be open? If so, when?"

"I'm certain Mum will ring by nine—surely."

"That's nearly three more hours." Lily yawned.

Phila yawned, too. "Last time I looked at the clock it was nearly three."

"What a friend you are, staying up to keep me company." She yawned again as Phila summoned tea.

Hartnell's rang early. They found the gown and would deliver it right away. Lily breathed freely again.

"God's in his heaven—All's right with the world!" Phila beamed. "Robert Browning from 'Pippa Passes'."

Lily shook her head. "Of course."

Los Angeles Memorial Coliseum
University of California at Los Angeles vs.
Texas Christian University

"Just like old times, huh Mike? You and me watching football?" Dan adjusted his baseball cap with the UCLA Bruins logo, topping off his gold shirt and blue shorts.

"Sure is Sport. Only your dad is missing." His uncle settled a Notre Dame Fighting Irish cap over his salt and pepper hair. Father Mike dressed in mufti today, gray trousers and green sports shirt—the only fan in their section not arrayed in the official colors of blue and gold.

A small cloud of sadness drifted over the sun. "I don't think either of you missed a single one of my games in high school or at Stanford either."

"After I forgave you for not going to Notre Dame. The least you could have done was to get your masters and doctorate at my alma mater instead of Columbia. That school seduced you away from the Lord."

"No preaching today, huh?"

"OK, kid. Sorry, occupational hazard." He chuckled.

"Today's crowd is a fairly good showing for the second game of the season. What d'you think . . . about thirty thou?"

A gaggle of boys scrambled up the aisle. "Hey, Professor McCauley!" A gangly kid with a sandy-colored crew cut poked his buddies. "Look who's here, fellas, my philosophy prof and . . . no date for the game, Prof?"

"Ah, Mr. Evans. No date either I see. This is my uncle. Mike, Jack Evans, who I thought was interested in getting a good grade in my class."

"Aw, Professor, you know you don't mind the joshing." Jack looked at Mike. "He doesn't, you know. He's the only fun prof I have. The rest are so old they love to tell how they fought in *the war*." He crossed his eyes.

Dan grinned. "Mr. Evans, *I* fought in *the war*."

"Naw. You don't say."

"I *do* say. I was way too young then, but I flew fighter planes protecting our bombers over France and Germany."

Jack's jaw dropped. "Were you a hero?" The boys hushed, gaping pop-eyed.

Mike's eyes gleamed. "Every pilot was a hero, Mr. Evans. Your prof received the Distinguished Flying Cross and Purple Heart. I am very proud of my nephew, young man." The boys gawked, mouths agape.

"Jackie," a beefy kid with a red face and red hair, elbowed Jack. "That's the priest from the Newman Center. Be polite."

Jack's eyebrows shot up as he goggled first Mike, then Dan. He opened his mouth to say something but stopped and frowned. "Uh, well Prof, see ya in class," he waved as the boys walked off.

"Obviously Jack was surprised your uncle is a priest. You're not proselytizing humanism to your students, are you Danny?"

"*Father* Mike, surely you don't think I would use my classes to convert these virgin minds to my way of thinking. Do you?"

"I hope not, but the kid's reaction—"

"Look Mike, I don't get personal in class, but sometimes the kids corner me outside class, and I answer their questions. I try not to go into detail on my beliefs, but I'll tell them about different ideologies. As for extoling Humanism, I leave that to my lectures."

"Regarding those, where in England are you speaking next month about how humanity is just fine on its own?" A smile accompanied the sarcasm.

"City University London, and the University of Liverpool—October seventh and ninth. The provost mentioned that someone from Oxford might attend to check me out. That's the big time, Mike."

"Would speaking at Oxford make up for losing your dream of flying jets? Has humanism filled that hole?"

"Nope. Nothing ever will but speaking at Oxford would come close." They stood to cheer at UCLA's third touchdown against the Horned Frogs. Only groans wafted across the field from the purple and white section.

CHAPTER 12

CINDERELLA HOPES

"A Dream is a Wish Your Heart Makes"
Song from Walt Disney's *Cinderella* (1950)
Written and composed by
Mack David, Al Hoffman, Jerry Livingston

Monday, 29 September
St Peters Vicarage
After breakfast, Lily knocked on the door of her father's study.

"Come." He rose from his desk and came over to her. "I'm happy your difficulty was resolved. However, should you decide to change your mind and join us, for any reason, I will leave some money for the train fare. Our schedule is here on my desk." He placed his hand on her head and blessed her. "Go with God, child. You have our love always no matter what and, of course, the Almighty's as well."

Why did she always misjudge her father? He had removed her guilt, and now promise grew in her spirit.

Lily threw herself into helping with the last-minute preparations.

The Earl sent János with the car to take her family to the station.

Euston Station
Stevie gave Lily a quick hug. "We'll miss you, sis. Knock 'em dead."

Tears running down her face, Kit clamped on to Lily. "It shan't be the same without you. I never got to see your gown."

Mum held on to her for a couple minutes. Although shorter than Lily and more delicate, there was strength in her mother's embrace and the faint scent of lavender.

"I love you so much, sweet child. I pray only for God to bless you with His very best. Remember always to look with your heart as well as your eyes. Really *seeing* takes the Spirit."

"Thank you for being on my side with Father."

"Do you really doubt he cares?"

There was a rush to stow the cases, a chaotic round of hugs and kisses and "don't forget . . ." and the dash to board. Kit and Stevie, noses pressed to the window, wagged their hands. Mum blew kisses and Father waved.

When the train pulled away, Lily felt a sudden draft and shivered. No, everything would be fine. Father had given his blessing.

János drove her back to The Havens. The gown had arrived.

Wednesday, 1 October
The Havens

She crept downstairs one last time to gaze at her work of art. Phila called it her *oeuvre*. Lily caressed the folds of the skirt. Molly had worked her magic.

What a fright on Friday. She had lain in bed recalling the agonizing wait till Saturday morning. Her dream was alive. She would meditate only on the future, picturing herself descending the grand staircase into the ballroom on Hugh's arm, to the oohs and ahs of everyone.

"Oh, the looks of surprise when those snobbish girls behold your exquisite gown."

She sat up bursting with pride, too excited to sleep.

"Of course, you will dazzle the young men. The noble ladies will whisper among themselves, wondering who the designer is."

She hugged herself in anticipation.

Conscience whispered: *"Oh dear, your heart is haughty, your eyes are lofty, You are exercising yourself in great matters, in things too high for you."*

On the following Wednesday, they would announce the winner of the contest.

Yes, it would be a week to remember.

Thursday, 2 October
Rivenwood on Thame, Oxfordshire
Lily always enjoyed the drive out to the Claiborne's country estate. It took a little over an hour via Uxbridge, High Wycombe, Stokenchurch, and Thame; with János pointing out sights the girls had already seen multiple times.

Phila had explained how the estate sat half in one shire and the other half in another. It was west of the village of Thame in Oxfordshire. The village of Haddenham in Buckinghamshire sat four miles north and east with the manor house by the River Thame in Oxfordshire.

Of course, this trip was different. Brimming with excitement Lily looked out the window at the moving scenery, not seeing it at all.

"Lil, you are like Cinderella going to your first ball, and we shall meet our Prince Charmings."

"I absolutely love riding in the *gilded pumpkin*." Lily laughed. Usually she dismissed her friend's flights of fancy, but today she felt like playing along. Their golden carriage advanced up the long driveway past the grazing sheep in the meadows on both sides and drew up in front of the palace.

"Oxymoronic, isn't it, sheep feeding right on the front lawn like it's some simple farm?" The *princess* preened.

"Oh, Phil. You and your *look-how-smart-I-am* words."

The carriage drew up to the front of the red brick grand mansion of the *King and Queen* of Wembley. Two giant ancient cedar trees stood guard on either side of the enormous home.

"It's a behemoth, isn't it?" Phila had said the first time Lily saw it.

"A what?"

"A monstrous creature that swallows people alive." Phila had enjoyed her joke.

The royal footman opened the carriage door for the princesses.

"Thank you, János." Her highness gave him a benevolent smile.

Lily never ceased to be amazed at the entrance. Ten columns supported the roof of the ivory-colored portico with the parapet of carved balusters and urns dressing up the rather stern simplicity of the red brick. Tan pavers framed the ground and first floor windows and building corners.

The royal butler opened the massive carved oak door. Like Alice in Wonderland, Lily marveled at the scene. The entry hall yawned before her from the stone floor to the wooden arches reaching for heaven. All the ceilings on the ground floor were so high, they reminded her of being in church.

The girls raced to the rear of the great house, where ten-foot windows of the solarium and French doors opened out onto a flag-stoned courtyard and fountain. Beyond beautifully manicured gardens flowed the narrow sleepy River Thame, with copses hugging the banks here and there. Alongside the stream, the girls had spent many lazy hours.

Lady Audrey welcomed them with smiles and hugs. Lily had taken to Phila's aunt straightaway on her first visit to the country estate. "Everyone adores Auntie Audie." Phila had said. "My aunt stayed after Uncle Lindy was killed in the war. She loves it here and actually manages it for Papa."

Auntie Audie sent the girls off to picnic by the river.

Phila had explained to Lily that the Thame was so narrow, it was pretty much unnavigable to boats save for canoes. From the Vale of Aylesbury southwest into the larger chief River Thames near Dorchester, it supplied about forty miles of recreational possibilities.

Years before, Phila had given Lily a detailed and boring rendition of how the Thame played a key role in the English Civil Wars during the seventeenth century. When the girls were ten, Phila recited the whole history lesson about the conflict between Parliament and King Charles I.

Only the part about the authorities chopping off the king's head sounded interesting. Lily had asked if King George and Parliament got along OK now. After Phila said she thought so, Lily had sighed, totally bored.

Today Cook had packed a lunch, and the girls walked down to the bank then settled on a rug under a willow tree. The strands of delicate lacy branches swayed and whispered in a gentle warm breeze. A swan family glided up to the edge of the bank.

"Look Lil, the cygnets are almost fully grown." Phila pointed to baby swans. "They look about ready to try their wings." Their jet-black eyes sparkled in the afternoon sun, as they squeaked, begging for bread.

"Tilly prepares the most scrumptious delights." Phila unpacked the basket with prawn sandwiches, potato crisps, cherry tartlets, and cold lemon squash. She arranged the feast on linen serviettes and poured the squash into crystal glasses balanced on a book of poetry she'd slipped into the basket.

They munched on the sandwiches, shared a few scraps with the swans, and sipped their drinks. Then Phila put the glasses away and poured tea from a thermos into china cups. Withdrawing a small package from the basket, she announced: "Cigarettes!"

"Phil, no! Our mums will have kittens!"

"Smoking outside, they won't know."

Phila lit the cigarettes. They inhaled, coughed, and blew out with aplomb.

"I absolutely love autumn." Lily laid back on the rug, looking up at the leaves gleaming in their seasonal spectrum of warm colors. "What were those words that American poet used to describe red?" She inhaled like Zsa Zsa Gábor in *Moulin Rouge*, exhaling dramatically.

"Emily Dickinson on autumn? Hue of blood, scarlet rain, and vermilion wheels?"

What a lovely way to describe red. Lily rolled on her side to sip her tea.

Phila recited the poem, lying down to face Lily. She puffed seductively. "Who am I?"

"That was lovely. Did Dickinson write about handsome princes?"

"There's one about cupid's arrow."

"I suppose that will have to do. Ah, Lana Turner in *The Bad and the Beautiful*." They giggled.

As Phila continued reciting, a dreamy expression blossomed on her face. Lily hoped that the dear girl would one day be vanquished by the archer's bow. "So, Cupid is armed for Saturday night?"

"I hope so." They touched their cups in salute.

"Have you any definite targets?"

"Well, there's Todd Thorndike, but he's had his sights set on Jacquie. Talk about charming, though. And handsome."

"Then there's my gorgeous brother, of course. You can bet all the single girls will be lining up to dance with him."

"Yes, Hughie." Lily couldn't imagine any chap more handsome. She'd hardly seen him in the four years he'd been in the States. But now, he'd taken leave to be home for Phila's ball.

"I know!" Lily sat up. "Ask him to pay attention to Jacquie so you can make a play for Todd."

"You're not *serious*!" Phila popped up. "He doesn't love me enough to make that sacrifice. And, you know what, I love him too much to ask." She wrinkled her nose. "I told you how Jacquie threw herself at Hugh when he was here last Christmas."

"Was she shameless?"

"His paying so much attention to Cicely Barker-Jones at one party sent Jacquie into a rage."

"That angry? What did she do?" Lily twitched with anticipation.

"Well, a rumor went around that Cicely was carrying on with her father's chauffeur. The poor bloke got sacked, and she was sent to Scotland for six months."

"Did Jacquie do it?"

"What do you think?"

"I think she's capable. What did Hugh do?" Lily's eyes widened.

"I never told him. He would have felt awful." Phila frowned. "For once Jacquie didn't get what she wanted."

"Poor Cicely and the chauffeur didn't deserve that. Whatever made Jacquie so mean?" Lily's brows knit together. "Thank heaven she didn't take revenge on Hugh."

"She's been that way as long as I've known her. Besides, what could she do to him?"

CHAPTER 13

EXPECTATIONS

There is only one success—to be able to spend your life in your own way.
                      Christopher Morley (1890–1957)

Saturday, 4 October
Rivenwood

Lily woke with a start. At last, the ball is here.

The maid pulled back the drapes to a rush of glorious sunlight and opened the window to a chorus of birds singing.

"H-here's your tea, M-miss." Molly set down the tray on the table by the window. The town staff had come to the country to help. She poured the steaming liquid into a cup.

"Thank you, Molly." This is the life. Her gown hung in the wardrobe, all pressed and ready to go.

Lily sat at the table to drink her tea. The liquid warmed her throat as the sunlight bathed her body. A robin sang his song, clear and bright. Her reverie returned. Oh, to be a lady and live like this all the time. She looked around the lovely room with rose-colored walls and dusty blue carpet. A crown of rose satin and white organza topped the maple four-poster bed, which was covered with a rose satin coverlet and white pillows. A delicate dresser was sculpted walnut. She closed her eyes giving in to a daydream.

"It would be a walk in the park to dazzle and beguile one of those noble young men at the ball to fall in love with you. Marry, become a real lady, and forget fashion designing."

"But when my gown wins?"

"You can become a lady on your own."

A china vase held orange mums. Fine bone china graced the tray—teapot, cup and saucer, the matching pitcher of milk and bowl of sugar. She traced her fingers along the white porcelain china's border of cobalt blue and gold. The handles were a sculpted gold and the rims delicately scalloped. She turned the saucer over—Haviland Limoges, 1894.

Molly returned. "Miss P-phila says to join her s-straightaway." She curtsied and left.

Lily slid into her slippers and wrapped her dressing gown about her, hugging herself. She went to the windows and gazed out on the rolling lawns, gardens, and stone walls. Surely, there couldn't be a lovelier place to live.

"Marry someone with station and means and buy your way into the fashion world."

"No, I'll do it on my own."

Lily crossed the room and opened the huge wardrobe to reveal a long looking glass on one door. She removed the couple dozen bobby pins holding her curls and combed through her hair. Taking down her gown, she held it in front of her, swaying from side to side. Drawing herself up to her full five foot nine, she announced: "Lady Lillian," while regally parading back and forth across the huge room.

"Ladies and gentlemen, may I introduce the star of Dame Lillian's Autumn Collection." She closed her eyes imagining the acclaim. Then waltzing around the room, Lily hummed a tune while imagining all the handsome young men she would dance with and captivate at the ball.

Lillian Grace Whitely was actually going to a ball! Life had begun at last, thanks to Phila. How uncommon her friend, not holding her nobility in high esteem like her peers—like Jacquie. That Phila *was* somebody didn't matter to her. She didn't put on airs like the other girls. None of the Claibornes were stuffy, well maybe Hugh a little. Since Phila's father never expected to hold the title or receive the inheritance, he made a life for himself in the Royal Navy earning his own way, that is, until six years ago.

Lily was so very grateful for their friendship—and, of course, for this delicious taste of society.

"Phila!" Lily jumped up. She hung the gown, closed the wardrobe door, stuck her hair in a ponytail, ran out into the hallway, and knocked on the door opposite. "Phil?"

"Come." Her friend sat at her dressing table scrunching her pug nose at her reflection in the looking glass. She wore a lavender dressing gown with her curly tangerine hair caught in a lilac ribbon. "Thank heaven Papa has a title and means now. I'm no catch otherwise."

"Phil don't put yourself down that way. This is your day."

Lily leaned back on the apple-green satin chaise lounge pulling a nylon stocking slowly over her leg. She wagged her foot back and forth, admiring the sheen of the sheer fabric up the narrow ankle and shapely calf. Straightening the seam, she fastened the stocking to her garter belt.

Phila twirled around on her lavender satin boudoir chair, smacking her lips. "Shall I wear the red lipstick or pink?" Turning back, she grabbed a tissue and wiped her mouth, applied another color and turned again. "Red?"

"Pink goes with your gown, but red is more . . . grown-up. And definitely more in vogue. However, red is not your color."

"Well, we are grown women now, silly goose. And, of course, you're the one learning all the fashion. Just think, one day I shall have my very own fashion designer."

"What a loyal friend you are, Phil."

"Of course, I know talent. I will discover you. Besides my gown will make me so scrumptious—a genuine Lily original—I'll have a full dance card."

"How many young men did you send invitations to?"

"Plenty for both of us to choose from," Phila grinned.

CHAPTER 14

THE BOMB AND BEST WISHES

> When you see something that is technically sweet, you go ahead and do it and you argue about what to do about it only after you have had your technical success. That is the way it was with the atomic bomb.
> *The Hope and Vision of J. Robert Oppenheimer,*
> J. Robert Oppenheimer (1904–1967)

Hugh entered the sunny breakfast room. "Good morning." He yawned.

"Good morning, son. These all-nighters are getting to be a steady diet with you."

"Aye, Sir." He went around to give a hug and kiss to his mum and then his aunt. "Here we all are again, Audie."

"It's always good to see you, nephew." She giggled. "What have you brought me this trip?"

"Are you charging me a fee, like a hotel, Auntie?" Although more like a sister, he enjoyed teasing her as if she was much older than six years. He admired how she exhibited an air of authority that belied her youth. Slim and athletic with straight dark blonde hair and hazel eyes, she possessed a spicy and fun personality.

He settled in his chair, yawning again. Good strong tea was just the ticket. That would wake him up. Hugh wrapped his fingers around the cup and drank. Why is it that tea always tasted so much better at home?

The door opened, and Duncan entered. "I've unpacked for you, and I'll see that your mess dress is pressed and returned to your room shortly, Commander."

"Thank you, Sergeant Major. I appreciate your gracious care." He expelled a loud sigh. "I have to take care of myself in the colonies. I've even had to learn to cook."

"My poor darling," cooed Mum.

Everyone laughed.

"Sorry, Commander. Life too tough in the Navy?" Duncan's eyes glinted.

"Sergeant Major take care how you address this officer, or I will report you and send you packing back to Aberdeen."

"I doubt Neptune and Triton would take lightly to that, *Sir*."

His father looked askance at the two of them. Dad was such a stickler for decorum.

"Good morning!" Phila popped in.

"The birthday girl has finally decided to grace us with her presence?" Hugh rose and gave her a hug. "Slept in, did you?"

"We've had ball things to attend to, if you please." Phila winked at her mum.

"Ball? What ball?" He glanced at his dad. "Is this the secret mission you had me fly home for last night?" A huge yawn overtook him. So much for the tea helping.

"*Hughie*. You're insufferable." Phila yawned back.

For once he refused to rise to the slight. His eyes fastened on the beautiful young woman behind her. "Sorry." Who is this vision?

"Hughie are you all right?"

"It can't be . . . Lily?" Damn, I'm staring.

"Hello, Hughie."

"What happened to our little miss?" He tilted his head to the right.

"We grew up, Genius." Phila rolled her eyes.

Lily certainly has. He hastened to her side, giving her a hug and kiss on the cheek, but somehow discomforted. He pulled out a chair and seated her. When he looked up and glanced around the table, all eyes were on him and Lily.

He couldn't say what had just happened, and he certainly didn't want to let any of them know. Time for diversionary action, Commander. "All this fuss over a ball when there is explosive news."

"Darling, do you mean that tea rationing ended today? Let's enjoy our Earl Grey."

"Pardon me, but we detonated our first atomic bomb off Australia yesterday."

"Hugh dear, I think your sister's birthday is a much happier subject." A scent of fish accompanied with an appetizing aroma of butter and spices announced breakfast. "Ah, the food is here. Thank you, Giselle."

The maid began serving.

"Of course, Mum. But this is earth-shaking news. It's taken a few years to catch up to the Yanks, but we're in the game now. Kippers and scrambled eggs with tomatoes and Flora's hot cross buns. I *am* home." Hugh dug in.

"Five years to be exact since the race began." Dad picked up his knife and fork. "It all started with the Americans in New Mexico."

"The prime minister announced the test in February." Phila took a roll from the basket Duncan held for her.

"By Jove, you do keep up." Hugh saluted her trying to keep his eyes off Lily. Strange, Flora's breakfast was losing its allure.

"And you thought my head was always in the clouds. Mum, this tea is scrummy, good and strong." She poured a little milk into the cup and stirred.

Keep talking, Genius. "And to think the colonists dumped over three hundred chests of tea into the harbor in 1773. They called it the Boston Tea Party."

"Can you imagine wasting all that tea." Mum took a sip.

"Why?" Lily's smile stirred Hugh's desire. Warmth rose to his face.

"In protest of our parliament's Tea Act, some Massachusetts blokes calling themselves the Sons of Liberty, and disguised as Mohawk Indians, did the deed. They viewed the act as an example of Britain's taxation tyranny, when it was actually enacted to save the faltering British East India Company."

"That's amazing, Hughie. I suppose you know all about America now." Even her voice has matured.

"'Taxation without representation,' they had a point." Pet's two cents, of course.

"Well, Americans did inherit the idea for the right of persons to certain basic liberties from our own evolved traditions. Later they set them forth in the Magna Carta, which was embodied in their constitution." Lily seemed absorbed in his delivery. He sat up straighter.

Phila grabbed the lead. "Then used it to gain their independence from the mother country. So, they owed their rights to the English barons who forced King John to recognize those rights and privileges in 1215."

"Americans, odd lot, them." He sneaked a peek at Lily. She's cracking. He hadn't seen a single woman in the States who could outshine her, not even Darlene. "But they owe us a lot."

"And have paid us back many fold in the last two wars," Dad sent him a stern glance.

"But you're enjoying your posting in Washington, aren't you, darling?"

"To be sure, Mum."

"So why are you off on the Americans?" Phila wrinkled up her nose.

"On the contrary, it's strange how alike and yet how different they are. A real melting pot, that. Each state has a distinct character with a certain cadence to their speech."

"You mean like England, Scotland, Wales, Ireland, Canada, and Australia?" Audie peered over her nose at him.

"That's telling you."

Dad pointed to his newspaper. "Speaking of Australia, it says here we detonated the bomb in the hull of an old frigate just off the Monte Bello Islands."

"Where is that?" Mum squeezed more lemon on her kippers.

"The northwest coast. That makes us the world's third atomic power after the Yanks and Soviets," Hugh raised his cup. "Cheers. And Sergeant Major, another of Flora's rolls, please."

"That's just marvelous." Phila pouted. "So, we all get the big bombs and start dropping them on each other. And, after two horrid wars that tore countries apart and damaged people's lives forever. Didn't anybody learn *anything*? We lost two uncles and a cousin, and Lily lost her brother. So many killed. The Japanese started the war with the States, but there was such slaughter when the Americans dropped the bomb on Hiroshima and Nagasaki." Her face clouded. "Suddenly my ball seems insignificant and self-indulgent."

"Oh, darling."

"Mummy, that dreadful bomb killed and wounded something like 225,000 people. Now we make bigger bombs to kill more people?"

Looking at her sweet face so sorrowful, Hugh felt like a monster. What did Lily think? "I'm sorry. The idea, Petunia, is that if both sides have a bomb it will serve as a deterrent."

Dad furrowed his brow. "Hopefully the horror of knowing what these bombs will do will keep nations from using them."

"Henry. Hugh." Mum gave them *the look*. "That is quite enough! What a subject to broach today, on Pet's birthday."

"Affairs of state, my dear."

"Fine. But not here. Not today. Off with you men! Pet, I love that you would consider the consequences of that business, but let's leave that for another day. Let's see how the preparations are going in the ballroom, shall we?"

Lily gave Hugh a shame-on-you, now-you've-done-it look, taking the wind right out of his sails.

4:00 p.m., Sunroom
Lily tried to sit still for afternoon tea. Just hours now. Phila fidgeted, too. How could they help it with the excitement building?

The Countess and Lady Audrey sat sipping tea, cool as cucumbers. Her ladyship had forbidden the men to join them, leaving them to take theirs elsewhere. She didn't want any further taint on Phila's mood.

Molly entered. "M-miss Lily. You've a t-telephone c-call."

When Lily took the call in the library a smile bloomed at the deep voice. "Father! Where are you?"

"At the vicarage, St John's, in Inverness. We're off shortly for Kyle of Lochalsh, then to Skye tomorrow. We miss you. I know you will grace the event."

"Is the tour going well?" Lily missed them, but only for a moment.

"Very well. The Lord has mightily blessed it. Thank you for asking."

"Your father has never preached so brilliantly."

Mum must be listening in next to Dad. Pride emanated from her voice. "Are you excited, Lily? Only a few hours to go."

"Mummy, thank you for understanding. Thank you for everything. I love you."

"And I love you, darling."

"Sis, you should have seen Edinburgh Castle!" Good heavens! Were they all crowded around the receiver? "And Loch Ness and the Highlands are *really* kind of *strange*. You'd like it. Sorry you're not here. Father and I are going fishing on Skye. Watch the gents at that dance."

"Stevie, that's the purpose, silly."

"Lily! Lily! They talk funny up here," chirped Kit. "Stevie says he saw the monster. You know—Nessie? I miss you *so* much. Have jolly fun at the ball."

"Lily, dear." Mum's tranquil voice washed over her. She had needed a holiday. "I'm so sorry you missed the shopping in Edinburgh. You would so have enjoyed looking at the tweeds. I'd never seen such an array. I bought you some pearl gray and silver — your favorite colors."

What a dear.

"Oh, and the tartans here in Inverness — such an assemblage in one place. I found some lovely MacEwan plaid, so you'll be proper in wearing that tartan. I can hardly wait to see what you make of it."

"I've never seen your mother more interested in shopping. Well, we must ring off now and leave for the station." Father coughed. "I love you, Lillian. I hope this evening is all you hoped for."

The sun rose and shone its warm light over her. The sun was Father and the light, love. In a second, she was cut to the quick. She had chosen not to be there for him in his finest moment, but he had blessed her anyway.

Maybe she could try to make up for it. Hear all about it. Show genuine interest, or maybe the chance was gone forever.

"Thank you, Father, thank you. I love you, too."

"But you don't love him nearly as much as he loves you."

Bother Guilt.

Sir Henry's Study

Hugh opened the door for the maid. "Thank you, Giselle. We appreciate your serving tea in two separate places."

"Of course, Master Hugh." Her eyes sparkled as she set out the tea things and left.

"Since we have been expelled from tea with the ladies, we shall have to make do." Hugh grinned at his father, and they shared good-natured laughter. "My fault, Sir. I shouldn't have brought up such an explosive subject." It would take some finesse to charm his way back into his mum's favor. And Lily's?

"I think your sister realizes that the dropping of those bombs by the Americans was necessary to finally bring an end to that long war. All the same, I would not have wanted to make the decision President Truman did." Dad lit his pipe.

"I reckon it keeps him up nights." Hugh poured and served the tea. "They do prepare tea properly at the embassy, but outside they just throw a bag in a cup and pour on hot, but not necessarily boiling water."

"Roughing it are you, son, in the colonies?"

"Tough duty, Sir."

"No one will ever know how difficult, Hugh." His eyes took on a serious mien.

"I would rather have seen active duty during the war." He still smarted from missing out on the action and acclaim.

"While I appreciate that—your intellect, knowledge, and qualifications were most effective at the Admiralty. I'm proud of you, son."

But Hugh wanted to be proud of himself. "Understood, Sir. That's what they tell me now." Hardly his preferred cup of tea being behind the scenes, but it appeared to be his lot in life.

"Considering the devastation caused by those atomic bombs, the help our traitors have given to leak those secrets to the Soviets is paramount to our attention. Not that I'm privy to your assignment, but I assume your efforts are as critical as ours were during the past wars."

"I appreciate that, Sir."

"I have not let on to your mother about my concerns as it would cause her much consternation. That is also why your sister needs to curb her vocal curiosity. You are your mother's only son. Losing your older brother so young and two brothers before their births was agonizing for her. She holds on to you with a mother bear's furious love."

"I know only too well." Smothering.

"So, take care son."

"You were in jeopardy many times."

"Hopefully, you will find that a man fears more for his children's welfare than his own."

"Granddad worried about you?"

"Yes, and when you have your own children you will truly understand."

"Can we not go there again, please?"

Dad took a puff and blew it out. "Actually, I think we should."

"Do you want me to marry just anyone to produce an heir?" Should I mention Darlene?

"No, I don't. Your mother is . . . everything to me. We share something . . . special. I want that for you and your sister. From what Phila tells me, you've had scores of females—I believe the term she used is 'throw themselves at you,' and—"

"Dad! That is getting personal!"

"Quite! I'll only say that your mother prays daily for you to find *the one*." He coughed.

No, mentioning Darlene didn't seem right.

"Also, for your sister. Obviously, you two need divine guidance. Phila especially. That girl has her sights set on some fairy-tale idea of a mate. You both have been blessed with superior intelligence, but I wonder sometimes if—"

"We have any common sense?"

"Quite."

"Affairs of the heart don't actually fall into the realm of common sense, do they? How reasonable were you about Mum?"

His father cleared his throat. "It made perfect sense."

"So, let me guess, what did you say to Mum when you proposed? 'Beatrice, it makes perfect sense for us to marry.' Huh, Dad?"

"Let's see, weren't we discussing your assignment?"

Thought that would change the subject. "As a matter of fact, I've a question. I don't think my promotion was really due to my work. Do you think it might be more about the next mission?"

"Dear boy, if you think I have intelligence on just what that might be, you're adrift." Dad sat back in his chair, enjoying his smoke.

"Surely, you don't think I would attempt to inveigle information out of my own father?" He looked wide-eyed at his dad.

"Don't try that innocent face with me, Commander."

Caught. The jig is up. "Aye, aye. Admiral." Was he now out of favor with Dad, too?

CHAPTER 15

THE BALL

> Dazed with a half-hour triumph, she held the crowd. She loved the boys that buzzed on her like flies, she loved the envy in the women's eyes.
>
> "Infatuation," C. S. Lewis

Lily could hardly breathe. At long last the grand evening had arrived. She and Phila watched the guests make their way to the second-floor landing, being announced, then descending the grand stairway into the ballroom. Lily pinched her wrist. It hurt. This was real. At last it had arrived. The Ball.

She had looked outside earlier, but the rain wouldn't ruin her night. The servants busy with umbrellas assisted guests from their autos. Inside, the decor shone warm and glowing. Lights from the chandeliers glimmered and twinkled like a galaxy of stars. From the walls, golden-gilded wainscoting gleamed. Fresh camellias bloomed on the small tables lining the huge dance floor. Guests gathered and sat on the cobalt-blue brocaded-silk chairs. A bouquet of fragrances wafted up the stairs. The soft buzz of conversation blended with subdued music.

"Lord and Lady Napier-Jones and Miss Jacqueline Napier-Jones," announced the Master of Ceremonies.

"I guess you had to invite them?" Lily whispered to Phila.

"Papa said so."

Jacquie's mother wore her usual haughty demeanor. The severe lines of her emerald silk gown only accentuated her manner. But Lily could hardly take her eyes off the woman's magnificent emerald necklace and earrings.

"Wouldn't Lady N-J make the perfect Wicked Stepmother?" A mischievous glint flickered in Phil's eyes.

"And Jacquie?"

"Oh yes, the absolute epitome." They giggled.

The *Wicked Stepsister* flounced down the stairs, her full skirt bouncing. The sea-foam color did nothing to flatter her pale skin and corn-silk hair, waved into a pageboy.

Lily studied the gown, strapless with coral rosebuds cascading down the midriff. Chiffon draped the front of the skirt, gathering in at the back. She looked down at her own skirt and caressed the fabric. It was more streamlined than the crinoline fashion so popular now, but she thought it more elegant. Besides it didn't require as much material.

"Not long now." Phila reached over and squeezed her hand.

More guests poured in and flowed down the stairway. What a display of nobility. Dukes, duchesses, counts, a couple of earls with their wives, many lords and ladies, and all the young people. Down in the ballroom flowed a sea of hues like flowers floating on the ocean interspersed with the formal black and white of gentlemen.

"OK, Lil, it's your turn. Go wow them."

Phila's brother walked toward her. He cut a stunning figure in his dark blue Royal Navy mess dress with gold accoutrements.

"You're going to be Cinderella and meet your Prince Charming," Kit had said before boarding the train.

Cinderella indeed, with Phila as her fairy godmother. But *she* had made her gown, not fairies. Hugh looked like a prince, but he wasn't *her* Prince Charming.

Still, he did wear a radiant grin and his dancing eyes were dazzling.

He strode up to her offering his arm. "Miss Lillian, may I?"

"Commander Hugh Claiborne and Miss Lillian Grace Whitely."

She beamed up at him as they started down the grand staircase.

"You are absolutely ravishing, my dear. I say, you've caught the eye of a host of young men." He waved his free arm over the throng below.

And, Lily noticed, the girls.

"Look at those snobby daughters of nobility."

Pride welled up inside her.

"See the jealousy in their eyes. Absolutely green with envy."

She floated down the steps, mesmerized by the magic all around her and reveling in the attention. Hugh led her to one side, where the guests were standing, awaiting the birthday girl.

Whisperings.

"How can a future earl, who could have any woman he wants, be with *her*? She's a *nobody*."

"She's just a poor mercy case of Phila's philanthropy."

"Look at that gorgeous gown. Where ever did she get it?"

Hugh frowned, glints of anger flashed in his eyes. "Lily, I'm so sorry. How rude and cruel." He tilted his head to the right, compassion shining from his eyes.

Yes, it hurt; but she wouldn't let them know. She lifted her chin. "No matter, Hughie. I'm used to it. To them, I'm just a commoner."

"Oh, Lily, there's nothing common about you."

And there's everything noble about you. She smiled back.

She and her gown were a sensation. Success tasted so good.

"Let the vixens eat their hearts out. Tonight, this future earl is all yours."

A general officer from Lindell Claiborne's Army regiment escorted Lady Audrey down the stairway.

At last, Phila stood at the top of the stairs.

"Admiral Sir Henry Claiborne, The Earl of Wembley; Lady Beatrice, the Countess of Wembley; and Lady Philomena Justine Claiborne."

Phila's father led them downstairs as everyone applauded.

Phila glowed. She truly looked lovely, her tangerine hair caught up in delicate lilac-beaded combs at the sides thrusting her curls atop her head and down the back in corkscrew swirls.

No one could have a more loyal chum. Lily had made her gown, too. She had designed it with simple lines that complemented her friend's shorter and more rounded figure. Lily had chosen an iridescent lilac silk with hints of darker purple for the strapless dress, which she nipped in at the waist with A-line panels flaring out at the hem. She had sewed a short-waist, quarter-length V-necked camisole out of a violet crocheted lace. Phila topped it off with a dainty necklace and amethyst earrings.

The Earl took his daughter out onto the dance floor to begin the ball. After Hugh danced with her, others took the floor as he whirled away with his mother, Lady Audrey, and then Lily.

She waltzed in a dream accompanied by music from heaven. Sir Henry had engaged the Oxford University Chamber Orchestra. The nearly thirty players just fit in the alcove of the salon under the great bow window.

Lily's dance program filled up quickly, as did Phila's. Hugh rescued them after an hour and ushered the girls into the dining room, where he filled their plates from the sumptuous buffet. At first, Lily hesitated accepting a glass of champagne.

She gazed down at the golden liquid and took a sip, then another. "It's lovely."

He held up his glass. "A toast to a beautiful lady." He tapped his flute to hers.

"My, my, my."

Lily turned at the scalding voice. Jacquie.

"If it isn't the vicar's daughter imbibing spirits. Are you planning on taking advantage of this *innocent* damsel, Hugh?"

Lily froze as heat rose to her face.

Jacquie leered at her. "Blushing, my dear?"

"Why, Miss Napier-Jones, delightful as ever. Do excuse us." Hugh smiled graciously. "I believe this is our dance, Lily." He set their flutes down and off they whirled, the *Wicked Stepsister* glaring after them.

"A gallant knight rescuing a damsel in distress." Lily's spirits lifted heavenward. "I should have you with me always."

"Yes, you should." Hugh pulled her closer.

"Oh, Hughie, you are so charming." And smell so good—musk, pine, with a hint of citrus. When he was away at university, the girls had sneaked into his toilet and found the scent he wore—Blenheim Bouquet by Penhaglions named from Blenheim Palace. It suited Hugh.

He grinned. "Do you expect anything less?"

"Not from my big brother."

"You're not a little sister anymore." His eyes locked on hers.

"I was when you taught me how to dance." She felt his hand warm on her waist. "Do you remember?"

"You were sixteen and learned quickly. As I recall we had near perfect synchronization. Like now." He twirled her around.

"You were a wonderful teacher. So patient."

"Pet didn't think so. She wanted to lead."

They laughed.

※ ※ ※

Phila barely sat down since descending the grand stairway.

"What do you know, you've learned to let the man lead." Hugh led his sister around the floor. He squeezed her waist and smiled down at her. "You look lovely and absolutely glow."

"It's not easy with you tall chaps, you know." What a sweet compliment.

He lifted his chin. "You must have had an exceptional instructor."

"Egotist." She pinched his shoulder.

He grinned. "I say, they are wheeling in the piano for you to play." He escorted Phila over to their father.

The beautiful Steinway grand piano beckoned. Papa led her to it and turned to announce her selection.

"Lady Philomena Claiborne would be delighted to perform Debussy's *'Jardins sous la pluie*—Gardens in the rain.' As many of you know, Debussy was a French Impressionist composer and is one of my daughter's favorites."

A hush came over the ballroom as the dancers seated themselves. Phila composed herself at the majestic instrument and began to play.

A few minutes into the piece she glanced around the room at faces illuminated by candlelight. Did the grace and beauty of the music lift their hearts like it did hers? As her fingers sailed over the keys, the musical notes rose as if on wings of joy, then fell gently as soft raindrops on opened red roses.

How she loved to play, particularly on the old Steinway. She was a bird in flight, flying to a heavenly realm, the music pouring forth from her heart.

When at last her fingers stilled, the company stood and applauded. Pride clapped loudest.

"Brilliant, Lady, just brilliant."

Hugh gave her his hand, lifting her up, then standing back as she took a bow. Phila felt positively *beautiful*.

"Brava, Pet. Never have you played so well. I'm proud of you. That was the most skillful and tender interpretation of that masterpiece I have ever heard. Exceptionally moving and uplifting. My sincere felicitations." He bowed low to her.

Is this my brother? What's gotten into him? Two lovely compliments inside an hour. He could be so infuriating, conceited, a procrastinator of the first order, and ridiculously formal to the point of annoyance, but how she did love him. *Can I ever find a man as exceptional?*

The orchestra took up the music again as Hugh guided her out onto the floor.

She was in seventh heaven. Nothing could ruin this night.

CHAPTER 16

MEOW

> She turned over the page . . . came to a spell which would let you know what your friends thought about you.
> *The Voyage of the Dawn Treader,* C. S. Lewis

Phila retired to the ladies' toilet. Managing inside the stall was cumbersome with all the skirt and petticoats to bother with. She heard the door open with the sound of swishing crinolines.

"Well, I never! You could have tipped me over with a feather when I saw that *person* coming down the stairs—and on the arm of the future Earl."

Miss Familiar Whiny Voice?

"And she's wearing the very gown I wanted at Hartnell's."

Jacquie. What?

"*That's* the one the Hartnell woman wouldn't let you have?" Phila couldn't place Miss Second Girl's voice straight away.

"Yes. Can you imagine? She told Mum that it wasn't theirs and had come in by mistake. I wanted it until the woman said that it wasn't a Hartnell original."

Phila grinned. So that's what happened at Hartnell's. And, of course, they wouldn't have told us. Wait till I tell Lily and Mum.

"So, how did this person end up with it?"

Veronica Sedgley-Milne. She and Jacquie were inseparable.

"I haven't the slightest idea, but I intend to find out."

"It *is* a gorgeous frock."

The door opened again with more ruffling of petticoats. Phila sat still. How delicious to eavesdrop and fortuitous to hear what had happened.

"Are you talking about Lily's gown?" Miss Third Girl. "Is it not stunning? That bright lapis blue is breathtaking. Did you see how all eyes turned on her when she came down the stairs?"

"That's because one doesn't usually see a commoner at a ball, *and* on the arm of the *most* gorgeous man here, not to speak of London's most eligible bachelor. Besides, have you no taste, Edwina?" That was Jacquie. "It's not a Hartnell."

Phila smiled, again. Edwina Endicott had excellent taste. And she didn't like Jacquie either.

"He's not the only British designer." Veronica.

"Perhaps it's French." Edwina. "The straighter skirt is so elegant and the off-the-shoulder bouffant sleeves—looks French to me."

"I'm sure the jewelry isn't hers." Jacquie.

It is too. Mum gave Lily the lapis lazuli beaded necklace and earrings. So there, you witch.

"I wonder if Hartnell's are so taken up with the Coronation gowns that they've farmed out for designs." Jacquie.

"Goodness gracious. Hartnell's wouldn't do that." Veronica.

"Come, come, ladies. We can afford to be generous, give Lily her due." Edwina. "Why doesn't she have as much right to be here as we do?"

Phila smiled at someone coming to her friend's defense.

"Edwina, you're so plebian, defending that girl.

"Jacquie, that's unkind."

"Ever since you spent last summer in America, Edwina, you've been in an equality phase. That commoner will always be beyond the pale."

"I think you're jealous."

Of course, Jacquie's envious and begrudging.

"And maybe just a little put out because Todd Thorndike has danced with Phila several times and not with you." Veronica.

"The boys *have* to dance with her, it's *her* ball. But Todd's *mine!*" Obviously, Jacquie.

A few very unladylike words came to mind.

"Well, they don't have to with Lily unless they think she's the most beautiful girl at the ball."

Well done, Edwina.

"Still, how did a dress at the queen's dressmaker end up on a commoner?"

Jacquie just can't let it go. Phila fumed.

"What if Hugh Claiborne marries the girl?" Veronica. "She'll be a countess someday."

Oh, if only.

"Dancing a few dances doesn't mean anything. He *has* to dance with her. She's his sister's friend." Jacquie.

"I don't know. Did you girls see how he was looking at her?" Veronica. "I reckon there's something there."

So, Veronica had seen it, too. I knew I wasn't the only one.

"Don't be ridiculous. He's just playing with her. Maybe she's *reciprocating*."

"Oh, Jacquie! Shame on you for suggesting such a thing." Edwina made points there.

"Being a vicar's daughter doesn't make one a saint, you know."

That's it! Phila gathered her skirts about her and burst from the stall. "Jacquie, how *dare* you even suggest that Lily would do such a thing! She's been like a sister to Hugh and me!"

Jacquie jumped back, her eyes bugged out, and her mouth wide open. The other girls seemed frozen, wide-eyed and gasping. Edwina's surprise melted into a grin.

Jacquie's shock turned to a sneer. "And would she be giving him a little *sisterly* love?"

"You witch!" Fury shot through Phila. She leapt at the odious girl, but Edwina stepped in front of Phila to stop her.

"Calm down, Phila. She's not worth it."

Phila glared at Jacquie. "Just so you'll know, *witch*, Lily designed and made that gown herself."

Jacquie stammered, "that's impossible, how could she—"

"Create a dress that has all of you thinking it was fashioned by a famous designer? Even a French one?" Phila stared the girl down. Jacquie started to speak, but Phila interrupted. "Lily is incredibly talented and will be famous someday."

"She *actually* made that dress?" Veronica's eyes bugged.

"And, mine, as well."

"Well, what do you know." Edwina lit up.

Phila beamed at the incredulous look on their faces. Jacqueline Napier-Jones speechless. What a night! She turned on her heel and left the lavatory. Back in the ballroom, her brother danced with Lily. They looked so perfect together. Hugh looked elated; his eyes fastened on Lily's. Ooh la la. Is there something there?

Later on, Edwina sought out Phila. They sat at a small table in the dining room nibbling cake and sipping champagne. "I just wanted to warn you. Jacquie has made it her business to spread the news about your gowns." She shook her head. "What a *quelle déception!*" Edwina saluted Phila with her flute. "Jacquie definitely needs to be taken down a peg or two. She can be so unkind."

"Catty, you mean? I appreciate you standing up for Lily."

"I've always liked her, and those girls were being so tacky. I didn't know she had such talent. Both her gown and yours are *absolument magnifique!*"

Phila saw Lily and waved her over.

Her friend was flushed and out of breath. "Thank heaven Hugh taught me how to dance. I can't think of anything more delightful. This has been a right royal night."

"Sit down. You need something to drink."

Edwina beamed. "Lily, I want to compliment you on your gown, the beaded camisole is brilliant. *Elle est magnifique!*"

Phila tittered. "Edwina is going to spend a couple months on the continent so she's studying her French."

"How lovely. I'd like to study design there some day."

"You should. Before Phila told us you designed your gown I thought it might be French. It shows a certain familiar flair."

Lily looked askance at Phila.

"Yes, I am so proud of you that I had to tell. And guess what?" She bubbled over about Jacquie seeing and wanting the gorgeous dress. "Besides Jacquie was bound to wonder when she saw you in it." Then she grimaced. "Perhaps I shouldn't have said anything. She's off gossiping now."

"No one would question that your gown is a Hartnell original, Edwina," said Lily. "The seed pearl work is exquisite."

Edwina's ivory chiffon-and-lace creation impressed Phila. Much too fussy for her taste, but it flattered the other girl's slim figure.

A handsome young sub lieutenant in Royal Navy mess dress approached the table and bowed. "Lady Philomena, Miss Edwina. I believe this is our dance, Miss Lillian." And off she whirled.

Edwina's eyes sparkled. "There are quite a lot of Navy men here. Their uniforms are so dashing. And Hugh's been promoted to commander. He must be doing very well."

"If Papa was any prouder he'd burst his buttons."

"Lily's barely sat down all evening. I noticed that Percy Hornsworth is challenging the Navy for dances."

"He's nice. I've known him forever." Phila smiled. "Lily wondered for a while if the junior officers would ask her to dance once they saw her with a commander."

"And he is so divine." She gazed wistfully at Hugh. "I envy you, Phila. You have a brain and are planning to do something with it. The rest of us—we're just looking for husbands, well-off and titled. Honestly, have you seen how Tansy Huntly has flaunted herself at Todd Thorndike? Jacquie looks livid. I wouldn't be surprised if she retaliates. She's a schemer."

"I would flaunt myself if I thought it would do any good. He is the epitome of tall, dark, handsome, and absolutely divine." What a dancer.

The rest of the evening flew by, Cinderella and her godmother dancing with dozens of charming princes and Royal Naval officers. Even the *Wicked Stepsister* with her gossiping about the gowns couldn't spoil the event. It was like a fairy tale, except no one lost a slipper.

CHAPTER 17

IN FATE'S FOOTSTEPS

There's a Divinity that shapes our ends.
Hamlet, William Shakespeare (1564–1616)

Tuesday, 7 October, 7:45 p.m.
The Havens

"It's Reverend Whitely ringing from the Perth station," announced Duncan to the family in the sitting room, after their evening tea.

Lily bounded out of her chair and ran ahead of the butler to the library.

"Father! Is everything all right?"

"Everything's just fine. We've decided to come home tonight to be there for the announcement. Here's your mum."

A thrill shot through her.

"Darling, it's your father's idea. Here's Stevie."

Father's idea?

"Good luck, sis. We all know you'll get the prize. Hey! Kit don't grab!"

"My turn! You'll win, Lily. I know!"

I knew, but now I don't.

"That's good, Kit," Father came back on. "We're taking the sleeper from Perth in half an hour, through Harrow and Wealdstone, arriving in Euston at 9:48 in the morning."

"I'll see you all then."

She turned to Duncan. "They're coming into Euston tomorrow morning."

He inclined his head. "János will be there to collect them."

She relayed that news. "I can't wait to see you all. I love you, Father."

"Tomorrow is your big day. We shan't miss it. We love you too, Lily, and I am so very proud of you."

They rang off, and Lily smiled. She could hear the angelic choir singing.

"Look who's on Cloud Nine!" Phila ran up and gave Lily a hug when she rejoined them.

"They'll be here for the announcement!" She twirled around and hugged her friend back.

The Earl and Countess smiled as Lily and Phila chatted excitedly about what they'd do after she won. Lily thanked her ladyship for sending János to collect her family at the station.

Duncan returned. "It's the embassy ringing, the commander."

"I'll take it in my study." The Earl rose.

"I beg your pardon, Sir Henry, but he's asked for Miss Lily."

"Me?" She flushed. *Father's coming home early for me. Now, Hughie is ringing from Washington? Heaven reached down to Earth.*

They were all looking at her.

"Yes, you, silly. Well?" Phila pulled her out of her chair and nudged her forward.

Lily went to take the phone again. "Hugh?"

"Miss Lillian are you excited?"

"Oh, Hughie, I think I may faint. I couldn't eat a bite at tea. I know I won't sleep a wink."

"Ask Duncan for a draught of brandy and relax. Your win is a sure thing. Right?"

"I thought so, but now I'm petrified."

"Have faith, Lily dear. I wish I could be there, but I'll ring tomorrow night when you're all celebrating with champagne."

He will? Oh, they all believe in me! What if I don't win? I was so sure. Now, I'm not sure at all.

Perth Station
8:45 p.m.

I'm going to miss me train. Ollie Ogilvie stuffed his book in his rucksack as the train came into the station.

In nearly thirty years of riding the train from Scotland to England, he couldn't recall the Dundee to Perth train ever being this late. A few minutes here and there, but over an hour behind schedule? If it was still wartime, the odd series of events that unfolded that night would not have seemed so unusual. But now?

The station manager had explained that the engineer was suddenly taken ill, so it took a half hour to borrow another engineer from an inbound train. Then, a quarter of an hour after departure, a farmer flagged down the engineer and pointed out damaged track. It took another twenty minutes for the farmer, engineer, and fireman to temporarily repair it. Another five minutes down the track, the train was blocked by a large flock of sheep. As if leaving nearly an hour late wasn't bad enough, the journey that normally required twenty-two minutes took nearly fifty.

Thanks to one delay after another, the train pulled in at 9:00 p.m.

Ollie tugged on his worn Army field jacket and, hefting a couple of duffel bags, disembarked. His gaze followed the track leaving the station. The station manager shook his head, apologizing to the London-bound passengers. The 8:15 p.m. London train had departed right on time.

Ollie dropped his bags, pulled off his cap, and scratched his head—no doubt further messing up his shock of wayward red hair.

"Sairy, soldier." The station manager bent his head way back to look up at him. "We'll git ye on the mornin' train."

"Thenk ye." Ollie flashed the older man a big grin.

"Ye're a muckle tall laddie."

The man's brogue was broad Scots and probably Glasgow. Of course, he'd mention his height. When a bloke towered head and shoulders over most men, it was rare when people didn't.

"Whaur du ye cum frae?"

"Arbroath."

"Arbroath, that also be near whaur the Duke of Angus an' Aberdeen's grand castle is? Funny name as I mynd."

"Aye, 'tis near. Lochlannach. Gáidhlig frae Viking."

"Och. There be some legend aboot a giant Viking wi' fire on his heid oop there, richt?" The man gazed up at him a wary look in his eyes.

"Aye, there be, back in the ninth century."

"Any relation, laddie? Ye kinda fit the bill."

"After all these centuries?" He hooted, accustomed to the mockery.

How about that joke of history? After all these centuries Bjorn lives on in your family, and you the spitting image including the big ears and fiery temper.

"Saw some action, did ye?"

"Aye. More than a mon should." Why dinna the memories fade after all these years?

"Gaein' back tae your ootfit, are ye?"

"Na. To university."

"Ye dinna say. Gude frae ye. Which one?"

"Oxford."

"Ye must be one verra gleg laddie. God bless ye."

"Thenk ye."

CHAPTER 18

A DAY LIKE NO OTHER

Have mercy upon me, O LORD, for I am in trouble: Mine eye is consumed with grief, yea, my soul and my belly.

Psalm 31:9–10, KJV

London, Euston, St Pancras Renaissance Hotel
Wednesday, 8 October, 6:30 a.m.
Dan buttoned up his western shirt, tucked it into his jeans, and strapped on the belt with the big silver buckle he'd won at his last rodeo. He could wear regular togs but felt most at home in western gear.

"Is this how all Californians dress, Dr. McCauley?" a brash young college reporter had asked last night after Dan's lecture on Humanism.

"No, but I grew up on a ranch, and this is my usual garb."

"You sure you're a real professor? You don't look old enough."

Dan had sighed. "You want to see my passport?"

Gazing in the mirror, Dan could see why people made that mistake. He leaned in closer. *Not my eyes. They've seen war and death and disappointment.*

Plunking down on the bed, he was pulling on his fancy leather-tooled boots when the phone by his bed rang.

"Hello."

"Good morning, Dr. McCauley. Devin Giles, University College London, here."

"Hi, Dr. Giles. Good group you rounded up last night. What can I do for you?"

"It *was* a good assembly of faculty and students. I've already received positive feedback on your lecture. You met Dr. George Grafton from Oxford, and he was suitably impressed. I'm certain that it would be quite a feather in your cap to speak there."

"That, Dr. Giles, would be the height of achievement for the son of an actress and a rancher, especially considering that I was born in Hollywood."

"Indeed. I say, may we intrude on your schedule? Aren't you planning on taking the Euston Down express through Harrow Wealdstone to Liverpool?"

"Yeah."

"Might you take a later train?"

"Sure. The provost from the University of Liverpool said the first thing on the agenda is this evening. I can hop a later train. What's up?"

"The President of City University arrived back late last night and was disappointed that he wasn't able to attend your lecture. He's having breakfast with Dr. Grafton and thought you might want to join them."

"I would indeed." Oh yeah!

"Brilliant. I'll collect you at eight."

London, Harrow and Wealdstone station
8:17 a.m.

"Mum, it's awfully foggy." Stevie stared out the window. "Do you think the engineer can see the station?"

"It's scary," squealed Kit.

Ruth cast a concerned glance at her husband. "Oughtn't the train to be slowing down, Jon?"

"The Lord's in control." The vicar wrapped his arms around his wife and daughter.

Then their world exploded.

"Mummy!" Kit screamed as luggage rained down. Stevie was thrown to the ceiling. Jon pulled Ruth and Kit into his body and bent down covering them. Shards of glass from the windows sliced through the air.

Jon held his family tight. Something must have hit the trai—

Everything around them burst into screaming metal, flying glass . . .

And death.

❊ ❊ ❊

Silence.

Then moaning, screams, hissing engines.

Gargoyles of twisted metal reared up in obscene shapes. Human flesh and bone, crushed and torn, had been tossed about like trash. Blood and fleshy matter splattered about like some nouveau-impressionist painter had, in an insane frenzy, flung globs of paint on an innocent canvas. Metal entwined with bodies and parts—so many parts—shredding so many lives.

All that remained was destruction and despair.

✻ ✻ ✻

The Havens, 8:30 a.m.
Lily hugged the quilt around her.

"Today's the day that will change your life forever."

Eyes still closed, she envisioned the scene at two o'clock that afternoon when Mistress Gianna would announce that Lillian Grace Whitely had won the contest for the most resplendent gown. A perfect Phila word.

And Mum and Father will be here for the announcement! Her heart was sure to burst.

She bounded out of bed, threw open the drapes—and gasped. She expected a glorious sunny morning. Instead a foggy murk loomed threatening to suffocate her. The dancing fauns atop the garden fountain just below her window had disappeared into the mist.

Disdain hissed in her ear. *"Isn't that just like God to blot out the sun today? Too much attention to worldly appearance."*

"No! I shan't let the gloom dampen my big day." She dressed and packed. "What a great homecoming it will be."

The antique gilded clock read nine o'clock. Breakfast with the Claibornes, then walk—or maybe run—home. Oh! She couldn't wait to see them!

The announcement this afternoon and celebration tonight.

"This will be the best day of your life!"

What luxury she'd enjoyed this past week, sleeping in the suite of rooms and having meals with Phila's family. Lady Beatrice seemed to glory in having her daughter and son home along with all the excitement of the ball. As always, they included Lily as family.

Hugh had flown back to Washington Monday morning. How dear of him to ring last night. Phila would return to Oxford soon. Although their country home was close to the university, she preferred staying in her rooms at St Hilda's College.

When Lily entered the dining room, Phila's face brightened.

"Today's the day, with the first of many accolades to follow. I'll go in with you and do the shops, then pop in for the grand announcement."

"You ladies are taking a lot for granted." Lady Beatrice lifted her eyebrows. "Although I don't wish to dampen your spirits."

Phila nearly bounced in her chair. "Lily's gown is a sure thing, Mum. Remember the reception it got at the ball?"

His lordship chuckled. "I suppose this is my signal to leave since Hugh isn't here, and I am not educated in the matter of women's frocks." He laid his serviette on the table and excused himself.

At quarter past ten, Lily left for home to await their arrival. But by half eleven she rang The Havens. Her ladyship informed Lily that there had been some mishap at the Harrow and Wealdstone station affecting all outgoing trains. Why didn't she come wait there? Walking fast, she hoped the exertion would still the disquiet growing deep inside her.

※ ※ ※

When Duncan opened the door, his usual smile was gone. In its place, tight, grim lips.

Lily shivered as she entered the great hall.

Phila ran up and hugged her. "Oh, Lil."

She froze, gripping her friend's arm. "What's wrong?"

Her ladyship followed behind Phila, her face pale, eyes glistening. She pursed her lips like Mum did when she tried to harden her resolve. "Lily, my dear, let's go into the library and sit down."

She took Lily by the hand and guided her to the divan, then sat next to her, holding both her hands.

I'm going to scream! What's going on?

When the Earl entered the room, a cold dread descended on her. Why is he home at this hour? She held her breath.

"Lily, breathe," Phila's mum commanded. "Henry?"

He took a seat in the big chair facing the divan and cleared his throat.

Lily tried to swallow, but her throat was too dry.

His eyes looked so sad. "Lillian dear, I am grieved to tell you that there was a railway accident this morning. There is no news of survivors at this hour, and it may take some time before we know exactly what happened."

Survivors? All the air sucked from her lungs. She sat there, staring at the Earl's chin.

"Breathe, child, breathe." Her ladyship rubbed her back.

What's he saying? A railway accident? But what did that mean? What about her family?

Looking at Phila's mum, Lily opened her mouth, but no sound came out. She gulped in air, but it wasn't enough. She couldn't get enough! She gasped and coughed, fighting for air.

"Pet, ring for Giselle to bring a paper bag. And a cold towel, please." Lady Beatrice patted Lily's arm. "We don't know anything yet. There is always hope."

The next thing she knew, Phila held a paper bag to her mouth encouraging her to breathe in and out. Her breathing slowed, and the panic began to ease.

Lady Beatrice placed a cold cloth at the back of Lily's neck.

"Lily are you able to listen now?" The Earl's voice sent dread slicing right through her.

She moaned. Phila's mum held one of her hands, Phila the other.

"János used a telephone at hospital and rang a few minutes ago. The authorities enlisted him to help transport the wounded there."

"B-but, my family?" She sat up and grabbed the Earl's hand.

"We don't know yet. He couldn't get close to the station for the traffic backup. Then a bobby recruited him to take the injured to hospital."

Lily fell back on the cushions and groaned. She tried to grasp what she was hearing, but only caught words and phrases here and there.

". . . spoken railway authorities . . . not tell anything this point . . . rang bishop . . . spoke assistant vicar . . . churchwardens . . . my men . . . rounds hospitals . . . take time find them . . . Mrs. Terrill ring if . . . *when* return."

When they return. No *if*!

British Embassy, Washington, D.C., 1200 hours

The naval attaché picked up the receiver, "Commander Claiborne."

"Hugh, honey. You haven't called." The senator's daughter crooned over the line in her soft syrupy voice. "When did you get back?"

"Monday afternoon, Darlene."

"Why didn't you ring her?"

Why didn't he? Hugh had no answer to the subliminal question. He tapped his pencil on the three-inch stack of papers on his desk, thinking. "I had to jump right back into work."

"Feeble."

"But darling, it's been a whole week. I missed you so. How about tonight?" Her seductive tone had slipped in, but today it had no effect. "I want to hear all about the ball. I really wish you would have taken me."

"As I told you, I didn't want you to outshine my sister and her friends. And I wouldn't have been able to give you the attention you deserve." Smooth enough?

"Hugh sweetheart, but that doesn't explain you not calling."

No, it doesn't.

"Did you run into an old flame. I'm sure you've had several."

"They're all married. Let's have this discussion when I'm not on duty, shall we?" Irritation cancelled out desire. He'd asked her not to ring him at the embassy. "I say, let's make it for Saturday, shall we? I won't be good company until I catch up."

"Oh, but honey, I can't wait—"

"Commander."

He looked up at the Royal Marine Sergeant Major.

"Office of the Naval Secretary ringing, the Secretary, Sir."

"I can't talk now, must ring off. Sorry." He replaced the receiver. "Thank you, Sergeant Major." Why was Dad ringing from his office? He should be home by now for the celebration. He picked it up again. "Dad?"

"Son, have you heard about the railway accident?"

"Aye, Sir. Horrendous, by the sound of it." But why is he ringing? A wave of apprehension swept over Hugh. He held his breath.

A moment of silence, then: "Lily's family was on the Perth train."

The direct broadside left him reeling. "Oh, no! Are they—?" He gripped the edge of his desk.

"We don't know. János tried to find them at the station but couldn't for the extensive wreckage. The authorities commandeered him to help. He finally made it home with no news."

"How is she?" Oh, Lily. With his heart in his throat he found it difficult to swallow.

"In shock, I think. Pet says she just stares out the window."

"I should come home." She needs me.

"Wait until we know more."

Hugh let the receiver drop. He stared ahead seeing nothing. He couldn't believe it. Sweet little Kit. Stevie trying to see if he could best him at some historical fact. Father Whitely's vibrant faith, and Mrs. Whitely's graciousness. No. Dear Lily.

Please God, not this family.

"Commander. *Commander Claiborne!*"

He looked up into the sergeant major's face. "Yes?"

"The First Secretary has asked us to help take calls from our citizens asking about survivors."

"Do we know any yet?"

"Nothing has come in on the teletype, Sir."

"I want to see them the minute they come through, Sergeant Major."

"Yes Sir."

Please . . . Let their names be on one of the lists.

The Havens

Phila detested waiting, but this was agonizing—like waiting for Hugh to come out of his coma. The day stretched on forever. Her father went into the city and returned late. Only horrifying news.

Lily could neither eat nor speak. It looked like she could barely breathe. Two churchwardens came by to pray with her. But she just sat there, staring into space.

If only Phila could help in some way, but it seemed so hopeless.

After a late tea, where no one ate much, they all sat in the drawing room. Lily huddled in a chair near the fire, shivering from time to time. The fire clearly failed to thaw the icy fear Phila could see taking hold of her friend.

The door opened, and in came János. "You wished to see me, milord?" The usually impeccable young man stood there; his uniform torn, bloodstained, and dirty.

"You equipped yourself admirably, János." Papa got up and poured cognac in a snifter handing it to the chauffeur.

"Milord?" János took the glass, his hand shaking.

"Drink it down, man."

He did, then turned toward Lily, his expression chilling Phila to the bone. The jovial Hungarian, readily laughing at his frequent errors with *the English*, stood stock still, his normally rosy complexion drained of all color. His dark eyes, red and dirt-stained face flooded with sorrow. "Miss Lily, no find family. Big *katasztrofa*. So much—"

"János, I want to hear everything." Papa worked his jaw. "Bea, take the girls upstairs."

"I can't listen to any more." Hearing this low whisper from Lily, Phila took her friend's arm leading her from the room. Though Phila understood, she wondered if hearing the truth wouldn't be better than their imagining.

The young women retired for the night, but Lily did not sleep. Phila had insisted Lily stay in her rooms, but she sat in a big chair all night. Every time Phila checked, Lily just stared into the dark.

Morning brought no news, no relief. Phila put her arm around Lily, who sagged against her friend and spoke in a heavy whisper. "The whole world has come to a halt."

CHAPTER 19

CRUSHED

Grief was overwhelmed in terror.
Surprised by Joy, C. S. Lewis

Thursday and Friday
Phila had an irresistible urge to forcibly move the hands on the clock. It was as though time had ceased to exist. Thursday came and went.

The newspapers were full of harrowing news of carnage. *Why am I reading this?* But she couldn't stop.

One article in a daily read:

> At 8:17 a.m. the speeding express from Perth barreled into the Harrow and Wealdstone station smashing into the passenger train from Tring. Seconds later the express from Euston crashed into the wreckage of the two trains, demolishing rail cars and ripping up the platform where passengers were boarding the eight o'clock express to Liverpool.
>
> Witnesses said they heard the brakes screech and groan as they grabbed at the rails. The crescendo of metal smashing metal reverberated throughout the station. Then an eerie silence. Then moaning, cries, screams, and the hissing of engines resounded everywhere.
>
> Rescuers said, inside what would have been the carriages, it looked like shards from the windows whipped through the cars like propellers from an airplane.

> The scene was horrendous. Man and machine ripped up and smashed together, reminiscent of direct hits during the Blitz. Debris rained down even at some distance from the station.
>
> So many lives torn apart.

Including Lily's. Phila breathed in gasps, shaken by the explicit description. Any other time she would have admired the writing. Now, it only made the horror more real.

Obviously, she would keep all these reports away from her friend.

Saturday, 11 October

Lily sat in a cane wingback chair peering out the big atrium windows.

It rained all day. Evening crept in without notice.

Mum would have told Kit that the angels were weeping. Oh, is sweet little Kitty Kat with the angels now? Or did she lay crushed and bleeding in some hospital? No, she and Mum and Father and Stevie are all right. They *had* to be.

But that didn't stop Fear from wailing. *"No! They are all dead, and you are alone."*

Then she heard Hope whisper: *"'He shall give his angels charge over thee, to keep thee in all thy ways. They shall bear thee up in their hands, lest thou dash thy foot against a stone.'"*

For a moment, those Bible verses warmed Lily, and she repeated them over and over.

"Lily, dear?"

The soft voice broke into her musing. She turned and started to rise.

"No, dear." Her ladyship eased her back down kneeling beside her. Phila and his lordship followed behind. They moved so slowly, as if in a dream. Their faces seemed to grow longer as they drew near. His lordship's voice was a low growl, like a 45-rpm record being played on 33.3 speed—the words drawn out like the first and last letters were in a tug-of-war. "I've haad baad ne-ews. They ha-ave found their . . . your fa-amily. What we fe-eared is true. They ha-ave all pe-erished."

Her heart stopped. She couldn't breathe. "*No!* They can't all be dead!" She jumped up—everything went black.

❋ ❋ ❋

Lily's head swam. Confusion clouded her thoughts. "Mummy. Mummy, where are you?"

"It's Phila, Lil. You fainted. But I'm right here."

She lay on the floor, her friend's face above her. A cold cloth covered her forehead. "What happen . . . no. no. no. Don't believe."

"I am so very sorry, my dear." Phila's mum wrapped her arms around Lily.

Dark closed in around her. A numbing cold gripped her heart, then spread all the way to her fingers and her toes. Her teeth chattered; she couldn't stop shaking.

"They're with the Lord now." Phila's mum's voice soft like the big wooly shawl she wrapped around Lily. "But we're here for you, as long as you need us."

"Gone. All gone." She moaned. "They've left me. Why? Oh, God, why didn't you protect them?" She sobbed, gulping in air, gasping as all happiness drained from her soul.

Phila held her.

"No!" She shook her head. "No. I won't believe they're all dead." She jumped up, throwing off the shawl, then doubled over vomiting. Shaking, she sank to the floor. Everything swam, and dots danced before her eyes. "Home."

She turned to Phila's mum. "Please, I need to go home, now. *Please.*"

"Have János fetch the Bentley. We'll drive but let me ring Mrs. Terrill first."

Lily shivered. Phila rubbed her hands and coaxed her to drink some ginger tea. Though hot, it did nothing to warm her.

All dead. They couldn't *all* be dead. Not Father, who preached, "God is my protector." Not Mum, dear Mum, who wrote such lovely poetry—delicately rhyming words that Phila said were "strung together like strands of fresh-water pearls." Not Stevie, dashing black-eyed, black-haired Stevie, her knight errant. Not Kittie-Kat—sweet, bubbling, purring, cuddly little sis. Not after losing Benjie in the war. That had been bad enough, but this?

Everyone's lying. It's a frightful nightmare—a farce, to make her feel bad for not going with her family. Sudden and utter confusion overwhelmed Lily.

She pinched herself. Ouch. No. It is real. Her mind reeled as Guilt reared its ugly head.

"They were coming home early especially for you because of your stupid gown. You killed them."

"No-o-o!" Lily moaned.

Squeezing her eyes tight, she tried to block out the picture of trains crashing and the din of accusing voices. She rocked back and forth, pretending Mum was rocking her. Soon she began feeling heavy, drowsy. Slowly she relaxed and dozed.

※ ※ ※

Darkness surrounds Lily. A light starts to grow and illuminates a tunnel — the sound of a train approaching at great speed.

"Come with us!" Mum stretches out both arms. "Hurry, girl."

Train wheels chant. "Wick-ed girl. Wick-ed girl. Wick-ed girl."

Lily is running. A whistle screams from behind; she snaps her head around. A second chugging steel monster bares down on her.

"I'm so s-o-r-r-y!" She screams. "I'm coming — wait!" Lungs bursting, legs straining, she stretches her arms out nearly six feet to reach them. Steam billows around her, blotting them from view.

"Such a sorry excuse for a sister." Blame hisses in her ear.

"Hor-rid girl. Hor-rid girl. Hor-rid girl." The wheels thunder.

Terror crushes in on her. Steam swirls. Breaks squeal. Screams.

※ ※ ※

"Lily. Lily wake up dear, we're here." Someone shook her gently. "My dear, you're absolutely flushed." Mum blotted Lily's forehead and cheeks with a handkerchief.

She opened her eyes. No, not Mum. *Phila's* mother bent over her in a car. How nice of Phila's parents to take her home. But she didn't remember leaving The Havens or getting into the auto.

Home!

Lily bolted out of the car, down the path, through the front door, and into the entryway.

CHAPTER 20

GONE

You can't go home again.
  You Can't Go Home Again, Thomas Wolfe (1900–1938)

St Peter's Vicarage
Lily stood in the entrance, calling. "Mum, Father, Stevie, Benjie, Kit?"

No answer.

She dashed through the house. Every room, empty. Around every corner, she expected to bump into them. Her mum's lavender scent lingered. Still no answer. No one gathered in the garden. She crossed it and, breathless, entered Father's study.

Charles Boyne, the curate, looked up from behind the vicar's desk.

She froze, staring at the man. "What are you doing here?"

"Oh, Lily. I am so very sorry." The plump man looked out of place. Her father gave off a quiet dignity and gentle authority. The curate always looked rumpled and thrown together.

"Where's my father?"

Just then, there came a knock at the door leading from the chapel. A tall, thin man wearing a black cassock with scarlet trim entered. "Charles, I—"

Lily twirled to face him. "Where's Father?"

The cleric bowed and stepped away from the desk. He spoke in a calm voice. "Lily, do you remember me? Bishop Osred."

She nodded. "Why are you here?"

"Come, let's sit you down." He led her to one of the chairs facing the desk. "Has Sir Henry explained?"

"We have, Bishop." The Earl appeared in the doorway, Phila and her mother following.

"Thank you, Sir Henry. I understand. Charles, if you would fetch the family's belongings please." He steered Lily to the brown leather couch and sat beside her. "Lily, my child, I know how difficult this is to accept. I'm so very sorry, but your family has gone to be with our dear Lord."

"No! It's not true. It can't be."

"Bless you, child, but I saw the—I identified them myself." His face was set in soft furrows and mercy shone from his eyes.

"W-w-won't believe." She shook her head. "Want to see."

"No, my dear, you do not want to see." His gaze was tender. "Won't you take my word for it?"

"No! They wouldn't leave me like this. God wouldn't do this! Would He? Why?"

"I don't know why, dear child. Not even after all these years."

She looked into his eyes. The kindness there brought no relief. She glanced at Phila, who wept softly. Tears filled Lady Beatrice's eyes. His lordship coughed and cleared his throat.

A knock on the door. The curate entered, carrying two suitcases and a clumsily wrapped package.

"Thank you, Charles."

Lily stared at the cases. The larger one belonged to Mum, the smaller one to Kit. How could her family be dead, and the cases look no worse for wear?

Mr. Boyne put the package on her father's desk. The bishop unwrapped the paper and handed her a well-worn Bible. Its leather cover was torn and stained dark red by—

Father's blood?

She shoved it back at the bishop, not daring to touch it.

"It is your father's Bible. Charles and I collected what we could recover." He laid a gold locket and chain in her hand. Lily peered at it for a few minutes, then opened it, staring down at the tiny photographs of her father and the four children. Mum wore it always. The bishop handed her a battered school notebook with the name "Steven Barnabas Whitely" etched on the front. Next came Kit's delicate silver chain and tiny cross.

She never takes it off.

Lily bent over, picked up Kit's small case and opened it. On top, she found the well-loved Narnia book. She caressed the volume, hugging it to her chest and closing her eyes.

Time stood still.

When she opened her eyes, she stared at her mother's case. She flipped the latch and lifted the lid. A soft package lay on top. She felt it, knowing it contained the tweed and tartan. She slammed the case closed.

After a few moments of silence, everyone but Phila and her mum filed slowly from the study. Phila tiptoed forward and took each item from Lily's hand. She removed some of the clothes from Kit's case and placed the mementos inside, wrapping a bit of clothing around each. Her ladyship took Lily's hand and helped her upstairs.

Lily let Phila and her mother put her to bed. Phila laid the suitcase in a chair near the bed and sat down next to Lily.

Lily looked up into Lady Beatrice's concerned face. "So c-c-cold, Mummy," she whimpered.

"I know, my dear. Pet go fetch some brandy and a couple of hot water bottles."

※ ※ ※

Phila pushed the door to Lily's bedroom open. She propped Lily up with more pillows, then tucked the water bottles behind her back and at her feet. She piled on another quilt and coaxed her friend to drink the liqueur.

Lily sputtered. "Burns."

"Here, try this." Phila handed her friend a cup of tea. "It'll warm you up for sure."

"No" Lily groaned. "Cold, so cold. Never warm, ever again." She moaned, then appeared to drift off into a restless sleep.

Phila sighed and sat back in the chair. She forced herself to take a few deep breaths.

Meow.

She cocked her head. The sad cry came again. She got up and opened the door. Kit's cat scampered into the room and hopped up on the little girl's bed, nosing behind the teddy bears. Phila lay on the bed and stroked the soft white fur until Snowy purred.

Lily moaned and tossed back and forth.

Phila closed her eyes and prayed.

Sometime later a man came in and patted Phila on the shoulder. She sat up.

Dr. Lowman examined Lily and gave Phila a bottle of medicine for her friend. After she spooned some into Lily's mouth, poor Lil seemed to settle down and sleep.

Phila wrapped a quilt around Lily, then lay down on Kit's bed. The cat's warm little body snuggled up beside her. She fell asleep to the steady purring.

※ ※ ※

Lily is running.

She runs straight into a huge Bible, its pages whipping at her. Words fly out of it, accosting her. Stevie bursts forth from the pages and starts hitting her with his notebook. Benjie, in his torn and bloodied uniform, flees a wicked-looking witch flying at him on a broom, twirling a big silver cross at the end of leg chains. Kit is climbing into the mouth of an enormous lion, which, in turn, is being eaten by a monstrous wardrobe with a dripping mouth and glittering eyes.

The lion roars.

Lily screams at him. "You're not supposed to growl with your mouth full!"

But he roars louder. Two trains come rushing out of the wardrobe's eyes bearing down on her. Lily's father stands atop one of the trains, shouting: "You will be judged for not coming with us!"

Mum hangs onto the other engine. "My locket is yours!" She opens the clasp and out fly Father and Lily's siblings.

※ ※ ※

She woke up screaming. Phila was at her side in a moment, wrapping comforting arms around her. "It's all right, Lil, it's all right."

Lily collapsed back into bed and sobbed. "Oh, Phil, I can't believe it. I can't believe they are *all* gone. It will never be all right again!"

Sunday, 12 October, 8:00 a.m.
Washington, D.C., Hugh's apartment

Hugh jarred awake at the shrill ring of the telephone. He forced his eyelids open and eyed the clock. Who was ringing at eight hundred hours

Sunday morning?

Dad!

He jolted upright, pushing his body out of the bed and groped his way to the living room to grab the receiver and collapse in a chair. "Hello."

"Son, it's Dad."

"Aye, aye, Sir?" He grabbed the armrests.

"It's bad, son."

He jumped to attention like he'd been doused with ice water. "Aye, Sir."

"They were all killed."

"Oh, no. Dear, dear Lily." His throat closed up. Words failed. Barely breathing, he couldn't move. He'd been expecting a blow, but the shock was a direct hit amidships.

His dad remained silent as well for some minutes. "Son are you all right?"

"Aye, Sir, it's just . . ." *Why, God, why?*

"I understand."

"She must be shattered." *I am.*

"She is."

"I'll come right home." *She'll need me.*

"Do you want me to ring Sir Oliver?"

"No, Dad. I'll have a go." He wanted to fly to her, wrap his strong arms around her, and hold her.

They rang off. Hugh flopped back on the bed, staring at the ceiling. The picture in his mind of the black-haired beauty wearing the appealing blue gown dissolved into a sorrowful vision of her in a black sack, her glittery pewter eyes melted into two charcoals.

He didn't know how long he lay there. The phone rang again. "Hello?"

"Did I keep you out too late, darling?"

Not now, Darlene. "No. Sorry, I have to ring off."

The phone again.

"Darlene, I'm not able to talk now."

"Hugh! You were so distant last night. What's wrong with you?"

"Darlene, my father just rang. Lily's whole family died in that railway accident. I need some time. Good-bye."

He ignored the next ring. *Not this time.* He headed for the shower. After dressing quickly, he went out. Walking at a fast pace, he made it just in time for the service at St John's Episcopal Church.

That evening Hugh's presence as an attaché was required at a cocktail party at the home of Dean Acheson, the U.S. Secretary of State. The commander worked the room going around greeting those whom he was obliged to acknowledge. Then he made his way to the bar. He was drinking his second scotch whiskey when a voice interrupted his reverie.

"Commander?" He recognized the soft British accent of Sir Oliver's wife.

He turned and stood. "Lady Barbara. Do you wish my assistance?"

"No. Perhaps *I* can be of assistance to you." Oliver Goldsmith's maxim, "Beauty is as beauty does," fit her to a tee.

"I beg your pardon, your ladyship?"

"Commander, what's wrong? I'm seeing a great deal of pain in your face and bearing tonight."

"I'm sorry to concern you. It's personal, Ma'am." Her expression of compassion reminded him of his mum. Time to weigh anchor. "If there is nothing, I should be leaving." He drained his glass and turned to depart.

"Hugh, sit back down and tell me what's the matter. That's an order." She slid onto the next seat and ordered a glass of champagne and a single scotch.

"The rail crash on Wednesday, the family of my sister's best friend were all killed." There, he said it. Hugh looked away.

"I'm so very sorry." They sat in silence for a while. "The young woman who designed her own gown? The photograph on your desk?"

He nodded. "I've known Lily for thirteen years. She and Phila are inseparable. She's . . . like, like a sister. Her brother was fourteen; Lily's sister, seven." The floodgates on the need to tell someone burst. "Her older brother was lost in the Battle of Britain. Her father was vicar of St Peter's. He and her mother and other siblings were unaccounted for until yesterday. They were on the train from Perth. My father rang this morning. Lily . . ." Hugh cleared his throat and ordered another drink.

"You want, you *need* to go home."

"Yes, Lady Barbara."

"But you've just taken leave and wonder if the ambassador will let you go again so soon?"

"Yes, Ma'am."

A young woman came up to Lady Barbara, casting a come-hither look at Hugh. "Mrs. Frank, who is your handsome sailor?"

"Marilyn, forgive me, but we're engaged in an important conversation.

I'll be with you in a few moments." Her ladyship turned back to Hugh as the woman left in a huff.

"The uniform." Hugh shook his head.

She grinned. "Oh, it's definitely more. Commander, I think you can help me with something, and I will have a word with Sir Oliver in your favor."

CHAPTER 21

THE UNCLE

Wherever I am I know that you will come and see me.
Letters of C. S. Lewis, W. H. Lewis

Monday, 13 October
St Peter's Vicarage
Lily lay on the bed hugging the three teddy bears and absently stroking Snowy, who was curled up against her midsection. The sun had set. Dark shadows crept across the bedroom, shrouding her in despair.

"Where's my Lily-girl?"

That powerful voice could only belong to one person! She catapulted out of bed, tossing the cat and bears in scattered confusion. She flew down the stairs and threw herself into her uncle's arms. They stood embracing for a long time as she cried herself out. Then he wiped her face with his handkerchief and led her into the parlor, settling her next to him on the loveseat.

She gazed at him, fresh pain piercing her heart. There sat a slightly younger version of Father. However, her uncle's thick hair was close-cropped, not long and slicked back, and a little gray showed through the black. He wore the uniform of the British Army, the Third Infantry Brigade, not the dark suit and dog collar of a vicar. But his blue eyes drilled deep into hers, like Father's, and the familiar smile warmed her soul.

Colonel Gordon Whitely sat up straight, quiet, waiting for his niece to regain her composure.

"Uncle Gordy, you came."

"Did you think I wouldn't?"

"Yes. No. But, how? Did you desert?"

"Goodness no, Lily-girl. Sir Henry arranged leave with the War Office.

Not a small miracle, mind you. You've made yourself influential friends. Not a small blessing either. Thank God. I wouldn't want you alone just now."

Phila knocked on the door and peeked in. "Colonel Whitely, we're so pleased you could come."

"Thank you, Lady Philomena."

Mrs. Terrill brought in tea and Phila poured. Pressing against her uncle, Lily stared into the cup in her hands. After a long while her uncle coaxed her to drink, then Phila took her up to bed. Hugging a Teddy, she drifted off comforted that Uncle Gordy was there.

※ ※ ※

The colonel held out Phila's chair for her then sat opposite, just the two of them. Slightly discomforted, she clasped her hands under the table as he said grace. Awkward silences had a disquieting effect on her.

"How is the situation in Egypt, Colonel Whitely? The news is disturbing. Is it going to be our next big war?"

"No, I think we've had enough of that for a while. Skirmishes, yes. Don't believe all you read. The press usually exaggerates. It's calmed down considerably since July when General Naguib overthrew King Farouk. Foreign Secretary Eden is attempting to negotiate. They want us out, plain and simple. I don't doubt it will come to that eventually. Countries are keen on being independent."

Mrs. Terrill served a lamb roast with potatoes and vegetables from the garden. Phila's taste buds whetted with the scrumptious aroma. The Colonel ate with relish. The pudding was a lemon tart, Lily's favorite. Where did Mrs. Terrill find the sugar?

Mrs. Terrill came to collect the plates. Phila smiled at her and mouthed "scrummy." The woman smiled back. She served coffee.

Lily's uncle sipped his. "Now, Lady Philomena, will you brief me on all that has taken place, please."

※ ※ ※

Lily tossed fitfully, sleep evading her. Wrapping her dressing gown about her, she stole down the hallway, halting at her parents' door.

She heard weeping. "Oh, Jon. Why you, not me? It was supposed to be *me*. Dear God, why? I don't understand. Jon was so good. He was *Your* man."

Lily stood still, afraid to breathe. Then shakily she reached out, and gripping the knob, slowly turned it and peeked in.

Her uncle knelt by the bed. "Jon, I swear I'll find a way to look after Lily."

She eased the door shut and crept back to bed. I'm not totally alone. She had Uncle Gordy. And Teddy Timothy, Teddy Thaddeus, and Teddy Thomas. But not Teddy Theodore. She hugged the bears tightly, dampening their fur with her tears. A warm living ball of fur plopped on the bed and burrowed under the mute creatures. Snowy crawled up on Lily's chest, and after turning three times and kneading her belly, settled down.

Her uncle would take care of her. Somewhat comforted, Lily drifted off.

※ ※ ※

Uncle Gordy marches at the head of a platoon of teddy bears. One bear veers off from the rest and runs down a railway track. A monstrous locomotive puffing billows of steam charges behind.

Teddy Theodore squeals as the train runs him down.

CHAPTER 22

DARK DREAMS

There is a sort of invisible blanket between the world and me.

A Grief Observed, C. S. Lewis

Tuesday, 14 October

"Teddy!" screamed Lily. "Teddy, the train!" She sat up in bed, trembling.

Phila bolted to her side. "It's OK. I'm here. Why, your nightgown is soaked." She tugged the garment off Lily's shivering body, rubbed her with a towel, and wrapped the quilt around her. Pulling a fresh gown from the dresser, Phila slipped it over Lily's head. Then guiding her to Kit's bed, she arranged the covers around her.

Lily tried to resist. "No. K-K-Kit's—"

"I know, but your bed is damp. I'm sure Kit wouldn't mind. How many times did she sleep in yours? I'll fetch you a cup of tea and a couple hot water bottles to chase that chill away."

Phila tucked a hot water bottle at her friend's back and one by her feet. The hot drink also warmed Lily a little. Snowy curled up in the crook of her neck, purring. Lulled by the warmth and cuddly little body, her tense muscles relaxed. Then the faint chords of a piano drifted through to her consciousness. Mum playing downstairs in the drawing room. The sweet melancholy tune soothed her hurting heart. Calmed by the tender music, she drifted back to sleep, her cheeks wet with tears.

Sometime later she woke, recalling how comforting the melody had been. Then reality hit a sour note. Mum couldn't have been playing. She was gone. They all were gone. "Oh, Mummy, how will I go on without all of you?"

Uncle Gordy.

Lily bathed and dressed, then descended the stairs and entered the dining room. Her face brightened when she saw her uncle rise to greet her.

"Bad night, Lily-girl?" He had dark circles under his eyes. "Me as well."

He seated her patting her hand. "Dreams?"

"They frighten me so."

"Dreams can be quite unsettling. And often extremely terrifying and confusing."

"You?" She couldn't imagine her brave, strong uncle ever being afraid of anything.

"Yes, my dear, frequently."

"The war, Uncle?"

"Yes, and now." His eyes took on a sad mien.

"Are they scary?"

"The dreams? Quite so."

"Oh." Lily looked down at the plate of eggs, bacon, beans, and tomato that Mrs. Terrill had placed there.

"But, Lily-girl, they aren't real. It's one way your mind works through grief. Like letting off steam, you might say. Usually, they're all jumbled up and rarely do they make much sense. Though some say it's our subconscious speaking to us. They'll wane with time."

Phila joined them.

Uncle Gordy smiled at her. "Was that you playing, earlier, Lady Philomena? Beethoven's Moonlight Sonata, if I'm not mistaken?"

"Yes, I thought it might soothe Lily. But Colonel Whitely, please call me Phila."

"As you wish, Lady Phila."

"Thank you, Phil. So lovely." Lily squeezed her friend's hand. "I thought at first it was Mum. She used to play us to sleep sometimes." Taking in a deep jagged breath, she swallowed.

"Ah yes, Lily-girl, your mother played beautifully, and Lady Philomena, your playing is exemplary. It assuaged me as well. Thank you."

"Thank you," Phila took in a deep breath. "Breakfast smells delicious, Mrs. Terrill."

Lily tried to pass her plate to her friend.

"No. If I start eating for the both of us, I'll gain another stone and will *never* find a husband. *You* need to *eat*. Be a friend, please." But she took the plate and asked the housekeeper for just toast for Lily.

"Lily-girl, eat. And that's an order."

※ ※ ※

The days yawned before them; Phila concerning herself with her friend's care, acting as a guide as Lily groped her way through the heavy fog of grief. Phila's parents and Lily's uncle took care of all the arrangements and business. The parish undertook funeral and burial expenses leaving the mere £100 in the vicar's bank account for Lily. The Claibornes stored the household goods. But still much remained to sort out.

※ ※ ※

While Lily rested, Phila went in search of the colonel and found him in the vicar's study, slumped in Father Whitely's chair, staring at a letter. A cup of tea sat untouched at his elbow. She gasped when she saw tears roll down the cheeks of the veteran warrior.

"Yes, Lady Phila?" He croaked.

She tiptoed to the desk. "May I help?"

He gripped the paper in his hand. "This is the letter I wrote my brother when his son's plane crashed."

He let it slip from his fingers onto a stack of documents. "I'd rather be facing an enemy battalion." He motioned to the piles of paper cluttering the desk. "I could handle that. This, this is, difficult—worse than when I have to write home to parents that their sons have died in combat."

Phila didn't know what to say.

"Never seen a soldier cry, milady?"

"No, Sir."

"We do, you know. Even on the battlefield. But mostly afterwards. Every time a man is killed under your command, it rips a hunk of life out of you."

"How dreadful. Oh my, Lily must feel like half her body has been gutted."

"And her soul. Where is she?"

"Upstairs, lying down."

For what seemed like an eternity, Phila just stood there. After a while she became aware of a purring noise and noticed that Snowy had settled herself on a stack of papers. The colonel stroked the cat absently. Suddenly Snowy started & jumped off the desk.

"I say, hello there." The colonel jumped to his feet.

"Audie! What a surprise." Phila's aunt gave her a big hug.

"Oh, Colonel Whitely, may I introduce my aunt, Lady Audrey Claiborne. Audie, Lily's Uncle Gordon."

He bowed taking her hand and kissing her fingers. "My pleasure, your ladyship."

"Oh, do call me Audrey, Colonel."

"And I am Gordon."

"Audie was married to my father's youngest brother who died in the war."

"My condolences, Madame."

"Well now, my sister-in-law said there was a great deal of sorting to do, and you could do with some assistance."

"Will Rivenwood do without you? Colonel, my auntie manages our estate in Oxfordshire. She is quite the businesswoman."

"I'm impressed. I salute you."

Audie beamed. "Oh, Mrs. Terrill handed me this."

"Lily's mum's favorite Irish knit shawl. I'll take it to her when she wakes. I'm sure it will comfort her." The scent of lavender lingered.

"I'll give Mrs. Terrill a hand." Audie smiled at Lily's uncle and left.

"Colonel Whitely"—Phila picked up his cup, "I'll fetch you a fresh cup of tea and come back to help."

After Phila and the colonel cleared out Father Whitely's study, they tackled the master bedroom where she helped pack some of the vicar's clothing.

Sorting through the drawers on the bed, Phila held up some jumpers. "They look about your size, Colonel, and hardly worn. Though I expect you shan't need them in Egypt."

"I won't be there forever. Perhaps I can get a billet here at home for my next assignment."

"I'm sure Papa could arrange a transfer. He has influence."

"I don't think even he has the influence to pull that off. Besides, I couldn't impose."

"Not even for Lily?"

"Should you be checking on her, Lady Phila?"

"Yes, Sir." His polite rebuke told Phila she'd overstepped.

✽　✽　✽

Cracking open the bedroom door, Phila saw afternoon shadows clinging to the corners of the room. Lily lay on the bed, motionless, but with eyes wide open.

"Lil, did you get any sleep?"

"Don't think so."

"I've brought you something."

"What?"

"Your mum's shawl."

Lily blinked, sat upright, and yanked it from Phila's hands like a starving child.

Lily sat there rocking back and forth, her nose buried in the shawl. "Mummy." She crooned the word over and over.

Phila held her friend till she lay back down and drifted off.

✽　✽　✽

Following afternoon tea, Lady Audrey packed up Stevie's things as Lily watched. She saved his rugby shirt and tin box of mementos—what he called his "somesings" when he was a wee lad. Kit's clothes were also boxed to give to the poor. Each article placed into the container tore little bits from Lily's heart.

CHAPTER 23

RUTH

There is no pain so great as the memory of joy in present grief.
Aeschylus (525–456 BC)

Phila led Lily into the parlor, but she held back.

"I haven't the heart to clear out Mum's desk."

"I'll do it." Phila found several prayer and poetry journals in Mrs. Whitely's graceful handwriting. Lily would treasure these. Phila opened one to a beautiful sketch of an ancient tree with her thoughts about a passage from Scripture:

> To appoint unto them that mourn in Zion, to give unto them beauty for ashes, the oil of joy for mourning, the garment of praise for the spirit of heaviness; that they might be called trees of righteousness, the planting of the LORD, that he might be glorified.
> Isaiah 61:3

> I think about the tall majestic trees, which have stood for hundreds of years. Every little passing moment, those trees strove toward the heavens, from tiny shoots to tall rooted and established beauty, they grew and flourished, never giving up but steadfast, faithful, and persistent.

> Now they lift their hands in praise to their Lord and Maker in the heavens above, and the birds make their homes in the boughs.

What an engaging picture Lily's mum had painted from that passage. Why did you take her, Lord?

Phila couldn't resist reading more.

> Father, I long for the courage, persistence, and steadfastness to overcome the grief and sadness in my heart, to rise above, for You, to flourish for Your glory and to have true courage in the face of life's challenges.

Phila flipped the pages, looking for a date. Sixteen November 1940. Just weeks after Benjie was killed.

> Help me grow in wisdom as Your beautiful trees, moment by moment, so that at the end of all things, I would be as a tall tree bearing precious fruit for Your glory. May "righteousness and praise spring forth before all the nations."

Now, suddenly, Lily's mum had been swept away to heaven. Her death seemed in vain; what beautiful bright fruits and flowers could bloom now? Lord, take the pain and hurt.

Next Phila found a poem that would be a beautiful tribute to Mrs. Whitely. Lily couldn't bring herself to read it but agreed that Phila could at the funeral.

※ ※ ※

Under Phila's direction, Lily packed up most of her little sister's toys, animals, dolls, and books—handling each with loving care before tucking them into boxes to go with the household items. Lily had worn the silver cross and chain since the bishop had given them to her. The three bears and Kit's favorite Narnia book, Lily tucked into her own suitcase.

"Let's pack up your things now, shall we?"

Lily sighed and walked toward her dresser. She stopped suddenly and stared at the sketches of her gown. It seemed like Lily was seeing them for the first time.

"Oh, Phil, my gown!"

"No question that it would win the grand prize."

Lily gazed at her, confused.

"Oh, Lil, it won! Madame Gianna rang expressing her condolences and said they had sent the gown to Hartnell's to be displayed."

"I won?"

"You did indeed."

"Doesn't matter now. But—why they came home early—why they died." Lily's face contorted in agony.

How can life be so wonderful and so horrific?

"I just don't understand." Lily sank down in a chair, sobbing.

"Neither do I." Phila bent over her friend, gripping her shoulders. "I can't imagine how much you are hurting."

"Will there be happier days ever again?" Lily gazed up at Phila, big tears filling her eyes.

"Yes, there will." Weeping now too Phila wrapped her arms around her friend and held her tight. "'Weeping may endure for a night, but joy comes in the morning.'"

Lily managed to speak through her sobbing. "Will it ever be morning again?"

CHAPTER 24

TREASURE CHEST

A faithful friend is a strong defense; and he that hath found him hath found a treasure.
Louisa May Alcott (1832–1888)

Wednesday, 15 October
Lily woke early and, gathering her courage, ventured up into the attic where her mother kept her treasure chest. She climbed the ladder, walked around boxes, an odd table, a shelf, a broken chair — all blanketed with dust. Unmindful of the dirty floor, she settled down next to the large cedar-lined trunk.

Lily ran her fingers over the intricate carving, tracing the figures. Uncle Gordy had given the chest to her mother years ago, shipping it all the way from India. Father thought it too gaudy and pagan, depicting the Hindu gods. He objected to foreign idols in their home. Mum yielded partially to him by keeping it out of sight.

Footsteps on the ladder. Lily turned. A mop of curly carrot-colored hair popped up through the hole. "Good, you've decided to come up."

"Is this where your mum stowed away Christmas gifts?" Phila moved closer.

"Yes." Lily laid her hands on the lid. "I'll be surprised if it's empty."

Phila grinned. "My mum starts holiday shopping as soon as the season is over, but she'd never let us know where she hides them.

Distracted from the task at hand, Lily looked up at her friend. "Surely you wouldn't peek now?"

Phila grinned. "The Disciplined Dignitary wouldn't. Me? I can't stand the suspense."

"Will you never grow up?"

"You sound like my brother." She stuck out her tongue. "Not if I can help it."

"You're hopeless," Lily almost laughed. "I've known Mum packed away gifts up here for a long time, but then, it has always been locked." She held up the key. "Mum told me where she hid it last year."

"She knew you wouldn't peek. You have the patience of Job."

A sudden chill wafted through the attic, and Lily shivered. "Did you have to bring up Job? He lost his family, all in one day, too." She took a deep breath. "I am *not* going to cry."

"Oh, Lil, I am so sorry. What a thoughtless mouthpiece I am. Please forgive me." Phila climbed over a couple boxes and sank down next to Lily, giving her a hug. The light from a tiny window sifted down as if spotlighting the chest. "There's hardly any dust on it. Must mean it hasn't been long since she's been here. Do you want me to open it?"

"No. I'll do it." Lily breathed in and out for a couple minutes, then rose up on her knees, unlocked the latch, and lifted the cover. Right on top was a large package of soft stuff wrapped in brown parcel paper and tied with a red ribbon. The envelope tucked under the bow read *Lily* in her mother's graceful cursive. She blew out all the air in her lungs and sank back on the floor. Dust particles danced in the filtered light. They both sneezed.

Phila peered into the chest. "She did it. Dash it all, Lil. Do you think there are more?"

She nodded but didn't move for a long time.

Phila nudged her. "Well, shall we?"

They lifted the large bundle out of the trunk. Beneath it they found a collection of smaller parcels and boxes all wrapped in butcher paper and tied with red, green, and blue ribbon. The box for Uncle Gordon was near the top, probably for Mum to post.

※　※　※

Spending the last few mornings packing only dragged Lily's sorrow deeper. She couldn't bear to look at her mother's journals, so she secured them in a special parcel. She cast the gown sketches and fabric swatches into a box.

"Lil let's change for the service and walk over to The Havens a little early."

They needed their coats, but at least no rain. Lily gratefully inhaled the fresh air. Phila seemed antsy, nearly skipping. Another time Lily would have suspected a trick. But she appreciated Phil not talking.

Life was empty and silent now. No joy.

CHAPTER 25

LILIES AND LAID TO REST

> Will nothing persuade us that they are gone?
> *A Grief Observed*, C. S. Lewis

The Havens

Lily followed Phila as she climbed the steps of her house. When the door opened, however, instead of the butler, Phila's brother stood there in his Royal Navy mess dress uniform.

"Hughie!" Lily fell into his arms, clinging to him as if she could draw his strength into her body. He held her close while she wept.

Finally, she quieted and looked up.

His eyes bathed her in compassion. "Lily."

"You c-came."

"I did." He handed her his handkerchief.

"H-how?"

"Sir Oliver was generous, but I'll have to wed his daughter."

Lily gasped. "Really? You did that for me?"

"No. Only joking. I hoped to see you smile a little."

"Hughie, thank you." She managed a half-hearted tug on the corners of her mouth.

They retired to the dining room. Regaining her composure, Lily talked, and Hugh listened.

✳   ✳   ✳

Hugh looked up when his father, sister, and mum entered the dining room. Mum gave Lily a squeeze from behind. "I'm so glad you two had some time before the rest arrive for lunch." Hugh stood to seat his mum.

"Lily, my dear." Before taking his seat, Dad patted her shoulder, then glanced at Hugh. "Son, sorry I missed you when you arrived this morning. Did you get any sleep?"

Hugh yawned. "A couple hours."

While he pulled out a chair for Phila, Lily reached up and tugged on her arm. "I knew you were up to something. A lovely surprise. Thank you."

Lily's uncle arrived in Royal Army regimental dress—black jacket, white belt, burgundy trousers, white gloves, wheel hat tucked under his arm. Multiple medals decorated his jacket and the silver epaulets on his shoulder displayed two bath stars and the crown of a colonel. Audie was on his arm.

Duncan snapped to attention, and Hugh thrust himself out of his chair striding over to introduce himself. "Commander Hugh Claiborne, Colonel Whitely."

"Commander. You won't remember, but we met briefly when you were home from Cambridge."

"Of course. You weren't in uniform then."

"Nor were you." After shaking hands, Hugh continued.

"You already know my father and mother, and apparently my aunt."

"Sir Henry, Lady Beatrice." The colonel bowed.

"Gordon, good to see you again."

"Sir Henry, thank you for arranging my leave."

"You are quite welcome, Gordon. It was the least I could do for our dear Lily."

"Lady Phila." He nodded, then embraced Lily.

"Colonel Whitely," Hugh waved Duncan over, "may I present Sergeant Major Duncan MacWhirter, retired, of the Seaforth Highlanders. He keeps this family shipshape now."

"Sir! My honor!" Duncan stood at attention.

"Sergeant Major, your Highlanders saw plenty of action."

"As did yours, Sir." Obviously, Duncan recognized the insignia of the Third Infantry Division. The black triangle trisected by an inverted red triangle insignia had been created by Field Marshall Montgomery to instill pride in his troops. "Monty's Iron Sides, I believe, Colonel."

"Yes, Sergeant Major, that's what they called us. But the Seaforth's served with distinction as part of the 51st Division in the Second Battle of El Alamein and the Allied invasions of Sicily and Normandy. Were you with the Second Battalion, Sergeant Major?"

"Yes, Sir."

"Then it is *my* honor, man." While shaking hands with the butler, the colonel's eyes lit up. "Forgive me. I have to ask, are the rumors true about a giant of a soldier in your battalion referred to as the *Red Pict*? A crazy redhead who went into battle with his face painted blue. He took out two Panzers single-handed at El Alamein. I believe he was awarded the VC for action in Normandy."

"Yes, Sir. My own young recruit. He ended up a sergeant and not dead like I feared." Duncan beamed.

The exchanged piqued Dad's interest. "Duncan, perhaps you and Colonel Whitely should take time later to discuss this further. I may even join you."

"Count me in too." Hugh sat back down and returned his attention to Lily.

St Peter's

Lily gritted her teeth, forcing her emotions to still. Bishop Osred conducted the services. The church was full to overflowing.

Phila mentioned that 112 people had died in the accident. How did one comprehend that many people being killed at once? Especially when she couldn't even grasp that her own family was gone.

Lily sat in the front pew, Uncle Gordy on her left, Hugh on her right. She wore the little black felt hat with the veil that her mum always wore for funerals.

She sat there, frozen in body and soul. Her only relief the warmth of Uncle Gordy's and Hugh's hands, which she clasped as lifelines. As pain throbbed, she grasped harder.

"Lily-girl, if you don't loosen your grip," Uncle Gordy whispered, "I shan't ever be able to handle a revolver again."

Hugh squeezed her other hand.

Lily offered a weak smile at her uncle through her tears and rested her head against his shoulder. She wanted to close her eyes tight and block out the view of the four caskets—three full size and one small. White lilies rested on top of all four.

Lilies.

She would loathe the flowers from then on.

After the bishop memorialized Lily's father, mother, and two siblings; he called on Phila. "As many of you know, Ruth was an accomplished poet. Lady Philomena Claiborne will read one of Ruth's poems, which she composed after losing her son, Benjamin, in the Battle of Britain."

Phila came forward and recited the rhyme. Her voice quivered.

> I'll fly away to some far country green,
> Where no more tears will fall and all that seems
> In vain will bear bright fruits and flowers divine,
> Where pain and hurt will fade and joy will shine.

Lily's eyes fell upon the white lilies again, her heart utterly overwhelmed. Pain. Hurt. Joy. She clung to Uncle Gordy. He held her tight.

The organ began playing. Then a pure soprano voice filled the cathedral.

> "Amazing grace! how sweet the sound,
> that saved a wretch like me!"

How her mum had loved the hymn. Now it tore at Lily's heart.

> "I once was lost but now am found,
> was blind but now I see."

But she was utterly *lost* and *couldn't see* for the sorrow.

Her uncle's and Hugh's touch gave some comfort as did Phila's hand on her shoulder from behind.

They remained beside her throughout the tortuous day. At the end of the service, Lily passed by each of the closed coffins, laying her hands tenderly on the wood. She finally broke down and sobbed over Kit's. Her uncle took her arm and helped her move along.

At the graveside, Uncle Gordy held the umbrella over their heads in the drizzling rain. Hugh stood right behind Lily.

The Vicarage

In the receiving line at the wake, Lily was flanked again by Uncle Gordy and Hugh with Phila directly behind her. Lily stood as people filed past, offering condolences. Her uncle greeted people graciously; Hugh kept them moving.

There were hugs, kisses, and tears as the mourners paid their respects. The less the people said, the more care Lily felt. *I'll scream if one more old biddy tells me they are better off where they are. Will this torment never end?* She looked down, biting her lip.

"I'm so very sorry, Lily." The speaker took her hands and squeezed them. Lily looked up. Tears glittered in Edwina Endicott's eyes. She said no more, just stood there. Giving Lily a hug, she moved on.

"That was thoughtful of her to come," Phila whispered in Lily's ear. "I thought she was leaving for France."

Lady Beatrice rescued Lily from the line, explaining that "the poor girl needs a cup of tea and a rest."

In the parlor, Lily pulled the shawl tight around her and sank into the first chair she saw. She refused the tea. "Please." It took all her strength to speak. "I just want to leave."

Phila escorted Lily back up to her room.

Later that night

Lily couldn't sleep. She lay there, shivering, eyes open. Her last night in the vicarage. Tomorrow she and Uncle Gordy would go to Rivenwood.

"Afraid, are you? You should be. You're all alone now."

That frightful voice again!

"See what happened when you had to have your own way."

"Go away! Please!"

Guilt pressed its advantage. Horrid voices pelted her. Anger boiled. She shot up and out of bed. Creeping out of the room so as not to wake Phila, she tiptoed down the hall, careful not to disturb Uncle Gordy. She stole quietly down the stairs and slipped through her father's stripped study into the cozy chapel adjoining it. She stood facing the tiny altar in the dimly lit chancel.

"God, where *were* You?" Her voice sounded hollow and flat. "Where *are* You?"

Silence.

"What did you expect? An actual voice?"

She balled her fingers into fists. "Answer me! Father said when we call, You will answer."

Silence thundered all around her.

"Well? I'm waiting." She shivered. Shouldn't she feel the warmth of His presence. Instead an icy draft chilled her bones as the last vestiges of faith drained from her soul.

"If You don't exist, they died in vain."

If her loved ones were with God, she'd feel it. But she felt nothing.

Lily stared several moments longer at the altar, took a deep breath, blowing out the air with a whoosh. "Good-bye, God!" She pivoted and stomped out of the chapel, letting the door bang shut.

She crept up the stairs, crawled back in bed, closed her eyes, and tried to settle her mind. But it wouldn't rest. Hot tears seeped out in the darkness. Cold rain pattered on the window. The hollow emptiness of the room closed around her. No clothes, no toys, no teddy bears, no books — no Kit.

Then in the stillness . . .

"Read it again, please," her sister's voice had pleaded.

"You have other books besides Narnia, Kit."

But the little girl chatted on about the characters like they were real people in her life.

"It's just a made-up place, Kit. It's not real."

"It's real to me." Kit pouted.

"You're a child."

"Phila's not a child. She loves Narnia."

Lily sighed. "Perhaps Phila needs to grow up, too."

"Lily, you were more fun before you grew up. I don't ever want to grow up." Kit had grabbed her bears and hugged them.

Now she would never grow up. Stevie wouldn't go to university and be a scientist. Benjie wouldn't preach like Father. Mum wouldn't have her poems published. Father wouldn't convert all of Scotland.

The only thing left — the nightmarish unspeakable *real*.

CHAPTER 26

BETWEEN SORROW AND SADNESS

Can I see another's woe, and not be in sorrow too?
Can I see another's grief, and not seek for kind relief?
Songs of Innocence, On Another's Sorrow,
William Blake (1757–1827)

Thursday, 16 October
Phila helped Lily into the Bentley for the ride to the country.

Lily looked around. "Uncle Gordy? Hugh?"

Mum patted her hand. "They went with Henry to Whitehall. He and your uncle have meetings and Hugh an errand for Sir Oliver."

Lily leaned back in the seat and closed her eyes. Phila shook her head, glancing sadly at Mum. "Do you think spending some time in the country will help Lily?"

"I hope so, darling."

Rivenwood
Phila sighed with relief when the thin and wiry Black Irish butler opened the door. It had been a grueling nine days.

"Thank you, Killian." She always appreciated his winning grin and agreeable nature, today subdued and respectful.

Killian's buxom wife, the housekeeper, had a sweet face, auburn hair, and green eyes. Together, they took Lily upstairs where their daughter helped Lily undress and get into bed.

"I'll keep an eye on herself." The youthful upstairs maid's freckled face, usually so full of smiles, etched with pain.

"Thank you, Kenzie," said Phila. "A break would be wonderful. It's been awful seeing Lily so numb."

After Killian brought up Phila's cases, she flung herself on the bed and closed her eyes. Could it really be less than a fortnight ago that she and Lily had shared the excitement of preparing for her ball in this very room? Now, no cheer remained.

Phila didn't know how long she lay there staring at the ceiling, but she started at the knock on the door.

Kenzie peeked in. "Miss Phila, it's half one, sure an' will ye be joinin' yer mum and auntie for lunch?"

"Yes, I'll be right down." She freshened up and plodded down the stairway.

※ ※ ※

"Are you all right, Pet?" Mum's brow wrinkled.

"Yes, Mum, just daydreaming a little. Will you mind if I go for a ride after lunch? I need to work off some stress or I'll go stark-raving mad."

"That's probably a good idea." Audie turned to the butler. "Killian, would you ring George please?"

After lunch, Phila charged up the stairs to change, then ran to the stables. The head groom had her horse saddled and waiting.

"Thank you, George."

He helped her mount, and off she rode down the paths crisscrossing the meadows. The damp air washed her face, invigorating her as she trotted and cantered her horse against the wind. She couldn't get enough of the revitalizing air.

On the way back, Phila skirted the woods and walked the horse along the river. The swans glided up to her, begging for offerings. Just two weeks ago she and Lily had happily picnicked in this spot and fed them and their two cygnets. They had been filled with hopes and dreams.

At dinner, Phila noted the continued absence of the men.

"Your father said that since they have more business tomorrow, they might as well stay in town. They're planning to dine at Simpsons on the Strand tonight." Mum's eyes twinkled. "I think your father is looking forward to an evening with *the boys*."

London

Hugh grinned. It was great to be back at the wheel of his Bentley Coup under his own power. "'Damn the torpedoes; full speed ahead.'"

He pressed the pedal.

"A little fast, son? Wait till you get out into the country, won't you? The young always want to speed, right, Gordon?"

"Straight on target, Sir Henry." Lily's uncle chuckled from the backseat. "I do like your wheels though, Commander."

Hugh drove from Eaton Square to Westminster in Central London and up The Strand. He pulled up at the Savoy Hotel, where a bellman took his car. They walked the couple yards to Simpsons.

"Right this way, Sir Henry." The headwaiter led them to a table.

Hugh's mouth salivated the moment they entered the restaurant. The delectable aroma of roasted beef and spices triggered his taste buds.

They all requested the beef. Dad ordered a bottle of cabernet sauvignon to be opened and to breathe.

The waiter delivered them three scotch whiskies. Dad sipped his. "Gordon, I have two meetings tomorrow morning. What is your schedule?"

"The Vice Chief of the Imperial General Staff has ordered me to present myself in the morning." The colonel fingered the rim of his glass. "Not sure what's up."

"Promotion?"

"He probably just wants an eyes-on report."

"Hugh?" Dad looked over at him. "More assignments from Sir Oliver?"

"Aye, Sir." Unfortunately.

Dad buttered a roll. "He was gracious to give you leave so soon again."

"I had to pay a price."

"Pay?" Dad's eyebrow shot up.

Hugh swallowed his embarrassment. "I have a shopping list from Lady Barbara for things for their daughter's birthday."

His dad and the colonel guffawed.

He glared at them. "Enjoying this, are you, *Sirs?*"

"I've an idea, Commander." The colonel's eyes glinted.

"Yes Sir?"

"Why don't you ask Lily to accompany you?"

Why didn't I think of that? "That's an ace idea, but do you think she's up to it?"

"It can't hurt to get her mind off her grief for a little while. You'd finish in half the time, and she'll save you, shall we say, some discomfort?"

"I say, Gordon, good show." Dad grinned. "You learned that from your wife, I presume?"

"Not married, Sir Henry, except to the Army—twenty-three years. I never found a woman who could compare to my brother's Ruthie." His eyes glistened. "Jon was blessed, indeed. Ruth was one special lady. I'm a confirmed bachelor."

"Yes, my son appears to be headed in that direction."

Here we go again. "Actually, Dad, I've been seeing a girl in Washington, the daughter of a California senator."

Dad's eyes widened. "American *and* Californian?"

"The king gave up his throne for an American. And the vice-presidential candidate, Mr. Nixon, is from California." Hugh inclined his head.

"Yes, that."

"And have you ever seen any of the gorgeous women from there?"

"Can't say I have. Shall we change the subject?"

Absolutely! The memory of the sexy, provocative, long-legged blonde, however, had begun to lose its allure. Still, maybe it would stave off his father's concerns for a while.

Dad seemed relieved as well. "So, Gordon, how was it that Father Whitely went into the church and you into the Army?"

"Jon had the *calling* as long as I can remember." A wistful expression took over his face. "He was eight years older. I started playing soldier as a small lad. So, we decided between us that we would be soldiers—he for God and me for the Crown. But we always thought I'd be the one to die first." His eyes clouded. He cleared his throat. "Sorry."

"I understand, Gordon, I've lost three brothers." His voice became husky.

"My condolences, Sir Henry."

"My eldest brother was killed in 1916. The next eldest became Earl after our father died. He died seven years ago. The youngest was killed in '42. Audrey is his widow." Dad signaled the waiter to pour the wine.

The colonel appeared surprised. "So, you weren't expecting to take on the title?"

"No. Neville didn't get the chance to marry. Rayner and his wife lost their son in the war, and his wife remarried. Lindell and Audrey were married just before he deployed. No time for children." Dad sniffed and tasted the wine, nodding to the waiter.

"That's ten years. She never remarried?" He gazed down at his goblet. "Such an attractive woman."

"Audie loves Rivenwood." Hugh smiled, relieved that the attention had been deflected elsewhere.

Dad joined in. "I guess you could say she's married to the estate. My sister-in-law has an incredible head for business. She has made the place pay for itself. We would have lost it to death duties otherwise."

Hugh nodded to his dad. "Audie's poured her life's blood into the place. We've been so grateful to her. Mum yields the position of lady of the manor to her, and Dad, management of the estate."

"That is gracious of you, Sir Henry. I'm impressed."

"Not at all, Gordon. I am relieved of the responsibility. Running a ship or a department is much more to my skills."

The waiter wheeled the wooden trolley up to their table and raised the magnificent silver cover to reveal a large joint of beef. He carved the meat and served it, then pouring more wine.

Silence fell at the table as the men began eating their beef and Yorkshire pudding.

"Sir Henry, this beef is excellent." The colonel put down his cutlery and wiped his mouth with his serviette. "I can't think if I've ever had anything as fine."

"It's Aberdeen Angus beef. I see the Duke of Angus and Aberdeen now and again in the House of Lords. Lord Malcolm told me he sells directly to Simpsons."

The colonel raised his goblet. "To the finest beef in the kingdom." Hugh and Dad met his toast. "Speaking of Scotland, I'm enjoying getting to know your butler and learning more about the Seaforth Highlanders. What an honor to meet one of the men captured by the Germans at Saint-Valéry-en-Caux after the Battle of France in '40, who actually escaped."

"I'm surprised the sergeant major granted you the privilege of his heroic tale." Hugh dipped a bite of Yorkshire pudding in the *sauce de bœuf*. "We've been requested to keep the knowledge under ships—a condition of his hiring."

"Not bucking a sergeant major is wisdom of command." He raised his goblet in salute. "How did you know then?"

Hugh sipped his wine. "He told us he was with the 2nd Battalion, 51st Division at the commencement of the war in '39 and disembarked in France in '40. Because he wasn't killed, he must have been one of the 10,000 from the 51st who surrendered. Of the 290 soldiers who escaped on the march to prison camp, 134 were from Duncan's outfit. So, when I presented him with the facts, he had to admit it."

"Amazing, Commander, your grasp of the details." The colonel nodded to Hugh.

"That's my son. He recalls everything he reads." His eyes sparkled with pride. "My father enjoyed the same impressive gift that humbles us mere mortals. Hugh was a natural for Intelligence."

Hugh grimaced. "And that's where they stuck me for the war."

"Without which the Allies would not have won." The colonel smiled. "Don't minimize it, Commander, be proud of your contribution."

"Exactly what I tell him, Gordon." Dad gazed over his nose at Hugh.

The colonel chuckled. "So, how did an *Army* man come to butler for a *Navy* admiral?"

Dad grinned. "He'd had enough soldiering and told a field-marshal friend of mine. When my brother died, his butler retired. It seemed a match made in military heaven. We saw eye-to-eye from day one."

Hugh chuckled. "And, may I add, that the Army has even taken charge of my labs, not to mention my sister."

"And that's no small mission—my daughter, that is." Dad and Hugh laughed.

The colonel smiled. "Lady Phila has been a blessing to Lily these past days. She helped me pack as well. We enjoyed some conversation, too."

The waiter removed their plates and served coffee.

"My daughter loves your niece like a sister. She's family to us as well."

Lily's uncle's face brightened. "It's such a relief to know that Lily has such caring support, especially the kind of tender affection your ladies give her. I'm her mother and father now and have no experience whatsoever in how to be that."

"Parenting carries with it grave responsibility, even for grown children." Dad glanced Hugh's way and coughed. "Of course, a father remains accountable for a daughter until she marries."

"Yes, that has me concerned." Colonel Whitely's expression had become grave. "I certainly can provide for Lily fiscally, but being here for her physically? That is weighing on my mind. I will need time to carefully consider my life path now. I actually have never imagined my life beyond the Army."

Dad smiled. "That's perfectly understandable, Gordon. Whatever we can do—"

"Sir Henry, you and your family have—" His voice got husky, "shown Lily and me such, well, my brother would have said, Christ's love. Thank you."

Friday, 17 October
Rivenwood

When Hugh arrived from London early that morning, he met his sister in the foyer.

"Lily's dressed and ate a little. I think this shopping trip is a good idea. Hopefully it will work."

As Lily descended the grand staircase, Hugh could see she hadn't taken her usual care in dressing, but even without cosmetics, dark circles under her eyes, and her black hair pulled back in a ponytail, she still radiated beauty.

Oh, Lily. He hated seeing her in such pain. And there was nothing he could do to make it better.

He escorted her out the door and into his coup. "You're sure you're up for this?"

She looked at him and nodded.

"I know what an imposition it is, but I'm a sailor on dry land with this assignment. Lady Barbara promised if I would shop for her daughter's birthday, she would see to it that Sir Oliver gave me the leave."

"I'm glad you didn't have to marry her."

Are you?

Since the ambassador's wife wanted gifts especially from London, Lily suggested Liberty's on Regent Street. Hugh didn't hear much enthusiasm in her tone, but at least she was talking.

"The shop was founded in the mid-1800s selling exotic silks imported from China and Japan, cottons and fine wools from India." Lily recited the information without emotion. "Liberty prints are created exclusively for the store and famous worldwide."

The prints were bright and distinctive. But Hugh found standing in the dress department while Lily looked over the frocks decidedly uncomfortable. He tried to look nonchalant. Did ambassadors give medals for duty above and beyond?

"Would you look who's searching for frocks?" A shrill female voice cut into his camouflage. "I do believe it's Hugh Claiborne."

Damn. I'm caught.

"No! I thought he was in the States." The second voice sounded friendlier.

He turned slowly in the direction of the voices. The two young women looked vaguely familiar, but he couldn't place them. "Ladies. How lovely to see you."

"I'll just bet. You don't recognize us, do you?" The first's strident tone matched her pinched face, red-lipped simper. "But then your eyes were only on your sister's friend."

"I beg your pardon." His lip twitched.

"We were at your sister's ball a few weeks ago." At least the second girl smiled.

"Hugh, do you think she'd like either of these?" Lily approached with three frocks in her arms.

"And who is London's most eligible bachelor with in a dress shop, but the girl he escorted at the ball." The first's harsh tone turned provocative. "The rumors must be true."

"And what might those rumors be?" He looked the speaker in the eye, ire building when he saw how Lily paled at her words.

"Oh, gracious. It's Phila's friend," piped up the second girl. "Lily, I'm so sorry." She hustled her companion away.

"Are you OK?" Hugh took the frocks out of Lily's hands, hung them on a rack, and took her in his arms.

The girls looked back at them.

Rumors? He didn't like the sound of that.

"I'm all right." Lily straightened up, a brave smile on her face.

They decided on two dresses and proceeded to Harrods for the other items on the list. Since money wasn't an object, Lily suggested the top department store in London. "Be sure to keep the packages with Harrods' labels on them. That's important."

Hugh felt totally shipwrecked in the lingerie department. Lily had picked out the personal items from the list, and he was paying for them, hoping they'd get underway before another female broadside.

"Don't tell me. It's Lily Whitely . . . and in Harrods?"

Too late. Direct hit. Now, what? Who? In here? I'm outed.

"Yes, Jacquie, it's me."

"You're out so soon. I'd have thought—" She stopped short when Hugh turned to face her.

"Jacquie Napier-Jones, in Harrods? Need something to make you lovelier?"

"How snide, Genius."

She stood there, mouth agape for a moment. "Hugh? All the way from the States to buy unmentionables? And, for Lily?"

"Not for Lily, as a matter of fact. Gifts for the ambassador's daughter's birthday—from her parents."

"Of course, Hugh."

Was this how the ancient Greek sailors felt when the Sirens lured them to their dooms?

"Be polite, Genius."

"Shall I have Lady Barbara send you a note?"

"By all means, you do that." She leered back.

The virago is returning fire. "Lily is assisting me."

Jacquie cocked an eyebrow. "How kind of Lily, and so soon. You must be utterly traumatized. My condolences." The lack of concern in her voice betrayed her. "Well, I guess it is true." She regarded Lily with hauteur.

"What's true?" Hugh barked.

Jacquie shot back. "That you two are an item."

"Hugh," Lily took his arm, "let's go, please."

Against his desire to launch another round, Hugh acquiesced. "Cheers, Miss Napier-Jones. Right now, Lily needs a cup of tea and lunch before we drive back to the country." He gave Jacquie a cold smile, then put his arm around Lily and strode away, leaving the shrew standing there with her mouth open.

Lily leaned against his arm. "Oh, Hughie. You'll be the talk of the town now that Jacquie saw us together."

"Why should I mind? But *what* are these rumors?"

"Don't bother yourself. You know silly girls, always spreading gossip."

"What gossip?" What's going on?

Lily flinched at his harsh tone. She flicked her hand.

"Look at me Lily. *What* rumors?"

"It's just jealousy, probably. They say that I was, reciprocating for your attentions."

"Now *that*—that I mind tremendously!" He gritted his teeth. "Where did a perverse rumor like that come from?"

"Your escorting me to the ball."

"What?" How could they discern such a tawdry notion from his chaperoning Lily? He was fuming as they walked to the car park.

"Hughie give me the packages. You're mangling them. It's *only* gossip."

"It's reprehensible! Have they no honor?" Ungentlemanly names for these ignoble females surfaced like bile regurgitating, but he remained silent.

"Don't be angry, Hughie. Don't you see, it doesn't matter anymore."

But it does matter. It matters tremendously to me. "It's your *reputation*! I hate that I'm the cause of such talk." He would ask Phila for details.

CHAPTER 27
THE MEMORIAL

Heaven knows we need never be ashamed of our tears.
  Great Expectations, Charles Dickens (1812–1870)

Rivenwood

Hugh was the lone male for afternoon tea, but he wanted an opportunity to quiz Phila, so he sat next to her.

"Poor Hughie." The corners of Lily's mouth twitched. "It was bad enough for him to be seen in a dress shop *and* the lingerie department, but they were so catty. I hope they don't tattle all over town."

"Oh, darling, how horrible." But his mum and aunt couldn't hide their merriment.

Audie goggled at him. "Why didn't you say you were going lingerie shopping, Hughie? I would have given you my size."

He glared back.

Phila's eyes lit up with amusement. "But, Hughie Louie, I think your selections of the Liberty frocks and *unmentionables* should delight Sir Oliver's daughter." She giggled.

"Lily did that." Hugh glowered around the room.

"Why, darling, I do believe you're flushed."

Mum, you too? When are Dad and the colonel getting here? He'd been at the mercy of females all day. Where's a decent naval battle when a chap needs one? I definitely should get a medal for what I did today. Finally, though, Lily had come out of herself a little, so he supposed the sacrifice worth it.

While Lily showed his mum and aunt the dresses, Hugh leaned over to his sister. "What did those girls mean about the *rumors* being true? What rumors?"

"If I were to guess, maybe that those single girls at the ball, who were green with envy at you escorting Lily, have been saying that you two are an item."

"Being *an item* is one thing, *reciprocating* is quite another."

"Oh, *that*?" Phila winced.

"Yes, *that*! So that rumor *is* out there?" He glared at her.

She glanced at her hands. "I heard it myself."

"When?" *Why won't she look at me?*

"In the toilet at the ball. Jacquie suggested it when the girls were talking about how you were looking at Lily."

"Why didn't you tell me?" *How was I looking at Lily?*

Phila continued studying her hands. "I didn't want to get you angry."

"I'm angry now!"

"I *told* Jacquie that Lily would never do anything like that."

"But *I* would?" *Take advantage of Lily? Never!*

"Oh, Hughie, you're a man."

And men are lechers, of course. "*You* need *to do* something."

"I was, but then it all happened." She gazed up at him.

"Do something!"

She shrank back. "But—"

"Greetings, ladies and Hugh." Dad breezed in.

Reinforcements! "As the Yanks say, 'Here comes the cavalry.'"

"What's the surprise?" Miss Curiosity burst from her chair.

"Where is Gordon, Henry?" Audie peered past him.

"Well, *Colonel* Whitely will not be returning."

Hugh caught mischief in his father's eyes.

"Uncle Gordy's not coming back?" Lily sounded panicky.

"I didn't say that, my dear. The *Colonel* is not returning, but may I present *Brigadier* Whitely."

In came the new brigadier beaming with *three* Bath stars and Crown on his epaulets.

Hugh sprang to his feet. "Congratulations on your promotion, Brigadier."

"Thank you, Commander. I understand you were just awarded one, as well." They shook hands.

Mum graced the brigadier with a lovely smile. "Congratulations. Well-deserved, no doubt."

"Gordon, I'm happy for you." Audie went over to inspect his new rank. "Lily has told me about your impressive career."

"Oh, Uncle Gordy. Father would have been so proud." Lily ran into his arms. They stood so for a time. "What does it mean?" She backed up to look at him.

"Well, Lily-girl, I shoulder more responsibility, command more men, and receive a bit more money." He glanced at her face, then brought her close to him again.

Victory and promotion—a warrior's reward. However, this only makes the brigadier's decision more difficult. And Lily has no idea—yet.

Sunday, 19 October
Holy Trinity Church, Harrow
The quiet serenity of Holy Trinity Church resonated in defiance of the turmoil in Lily's heart and soul. When her father was vicar, this church had brimmed with joy. Childhood memories teased her brain like butterflies flitting by, then darting away before she could grasp them.

Sandwiched between her uncle and Hugh like military bookends in the front pew, she ached to draw some warmth from their bodies. But nothing seemed to help thaw her frozen state. Not tea. Not brandy. Not a roaring fire. Not living bodies.

I might as well be cold as . . . as Father, Mum, Stevie, and Kit in their caskets— now in the cold ground. She shuddered. Uncle Gordy put his arm around her and squeezed. Hugh warmed her hands in his.

She stared at the altar drowning in a wave of white lilies. Why does it have to be lilies?

There had been a time when the white flowers signified celebration, like when Lily was seven-years-old. She'd been dressed in a hand-me-down frock and hat, sitting in the front pew with her mother, still as stone, her gloved hands clasped in her lap. All prim and proper, she listened to her father's Easter homily. Benjie, in his brand-new Royal Air Force uniform, sat on her left and little Stevie perched on her lap sucking his fingers. She hadn't known then that they would all be taken from her; catapulting her comfortable, promising, young life into chaos.

"*This is what you deserve. They returned early for you. It's all your fault.*" Guilt's arrow pierced her heart. Surely, she'd die of the pain.

The bishop's words invaded her reverie. "Can we, like Job, that staunch man of God, accept the Lord's will and also say: 'Though He slay me, yet will I trust in Him.'"

No! I cannot! I will not!

As though he could hear her thoughts, Bishop Osred gazed right at her. "Can we admit also—to quote Job again—that 'we do not understand things too wonderful for us to know?'"

I am not Job! she shouted silently, staring right back at the bishop. I will never understand why they had to die. *No, I will never trust God again!*

Monday, 20 October
Rivenwood

For the eleventh morning since the wreck, Lily woke rocked by the crashing awareness that her family was gone. Oh, how she'd welcome Father's preaching now, Stevie's messing the bathroom, reading about Narnia to Kit again and again, Mum's comfort. She was alone.

But, no. Uncle Gordy is here and Hugh. Are they really? She threw on clothes and hurried down to the breakfast room. Sir Henry and Uncle Gordy sat together at the round table. Lady Beatrice, Lady Audrey, and Phila on the other side. Hugh entered wearing breeches and boots.

It *is* real.

After breakfast, she and Phila changed into riding breeches, boots, turtleneck jumpers, and jackets to join Hugh; while Lady Audrey took Lily's uncle on a riding tour of the estate. Though smothering grief threatened to engulf her, the sun shone, and for the moment a slight breeze chased the black thoughts away. The three cantered down the country road past sheep grazing, the bare harvested fields, and the orchards where farmers picked apples.

For a while, Lily almost felt alive. The brisk wind blew away the blanket of mourning that had engulfed her. The sun glimmered on the grass, wet from rain the night before. *It's golden autumn.* She delighted in the fashion show of russet, tangerine, and copper.

Memories of years past, riding with Phila and Hugh, enveloped her. Happy years with a glorious future unfolding, dreams on the horizon, hope beckoning, nothing but promise. But the dark demons of grief chased after her.

CHAPTER 28

INTERNATIONAL INCIDENT

If I be waspish, best beware my sting.
The Taming of the Shrew, William Shakespeare

Later that day
London
Lily sighed. Another good-bye.

Hugh was leaving. Lily leaned her head on his shoulder as they sat in the back seat of Sir Henry's Bentley. Hugh had invited her to accompany him when János drove him to the airport for his flight back to Washington. Uncle Gordy rode in front with the chauffeur, so she wouldn't be alone on the return.

Hugh held her hand. She felt the warmth of his body next to hers. Tears crept down her cheeks. She tried to wipe them away with her free hand. He handed her his handkerchief.

"You were so wonderful to come. I wish you didn't have to go back."

"So do I, Lily dear. So do I."

She couldn't see his face in the predawn darkness, but knew what was there: love, kindness, caring.

"How I wish it was in my power to undo what's happened. I'm sorry I can't do more."

"I feel so alone." She sniffed.

"Of course, you do. But you're not. We're all your family now. You have Pet, Mum, and Dad, and all the staff loves you and are there for you. Let them help you."

"I know." But they wouldn't fill the huge hole in her heart. "But why did it happen?"

"I don't know." He put his arm around her and held her close until they arrived.

"You are strong, Lily. You will make it through this. I have faith in you." His eyes glistened as he put her hands in her uncle's, took his cases from János, and walked toward the terminal. Before going in the door, he turned and waved.

Saturday, 25 October
Washington, D.C.

It took thirty minutes for Hugh to walk from his apartment near the British Embassy to the Churchill Hotel. He might have enjoyed the brisk and refreshing breeze if not for what awaited.

Hugh had procrastinated long enough. Better to get it over with now. Darlene had rung less than two hours after his return. He'd put her off as long as he could, but she'd rung yesterday at the embassy again.

"I have to attend this cocktail party of Daddy's for Californians tomorrow afternoon at the Churchill on Embassy Row. Meet me in the bar afterward. *Be there.*"

He didn't think the occasion called for a uniform, so he dressed in tan trousers and a tweed jacket, open shirt, ascot, and jumper waistcoat. Might as well look the part of the British gentleman. After ordering a scotch at the bar, he spotted Darlene on the arm of a tall young man wearing jeans, a brown leather jacket, a western shirt, and cowboy boots.

Could this fellow be a new interest? Perhaps she prefers a younger chap this time. Maybe Hugh could get out of this easier than he'd thought. He signaled her.

She waved back.

No denying, Darlene looked good—very good—in a black frock, low-cut and pinched in at the waist. He stood as they approached.

"Hugh honey meet *Dr.* Daniel McCauley. Dan, this is *Lord* Hugh Claiborne. He's English and will be an *earl* someday."

Hugh offered his hand, "Dr. McCauley."

The cowboy took it. "Lord Hugh." They stood eye to eye.

"Thank you, Danny, for the escort. You can go now. Bye." She dismissed him with a flick of her hand.

Grinning, the American nodded to Hugh and left. Did he detect a hint of warning in the Yank's eyes?

She slid onto the stool next to him. "I'll have a martini."

He gestured to the barkeep and ordered. "A friend?"

"Yeah. His father ran a huge ranch in the San Fernando Valley, a constituent of Daddy's."

"Ran? Past tense?"

"He died. Dan runs it now." She grabbed the drink as soon as the waiter delivered it and drank. "Would you believe he's a professor? Looks like a kid, doesn't he?"

"A child prodigy?"

"Whatever that means. No. He's just smart. You'd never guess he's thirty." She nibbled on the olive, then looked into Hugh's eyes. "You've been avoiding me."

"Darlene, I just returned Tuesday night. I have to catch up after two leaves."

"Yes, *two*. First the ball and then the funeral," her tone frigid.

Already, this was not going well. He looked away and saw the cowboy seated a few stools away with some other men. The bloke glanced his way a couple times as if expecting something.

"Hugh honey are you paying attention?"

"Sorry, still fighting the time change."

"Why did I have to call you first?"

"The trip was, frankly, gutting. And, I needed some time to collect myself. Our families are close." Why did she have to be so irritating? He folded the cocktail napkin back and forth.

"Excuses. Will you be going to all your sister's friend's family funerals?"

Maybe she's going to make this easy. "Lily is special. She and my sister have been inseparable since they were children."

"Lily? The way you say her name sounds *special* to me."

Does it? "Darlene! She lost both parents, her little sister, and brother, *and* her older brother was killed in the war. We're her family now. Have some compassion." Does she not have a heart?

"OK, don't get all huffy."

"I care a lot for her."

"I think you care *a whole lot* for her."

"Darlene, I've been like an elder brother after she lost hers. Lily is devastated."

"Ah, but I think she is much more to you. Just the way you say her name."

Enough. "Is this why you wanted to see me?"

"Bartender," she called out, "I'll have another."

Not that she needed it.

"How long have we been seeing each other?"

He eyed her. "I didn't know this was an examination."

"Not too smooth."

"You *men*! Six months, for your information. I've made myself *totally* available to you, even staying in DC a lot, and you've yet to make a move. I really thought you wanted to marry me. Well?"

"So, Genius, now what do you say?"

"I have entertained the possibility."

"Pitiful."

The barkeep delivered her drink.

"Hugh honey, do you love me?" She grabbed the glass, her knuckles white.

"You're a beautiful woman, Darlene."

"Absolutely abysmal."

"You love *her*! *I knew it*. You've just been toying with me. I've wasted six months of my life." She stood up, tossed the martini in his face, slammed the glass on the bar, and stomped off.

"You expect a medal for getting gin thrown in your face by an irate American female? Well, Genius, you deserved that for being downright pathetic."

Before he could collect his thoughts, someone put a serviette in his hand. Probably the barkeep. Mopping his face, Hugh turned to thank him, but who stood there but the cowboy.

"'Hell hath no fury like a woman scorned.'" Laughter resonated in his voice and a grin burgeoned on his boyish face.

Hugh dabbed the moisture from his shirt. "William Congreve coined that phrase."

"Hasn't changed since the seventeenth century, has it?" The cowboy chuckled.

What do you know, an informed Yank? "Alexandre Dumas wrote that

'Women are never so strong as after their defeat.'"

"*The Count of Monte Cristo?*"

Well, not entirely. "*Marguerite de Valois.*"

"Got me there, Lord Hugh, let me buy you a drink—one you can actually swallow."

"You're on, Doctor McCauley."

"Scotch, neat?" Hugh nodded. The cowboy ordered two, one with ice and one without.

"Call me Dan."

"And I'm Hugh."

"I thought I might do one for my country and try to avoid an international incident by making amends for a fellow Californian."

"I accept on behalf of the British government. But aren't you a friend of Darlene's?"

"Our dads were friends. She and I dated, but I prefer my ladies a bit less... temperamental? Can't say she and I parted in such a liquid fashion, though."

Hugh joined the cowboy in a good laugh.

Their scotches arrived. Dan lifted his glass to touch Hugh's. "Here's to continued Anglo-American relations."

"Cheers."

"You're with the embassy?"

"Naval attaché."

"Still in then?"

"Affirmative. You're a professor?"

"Of philosophy, UCLA, oh, University of California at Los Angeles. But I spent three years in your county while in the Army Air Forces—flew P-51s."

"Tough duty."

"Yeah. You?"

"Naval intelligence. No action." Shame always surfaced around the chaps who risked their lives in combat.

"Without guys like you, we'd have lost the damn war. I imagine intelligence is even more critical these days with the Cold War."

They discussed the divisions of Germany and Korea and parried about the differences of British and American women and universities. Hugh liked the chap. He had a keen mind and the casual winsomeness of an affable American. Dan ordered another round.

Hugh took a long swig of his drink, then stared down into it.

"Forgive a nosy Yank, but are you bummed about getting the dust off from Darlene?"

"Huh? No, actually, I'm relieved. I was . . . um . . . losing interest."

"I could tell she was brewing for a blowup. None of my business, though."

"I'd gone home twice then not rung her when I returned." *And what she said about Lily is disconcerting.*

Dan chortled. "I didn't think you Brit gents were as inconsiderate as us Yank churls." Though Hugh tried to pay for the next round, the Yank wouldn't hear of it.

When the third round arrived, they toasted. "You're a free man, Hugh. But you still look sad."

"Not that. I went home for the funeral of a family killed in a tragic railway accident."

Dan paled as his glass nearly slipped out of his hand.

"Are you OK man?"

Dan took in a couple gulps of air. "Harrow Wealdstone crash, right?"

"Yes. You know it?"

"Yeah. I was scheduled to take the Euston train to Liverpool that morning and had a last-minute change."

What a damned coincidence. He gave the chap a weak smile.

"Yeah, I dodged the bullet again. I thought I'd used up all my luck in the war."

"Is that why you got out?"

"No. All I ever wanted to do is fly, especially jets in the Air Force. But I was grounded after a crash."

"Rotten luck, old man. Sorry. Life has a way of demolishing dreams."

Anglo-American relations flowed as smooth as the scotch of the fourth round.

Normally, Hugh's British reserve would have kept him from such hasty camaraderie, but he found the chap quite engaging. "Dan, how about we drink to the genesis of new dreams."

"Here, here!"

Down the bar, the men Dan had been with motioned to him. "Hey, Dan, we're off to dinner. You coming?"

"No thanks. I'm hot 'n heavy in peace negotiations," he called back. "You know, Hugh, dinner is a good idea. Let's get some grub in the dining room."

"Only if dinner is on me."

"OK, but the wine is on my tab, Californian." He clicked his glass to Hugh's. "Hey, here's to the women in our futures."

"I'll drink to that." *To a future with Lily?*

They moved on to the dining room and ordered dinner.

The waiter presented the wine. "Chateau Montelena Cabernet Sauvignon '47, sir." He poured a splash into Dan's goblet.

Surprisingly, Dan sniffed the bouquet, sipped, swishing it around his mouth, and swallowed like a connoisseur. "Excellent my good man." The Yank regarded the Brit with feigned hauteur. "Hugh?"

He sniffed, sipped, swished, and swallowed—and was again surprised. "Superlative selection; Californian you say?"

Now the Yank's eyes twinkled. Obviously, he had put one over on the Brit. "Yes, from the Napa Valley, the winery was established in 1882. This wine is a blend of Merlot and Cabernet Franc. Their Chardonnay is excellent as well."

"I did not realize California wines were gaining prestige."

"Spoken like a true European." But the smile and tone were amiable.

Hugh's steak, French fries, and Caesar salad also agreed with his palate. "Tell me, what were you doing in London when you missed that fated train?"

"I had given a lecture at City University London and was booked at the University of Liverpool."

"Lecture?"

"Humanism."

"Ah yes, Jean-Paul Sartre in his *Essays in Existentialism* wrote that there is no such thing as human nature because there is no God to conceive it. Man is only what he makes of himself. Man is responsible for himself, his own individuality, and is responsible for all men." Hugh took a long pull on his wine. "That's a heavy responsibility for man to carry. Frankly, I'm thankful I share my yoke with God."

"You're a man of faith, then? Though not an uninformed one, having read Sartre." *This cowboy keeps surprising me.*

Dan inclined his head.

Hugh studied the Yank. "Read, but frankly much of what he postulates as truth astounds me. Take his statement; 'Man is at the start a plan which is aware of itself; . . . nothing exists prior to this plan; there is nothing in heaven; man will be what he will have planned to be."

Dan sat across from him smiling like a Cheshire cat. "Perhaps you need more wine." He signaled the waiter.

Hugh gazed into the ruby liquid. "That's the chicken or the egg conundrum. Man created *the plan*, but which man, and when? Did he make the earth, the sun, the moon, the stars—the galaxy? And how *is* man doing on his own?"

"On the other hand, how has your God done with mankind?"

"Consider this; 'Man is now a horror to God and to himself and a creature ill-adapted to the universe not because God made him so but because he has made himself so by the abuse of his free will.'"

Dan's eyebrows shot up, then drew together as he pursed his lips. Seconds slipped by. Then a grin splashed across his face. "What a profound riposte. You just came up with that?"

"Me? No. C. S. Lewis did in his book *The Problem of Pain*. Are you familiar with his works?"

Dan looked thoughtful again. "Should I be? Is he a Brit?"

"Yes, a don at Oxford. Probably his most famous book is *The Screwtape Letters*."

"Ah, yes. My uncle gave me that book back in '45. Devilishly entertaining. Hang on though, am I debating some genius whose brain is stocked with a plethora of profound rejoinders?"

"Sorry, photographic mind."

But the Yank didn't seem put off, and their debate over faith versus fate continued through coffee and cognac.

Hugh set down his brandy snifter. "So that's your topic on tour, humanism? Will you be visiting my country again?"

"I hope to. It was a breakfast with a representative from the British Humanist Association, that kept me from taking the train that morning."

"Or perhaps an act of God to keep you from the station?"

Afterward they caught a cab dropping Hugh off at his apartment.

"A pleasure, Hugh." They shook hands. "by the way, Darlene has a vindictive streak. Hope you don't incur any repercussions. So long."

"Cheerio Dan."

Wednesday, 29 October
British Embassy
Hugh walked into the office and settled at his desk when the commanding military attaché came by and invited him to have morning coffee in the commissary.

After commandeering their coffee, the men sat at a table across from each other. At that hour, the small dining room was half-filled with embassy personnel.

The Army colonel took a drink, then looked Hugh in the eye. "Commander is there anything you'd like to share about your social life that might impact your future?"

"Sir?" Hugh put his cup down without drinking.

"Say, a certain incident Saturday night?"

Damn, he knows about that? Who else does? "That was personal, Sir."

"Commander, I'm sure you are well aware that everything we do when representing the Crown in a foreign country reflects on the Crown and is *not* personal."

"Yes Sir. I've done nothing to embarrass the Crown or the embassy. The young lady simply broke off a relationship with me."

"Simply? As I understand, it made quite a splash." His expression dead serious except for a momentary flicker in his eyes.

"Quite." He couldn't recall seeing anyone he knew there.

"Was the relationship of an intimate, amorous nature?"

"No, Sir. That would have been unwise."

"That's good, because Sir Oliver wants you in his office at ten hundred hours."

Who witnessed my dousing? Who said what to whom? Darlene?

The next hour and sixteen-and-a-half minutes dragged by.

❋ ❋ ❋

The tall, dignified, middle-aged ambassador stood, "Commander Claiborne, you remember Senator Hunter." Sir Oliver wore the same expression Dad exhibited when Hugh had been in serious trouble as a young lad.

Darlene's father. Now, that's a shot across the bow.

The senator did not offer his hand. A vein in his neck pulsed and swelled.

His eyes smoldered in his beefy face. Sir Oliver's glare was scorching.

Hugh swallowed hard but stood at attention. "Sirs?"

"Your future is sinking fast, Genius."

Darlene's father cleared his throat. "This is awkward, but I must ask, have you had your way with my daughter?" He scrutinized Hugh's face, his eyes boring into Hugh's. His tone and expression conveyed that Darlene had said he had.

"No Sir!"

"Have you dallied with her affections?" His eyes narrowed.

Hugh gulped. He guessed he had, according to her. But then, she had dallied with his. "Sir, I have comported myself as a gentleman."

"Did you lead Darlene to believe you wanted to marry her? You've been seeing her for some time." He furrowed his brow and pursed his lips. Sir Oliver glowered.

"I considered it, Senator, but never said anything to her."

"But you don't love her."

"No, Sir. I realized I did not."

The senator's eyes turned icy. "Because you are in love with your sister?"

Hugh choked. He glanced at the ambassador.

His expression read, let's see how you get out of this, Commander.

"Make this good, Genius."

"Sir, Darlene must have misunderstood." Although, of course, she hadn't. "Lily is not my sister. She's been my sister's dear friend for thirteen years. I've been like an elder brother to Lily since her brother was killed in '41. Lily lost her remaining family in that London railway crash. Losing them has been—shattering." He had to force out the last words as his throat closed.

"I see. Darlene's been counting on a proposal. I expected one as well. Very disappointing, young man." Sadness had replaced anger in his eyes. "I had hoped you were *the one*. You would have been good for her, Commander." He exhaled and seemed to age before Hugh's eyes.

"Sir Oliver assured me you were not the kind of young man who would have disrespected his position to have committed such an irresponsible and imprudent act. "Darlene has a way of letting go of the good ones, like the son of a rancher friend of mine. I regret to say that the girl takes after my ex-wife."

Whew!

"Commander, you're dismissed." Sir Oliver tilted his head toward the door.

"Yes Sir."

This time the senator offered his hand. Hugh took it.

"You're a gentleman, Hugh. I'm sorry my daughter isn't more of a lady."

"Thank you, Sir."

Outside he inhaled deeply.

"You just about sank the ship, Commander. And over a woman!"

He swore he could hear cackling. Dad's right. I'm a nit when it comes to affairs of the heart. Some intelligence operative.

A half-hour later he presented himself in the ambassador's office, standing in front of Sir Oliver's desk.

"Well, Commander, you got out of that with your career still intact. As the father of three daughters, I'm not certain I would be that understanding."

"Yes Sir."

"I would not have expected reprehensible conduct from Sir Henry's son, say, like that of Burgess. His personal actions were an embarrassment to me and the Crown, not to mention suspicion of his traitorous activities. I certainly did not want another blight on my time here like he and Maclean put on it, and likely Philby, as well."

The ambassador had been mortified at their suspicion and probable defection to the U.S.S.R. "No Sir, as Secretary of the Combined Policy Committee on atomic energy matters and our representative with the American-British-Canadian Council on the sharing of atomic secrets, Maclean could have done serious harm to us and the Americans spying for the Soviets."

Sir Oliver's tall forehead creased. "I will not be surprised if we learn that the suspicions about Philby prove true in the long run. Talk about an embarrassment to our government, if the chief British intelligence representative and liaison here with the CIA turns out to be another spy."

"I hope we're wrong there, but I fear not, Sir." Hugh frowned, but at least he was off the hot seat.

"By the way, I would have given you leave for the funeral. You didn't have to take on my wife's mission. That was above and beyond the call of duty, Hugh."

"I know, Sir. But Lady Barbara was so understanding."

A faint smile crossed the ambassador's face. "She is that. Some advice, Commander—bachelorhood has its pitfalls, especially in this arena." A polite but stern warning. "Now, shall we get back to the Crown's business?"

"Yes Sir. With pleasure!"

Hugh respected Sir Oliver. He had been knighted with the Order of the British Empire at thirty-seven, made Knight Commander of the Order of the Bath at forty-one, and appointed ambassador at forty-three.

Perhaps the Foreign Service is the path to follow.

CHAPTER 29

WHISPERERS

My Dear Wormwood . . .

. . . There is nothing like suspense and anxiety for barricading a human's mind against the Enemy. He wants men to be concerned with what they do; our business is to keep them thinking about what will happen to them.

The Screwtape Letters, C. S. Lewis

November
Rivenwood

Lily and Uncle Gordy joined Lady Audrey for lunch at the small table in the sunroom. She greeted them warmly. "I have two letters for you from the embassy in Washington, Lily."

On one envelope, Lily recognized Hugh's bold neat cursive. The other address was typewritten. She opened that one first. "Hugh, of course, and this one is from — oh, my — Lady Barbara Franks, Sir Oliver's wife."

"Do read that one if you want." Hugh's aunt smiled graciously.

My dear Miss Whitely,

Firstly, may I extend Sir Oliver's and my condolences on the tragic loss of your family. I cannot begin to imagine the sorrow you are experiencing. We will keep you in our prayers. It is obvious that Commander Claiborne is grieving as well. He is so concerned for your welfare.

Secondly, I am most grateful for your assistance in purchasing gifts for our daughter, especially so at this sad time. She commented that she couldn't have done better herself. The commander could not have found a more expert assistant.

He showed us the photograph of the two of you at his sister's ball. What a handsome couple you make. Your gown is exquisite. Perhaps we might meet when we return to Oxford soon. Our eldest daughter was excited by the design and expressed a desire to have one like it.

Gratefully yours,
Lady Barbara Franks

"Brava." Uncle Gordy clapped.
"What a compliment on your gown. No need to read Hugh's aloud." Lady Audrey's eyes twinkled. "Gordon and I will chat."
Lily opened Hugh's letter and read to herself.

Dearest Lily,

Since I am not there to support you, I am pleased that your uncle's leave has been extended. He must be of great comfort to you.

I introduced him to Orion and said I would be grateful if he would ride him whilst he's there. Pet says he's been riding with Audie. I know Epona would like your riding her. She liked you from the first. You and Pet and I enjoyed such good jaunts. I realize you probably don't really feel up to it, but it would do both you and Epona good to get out. Do consider it.

I think of you a lot. I'm even attending church services without Mum's "encouragement."

Fondly, H

Oh, how she still missed Benjie, even after all these years. But the pain of missing Stevie, even sporting his smartness and making messes, throbbed. What a dear Hughie had been, standing in for them, and comforting her. She couldn't have made it through without her uncle and adopted brother.

Lily tittered.

"What's funny?" asked Lady Audrey. "Do you care to share?"

"Wasn't it dear of him to come for, for everything. And to think of our very proud Hughie agreeing to shop for feminine things in order to get leave to come."

"Oh, dear. Men will do even the most humbling thing for the love of a woman, you know." Her ladyship gave a gleeful smile.

"Yes, he is such a dear."

Uncle Gordy raised an eyebrow.

* * *

In the following days, Lily did ride with her uncle and Lady Audrey a few times, and Phila when she wasn't at university. Yet Lily didn't enjoy the animal's companionship as much as before. Some days she just walked down to the stables and stroked Epona's nose, feeding her an apple or carrot.

How comforting to lean on Uncle Gordy, but an unwelcome thought assaulted Lily's mind again and again—

"He'll leave you. You wait and see."

Will that voice never leave her alone?

No, Uncle Gordy wouldn't leave her. Already he had stayed at the Earl's country estate for over a fortnight past the funerals.

Nearly every day they walked hand-in-hand along the paths through the gardens. The last of the roses struggled, stunted but hanging on, giving off a slight fragrance. Some days they took long strolls around the grounds and into the deer park. The leaves decked out in their autumn costumes—crimson, marigold, amber, and a blush of currant—fell swirling around their feet.

Winter threatened though. Soon the trees would be stripped bare, stark and alone, like her. No frost yet, but a chill grazed Lily. Grief and fear stalked her like a threatening cold front holding off just out in the Atlantic. It would arrive eventually, singeing the last of autumn's life.

Lady Audrey was a gracious hostess, looking after their every need. Phila commuted back and forth to university, Uncle Gordy driving her in Hugh's coupe.

Magdalen Bridge, Oxford University

Ollie Ogilvie stood on the bridge spanning the River Cherwell, his hands resting on top of the ornamental parapet wall. He gazed down at the boathouse, where people hired the punts to cruise along the river.

Would he ever take her on one?

He had first seen the wee lass on the bridge a year-and-a-half ago. At first, he thought her a child with that froth of carrot-colored curls, but when she turned around her face proved more mature with bright knowing eyes—and his heart awoke.

Then he observed her at Mr. Lewis's and Professor Tolkien's lectures. Her astute questions and insightful comments intrigued him. Ollie sensed a fiery nature and upon first hearing her melodic giggle, lost his heart.

For three terms Master Sergeant O. C. Ogilvie, late of the British Army's Seaforth Highlanders, a hero of the Battle of El Alamein and recipient of the Victoria Cross for bravery in Normandy, fought for the courage to approach her. It wasn't that she appeared unapproachable, like so many of the upper-class English girls who put on airs.

He was the problem.

A hard-core soldier, he hardly passed for a gentleman. And she looked so very young, while he, even though only twenty-nine, felt so very old. However, after missing the Perth-to-London train that crashed in October, he'd made up his mind that he'd speak to her this term. After all, that was just the last time he had cheated death. How many lives had he left? Surely, he'd beat out a cat's nine?

Should he tell her who he was? Naw, that wasn't his style.

Ridicule slammed his heart. *"You actually think she would like you for you?"* Glenda had loved him.

"Seriously, the petite miss will take one look at you and run."

Glenda paid him compliments him calling him ruggedly handsome.

"Who are you fooling, a proper English girl going for a Scot?"

Glenda was English and a commoner. No doubt this bonnie lass hailed from nobility the way she comported herself.

"*Admit it. She scares you.*"

Heat rushed up his neck to his face and ears.

"*The mighty hero is afraid of a girl! Where's the courage that got you through the war alive? Did you leave all your guts back in those sand dunes and French beaches?*"

He could swear he heard faint howling.

The confidence Glenda had instilled in him a decade ago had long since dissipated. Ten years? The ache remained, but not so acute since the wee red-headed lass made off with his heart.

But he had barely seen her this term.

He always sat in the back row of the lecture hall and could pick her out without difficulty thanks to being six foot six. He'd caught sight of her in several of Mr. Lewis's and Professor Tolkien's lectures, a faithful attendee like himself. He knew her name because she often asked questions and the dons addressed her by it.

Finally, he got up the nerve and rang the porter at St Hilda's. "May I leave a message for Miss Claiborne, please?"

"You may, but she's not residing at college this term."

"Naw?"

"Oh, she is attending university, but not staying here, sir."

"Thenk ye." What could that be about?

"*You miss her, you fool.*"

Rivenwood

Lily and her uncle drifted through the days as if in a silky dream. It would have been a lovely holiday if not for their terrible loss. Somehow, it seemed as though some great hand kept the nightmares in abeyance. She ate again, breathed more deeply, and even smiled on occasion. Sweet notes arrived every week from Hugh. She even wrote back twice.

The second week in November, her uncle accompanied Sir Henry to London for two days. Upon their return, they spent a couple of evenings closeted in the Earl's study. Afterwards, Uncle Gordy hardly said a word. The next day he went out alone, returning with a grave expression.

"We'll take a stroll, shall we, Lily-girl?" He fetched her coat, helped her on with it, and led her into the garden.

The sun retreated behind the cloudbank rapidly overtaking the sky.

A nippy wind blew brown leaves across the path. The final rose blooms hung their dried and shriveled heads, but all she could smell was dust. Stillborn buds drooped on wilted stems. She shivered. She *knew*. Darkness crept in and surrounded her.

"Lily-girl, I've been to the War Office." His tone was gruff and forced. "Sir Henry extended my leave as long as he could. Now, I must return."

"But I thought you would leave the Army and stay with me." She stared at him as fear invaded her soul.

"I considered it, believe me, I did. His lordship and I explored my options. He was jolly good in advising me, but in the end, the Army is my life. I would be ill-equipped for little else. And I owe it to my men to see this Suez mission through." He looked down at his boots.

"Don't you owe it to me, to stay here?" Her cheeks burned, and she balled her fists.

"I do owe you, not only as my brother's beloved daughter, but also as my precious niece." He grasped her hands in his. "You are very dear to me, Lily. Sir Henry and Lady Beatrice have promised to look after you until I complete my assignment and get a billet here in England. I will take care of you. I have opened an account for you at Sir Henry's bank. I will allocate funds to you every month that you can withdraw for your living expenses. Whatever you need, you have only to ask."

Lily snatched her hands back. "But you promised Father."

He peered at her, questioning.

"I saw you that night you arrived. I heard you in their room. You *promised*."

"I did, that. And I leave you in God's hands here on earth and under His protection."

"Did He protect our family? What about you? You'll be killed, and then I'll have no one. Why did you come back only to leave again? I *hate* you!"

"Lily-girl?"

But she turned and fled.

※ ※ ※

Alone in her room, Lily flung the window open, breathing in the chill air. All she could smell was betrayal and fear. When she turned, she sensed a frigid presence.

"*Told you so,*" came the smug snarl. "*He cares only for himself and his career.*"

"He does care for me." Lily looked around the room. Where was that voice in her mind coming from?

"*Why then is he not staying?*"

"Duty. It's his duty."

"*Duty? That's what men always say — duty to their country, their god, themselves. They always love something more.*"

"He loves me." She collapsed onto the bed, hugging a pillow to her chest. "Where are you? Who are you?"

"*I'm you. There's no one else here but you. I'm the thoughts you daren't admit to yourself.*"

"No."

"*No one loves you anymore.*"

"*Liar! Don't listen, Lily!*" A warm breeze filtered through the chill air. A robin alighted and sang a sweet song outside her window.

"*God loves you.*" But the soft, loving voice was immediately drowned out by the shrill one.

"*If God loves you, why did he steal your family away? It's your fault!*"

Frightened, she dove under the quilts, slamming a pillow down over her ears. But the voices wouldn't be stilled.

"*The Almighty is not the thief who comes to destroy.*" She could hear Father quoting Scripture to her.

"*Who then has destroyed your life?*"

Lily screamed, "God!"

"*The Holy One comes to give life,*" Father whispered.

"*What kind of life have you got now? Poor little orphan, how will you live?*"

"Stop!" Lily flung the pillow across the room, sat up, and cried to the ceiling. "What ever will I do?"

"*The Comforter will give you the grace. You are never alone. You are with godly people who will help you.*" So faint, the sweet voice now.

The robin sang again. Then a flutter of wings.

"*Who? This lord and lady and silly girl? You are just a charity case.*"

Lily batted away at the air around her head. "Leave me alone. Go away."

Phila knocked on the door. "Are you OK? You locked the door. Lil?"

"Go away." Charity? "I will not be someone's charity."

"Whatever gave you that idea?" Phil banged on the door. "Dash it all, Lil, let me in."

"I just want to be alone." It was a lie, but better to lie and not be hurt than open herself to abandonment again.

"OK, if that's how you're going to be!" Lily heard Phil stomp away.

CHAPTER 30

DARK NIGHT OF THE SOUL

> Misery, my sweetest friend . . . Thou wilt not be consoled.
> "Death," Percy Bysshe Shelley (1792–1822)

Phila stomped away from Lily's door. Halfway down the hall, she turned sharply around, marched back, and lifted her hand to knock.

The door flung open. Lily pulled her in, slamming it shut.

"You're pale as a ghost, Lil." The bedclothes were askew. Her friend's hair was messy, and she trembled. Phila had heard shouting, but there was no one but Lily in the room. "Tell me what's wrong."

Lily sat down shaking her head. There was a definite chill in the air so Phila lit a fire. "I'll ring for tea. A good hot cuppa always helps. Sure you don't want to tell me about it?"

"No!"

When Kenzie knocked, Phila asked for tea. The maid glanced at the bed. Phila shrugged, and the girl left.

"Uncle Gordy is leaving." It was the most pitiful cry.

"I know. Papa tried to extend his leave again, but the Army promoted him to command his brigade at the canal."

"But I *need* him."

"Of course, you do, but you know he can't desert. Besides, you have me and . . ." She ducked out, dashed to her room, and returned carrying a fluffy bundle. "And, you have Snowy." She deposited the cat in Lily's lap.

After Kenzie delivered the tea tray, Phila settled into a chair and poured. The cat hopped down from Lily's lap and bounded up into Phila's.

"Oh, Snowy." Poor Lily.

"It's all right. She was always Kit's." Sorrow etched Lily's face.

"Do you know what?" Phila brightened. "That wee kitten has made friends with Neptune and Triton. I feared they would eat her for tea, mistaking her for a fox or a furry ball, but they're actually quite taken with her. I'll show you. Why don't I leave her with you tonight?"

"No. She'll just stand at the door crying to get out and go to you. I think she's found her new mistress. Kit would have liked that. Snowy needs love now, and I just don't have any to give."

They sipped their tea. Only the sound of purring stirred the quiet.

"The last couple of nights, I wanted to come to you."

It was just a whisper, and Phila nearly missed it. *Oh, Lily.* Her heart ached. "You should have, I'm here for you."

"I know, but I need to learn to be alone."

"You are *not* alone, ever."

"I know you're here. What a friend you are, staying here instead of at college, and only going for lectures and your tutor."

Tears welled up, and Lily began to sob. "Phil, I'm so frightened. What am I to do? Where am I to go? I've no family except Uncle Gordy, and he's leaving. What if he's killed?"

"Oh, Lil, don't think that way." Phila gently moved Snowy off her lap and went to her friend, hugging her. "We're your family now."

The cat jumped up on the bed, kneaded the pillow, then settled down on it.

"I'm not charity?"

Phila stared at Lily. "Charity? Where did you get that idea?"

Lily started shaking again and appeared frightened.

"Lil?"

"A voice in my head claiming I'm just a charity case for you and your parents."

Poor Lil. That dastardly devil dishing out poison and she too weak to fight him off. "A voice straight from the abyss. You don't believe that, do you?"

"Why are you all being so kind to me?"

"*Lillian Grace Whitely.* How*ever* can you ask that? We've been chums for so long. You're my very best friend. Am I not yours?"

"Uh huh." Lily sniffed and blew into her handkerchief.

"We all love you."

"But the voice said no one loved me anymore."

"Oh, Lil. Don't mind anything that despicable voice spouts."

"But there were other voices."

"Other voices? Ah, those voices Mum talks about." Phila grinned.

"A sweet soft one saying comforting things. Father quoting Scripture. They made my head swim." She sighed and sank back into her chair.

"Angel football." Phila giggled. Now it made sense. No wonder Lily was so shaken.

"What?" Lily gaped at her.

"That's what my grandpapa called it when we allow the good angels and the bad angels to play with our heads like a tennis ball."

"A children's story is not going to help me." Lily screwed up her face.

"I'm only using it as an illustration. He said that the devil sends these voices to taunt us to think or do wrong, but God also sends His messengers to motivate us to be good and not give the demonic suggestions an opportunity to take hold." Phila leaned back, proud of herself.

"You sound like Father. Don't quote Scripture or I'll scream."

I sounded like a preacher? "It does sound like nursery stories, doesn't it? I imagine it's quite common for a person who has suffered a tremendous loss to encounter episodes like that. I can't imagine what depressing thoughts would assault me if I lost Papa, Mum, and Hugh or if something horrible happened to me. Oh, and I don't have to be grieving to constantly hear Mum quoting the Bible to me."

Lily's bottom lip curled.

"If those voices attack you again, you run straight to me. We'll get rid of them together." She squeezed Lily's hands.

Lily seemed relieved. Phila talked her into taking a long bubble bath, then went down to join her parents, aunt, and Brigadier Whitely in the drawing room.

Snowy trotted down behind her and promptly hopped up in Mum's lap. Neptune moved over beside Mum, putting his nose in her lap also, and whined. Triton moved to her other side, and she stroked both heads.

"How is Lily?" Concern creased the brigadier's face.

"She's distraught that you're leaving, Sir."

"I expected that—poor child." Apprehension creased his face. "It's difficult enough for me to come to terms with a loss like this, but for Lily, it must be devastating. What more can I do? I've provided for her financially. Should I fall in action, she is my heir."

"Don't even consider that, Gordon. You've been an enormous comfort to her since you arrived," Audie patted his arm.

"My good man," Papa's expression was stern, "you have no choice but to return to your brigade."

"We *are* nearly family." Mum blinked back tears. "Please don't be concerned. We will look after Lily as if she were our own. How I wish—"

"That she'd fall in love with Hugh." Phila beamed. "Then they could get married, and everything would be OK."

"Your son, Lady Beatrice?" The brigadier's eyes widened. "What about the gorgeous senator's daughter he told us about at dinner?" Gordon glanced at the Earl.

Phila pouted. "He didn't tell me about her." But Mum's expression said that she knew.

"I suspect that was subterfuge," muttered Papa.

"Henry reminds the boy of his responsibilities now and again." Mum laid her arm on Papa's. "Hugh has always been fond of Lily, but we think his devotion may be growing into something deeper."

"Yes, it seems obvious to everyone except Lily *and* Hugh." Audie's eyes sparkled.

"Hardly *that* obvious," huffed Papa. The brigadier agreed.

Mum smiled. "Of course not, Henry. I had to *tell* you."

"Harrumph."

"Surprising, isn't it, how different men's and women's perspectives are?" An odd grin danced across her auntie's face. "It's as though we females always have our antennae out for affairs of the heart."

Phila cocked her head. That comment seemed aimed at Lily's uncle. Was Audie flirting?

Mum grinned at Papa. "Hugh will be home for a first of the year leave, I expect. Perhaps—"

"Ladies." Papa frowned. "Perhaps we can return to a more acceptable discussion."

Phila, her mother, and aunt exchanged amused glances. Were they also considering how they might help that romance along?

✳ ✳ ✳

In mid-November, Papa brought home a copy of the *New York Times*. The main story had been chilling: "The Atomic Energy Commission announced tonight 'satisfactory' experiments in hydrogen weapon research amid informed speculation that this meant a super-atomic bomb had been exploded in a recent United States test." The article went on to state that the commission did not go so far as to announce that a full-scale hydrogen bomb had been detonated. However, it did say "experiments contributing" to hydrogen bomb research had been completed.

As the world reeled from the fear of escalating war weapons, Phila watched Lily slip into a deep depression. Struggling to keep from being sucked down into the doldrums herself, Phila poured out her anxieties in a journal.

> When the brigadier left with János for the aerodrome, Lily waved good-bye, fled to her room, and hasn't come out for days.
>
> My heart aches for her. Is she going through a dark night of the soul, like the fourteenth-century Catholic mystic, Saint John the Cross? His poem speaks about the body and mind with their cares being stilled, but on their path to divine union. Would this darkness lead to the Light for Lily as it did for the saint?
>
> Oh, Lord, let it be so.

✳ ✳ ✳

The days passed in a blur. Daylight interrupted Lily, unwelcome when it came barging through the curtains each morning, demanding that she attempt to function. Facing the day was overwhelming. To crawl out from under the eiderdown seemed impossible, to bear the weight of her body, the weight of her mind and her heartbeat, unfathomable.

There were so many minutes in the day to breathe through, like tiny jigsaw puzzle pieces needing to be fitted together to make a bigger picture. The pieces of her life were disjointed, shattered. She saw no clear picture. A formidable desire engulfed her to let life and its accompanying heartache pass over her like wind over the treetops and to sleep forever. Not to think. Do. Or feel, anymore.

Just sleep.

※ ※ ※

Phila poured her concerns into her journal.

> How I wish I could help. Lily barely responds when Bishop Osred and Doctor Goodly-Smyth visit. They agree her uncle's departure was another blow her psyche can't manage. We are not to leave her alone much. She is critically depressed. It will take time, love, and God's grace to bring her back.
>
> She is catatonic, like one of Narnia's frozen statues under the spell of the White Witch. She is barely able to accomplish even the most elementary movements to sustain life. At night I hear her moaning, and find her nightgown and bedclothes soaked. After I change her nightgown, I often rock her for hours.

Friday, 5 December

Phila returned from university and marched into Lily's room. "It's brass monkeys out there." She dragged off her coat, knit cap, and gloves. "All this cold and snow for days and days, and winter's not even here yet."

Mum and Papa arrived in time for tea, commenting about the dense fog in town.

By morning, the dangerous fog had thickened with visibility of just a few meters. János and Lefan were sent to collect the staff and their families. They returned, all coughing, their eyes red. Even the Schultz was ill.

Sunday and Monday the chauffeurs and Duncan in Hugh's coup collected the families of Papa's naval staff and others.

Duncan, his voice raspy, reported. "It's a putrid yellow-brown and foul-smelling poison. London's at a standstill, no rail or air service. Worse than November of '48. I fear we will lose many souls." János and Lefan had terrible coughs by then, and their eyes red and runny. Several of the rescued people had nasty rashes besides.

Phila journaled her thoughts:

> Rivenwood is overflowing with people, including the stables and other out buildings. People are camped in every room. General Audie has organized us to feed and bed them all. The grooms are giving the children rides to entertain them.
>
> Even Lily works in the kitchen with Tilly, Flora and me. I share my bed with Lil, too. Other young girls sleep on the floor.
>
> Horrendous reports flood the wireless of the number of people sickened and dead—the East End being the hardest hit.

The smog cleared by Wednesday leaving thousands dying and dead. János and Lefan returned the refugees to London.

By late December the death count rose to nearly 4,000. The family and staff sat in stunned silence listening to the reports just before the holidays. The authorities affixed blame on the toxicity of factory gases and smoke from coal fires in homes as people tried to stay warm in the unusually cold weather. People angrily held the government responsible for not doing more to warn them and get more people out.

"How utterly bizarre," Audie broke the hush. "This anticyclone—an atmospheric pressure that's usually a good thing—causing an inversion that trapped all the toxic smoke and gases in the wet fog, so it couldn't rise. As a result, it actually smothered people. How tragic."

Journaling continued helping Phila process her emotions.

It's almost impossible to come to terms with this tragedy. And Lily—she's being smothered by grief. My attempts to rescue her are of no avail. I fear she will die of heartbreak. She eats so little and has grown so thin. Both the brigadier and Hugh write every week. Their letters pile up, unopened.

She wallows in the pit, the weather as dark and frigid as her mood. Once the crisis was over, she returned to her room and never leaves, just sits and stares out the window.

※ ※ ※

24 December
Knocking intruded on Lily's gloom.

"Lil, it's me." Phila breezed in and pulled Lily's dressing gown around her. "It's Christmas Eve, and Hugh has rung. You *are* going to talk to him."

"No."

"*Yes.*" Phila dragged Lily downstairs to the library. Phil's mum was seated, her father standing, the telephone receiver in his hand. He said something into it, then held it out to Lily. Phila put it into her hand. The three of them stole from the room.

"*Lily!*"

She lifted the receiver to her ear. "Hugh?"

"In the flesh, well theoretically, Lily dear." She just stood there.

"Are you not going to wish me a Merry Christmas? Here I am miles away from home across the pond, alone, away from all my loved ones."

She couldn't think of anything to say.

"You are not even going to pay me the courtesy of an answer?"

Lily looked at the receiver like it was a snake. She started to drop it on the phone's cradle.

"Don't you dare hang up on me! Have you read my letters? You haven't. You haven't even opened them, have you?"

He was lecturing. Her eyes watered.

"You are turning your back on everyone who loves you and trying their utmost to help you. Pet is beside herself. Mum is bereft. Dad is running out of patience. And your uncle, who is in a dangerous place, is worried sick about you."

Why is Hugh angry with me? Tears ran down her cheeks. She sniffed.

"I've made you cry." He cleared this throat. "I'm sorry." He was silent for a couple minutes. "Aren't you still the independent, obstinate girl I know? I want you to pull yourself together. Where is that strong-willed miss? Surely, she hasn't died, too."

She heard a loud exasperated sigh. "Lily are you listening?"

Dropping the receiver, she rushed past Phila and her parents—Hugh's words chasing her as she fled to her room.

CHAPTER 31

A FIRE WITHIN

Part of my life is dead, part sick, and part is all on fire within.
"Three Stage Lyrics," Christina Rossetti (1830–1894)

Christmas Day
What did Christmas matter to Lily? Or that God's Son was born in a manger to a peasant couple? What good if He came to save the world when He didn't save her family? What good, Christmas?

Lily never cared much for winter. It was cold, foggy, damp, wet, and sometimes snowy. The holiday season had made it all tolerable—the preparations, the shopping, and the parties. She had loved all the activity with its decorations, festivities, dressing up, giving and receiving presents, even the nativity celebrations at the church. How she loved trussing up the packages and trimming the tree. Presents . . .

Now—the day brought no warmth. No joy. No wonder.

Christmas was dead, like everything else in her life. The Almighty took that from her, too.

"Curse God and die." That's what Job's wife told him. *"What right did Hugh have to yell at you like that?"*

Something ignited deep inside her. Her nostrils flared, and her heart hammered. "I'll show you, Haughty Hughie! And the Almighty, too."

Lily stood staring out at the rain. She turned from the window and marched over to the wardrobe and reached inside for Kit's suitcase. It hurt recalling Stevie and Kit making a game of scouring the vicarage for the hidden gifts. One year they found them. Lily had carefully rewrapped the packages, but Mum knew, and the following year she hid them in Father's study where children were not allowed. After Stevie breached that ban, their mother had hidden them in the attic chest—locked.

"Mummy, I miss you all so much."

Lily placed the suitcase on the bed and opened it. One by one, she took out the wrapped parcels. Her fingers caressed the packages and fiddled with the ribbons.

A light tap sounded at the door. "Lil, it's Phil." Her friend peeked in. Spying the parcels, she smiled. "Oh, your Christmas gifts." She scuttled to Lily's side and perched on the bed. "Shall we put them under the big tree or do you want to open them now?"

Lily shook her head.

"Aren't you just a little bit curious? I would be."

"No."

"I'm sorry, of course, you're not. Not for now. Shall I put them back?"

"Please."

Phila carefully packed them back into the case and replaced it in the back of the wardrobe. "Won't you come down for Christmas dinner?"

"No, thank you."

Phila moved to the door and turned. "I'll bring up your tray later and perhaps a little mulled wine."

"I'm not really hungry, but the wine would be nice." She watched her friend latch the door, then turned her gaze back to the wardrobe. It called to her.

Oh, precious little Kit and her book about the wardrobe. If only I could enter a magic place where the last few months hadn't happened, and I could be happy again. But Defeat cut her yearning short.

"Make-believe doesn't happen. There are no magic wardrobes, and no one can undo the past."

She stared at the wardrobe for a long time, then rose as if in a dream, walked over to it, and took out the box of their "effects"—the authorities had called them. Lifting the box from the shelf, she carried it to the chair beside the fire and sat down, cradling it in her lap for the longest time.

Hesitantly she took each article from the box, setting them on the table— her Father's worn blood-stained Bible, Stevie's notebook, the wrapped tweed and tartan, and Kit's book. She recalled the part where the lion breathed on the statues, and they came back to life.

That's what I feel like, a frozen statue.

Is that what it would be like from now on? That place where her heart had been, that empty vacant space seemed to expand throughout her body till she sensed she was nothing but an empty shell.

"You've been robbed—your family, your home, your life, the joy of the Christmas season. Gone. Forever."

Not again. Was it really the voice of an evil angel or her own dark mind?

Lily looked back at the case full of presents. She rushed to the bedroom door, locked it, then returned to the wardrobe and took the gifts out again. She started to open the large parcel addressed to her, then she stopped. No. She couldn't. Putting the package back, she came across the box wrapped in brown paper addressed to Uncle Gordy. She had forgotten to give it to him. Kit and Stevie, Mum and Father didn't have a choice. But Uncle Gordy did. He could have stayed.

Lily tore the paper off and opened the box. Books. She read the titles—*The Screwtape Letters* and *The Great Divorce*—strange names for books, the author's name—C. S. Lewis. Why, that was the same person who wrote Kit's book.

Lily ripped open the envelope. The note read:

Dear Gordy,

You noted that you had heard some of Mr. Lewis's talks on the wireless during the war. I thought you would enjoy these. I have become quite interested in his theology. I look forward to hearing your thoughts on the books.

Your brother in Christ and in blood, Jon.

Lily started to repack the books.

"What kind of a man doesn't keep his word to his own brother or his god?"

Uncle Gordy had promised.

"Broke his promise, didn't he?"

"I hate him!" She ripped the first book apart and threw it into the fire.

"That felt good, didn't it?"

"Yes!" She tore the pages from the other and tossed it in.

"He doesn't deserve gifts."

"I don't care if he is worried sick! He deserves to be. And Hugh should keep his opinions to himself."

She stared into the fire, watching the flames lap up the pages of the books. As the flames blazed and burned higher, so did Lily's anger.

"That's right. Do you feel warm now?"

Yes!

She had been like one of those ice statues she once saw in the dining room of the Goring Hotel. But now, she was thawing. A flame flickered and ever so slowly began to grow within until it burned deep inside. Feelings sparked.

Heat pulsed through Lily. She took off her dressing gown and stood in her nightgown. The room glowed brightly. She gazed at the fire burning, transfixed.

Father always told them to look to God for light.

"You can make your own light."

"I won't be charity!"

"Faith, hope, and charity. The greatest of these is charity." The faintest murmur reminded her that charity also meant love.

"You don't have to listen to your father's words anymore. He's dead."

A whisper. *"He lives."*

"You are alive. Let the dead be."

"Yes, I will live in the world—with all its pleasures."

"You cannot serve the world and God."

She clenched her fists and bawled at the ceiling. "I'm not *Yours*! I am my own!"

"Jolly good show, that's telling him."

Lily waited for a soft protest.

Silence.

She knew what it was to be turned into stone, but she didn't need any magic lion to breathe on her.

She would come back to life on her own.

※ ※ ※

Phila brought up a tray for Lily. The moment she entered the room, she knew something had changed. The former gloomy atmosphere pulsated with an eerie energy. She sensed the presence of something ominous. Looking around, nothing appeared altered, so one else in the room. She looked at Lily and—

When Lily turned around in front of the fire, Phila knew.

Her friend had changed.

Lily's face was flushed, her eyes glazed.

"Are you ill?" Phila noticed how warm it was. "Goodness, it looks like you had quite a fire going."

"I was cold."

"Surely, you're not anymore."

"No. I'm not cold anymore."

Phila sensed her friend meant more.

"You brought dinner. I'm famished." Lily took the tray from her, sat down, and ate ravenously.

Lily had undergone a metamorphosis. "I wish you had joined us."

"I should have. It was impolite of me. I'll be down from now on."

"That's excellent news." Phila poured tea in the cups and sat down across from her friend. She sipped while watching Lily eat.

"Has . . . has something happened?" But what could have taken place? Lily hadn't been out of her room. "Lil?"

"Happened? I've decided it's time to move on with my life, that's all."

"That's wonderful." Still, a knot formed in the pit of her stomach. Is it just her imagination? She didn't think so. "Will you open your gift from your mum now?"

Lily glanced at the wardrobe. "No."

Phila had to broach the subject. "What did Hugh say to make you hang up on him?"

"He yelled at me like I was a child."

"That doesn't sound like him."

"You made me talk to him, and I had nothing to say." She sounded piqued.

Phila swallowed her ire. "He wanted so much to talk to you. When he rang back, Mum said he sounded hurt. He loves you, Lil. He's only trying to help."

Boxing Day, 26 December

Lily stood at the door of the dining room, working up courage enough to go in. She gasped when Duncan opened the door, then stood back to let her in and seat her. But she refused to sit. She stood there shaking.

Phila, her parents, and aunt glanced up, their eyes blinking. But Lily sensed a coolness from them. She half expected Hugh to be sitting there growling.

"I, I owe you all an apology for my actions last night. I don't know what to say in my defense. I . . . I'm so very sorry. You have all been so kind and generous, yet I was frightfully horrid. I hope you can forgive me."

Phila's mum rose and gathered Lily in her arms. "Of course, darling."

The Earl's graceful smile put Lily at ease. "Good show, Lily. Thank you."

Her friend pursed her lips, but her eyes gave away her glee. "I should think so. You were absolutely shirty last night."

"Really, Pet." Her mum shot her *the look*.

"It's all right, Lady Beatrice. I was horridly shirty, especially to Hugh." She looked down.

Phila rose and encouraged Lily to sit. "Enough of the hair *shirt*." She tittered at her pun. "You don't need to do penance." Phila always found a way of finding humor in everything.

Lady Audrey reached over and patted Lily's hand. Duncan smiled.

"I want to apologize to Hugh when he rings again, please."

"I think that can be arranged." Phila's father looked pleased.

Sometime later, after Lady Audrey had presented the staff with their Boxing Day Christmas boxes and they left to be with their families, Phila and Lily came in from walking the labs.

Duncan inclined his head to Lily. "Miss Lily, you're wanted on the telephone."

"Hugh?"

Duncan nodded, and Phila ran ahead. Lily shuddered, working up her courage again as she plodded to the library. Phila stood there holding the receiver.

Lily took in a deep breath, grasped it, and—"Hughie, I'm so very sorry. I was such a shrew. I . . . I—"

"Yes, you were."

Lily gulped.

"And you do owe me an apology. However, I will forgive you, but you owe me."

Hughie and his droll humor. "Don't make me feel worse."

"Lily dear, I was gutted."

Shame pierced her heart. "Oh, I feel worse than awful. Naturally, you'd be horribly upset." Still, she did think he had given her reason. "Phil dragged me to the phone. She made me. Then you yelled at me like I was a child."

"You acted like a child. First, you didn't say a word, then you rang off."

Please don't start yelling again. "Hughie Louie, I'm sorry."

"Why didn't you want to talk to me and on Christmas?" His voice quavered.

Lily fiddled with the phone cord. "I should have, but I didn't want to talk to anyone. Not anyone at all."

"I'm not just anyone."

"No, you're special. I do love you, Hughie."

※ ※ ※

Phila journaled her relief.

> I eavesdropped on Lily talking to Hugh. Thank heaven all's patched up.
>
> It appears she is making a move back to normalcy. I hope her weird behavior yesterday was just a fluke. Now, she's taking long walks by herself during the day, and I can hear her pacing at night.
>
> At least there is color in her cheeks. But the gleam in her eyes—I'm not certain it is a good fire. I fear Lily has abandoned depression for anger.
>
> And, perhaps something more pernicious.

CHAPTER 32

THE BROTHER

> Unless a man starts afresh about things, he will certainly do nothing effective.
> *The Wit and Wisdom of G. K. Chesterton*, G. K. Chesterton

The Havens
New Year's Eve, 11 p.m.
Hugh rapped softly on her door. "Lily?"

"Yes?"

"Were you asleep?"

"Hugh?"

"In the flesh. Are you in bed?" He hoped not.

"No-o-o. When did you get home?"

"A couple of hours ago. Would you care to join me for a late supper and perhaps a glass of champagne?" She didn't answer straight away. "Lily?"

"Yes. Why not? I'll be down in a few minutes."

Encouraged, Hugh bounded downstairs. He poked around in the pantry when a deep voice startled him.

"Commander?"

He turned to find Duncan behind him, an odd expression on his face. "I was looking for something to eat, Sergeant Major. Lily is joining me."

"Ah, yes, Sir. A light supper and champagne? Allow me."

"I thought you'd turned in."

"Waiting for the lord and lady, Commander."

"Expecting to establish a beachhead, Genius? What's that African proverb? 'Only a fool tests the depth of the water with both feet.'"

Hugh lit the fire in the small sitting area off the dining room. He rose and turned. Lily stood there dressed in gray jumper and slacks, her hair flowing softly on her shoulders. With a wispy smile, she seemed almost hopeful.

"Lily." He felt like a nervous lad on his first date. By Jove! She looked cracking. It struck him he was seeing her for the second time, the first as they stood on the threshold of the stairway leading down into the ballroom at Phila's ball.

"Hughie, thank you for being so understanding." A slight blush glowed on her cheeks.

"You still owe me, Lily. I will collect."

"Here we go, Mademoiselle et Monsieur, supper for two and some bubbly." Duncan came in with a tray and a champagne bucket, the two labs in tow.

Lily giggled, glancing at Neptune and Triton. "Chaperones?"

"Yes, Miss Lily. Never trust a sailor." He winked. Hugh scowled.

Duncan arranged the small table, popped the cork, and set the bottle in the ice. Two noses and four ears rose to attention. "Lads, you're on duty."

Lily laughed.

What a heavenly sound. "Thank you, Sergeant Major. You're dismissed." Hugh winked and handed Duncan a record album.

"My pleasure, Commander." On his way out, Duncan switched on the gramophone. First came the hiss of the needle in the groove of the vinyl disc, then the music.

"Do you like jazz?" Hugh hoped so. "This is Nat King Cole's new instrumental LP album, *Penthouse Serenade*."

"He's the American negro jazz pianist and singer, isn't he?"

"Yes, quite the rage."

"Hughie, what a lovely idea. Thank you. I don't deserve it after—"

"Forgiven and forgotten. *My* pleasure." He seated her at the small table, then sat across from her, the labs flanking him. "I thought we might close out the old year and ring in the new one together." He poured the wine. "Here's to a year full of promise." He touched his flute to hers.

Her eyes glistened. "I'm not going to cry." She stiffened. "I'm moving on. I'll manage on my own." She pursed her lips and squeezed her eyes shut for a few seconds.

"You don't have to do it on your own. We're all with you, you know."

"Yes, but I need to know I can."

A strange glint in her eye troubled him, as if something had disturbed her innocence. Of course, considering what she had been through, but still . . . Get a grip, man. You must be seeing things.

"You're doing better than I hoped for."

"Thank you for your letters. I'm sorry I didn't reply. I have read them all now."

"I didn't expect you to respond." But I hoped.

He poured more champagne. They supped on cold lamb, watercress salad, and cherry tarts. She nibbled. He ate earnestly.

Lily sipped her wine. "Why didn't you join Phil and her friends partying? By the way, isn't this quite late for a flight arriving?"

"I begged a ride on a Navy plane. And cavort with the youngsters?" He scoffed. "Besides, I wanted to see how you were. You didn't go either?"

"I'm not ready to party."

"But a party for two?"

A smile lit up her face.

"I'm sorry I wasn't able to make it back for Christmas. Speaking of party-time, it's quite the event in Washington. Since 1923, they bring a huge evergreen tree into the city near the White House and decorate it. Early in December, the president turns on the lights and makes a speech. Quite impressive for the Yanks."

He looked at his watch. "Three minutes to midnight." He got up and changed the record. The labs stood at attention. "I trust you like Bing Crosby."

"Phila and I loved him in *A Connecticut Yankee in King Arthur's Court* and *Road to Bali*. His voice is so dreamy."

The seventeenth century grandfather clock in the hall chimed a dozen times.

Bing Crosby's voice crooned—

> "Should auld acquaintance be forgot,
> and never brought to mind?
> Should auld acquaintance be forgot,
> and days of auld lang syne?"

"At ease lads." They laid down as Hugh took Lily in his arms, and they danced. "Happy New Year, my dear." He handed her his handkerchief since her tears had damped his shirt.

She blew her nose. "Oh, I'm sorry." She looked forlornly at the crumpled-up mess in her hand. "Hughie, I've gotten lipstick on your shirt."

He chortled. "I'm home; The Schultz can see to the laundry." They guffawed.

> ". . . we'll take a cup of kindness yet,
> for auld lang syne."

Hugh picked up their flutes and, giving her one, touched his to hers. "And I believe custom calls for a kiss." He leaned down and kissed her on the forehead. He longed for a real New Year's kiss, but all in good time.

"I guess you're officially my only brother now." She smiled bravely.

"I guess so."

That took the wind out of your sails, sailor.

He heard faint laughter, but Lily's expression was solemn.

"I've thought of you that way since Benjie was killed. Now, with Stevie gone, you really are."

He smiled bravely. "You can think of me however you want." Damn.

They sat quietly before the fire. She talked about her memories of the last two months, and he listened. When she cried, he took her hand.

"Well, well, what have we here?" A male voice cut in.

They turned to see Mum and Dad. They exchanged New Year's greetings. Hugh and his father shook hands. Mum hugged and kissed him and Lily. She gave him an especially approving glance, while glancing at his shirt. Then his parents left.

Hugh poured more wine. Lily reminisced about family moments. Then they resumed dancing. She fit so well in his arms. He kissed her temple bringing her closer.

"Lookie here, a very *private* party!" Phila burst into the room.

Bloody timing Petunia!

"Now I know why my invitation wasn't accepted. You two had other plans."

Lily backed away. "Oh, Phil, it just happened."

"Spur of the moment, Pet."

"Sure."

"Phil, it's a new year." Lily rose and hugged her.

"It is. And it *will* be good, I just know it."

"Let's toast to that." Forcing a smile Hugh handed his sister a flute. They tipped glasses and drank.

Zeroing in on the smudges on his shirt, Phila smirked.

"This is where the dramatic thing to do is for us to throw our glasses in the fire," Phila giggled. "But, of course, we won't. The Schultz would make us walk the plank." They all laughed.

"Now, isn't it past my *little* sister's bedtime?"

"And don't *older* men need their rest to keep up with us?"

"Touché." He gave his sister a big hug and a kiss on the cheek. "I hope it's a good year for you too, Pet. Lily tells me you couldn't have been more wonderful to her. Good show, ole girl. Happy New Year, sis."

"Well, I'm no party crasher. Good night you two. Happy New Year."

1953, New Year's Day
Lily woke suddenly.

"Get up. This is your day to seize your own destiny."

Sitting up, she looked around. It was dark. She pulled on the light. Twenty-eight minutes past six. She slipped on her dressing gown and walked over to the multi-paned French doors opening out onto the garden balcony. Night still lingered. It was chilly, but the fresh air was a tonic.

A solitary robin perched on a branch near the window. Its song sounded so hopeful. Slowly the blush of the new morning rose over the rooftops. She stood there as the outline of red softened into a rosy glow, then up peeked the golden ball.

As she stood transfixed, watching the ball grow bigger, a fresh resolve filled her. The lighter the sky grew, the clearer she could see — everything outside and the future beyond.

Today was the first day of a brand-new year. One week ago, she forced her way out of that suffocating darkness, deciding to take on life, but on her terms. On this red-letter New Year's Day, she felt reborn. Lily declared her independence to the dawn. She would be controlled by no one, influenced by no one, compelled by no one other than her own self.

"So, you think."

The snide retort floored her. "I will!" Leave it to God to try to discourage her. "You left me alone. I'll show You and make it all on my own."

"You've already begun."

Winning the grand prize for her gown had been only the beginning. The day after Christmas, she'd gone through the pile of mail and found Mistress Gianna's note. The news that had refused to break through the black cocoon surrounding her had burst upon her like fireworks. "I won!"

"Despite everything," Lily told the rising ball, "I'll keep winning."

"Will you?" sneered Contempt.

"I *will* find a way." She wanted to yell it to the world. *"I will!"* There had to be a way to support herself. She gazed out the window at the garden, at the leaves glistening after the rain. The newly born sun sifted through the dissolving clouds. Longing awakened as Lily's depression lifted. The little robin fluttered away and started his song again in a distant tree.

Dare she hope?

"Hope? Where has that gotten you?"

Did she hear a snicker?

"Go away you disgusting voices! I'll make my own hope!" She closed the doors.

Perhaps she could return to St Martins. Could she qualify again for a stipend? Was there enough in Father's account to sustain her and provide the remainder of the tuition? She would not ask the Claibornes for support. Uncle Gordy had offered, but she would not accept his guilt money.

She lay back down, mulling over the possibilities, and soon drifted off. When she rolled over she saw the time: 9:43 a.m. While dressing, she considered her options. First thing, she needed to find a position and a place to live.

A tap on the door.

"Hugh?"

"No-o-o. It's Phil. Are you ready to go down?"

She opened the door to a puzzled Phila.

"You were expecting *my* brother?" Phila's eyes were as big as saucers.

"Well, after last night I—"

"Ah, after last *night?*" Phila's eyes narrowed.

"Not *that*, you goose. He knocked just like that when he asked me to join him."

"Oh, and after?" Her eyes sparkled with suspicion.

Lily spied Hugh rising up behind his sister. "After?" Lily flashed a sheepish smile, hoping she looked guilty. "*Nothing* happened. I *swear*."

Phila's eyes widened, her mouth agape.

"Lily, you *swore* not to tell." A grin blossomed across Hugh's face.

Phila flipped around. "You snuck up on me and eavesdropped."

"Moi?"

"Yes, *you*!" Phila looked from one to the other and back. "You didn't, did you?"

"We'll never tell." Lily giggled as she followed Phila downstairs and into the dining room.

The Earl rose when they entered. "Well, well, Bea, are we not delighted the young people have joined us for, let's see, is it lunchtime?"

Hugh gave his father a mock salute. "I believe it is still morning, and we three are all shipshape and Bristol fashion."

Duncan came from behind his lordship grinning. He seated Phila while Hugh drew out Lily's chair, across from him and next to Phila.

"Lily, darling, we are so pleased that you felt up to celebrating last night."

"Hugh was so kind to give me a happy way to start the new year."

He beamed back at her.

"Yes, son, that was gentlemanly and gracious of you." He gave his son a thumb's up.

"Oh, yes, that was so-o-o *gentlemanly* and generous of you." His sister leered at him.

"Am I not a gentleman?" He faked a hurt look.

"Could we possibly begin a new year with you two making a resolution for less quibbling?" Their father scowled at them.

"What a brilliant idea, Henry. What a pleasure it will be to enjoy conversation without the argumentative parrying of our progeny."

Both Hugh and Phila wore expressions of shame.

"Aye, aye, Sir. Petunia and I hereby resolve to quibble less. Do I have an aye Pet?"

"Aye, aye, I hereby resolve."

"Son, you didn't say why you're home."

"Sir Oliver has a meeting with the PM tomorrow. A rush, rush, hush, hush thing. I'm the nanny."

"I thought you didn't like being a nanny." Phila's fingers flew to her mouth. Oops, that was a short-lived resolution.

"Good one, Pet. Being one to two little girls is a cut of a different jib than being one to an ambassador."

"It may take these resolutions some time to take effect, but I am sure they will." Her ladyship sent them both a look like Lily's own mum used to telegraph to the Whitely children that she meant what she said.

What I'd give to see that look again. Lily looked down at her plate.

"How is it that they still have their mother and father and you don't?"

The vile thought scared her.

"Lily, you've gone pale." Concern flooded Hugh's face. "What's wrong?"

They all turned to look at her.

"I . . . I just had a ghastly thought that frightened me."

Hugh hastened to her side. Phila moved to his chair so he could have hers. "What was it?"

Lily just shook her head.

Phila's mum rose and took Lily's hand. "Sometimes those horrendous evil-sounding thoughts fire in our brains just when we are enjoying ourselves. It's not coming from inside you. Can you go back to savoring this New Year's morning with us now?"

The love in the dear lady's eyes and voice melted Lily's heart as warmth returned to her body. "Thank you, milady."

Hugh's arm hugged Lily's shoulders.

After a cup of tea and some small talk around the table, Lily's good spirits returned. Duncan and Giselle served breakfast.

The blood oranges, creamed Finnan haddie, and hot scones with clotted cream and marmalade actually looked appetizing for a change and smelled divine.

Giselle served coffee.

The conversation homed in on Phila approaching her final term at Oxford. She expressed excitement about Professor Tolkien's lectures.

"Lily, here's a quote for you." Hugh's eyes twinkled. "'Where there's life, there's hope.'"

"Hughie, that's lovely, and perfect for New Year's Day. Thank you."

Phila's mouth and eyes popped open. "I don't *believe* it. You actually *have* read *The Hobbit*. When?"

"OK, I admit it. After coming out of the coma, I *was* bored stiff."

"You actually admit it." Phila grinned from ear to ear. "And 'The road goes ever on and on.' And, my *Hobbit* quote checkmates yours."

"You two are something." Lily marveled at their memories.

Her ladyship beamed. "Imagine them recalling those lines."

"I may write a book for children after I graduate."

Hugh inclined his head. "Why not, Pet? You certainly have the imagination."

Phila stared at her brother. "What? That was a resolutely sanguine comment, wasn't it?"

"Yes, darling." Her ladyship smiled.

"Good show, son. By the way, how long will you be staying?"

"That depends on the meeting tomorrow."

"Have you more plans of shopping for *unmentionables?*" Lady Audrey snickered. "I require a few items."

Hugh glared. "Rubbish. That was duty above and beyond."

"I need to make plans, too. I must find a position." Lily set her chin.

Hugh winked at her. "How about going up to Oxford with Phila?"

"Hughie, I've no brain for that."

"You have a lovely brain."

Lily blushed.

"What about returning to St Martins?" Lady Beatrice patted her mouth with her serviette.

"You've all been most kind, but I really must begin to support myself."

"Of course, darling, we will do whatever we can to help."

Lily excused herself and left.

✳ ✳ ✳

Hugh followed Lily out into the foyer. "Lily?"

She turned.

"Your uncle has left you funds. You don't need to support yourself."

Lily's chin shot up. That glint in her eyes returned. "Hugh, please don't tell me what I should do. He chose the Army over me, and I want none of that money."

"Oh, Lily dear. You don't understand a man's life. The brigadier has his calling, his work, and he must follow that."

"Over everything else?" She looked about to cry.

"A man's work *is* his life; you need to understand that."

"No, I don't understand that. I don't *want* to." Her lower lip jutted out.

"You're being bullheaded again. Give your uncle some grace and accept what he is able to give you." He gazed at her, imploring.

"No, I don't have to accept his abandoning me. I can make my own way."

Hugh laid his hands gently on her shoulders. "I don't think you have much chance all on our own. You will need help. I—"

Lily shook off his hands and backed away, her eyes on fire. "Phila's right— you *are* a chauvinist. You don't think women can make it in a man's world."

"I am not—" He *was* going to say then that he believed in her. But, he didn't get a chance.

"Well, I can, and I will!" She stared at him, bristling.

What had happened to his gentle Lily? "Be reasonable, you—"

Her hands shot up. "Hugh, please. No more lectures!" She turned on her heel and dashed up the stairs.

What just happened? He watched her go and heard a door slam.

"You made a mess of that, Genius."

Aware he wasn't alone, he turned to face his father standing in the door of the dining room, an amused expression on his face.

"Nothing like being humiliated in front of your dad."

"How long have you been there?"

"Long enough, son."

Might as well face the music. "I'm tossed overboard. Throw me a ring buoy?"

"I won't always be here to save you from yourself."

"*Dad!* I'm a little old for an admonition like that."

"Not from what I just witnessed. I fear your education has been neglected in the manner of handling the fairer sex. Lectures *never* work."

"You've given Pet many."

"She's my *daughter*, not a woman with whom I desire a relationship. Come to think of it, how many positive results have we seen?"

"What are you saying Dad?"

"That for a young man of exceptional intelligence, you show a great deal of ignorance about women."

"And you, obviously, have the knowledge. Did Granddad teach you *all* about women?"

"No. All that I know about women I learned from your mother."

"You mean *after* you were married?"

"Yes. I doubt men actually learn much before."

"Will you educate me?"

"I can give you some pointers from a male perspective. The giant's share you will need to learn from the horse's mouth." He cracked a smile.

"Can you tell me anything right now?"

"If I can hazard a guess, you were talking to Lily like you would have to your sister. As a son and a sibling, I remember not wanting to take advice from my parents or my brothers—*especially* my brothers. And if I felt that way, just imagine how little a young woman of Lily's strength and tenacity would care for it."

Hugh sighed. He didn't have to imagine it, he'd seen the results in full glory.

CHAPTER 33

TEA AND TALK OF COLD WAR

> Human life has always been lived on the edge of a precipice.
> *The Weight of Glory,* C. S. Lewis

8 January
The Havens
Lily crossed the foyer as Duncan was opening the door. Lord Henry lumbered in, stamping his feet and handing his dripping coat to the butler. "A pair of dry shoes would be welcome, Duncan. Is her ladyship in the sun room?"

"Yes, milord."

"Shall we join her Lily?"

Lady Beatrice rose to greet him. "Darling, you made it."

Hugh stood and waved Lily to a chair. She returned his warm smile. Thank heaven they had made up. He took her out to dinner. He apologized. She apologized. He promised not to act so much like a big brother. She had promised not to get miffed so easily.

The Earl settled in. "And a wonder too, the roads are swamped. However, János is an expert at driving in a torrent." He gave his wife a kiss, Phila a hug, and saluted Hugh. He smiled at his wife. "A cup of tea, woman, please."

"How was your day, darling?" She filled a cup and handed it to him.

Lily looked around at the family that had embraced her, so why did she still feel so very much on the outside looking in?

"Whitehall's in a dither, all this palaver about President Truman announcing last night in his final State of the Union speech to their Congress that the United States detonated a hydrogen bomb." There was a hushed silence.

Sir Henry took a piece of paper from the inner pocket of his jacket. "This is a copy of Mr. Truman's speech." As he unfolded the paper, Lily got the impression everyone was holding their breath. But what did it mean?

He cleared this throat and read. "'In the thermonuclear tests at Eniwetok'—that's the Marshall Islands—'we have entered another stage in the world-shaking development of atomic energy.'"

"Dear me," lines of concern etched her ladyship's face.

"Where?" Phila held her cup in mid-air.

Hugh stared at his father. "It's in the South Pacific near the equator between Australia and the Hawaiian Islands Pet."

Sir Henry's voice became intense as he continued. "Mr. Truman said, 'From now on, man moves into a new era of destructive power, capable of creating explosions of a new order of magnitude, dwarfing the mushroom clouds of Hiroshima and Nagasaki.'"

He could have been speaking some foreign language. Lily couldn't wrap her mind around what he read. The silence in the room was deafening— everyone glazed with shock.

Finally, her ladyship recovered. "What an inconceivable course of action for the human race, making something so powerful it can destroy us all. Are we that close to what it says in Revelation?"

"The sixth chapter of Revelation, you mean?" Hugh closed his eyes and began to recite:

> "'And I beheld when he had opened the sixth seal, and, lo, there was a great earthquake; and the sun became black as sackcloth of hair, and the moon became as blood; and the stars of heaven fell unto the earth.'"

He opened his eyes glancing around at them all.

> "'And the heaven departed as a scroll when it is rolled together; and every mountain and island were moved out of their places.'"

"Of course, you'd remember, darling." His mum's face had paled. "I never expected to see any of the end."

"Bea," Sir Henry took her hand in his, "I don't think we're there yet."

"At least they beat the Soviets!" Hugh shrugged. "But 'it's time to bite the bullet.'"

Phila grimaced. "A Rudyard Kipling quote from *The Light that Failed*. How appropriate, Hughie."

"I feel like I've lived too long." The Earl took a draught of tea. "We're sailing too close to the wind in this new cold war."

"*Cold* war?" Phila wrinkled her nose. "How oxymoronic. However did they come up with that term?"

"Actually, I know." Hugh regarded her critically. "Eric Arthur Blair coined the term in his essay "You and the Atomic Bomb," published in the *Tribune* in '45, I believe. He wrote that we're a world living in the shadow of the threat of nuclear war. It's a peace that is no peace, which he called a 'permanent *cold war*.'"

"How comforting," his mum's tone thick with irony.

"I say, wasn't that George Orwell?" said the Earl.

"Righto Dad, his pen name. He died recently. He wrote *1984*. Did you read that book, Pet?"

"No, too depressing. This whole discussion is too depressing."

Lily found it difficult to take in what they were saying. She had thought that only *her* world had ended. Now the whole world could end?

"I didn't like that book at all," Sir Henry grumbled.

"Quite so, Dad, you weren't supposed to."

"Would you care to enlighten the rest of us, darling?"

"Yes, since you appear to be so knowledgeable and informed." Phila feigned admiration.

"I didn't attend Cambridge for nothing."

"It certainly relieves me to know our funds weren't squandered." His dad smirked.

"And I wasn't seduced by socialism or communism?"

Phila's eyes widened. "Like those chaps at Trinity in the thirties — the two from your embassy who disappeared?"

"Leave it be, Pet. I am grateful Hugh remained loyal to God and country. However, speaking of Orwell, wasn't he a socialist? Opposed to totalitarianism though."

"And the book is about, darling?"

"Right, Mum. I dare say you wouldn't have cared for it. It's science fiction, takes place in 1984, some thirty years from now when *The Party* rules the state and the people. Big Brother—government surveillance—is always watching, controlling the minds of the people and voiding all their rights."

"Like some overbearing big brothers?" Lily whispered to Hugh. He winced.

"How frightful."

"That was the point, Mum, to wake us up to the possibility." Hugh stood and gave his mother an affectionate hug. "So, we won't let it come to that."

"I should hope not." Phila's cup smacked its saucer. "Science *fiction*, indeed. How on Earth could someone watch everybody all the time? Movie cameras on street corners, inside homes? What a crazy idea. However, would they keep up with it all? And you think I fantasize?"

"Although it's difficult to imagine now," Papa held out his cup for more tea, "not a decade ago, we would not have envisioned these bombs."

"Righto." Hugh nodded. "Jet planes were introduced at the end of the war. Now the North Koreans are flying their Soviet MIG-15s against the Yanks. The dogfights now are quite spectacular, I hear. A long way from the Great War." At the mention of the word *dog*, the two labs jumped up, tails wagging.

"Look what you've done, gone and roused Neptune and Triton." Phila huffed. Whoever coined enemy fighters battling each other with that term?"

Hugh settled the dogs down. "I understand it derived from observers watching World War I fighter planes in combat. Close to the ground the engines made growling noises and their maneuvering looked and sounded like two dogs fighting. Not that my lads would behave in such an ungentlemanly fashion, would you?" He stroked their regal heads.

Phila giggled. "I do believe they actually look innocent."

"Come, boys," Phila's mum bent over, kissing the labs' heads and scratching beneath their ears. "Let humans scrap that way. How sad that we find more horrendous ways to kill each other."

"Really, Bea, kissing? You spoil them. Do keep in mind that all our innovation does not go into killing each other. Think of how much faster the jet aircraft fly and how that's improving commercial service. Take the de Havilland on its maiden flight in May, only twenty-four hours from London to Johannesburg."

Her ladyship finished loving on the labs, so they moved on to Phila for similar treatment. "I read it stopped in Rome, Beirut, Khartoum, Entebbe, and Livingstone."

"That beat out Lockheed. You do have some memory, Pet. You should put it to use."

Phila sniggered, which excited the labs again.

"Where were we before jetting off the subject and giving you two a stage to show off your exceptional memories?" Their mum smiled at Phila and Hugh. "And I have difficulty recalling names."

Sir Henry chuckled. "That, they inherited from my father. That man left Oxford with three firsts and never forgot anything. He even recalled my transgressions to the day he passed."

"Bully for Granddad. Glad you didn't take after him in that regard, Dad."

"But our progeny did inherit you and your siblings' proclivity for bickering, Henry."

Hugh reached over and tweaked Phila's ear. Triton looked at him and growled. Phila smiled and stroked the dog's head.

Hugh cleared his throat. "So, back to *1984*—or should I say forward—we just might encounter Big Brother in the future considering how rapidly these breakthroughs are proceeding."

"Gracious, let us pray the Americans and Russians don't blow us all up." Her ladyship sighed.

Lily shuddered. What was wrong with people? Life was hard enough without worrying about being blown up. Another war? Was Benjie's sacrifice worth nothing?

"We have to face up to it and not get blindsided again." Hugh slapped his knee for the labs to come.

Phila clunked her cup down. "So, we get a bomb big enough to blow the other fellow up in order that he won't blow us up?"

"*Enough*, all of you. This is much too serious talk for tea. Dear?" She gestured conspiratorially to her husband.

"This bomb business *is* very serious, my dear."

"Of course, Henry, but life must go on." She tilted her head ever so slightly toward Lily.

"Ah, yes, and have you given more thought to your future, Lily?" He added milk to his tea and drank deeply.

Lily stared at the Earl.

"I say, are you all right, my dear?"

"All this talk of bombs, I—"

"How insensitive of us." Hugh's expression resembled Triton's when he was scolded. "Forgive us, please?"

She mouthed, "yes." It's just talk. Frightening talk. That's all it was. "What did you ask me, sir?"

"About your future, my dear?"

"I rang the design school. Since I left mid-term last autumn, I'm not allowed to return until next August. I have been searching the *Times* for positions."

"I may have some good news, then, if you are determined to find employment."

"Yes, your lordship, I am."

"Well then, you're well aware of Norman Hartnell, of course."

"Yes, sir." His fashion house had her prize-wining gown on display. Phila would take her to see it. "He's made London a fashion center and has been chosen by the Queen to design her ensemble for the Coronation."

"Quite so. He and I read 'modern languages' at Magdalen College at Cambridge in — well, some years back."

"Oh, Papa, you got the Queen's couturier to give Lily a position designing the gown?"

"Not *the* frock, but his house is extremely occupied with the wardrobe and other regalia, so he is seeking extra help. We were having a drink at the club, and I mentioned Lily. He's agreed to give her a chance. What do you think Lily?"

"He wants *me*?" She held her breath.

The Countess winked at her husband.

Lily felt faint, overjoyed, wanting to laugh and cry all at once. "Y-e-s-s. Yes! Oh, thank you, Sir Henry." She stood up. It was all she could do not to run over and embrace him.

Obviously, Phila did not feel any reluctance. She rushed over and hugged her father fiercely. "Papa, you're absolutely brilliant."

"Good show, Dad." Hugh slapped his father on the back.

"Let's have a little restraint, please!" But his lordship looked gratified.

When he had dislodged himself from Phila's grasp, he reached in his pocket and brought out a card, handing it to Lily. "You're to ring his sister, Phyllis, in the morning at ten sharp."

Lily gripped the card and stared at it.

Lady Beatrice smiled at her husband, touching her fingers to her lips and extending her hand in his direction. She turned and faced Lily. "We have that small guest cottage near the gate of this property. We'd like to offer that to you until you're ready to let a flat in town."

"I don't know what to say." Emotion threatened to engulf her. Lily forced back tears, her knees wobbling.

Hugh stepped to her side instantly, enveloping her in his arms and handing her his handkerchief. It was nice, hiding in his embrace and regaining her composure. He was so sweet, when he wasn't being domineering.

"Oh, just say, 'thank you,'" Phila nudged her friend. "Let's go see what fixing up the cottage needs."

Her ladyship moved over to her husband's chair and kissed him on the forehead. "You're a dear man."

"I know."

CHAPTER 34

LILY IN WONDERLAND

I can't go back to yesterday because I was a different person then.
Alice's Adventures in Wonderland,
Lewis Carroll (1832–1898)

9 January

Lily rose early. At breakfast, she declined the fare Giselle offered, asking only for a piece of toast and a cup of tea. Phila coaxed her to eat that and sent her off with a bouquet of encouragement. Lady Beatrice said she would be praying.

Lily rode downtown with Sir Henry and Hugh, whose work kept him in London for a few more days.

He looked over at her. "You look lovely. But then, you always do. Have lunch with me?"

"We'll see." She couldn't think beyond the next hour.

After they dropped his lordship off at the Palace of Westminster, János drove to Mayfair, but Lily insisted on getting out at the corner.

The chauffeur opened the door for her. "Goot luck, Miss Lily." He gave her a thumb's up, a gigantic smile blossoming. She grinned back, but her top lip trembled.

"Break a leg, Lily!" Hugh gave her a hug, a kiss on her forehead for luck, turned her around, and propelled her up Bruton Street toward number twenty-six. The sun seemed hesitant to work its way through the mist. She trudged ahead, working up her courage, holding on tight to her portfolio.

House of Hartnell

Lily showed Miss Hartnell's card to the elegant doorman wearing a military-type wheel hat, a long coat belted at the waist and fastened with five gold buttons on each side. He ushered her into the reception area and handed the card to the smartly dressed young woman behind the reception desk.

"I didn't know we were interviewing mannequins today." The receptionist gave her a full once-over.

Phila would call her "Miss Very Chic."

Wait. What did the girl say? "Excuse me? I'm here to see Miss Hartnell, Lillian Whitely?"

"Of course," she glanced at the card. "It's just, well, you certainly *could* model."

A model? Lily smiled. The receptionist picked up her phone and spoke a few words into it.

"May I take your hat and coat?" Miss Very Chic offered a practiced smile. "Quite impressive, your gown, Miss Whitely. Congratulations. Miss Felicity will come and collect you shortly. Please have a seat."

But Lily preferred to look around. Taking off her gloves, she turned slowly, absorbing the grandeur. The entrance hall was paneled in pale and dark green marble. Plush carpet in a subtle creamy shade of green led the way further in and up the stairs. Long velvet curtains in the same hue fell from the high ceiling.

Lily removed her coat and hat, handing them to the receptionist. She straightened her skirt, buttoned her jacket, tucked a stray curl behind her ear, and sat down. Then she saw it. Her gown—displayed on a mannequin standing on a dais. The sign read: *Central Saint Martin's College of Arts and Design, Grand Winner of the Coronation Gown Contest, Miss Lillian Grace Whitely.* The lapis blue stood out, complemented by the verdant background.

Pride welled up at the sight of her heart and soul's work, set in such a place of honor.

Then, like a sudden draft of icy air—

"So much attention to a mere dress."

The words were her father's, but not his kindly voice. Rather, it rasped with scorn.

Shaken, she closed her eyes. Not now, please.

"This dream will only disappoint. What kind of a realistic future have you really?"

The disturbing accusation threatened to crumble her resolve.

"Run! Now! Before you embarrass yourself."

No! She took a couple of deep breaths. Go away. Leave me in peace. Focusing on her surroundings, she struggled to regain her composure.

The room blossomed with splendor, light gushing in from the encircling windows. The velvet Queen Anne chairs and intricately carved antique tables all emanated opulence. Snow-white roses bloomed in a crystal bowl on an elegant ball-and-claw table in the room's center. How cheap her navy skirt appeared in comparison, though it was the best she possessed. Even the stillness bespoke luxury.

"Lillian Whitely?" A clear, flutelike voice broke the silence. A fair-haired sprite in a pale-blue shirtwaist dress, skirt billowing, floated down the graceful staircase. "I'm Miss Felicity. I'll take you up to Miss Hartnell's office."

Blue Sprite flounced ahead of Lily toward the stairs, her golden curls bouncing. Oh, what fun Phila would have labeling people here with descriptive monikers. The girl stopped and turned, gesturing at the display of Lily's gown, "Before I give you the tour and a history lesson, I must say how absolutely brilliant your gown is. It caused quite a stir in The House and—well, let's move along, shall we?" She started up the stairs.

Panels of faceted mirrors lined the staircase on both sides. Multiple images of Blue Sprite greeted her like bubbles of pale blue bobbing all around her. Lily's reflection surrounded her a dozen-fold as she climbed. She looked down at her feet tucked into sensible navy pumps, following after the pale-blue high heels.

The images disappeared into awe at the splendor that greeted her. I will not be intimidated.

"Unbelievable opulence, isn't it? Mr. H and Miss H devised the décor. The green he created himself and calls it *Hartnell green*, of course. The velvet was specially dyed in Paris and the marble is from Sweden and Italy." She pointed to the dozen coruscating chandeliers. "Original Regency and Waterford crystal."

"Of course."

"This is the salon. It's still early for clients, so we can go in."

The tranquil aura of the room soothed her. Gold-dusted mirrors lined the walls. Lily stared at the two giant crystal chandeliers. Gilt-encrusted, embroidered chairs surrounded the sides of the grand room. Taking a deep breath, she savored the spectacular ambience. What must this room be like when it's filled with the *noblesse oblige*, parading models in sparkling finery? She sighed. Thank you, Phil, for teaching me impressive words, even in French.

"Incredible, isn't it?" Her guide sounded breathless.

"Oh, yes."

"*Naturellement*, the Royals don't come *here*. Mr. Hartnell goes to *them*. But we see only the very best of society and nobility for balls, weddings, and the like. They gather to watch the showings of Mr. Hartnell's collections. And during *the season*, well, you can't imagine how hectic it is. But really exciting."

Felicity dropped down on a chair by the door and motioned for Lily to sit. "Enjoy now, while you have the opportunity. If Miss H takes you on, you won't have much of an occasion to be here in the inner sanctum."

Lily drank it all in. Perhaps there is a chance for a life and hopeful future.

"Well, here goes—the background you'll need to know." The girl fluffed her crinolines. "Mr. H opened his business in 1923. In '27, he created Dame Barbara Cartland's wedding gown—the romantic novelist, you know, and his oldest client. She says he's the designer who makes every woman look like a fairy queen."

"When George VI became king, Mr. H was commissioned to design the Coronation dresses for the maids of honor. He saw some portraits at the palace that gave him the idea for his crinoline dresses, which, by the way, are said to have influenced Dior's new look in '47. That's when designs became more feminine." Felicity rose, pirouetted, and bowed.

Lily glanced at her hands in her lap. How out of fashion the plain straight skirt.

Felicity chattered on, rattling off names of legendary film stars and gesturing to the front row of chairs. "They've all sat right here. Even that woman, Eva Perón—the one married to the president of Argentina—bought from Mr. H's collection when he showed it in South America. That was in '46. Señora Perón died last year of cancer. Only thirty-three. How sad. She was very beautiful—and very powerful."

Why did people have to die young? So sad. So unfair. Grief welled up, threatening to engulf her. Benjie, Stevie, and Kit's faces flashed painfully in her mind's eye.

"Oh dear, did I say something upsetting?"

"I . . . I . . . I lost my . . . brother in the war." Lily wrestled with the sudden impulse to tell this girl her whole loss, but she knew if she did, she'd fall apart.

"I'm sorry."

Thankfully, Felicity didn't carry on but directed Lily out into the foyer.

Once out of that room with its echoes of fame, she found her voice. "How long have you been here? You are quite informed."

"Three years, next month," the girl beamed. "It's my job to know all about The House. I give tours to schools, design classes, tourists, and prospective clients." She halted at a huge elaborately carved double door.

Lily stopped to stare.

"Quite something, isn't it? That's Mr. H's office. He had the door made when Gerald Lacoste designed all this in '34."

"It must have taken years to carve it."

"I should imagine. As you will see, he prefers the ornate." Felicity waved her arm about, then spouted in an affected tone, "Mr. Hartnell despises simplicity and believes it to be the negation of all that is beautiful."

"He what?"

"Sounds a bit too posh, doesn't it? But that's what he actually said. I read it in the *Times*. It's the embroidery and beads. He's known for it. It was difficult to be glitzy for a while due to the General Austerity Regulations during the war and afterwards. Better now."

"We studied his work at St Martins."

"I should think so. Mr. H *is* the royal dressmaker since '38." She led Lily to a collage of wedding gown sketches, then pointed to one hanging alone. "This was Her Majesty's."

"Extraordinary." Lily stood gaping in front of the drawing and the huge photograph of Princess Elizabeth's famous garment.

"Heady stuff, huh?"

How had this happened, that she should be in this magical place? That she might even get a position! "Oh, yes." She leaned close to the picture, her eyes devouring the details.

"The dress was made of ivory silk satin, mostly from Lady Zoe Hart Dyke's silk farm in Kent. It took four hundred girls working nearly a month to transform it into the dress."

"All for one dress?"

"Yes, but what a dress. Look at the embroidery—incredibly intricate, isn't it? See, the pearls and crystals form orange blossoms, ears of wheat, and roses"—she affected the just-too-sophisticated voice again—"inspired by Botticelli, *naturellement*. Over 10,000 seed pearls came from America. *The* famous *Mam'selle*, Madame Germaine Davide, had the honor of making the wedding gown for Her Royal Highness. Mr. H delivered it personally to Buckingham Palace in a shiny black box, if you will."

"Is she making the Coronation gown?"

"No. She retired."

How like Phila, this Blue Sprite rattling off huge amounts of information.

Felicity smiled. "The press was infatuated from the start—from the announcement of the engagement in July to the November event. The wedding, as well as the dress, was considered a much-needed boost for public morale. Wouldn't it have been marvelous to be a part of that? Of course, the Coronation will be even more spectacular."

"I should imagine so. But look at that gown, how much more magnificent can the Coronation gown be? Do you know?"

"Even if I did, I couldn't tell—not yet." Her eyes widened.

The girl's confidence impressed Lily. "I was sure you'd know. I'm amazed at your knowledge."

"I've a photographic memory." Felicity beamed.

"That's quite a talent. I know two people like that."

"Everyone at Hartnell's has talent. Obviously, you do, too, or you wouldn't be here." Felicity flounced ahead.

"I'm not here yet." Lily took a last glance at the Queen's wedding dress and followed.

The girl faced Lily. "I'd say you have skills and connections. Right? All you need is to hit it off with Miss Hartnell. Not a plum pick. She likes, or she doesn't."

Lily shivered.

"I don't miss a thing. You don't get this far without paying close attention to everything." She flashed Lily a superior grin.

Soon they came to closed doors. "That is where they are fashioning the Coronation wear. It's all very hush-hush. Been going on since a year last September. The gown will be Mr. H's masterpiece. They are on the ninth design. The first fitting was at Christmas. Apparently, Prince Phillip had some say in the last design."

"I thought you said it was all secret."

"Oh, it is, but one hears whispers."

Felicity ushered Lily into a small room, tastefully decorated in golds and tans. "Good luck. I hope she takes you on." The girl pranced off, crinolines bobbing.

A young man in a cedar-brown suit, starched white shirt, and carob tie motioned her to sit, as he spoke on the telephone. When he finished, he told her Miss Hartnell would see her soon. "Brilliant gown, by the way. Good show Miss Whitely."

Lily felt like pinching herself. Compared to the rest of the establishment, this room struck her as austere. She toed the beige carpet with the tip of her pump—plush, but plain. The furnishings were modern, simple in design, clean lines, and dark wood. Actually, quite restful after her *Alice-in-Wonderland* tour through the House of Hartnell.

On the table, she saw the latest issues of *Vogue* and *Harper's Bazaar* featuring gorgeous models in stunning ensembles. She leafed through one, looking but not seeing. She closed her eyes and gathered her composure.

At a soft ring the young man stopped typing and picked up the phone. "Miss Hartnell will see you now." He got up and opened the door for Lily.

She took a deep breath, patted her hair, smoothed her skirt, and walked in.

CHAPTER 35

THE INTERVIEW

Not knowing when the dawn will come, I open every door.
"Nature," Emily Dickinson (1830–1886)

"Miss Hartnell, this is Lillian Whitely."

"Thank you, Mr. Fontaine."

The woman standing behind the desk struck Lily as unremarkable yet striking in her simplicity—trim and stately with a high forehead, long straight nose, and russet-tinted lips. Silver streaked through her neatly waved chestnut hair. She wore a tailored and precise cream-colored linen suit, short-sleeved with an open collar, and belted at the waist. All this elegantly accented by a single strand of pearls and matching earrings, no rings. The phrase, "perfectly put together," came to mind.

"Why are you here, Miss Whitely?"

Lily gasped.

A slight hint of a smile softened Miss Hartnell's face. "I've startled you. Take a breath and tell me why you are here." Her voice rang with authority, but with a gentle quality as well.

"I-I'm here because Mr. Hartnell invited me to come?" Lily felt clammy all over.

"This is your first job interview, am I right, Miss Whitely?"

"Yes, ma'am."

"It won't be fatal, I assure you. And, rumors aside, I do not bite." The woman's eyes mellowed a fraction, and her smile widened.

"I haven't heard any such rumors, Miss Hartnell."

"But Miss Felicity did give you the tour?"

"Yes, ma'am, but she didn't—"

"Say anything unflattering? Undoubtedly, no. Miss Felicity is proficient at her job and suitably informative. Going beyond what's appropriate, would be unwise. Please sit." Miss Hartnell gestured to one of the two straight-backed cane chairs facing her desk. "First, may I extend my sympathy for your tragic loss." Compassion shone through her eyes.

Lily swallowed hard and clasped her hands together. *I've got to get used to this.* She gritted her teeth and took a deep breath as Miss Hartnell continued.

"You are very fortunate for Sir Henry's protection. I'm informed they look upon you as a daughter, which is one reason you are sitting in my office. I admire that you desire to make your own way. That has gotten you this far."

Lily doubted this woman gave many compliments.

"Also, I may add, the outstanding job you did designing and sewing your gown. Another reason you're here. Congratulations on winning the contest. Quite deserved. You show considerable potential. However, where you go from here depends on why you want to be at Hartnell's." She lifted her eyebrows. "Other than to earn a wage. So, you are here because?"

"I, I want to design lovely clothes."

"Splendid. Now we are getting somewhere."

Lily unclasped her fingers, loosened her shoulders, and drew in a deep calming breath. The rest of her body relaxed ever so slightly.

"Miss Whitely, I had my secretary inquire of your instructors at St Martins. They all think quite highly of you. A hard worker, they say. Obviously, you have talent." She held out her arm, motioning with her fingers. "Let's see your designs."

Lily handed over her sketches and waited. Cautiously, she allowed her eyes to gaze around the room. The room was large like the rest, but its neutral shades were subdued and unpretentious. Beige carpet and chairs covered in ivory and vanilla raw silk accented the plain, but delicate desk carved of dark polished wood. It made a dramatic statement set against the white-on-white tones. Light filtered softly through the windows. Framed covers of *Vogue* and *Harper's Bazaar* adorned the pearl and seashell papered walls.

Miss Hartnell caught Lily gazing around the room. "Do you approve?"

"Oh, yes, it's—"

"More tranquil?"

"Yes, actually. But that doesn't mean I don't—"

"Appreciate my brother's taste?"

"Yes, ma'am."

"Mr. Hartnell believes that 'simplicity is the death of the soul.' I, on the other hand, am of the same opinion as the great Italian polymath, Leonardo da Vinci, that 'simplicity is the ultimate sophistication.' You are familiar with him, I trust?"

"Yes, ma'am." Thank you, Phil, for all your history lessons. "He painted the *Mona Lisa* and *The Last Supper* and is considered 'The Renaissance Man,' whose talents spanned so many areas."

"Excellent. It takes all kinds to make a world, doesn't it, Miss Whitely?"

"Yes, ma'am." A shiver went through her body. Mum used to say that.

"We have many young people recommended to us, as you can well imagine. I'm not in the habit of accepting just anyone, even with such favorable recommendations." She paused.

Lily tensed.

"Connections get introductions. Ability and work ethic secure a position."

Another pause, this one so long Lily thought she would wilt right then and there.

"However, as I have said, you do indeed show promise, and such gifts must be fostered."

Lily breathed again.

"As it so happens, we've transferred some of our people over to the royal side with all the work for the Coronation, so we need to fill those positions in ready-to-wear."

Lily nodded. Did that mean what she thought? From the look on Miss Hartnell's face, the woman could read her thoughts.

"Yes, my dear, you have a position here if you want it."

If she wanted? "Oh, yes, ma'am, I do!"

"We will make use of your drawing ability eventually, but first you will need to work with the ladies who transfer the creation of drawings to actual clothing. I hope this arrangement works out for you, and for The House." She handed back Lily's portfolio and picked up the phone receiver. "Mr. Fontaine, ring Miss Felicity."

"Thank you, Miss Hartnell." Lily's face flushed with happiness.

Miss Hartnell's expression returned to her former serious mien. "And Miss Whitely?"

"Ma'am?" Lily held her breath.

"You will have nothing to do with the Coronation planning, but no doubt, you will hear whispers. Nothing—and I do mean *nothing*—said within The House is to be shared outside, not even with the influential—*especially* the influential. That includes Lady Philomena and her parents. *Especially them.* Is that understood?" Her cold gaze penetrated Lily's heart.

"Yes, ma'am." Her voice quavered.

"Welcome to the House of Hartnell." Lily hadn't thought the woman capable of such a broad smile. Lily felt she might burst with excitement.

The brown-suited man ushered her out of the office and into Felicity's care.

Miss Blue Sprite greeted her. "What big eyes you have."

"Pardon me?"

"You got the position. Congratulations."

How lovely to breathe again. "Miss Hartnell is quite frank, gets right to it."

"You know right where you stand with Miss H. Not like some." Felicity lifted her delicately shaped eyebrows.

"Some?" That sounded dubious.

"I don't want to prejudice you. You'll discover for yourself." She flicked her hand nonchalantly.

"What about Mr. Hartnell?"

"Oh, he's charming with the clients." Felicity tossed her curls. "When he's in an artistic state—a creative mood, and it's not going well—he pretty much stays to himself. The great door stays closed. No one enters except Miss H, the Directrice, and the madams. He rarely addresses the rest of us."

"Mr. Hartnell is all glitz and glamour for the *crème de la crème*, and Miss H caters to the common folk. That's brothers and sisters for you. My sister is quiet as a mouse." She shrugged her shoulders. "My brother—well, there's no other word for him but dour. Me—my dad says I was vaccinated with a phonograph needle because I talk so much."

"Takes all kinds to make a world."

"Now you're quoting Miss H. What about your siblings?"

Another heart squeeze. Lily grimaced and looked down.

"That bad, is it? Don't want to talk about it? So, we shan't. We'll talk about men. Surely you've lots." Felicity's face brightened.

Lily shook her head.

"I don't believe it. You're such a looker. You could model, actually. *I know,* no doubt you're just getting over a disappointment. Well, give it time. You'll have more after you than you can count."

You have no idea what I can't get over, and I doubt time will ever help. She forced a smile. "You're too kind."

"Just being frank. Ready for the rest of the tour, Miss Lillian?"

"Lily."

"Welcome to Hartnell's, *Miss* Lily."

Felicity showed her the rest of the facilities and the ready-to-wear workrooms. She explained that Hartnell's began the department store collections in 1947. The house had also created uniforms for the British Red Cross and the Women's Royal Army Corps during the war. When they finished, her tour guide left Lily at the top of the stairs. "See you Monday."

Lily floated down the mirror-paneled staircase, feet barely touching the steps. Her half-dozen reflections smiled back at her. Alice had been accepted into Wonderland. And Miss Hartnell was not the Red Queen. And, who was waiting in the foyer, but Prince Charming. Phila and her fairy-tales. But, what is all of this if not make-believe come true?

"Once upon a time Lily went to work for the Royal Couturier . . ."

At last, the voice of Joy!

"Lily, you got the position." Hugh gave her his hand. "It's written all over your face. Let's celebrate!"

She turned to wave good-bye to Felicity.

The girl wore a huge smile and envy in her eyes. She waved, but her focus was centered on the debonair man opening the door for Lily.

Dear Hugh. He had that effect on all the girls.

CHAPTER 36

CELEBRATION

All human wisdom is contained in these two words—
Wait and Hope.

The Count of Monte Cristo,
Alexandre Dumas (1802–1870)

Hugh escorted Lily out onto Bruton Street, fighting to keep his eyes off her. She positively glowed. "How about lunch at Claridges?"

"Oh, thank you, Hughie, but I couldn't possibly eat. I'm still a bundle of nerves. Can we just walk?"

"Certainly." They strolled toward Piccadilly, and since she seemed about to burst, he waited for her to speak.

"Hughie, I was absolutely petrified. I wanted to run away."

"But you didn't."

"Guess what? The receptionist thought I was a mannequin at first. Do you know what that is?"

"Of course, I've dated a couple. They hardly eat anything. And I'm not surprised."

"Oh, Hughie, do I look that skinny?"

"And you criticize Pet for not thinking before she speaks."

Regroup Genius. "You look perfect."

They skirted Green Park.

"Did you see my gown displayed right there in front?"

"I did! Real ace, Lily. What an honor. But it looked more spectacular on you." He was hoping she would turn and shine on him.

"Hughie! Do you know that every single person complimented me on it?"

"I'm not surprised." But her thoughts were in the clouds and not on him.

She babbled on and on as they strolled. He'd never heard her talk that much. But then, his sister probably never gave her the chance.

"Can you believe, Mr. Hartnell has designed for people like Tallulah Bankhead, Gertrude Lawrence, Marlene Dietrich, Merle Oberon, and Elizabeth Taylor. Legendary actresses. Think of all the famous people I'll see."

They circled the Marble Arch, entering Belgravia.

"The girl who gave me the tour has a memory like you and Phil. The information she rattled off left me spinning. A cocky little miss, but thoroughly captivating. She almost reminded me of Kit. I wonder if that's how Kit would have been as a young woman."

He saw the telltale sparkle of tears in her eyes and handed her his handkerchief. *Is this my lot in life, handing Lily handkerchiefs?*

"Hugh, do I have a right to be happy when they can't?"

Her words melted his heart. "Lily, their memory will always be with you. They would want you to be happy." He lifted her chin with his fingers. "You know that, don't you?"

She laid her head on his chest.

Steady, man.

"Hughie, your heart is beating so fast. Are you OK?"

"It's walking this far. I must be getting old."

The Havens

Hugh led Lily into the observatory. "Ladies and gentlemen, the lady of the hour." He propelled her forward making an exaggerated bow.

Mum, Dad, and Phila all stood and applauded. Neptune and Triton sat at attention. Lily blushed.

"Good show, Lil!" Phila beamed. She came to stand next to Hugh. "Lily is returning to the light," she whispered. "And now the limelight too."

The room glowed illuminated in the late afternoon sun, little rainbows dancing on the walls as beams glanced off the cut glass flutes lined up on a silver tray.

"We are all so very proud of you, my dear." Mum gave Lily a big hug.

"Good show." Hugh's father laid his hands on Lily's shoulders and gave her a kiss on the forehead.

"It couldn't happen to a lovelier lady." Hugh gave Lily a quick squeeze.

Pop.

Triton jumped letting out a startled ruff. Neptune looked up as if to ask what was happening. Duncan had uncorked a bottle of champagne. The labs were standing now expectantly, their tails thumping against Hugh's trousers.

The butler touched the bottle to a glass. "On behalf of the staff, we are delighted for you, Miss Lily."

Giselle and Molly giggled. János grinned, Flora curtsied, even The Shultz smiled.

Lily beamed as Duncan poured the golden liquid into the crystal flutes, passing them around to everyone.

Papa raised his goblet. "To Miss Lillian Grace Whitely of the House of Hartnell."

"Hear! hear!" They all replied and drank.

"I, I don't know what to say." Lily gazed into her glass, overcome.

"Drink up, girl."

"Sir H-Henry, thank you so very much—for everything. And you, too, Lady Beatrice." Her eyes looked glassy, but she managed a sip.

"I expect you shall take it from here and exceed all our expectations." Mum smiled at Lily.

The staff added their felicitations, then slipped out of the room taking their flutes with them.

"I am overwhelmed by your love and kindness." Lily looked around at them all. "I'm rather fearful of the unknown, but hopeful. I do hope to fulfill your expectations."

Hugh polished off his wine. *And, mine?*

※ ※ ※

What were his expectations? For life? For love? For the future? At the moment, Hugh simply wanted to get out of the house and away from everybody. In lieu of a long ride in the country, he took the labs on an ambitious walk in Hyde Park. At first, he had to run to keep up with them so excited were they for the adventure. The brisk air and exercise were invigorating. After a while the dogs slowed down to sniff and mark the trees.

Thoughts pummeled Hugh from all directions. His life had executed an about-face. *I'm back in the city I love—home, strolling with my lads in one* of the greatest city parks in the world. They walked at a brisk pace on the west side of The Long Water. Then why have I chosen a life that takes me away from London? Did that Hemingway quote he threw out at Pet have subliminal significance? "I can't stand it to think my life is going so fast and I'm not really living it."

Not that his job hadn't proved exciting and worthwhile, critical to the peace of the world. Except for the fighting in Korea, the Cold War presented a clear and present danger. And, he was a frontline warrior with riveting challenges.

But that presented a quandary. An only son is required to sire an heir, but an intelligence operative's lifestyle is not particularly conducive to marriage and family. Hugh sat on a bench by the lake and watched the nannies with their charges running about and playing. A small boy seemed taken with Neptune and Triton.

"Sir, are they friendly? May I pet them?" The lad received a hand and face washing from the labs. His delight tugged at Hugh's heart. What would a son of his . . . and, say, Lily's look like? The thought jarred him. He got up and called the dogs. What were his expectations about Lily?

And, what about a career in the Diplomatic Service? Sir Oliver was a rising star and impressive role model. Baron Franks, an Oxford academic and philosopher, had been the Minister of Supply, achieving fame replacing military supplies after Dunkirk and the Battle of the Atlantic. However, Hugh's chances of scoring renown and gaining a knighthood and an ambassadorship were next to nil. So, what choice does that leave? A mediocre life in the Diplomatic Service or an opportunity to gain honor as an intelligence operative?

He had told Lily that a man's work *is* his life, that her uncle had to follow his calling. Hugh had been disappointed when the Navy assigned him to Intelligence during the war, but he actually found the work exhilarating, and rewarding in Washington. Is this my calling?

He and the lads raced back to Belgravia. The three of them panted as they entered the house. The dogs collapsed on the floor, and Hugh leaned up against the banister as Lily floated down the stairs.

"Hughie, I thought you were tired out just walking with me." She leaned up against him and put her hand over his heart, her head on his chest. "Should you have exerted yourself like this?"

Lily don't do this to me.

CHAPTER 37

SEPARATE PATHS

If you love somebody, let them go, for if they return, they were always yours. And if they don't, they never were.
Khalil Gibran

Saturday, 10 January
Phila trotted down for tea. Not permitted in the dining room, Neptune and Triton lingered just outside the door, anticipating attention. Snowy followed Lily down the stairs, settling on the bottom step.

In a festive mood they all enjoyed a final meal together though Phila's emotions seemed divided. She was excited to be off on Saturday for Oxford, but apprehensive about leaving Lily.

Duncan brought in the roast beef and Yorkshire pudding and went around the table serving.

"I need to tell Flora this smells as good as Simpsons." Hugh wore an expression of absolute delight. "Sergeant Major is this Aberdeen Angus beef?"

"Aye, Commander."

His father glanced up. "What time does János need to drive the ambassador's attaché to the airport?"

Hugh shook his head. "No need for that, Dad. Phila will drive me. Of course, if I don't survive, you'll need to find a replacement for the ambassador."

"If you think so poorly of my driving, why risk your life?"

"Because I'll treasure those last moments with you. Actually, I'd prefer Lily's company, but she's a working woman now."

"And I don't drive." Lily grinned at them.

"I doubt that would be much improvement over Petunia."

"Such brotherly love. I'm overcome with filial affection." But she would miss him.

"Driving has to be safer than flying in these new jets." Mum's facial muscles twitched nervously. "You are flying out on this new de Havilland to New York?"

"It's proved quite safe, Mum. The pilots have had a lot more flying time than Pet has driving."

"You're an excellent driver, too, darling. You actually risk operating an automobile in America. I can't imagine, seated on the left side and maneuvering on the right."

"Tricky, that."

"I imagine so." Papa pursed his lips. "I'll leave you young people to deal with the idiosyncrasies of the colonies."

Hugh chuckled. "I read they actually followed English driving customs until they parted with the mother country and wanted to cast off all links with their British past."

"Surely, darling, you're not going to be driving next week whilst Washington is crowded with all those people for Mr. Eisenhower's inauguration."

"No, I'll leave that for the chauffeurs."

"You'll be in the ambassador's entourage?" Mum beamed at Hugh.

"Quite so. What an honor to be present at such a historic event."

"Interesting election, that." Papa took a helping of creamed leeks and green beans.

"I was sorry Governor Stevenson lost." Mum sipped her wine.

Hugh smiled at her. "It wasn't a landslide, as the Yanks say, like President Roosevelt, but Ike won by over six million votes."

"It's not difficult to understand, son. Obviously, the American people wanted a strong man of action to take the helm in the rough waters ahead. The Supreme Commander of the Allied Forces certainly proved himself in supervising the invasion of North Africa, France, and Germany for the Allied victory. He'd have had my vote."

"Mine too, Dad. Though he was aided by the press, who painted the picture that the nation wanted a father figure, what with all the concerns over this new war in Korea. However, it must be said that Stevenson made a good show of it, polling more votes for a Democratic candidate, except for Mr. Roosevelt of course."

"I liked everything I read about Mr. Stevenson." Mum served herself salad from the bowl Duncan held. "Quite an intellectual. I rather fancied that. And such a brilliant speaker. Interesting that he was born in California."

"Are you saying that Californians aren't up to snuff?" Phila tapped her mouth with her serviette. "The new vice president, Mr. Nixon, is a Californian."

"Well, I don't wish to discriminate, but one always thinks of Hollywood and their rather Bohemian lifestyle."

"I can't imagine actually living there." Lily scowled. "However, the fashions coming out of the movies are so intriguing. Weren't those gowns in *Sunset Boulevard* gorgeous, Phil? Edith Head designed them. She's one of the best."

"I do like General Eisenhower's wife, Mamie, with those short little bangs and perched up hats." Mum touched her hair. "Quite refreshing."

"I am looking forward to viewing the inauguration—not up to standard with the Queen's Coronation, *naturellement*. It's certainly possible that we'll never see another British monarch crowned in our lifetimes. Now the Yanks inaugurate a president every four years."

Hughie sounded so knowledgeable. He obviously loved his position.

Giselle brought in the pudding and started serving Hugh.

"Flora made Spotted Dick." Hugh took a serving of the suet pudding with currents and spooned custard and brown sugar onto it.

Papa sniggered. "I wonder if we will eat as well as we have these past ten days with the crown prince." Hugh grinned sheepishly.

"Darling, we haven't called you that in years." Mum tittered. "Lily, you are most welcome to dine with us, if you wish."

"Yes, milady, but I do have to begin to make my own way."

"I understand that, but with Pet and Hugh gone, we would enjoy the company, all the same."

"Thank you, milady. I will sometimes."

After coffee, cognac, and more conversation in the drawing room, the family said good night and Hugh walked Lily back to the cottage. Phila hung around downstairs at the foot of the stairway until he returned. She was dying to ask if they had moved beyond their brother/sister relationship now after spending so much time together since New Year's Eve.

When Hugh returned, she pounced. "Have you told her yet how you feel?"

Hugh backed up and stared at her blankly. "Which is what?"

"You *love* her." She gave him a dreamy look and studied his face.

"Of course, I love her." His eyes shifted looking past Phila.

She frowned. "I don't mean like a sister. You love her. You've been absolutely starry-eyed lately." Why won't he admit it?

He blanched. "What if I have someone in America?"

"*Sure,* you do. You know you've fancied Lily for years. That's why you haven't married, isn't it?" That's getting it out in the open.

He recoiled, blinked owlishly, then steeled his jaw. "For your information, Miss Busybody, I have a girlfriend. She's the daughter of a senator and quite a looker, actually."

He's lying. "I don't care. I know what I see. Besides, Papa said that was subterfuge on your part." Oops!

"Talk about a Freudian slip, dunderhead."

A dark, smoldering look clouded her brother's face. "You were discussing my *personal* affairs with *Dad?"*

"Well, if you are having an affair with that girl, I'll bet she's just a diversion."

"Petunia! I *am not* having an affair, and even if I was, it's not any business of yours." His eyes blazed. *"And* certainly not up for discussion, especially with Dad!"

"*I* didn't bring it up."

"Now you've done it, Bigmouth."

"Who *did?"* His eyes bored into hers.

"You are in the drink now."

"Lily's uncle asked about the girl."

"Just who was in on this discussion?"

"You're past the point of no return. Now who's the genius?"

Uh oh. If looks could kill—she whimpered, "Papa, Mum, Audie, Lily's uncle. We were talking about how you feel about Lily and—"

"Why were you *all* discussing me?" The veins stood out in livid ridges along his temple and throat.

"We-ll, I said you loved her."

Slamming his left hand down hard on the newel he winced, his face contorted, and he snarled. "How I feel about Lily is a subject for conversation with *everyone,* including her uncle?"

"We-ll, Audie said that women are more aware of the affairs of the heart than men."

"*You are not getting out of this predicament, numbskull.*"

Hugh's face glowed scarlet, his eyes flashed. "What is it about all you women thinking you know how a chap feels before he even knows himself?"

"Hughie?"

"*Enough!*" He stormed up the stairs.

Phila stood there, staring after him. *It can't be possible, he doesn't know.*

❋ ❋ ❋

Hugh stomped down the hall to his room, slamming the door. He bent over, holding his left hand with his right, putting them between his knees. He stayed in that position until the pain lessened a bit.

"Damn it, Petunia," he yelled at the door, "you aren't making this any easier. When will you stay out of other people's lives and *shut up?*" He sank down in his old brown leather chair by the window in the small sitting room off the bedroom, nursing his hand.

For a long time, he sat there in the dark. *When will that busybody stop pushing? This was all new to him, looking at Lily other than as a sister. Has it been there all along? What had Lily's uncle said about never finding a woman who could compare to his brother's wife?*

"Is *that* why *you* never married?"

He stared into the blackness, but it offered no answers.

"*What, were you waiting for her to grow up?*"

The heavens opened. Light blazed, blotting out the darkness.

Yes! The answer is *yes!*

"*About time you woke up Genius. Didn't Aristotle write that 'Knowing yourself is the beginning of all wisdom'?*"

"Enough of this!" He shot up, trooped downstairs, and out the back door, striding by the cottage and out onto the alley. *This was new territory, indeed. Should I say something to her?*

"*Face it, Genius, you're thinking like the male animal you are, ruled by your natural cravings instead of human compassion. Thought you were above that, didn't you?*"

Guilt trumped pride.

I'm a blackguard. She's still grieving. Although it appeared she had pushed it aside for the moment. Could she even comprehend a relationship other than of siblings?

He started back toward the house but stopped and turned. There were lights inside the cottage. He knocked on the door.

"Yes?"

"Lily, it's Hugh. May I come in for a few minutes?"

She opened the door, wearing a dressing gown. "It's a mess." Unpacked boxes and cases and pieces of clothing littered the tiny sitting area. She cleared some things away from a couple of chairs then walked into the bedroom and closed the door.

Now that he was there, he didn't know what to say. Could she hear his heart beating?

"So why are you here, Genius?"

She returned, wearing slacks and a jumper. "I'm trying to decide what to wear Monday for my first day at Hartnell's. We females fret about clobber like that. What did you do to your hand? It's frightfully red and swollen."

"Oh, this? I hit it on the banister. It's nothing." He ignored the throbbing. "I'm certain you will look lovely as usual."

"Of course, you'd say that. But the receptionist, the tour guide, and the salesgirls were all dressed in style. My clothes are not stylish."

"You've lucked out for the moment. She's doing the talking."

"I would venture to say that you will have a fine wardrobe in short order."

"You are so sweet, Hughie."

"Sweet? That ought to warm the cockles of your heart."

"Did you want something special?"

"Think fast, Genius."

"It's going to be so rushed in the morning, I just wanted to tell you how proud I am of you securing this job. What a promising opportunity it is for you. I know you will outdo yourself."

"Pretty good save, Commander."

"You think so?"

"I know so." He rose. "Now you need your beauty sleep, and I need to pack up."

"Coward! You're going to leave without a word of truth, aren't you?"

"Ah—"

Her eyes glinted bewitching him. "Yes?"

He stepped back close to her, gazing into her eyes. "Lily, I love you. I—"

"I know you do. And it's so comforting." She gazed up at him, blinking.

"Comforting?"

"I want to take care of you—"

"But, Hughie, *I* want to take care of myself. I love that all of you want to look after me. But, I've *got* to do it myself."

Why don't you just blast me out of the water, Lily?

"See the HMS Hope list deep on one side. Will it capsize altogether?"

"Good night, Lily dear."

"Weigh anchor, Commander, and put out to sea."

CHAPTER 38

VOICES OF FEAR

"What do you fear, my lady?" Aragorn asked.
"A cage," Eowyn said. "To stay behind bars, until use and old age accept them, and all chance of doing great deeds is gone beyond recall or desire."

Lord of the Rings: The Two Towers,
J. R. R. Tolkien

Lily stood at the door of the cottage for a long time after Hugh said good night. He seemed so sad when he left. Did he really think she couldn't do it on her own? Fear replaced her resolve of the last few days. For someone who yearned to make her own way, she realized she had come to depend too much on Phila and her family. Also, the servants.
"Well, let's just see how you do on your own."
She looked around the sitting room. No one was there.
"You actually think you have enough talent to make it at the Queen's couturier's?"
Fear charged the air.
"Oh, go away!" Lily started to cry.
Guilt stabbed. *"You don't deserve to succeed."*
"Go away."
"Away? I'm your deepest thoughts. I won't go away."
She sobbed.
A knock on the door.
"Hughie, I can't talk now."
"It's Bea, Lily."
Oh dear. "Coming." She dabbed her eyes with a handkerchief and blew her nose.

Lady Beatrice stood there, her eyes full of compassion. "My dear, you've been crying." Phila's mum steered Lily to the loveseat. "Please tell me what's troubling you?"

Lily started shaking and sobbing and fell into her ladyship's welcoming arms. "'Fraid. So afraid." Waves of panic and dread washed over her as she dissolved into the warm embrace.

Phila's mum held her tight without a word.

Finally, Lily's sobs turned into gulps for air, and slowly she regained her composure. "S-sor-ry."

"No need. A good cry always helps." Her ladyship smoothed Lily's damp hair back and dried her face with a handkerchief. They sat there for a long time, neither speaking.

Lily wanted so much to confide in this dear woman.

"Are you going to air your dirty laundry? Tattle about your fears?"

Shame threatened to silence her. She shook her head and whispered, "Won't go away."

"Are they the voices inside your head, child?"

Her head shot up. Those kind eyes pierced her heart. Feeling naked, she covered her face with her hands, turning away.

"No, darling, don't look away." The dear lady pulled Lily's hands down and placed hers on either side of her face. "They are like someone else's voice, but come from inside your head?"

"Uh huh. So frightening. Won't let me alone."

"Those thoughts are from the enemy." Her mouth pursed but her eyes gleamed.

"No, they are from the wicked part of me."

"Oh, child. We all have them." Now a smile appeared.

"Not *you*, milady."

"Yes, me. Voices of doubt, fear, spite."

No. Phila's mum was the most loving person. She never said a bad word against anyone. She wasn't cross and always so patient with Hugh and Phil. "Can't believe that."

"Oh, yes. When I was first seeing Henry, there was this girl who was throwing herself at him. 'Scratch out the hussy's eyes,' hissed the voice."

A guffaw escaped Lily. She couldn't picture the Earl and Countess as young people in love.

"*'Please bombs, fall on the Napier-Joneses,'* the voice whispered in a vile tone."

"No!" This time a full-throated snicker erupted.

"Oh, the hateful things I've come up with to punish Lady N-J for her arrogance and Jacquie for hurting you. I can't repeat those awful hopes of mine." Her ladyship laughed now, and Lily joined her.

"You won't tell?"

"No, milady."

"And I won't repeat what you tell me either. It will get it off your conscience and give you power over those notions."

Lily felt her resolve melting. "I was so wicked to go against Father and refuse to go on the trip. God is punishing me." Now it all tumbled out like a gushing waterfall. "I don't deserve to be happy. They came home early just for me. God is dangling a carrot in front of me, and then He'll whisk it away. I'll fail miserably and never realize my dream."

"Lily. Look at me. I'm sure your father was disappointed, yes, but God wouldn't punish you for not going."

"Then why?"

"I don't know. I do know God did not cause the wreck. He did, however, allow it. For what purpose, we'll never know this side of heaven. But He will bring good out of that evil. He always does."

"But why must evil happen?"

"Child, I haven't an answer for your question, but I'm certain God has thoughts toward you—thoughts of peace and not evil—thoughts of a future and of hope."

"That sounds familiar."

"It's from the book of Jeremiah. He says we are to work for the welfare of where we are sent and pray for it. So, if you do your utmost in your new position and work for Hartnell's success, you will succeed. Phila would say 'the sad prophet according to Mum.'"

"Father always recited word-for-word from the King James."

"He was correct, but a little paraphrase can't hurt. God speaks in many ways."

Lily gave a half-hearted smile.

"I think the Lord would have you know that He will listen if you call and pray. But my dear, you will need to seek after Him with all your heart. This may be hard now, but I promise if you do, you will find Him—and the peace you crave."

Lily wanted to believe it. But God had a lot to make up for.

"Meanwhile, we need to come up with a strategy to combat these attacks of the enemy." She stroked Lily's hair as she closed her eyes.

"Prepare yourself for the battle, my dear, beforehand. And it *is* a battle. The enemy is firing thoughts of guilt, failure, hate, revenge, and rebellion at you."

How did her ladyship know?

"Prayer first thing in the morning is your best protection, as I'm sure your parents counseled. By putting on God's amour—wielding the shield of faith and the sword of the Spirit, God's Word—you will be ready to repel those accusing voices. The Lord will be a shield about you and the One who lifts your head."

"Oh, that old litany?"

"I know you already know this."

Lily nodded, but a lot of good it would do her. Even though those verses were engraved in her mind, they hadn't helped her family.

"Resist the devil and he will flee."

Resolve welled up within her, and she knew that she would stand up to future bombardments. But all the armor she needed was a resolute will. She'd do it in her own power. She didn't need God. She would defeat the voices of Fear on her own.

Sunday, 11 January
The Lion and Lamb, Oxford

Ollie walked in the pub and up to the bar and ordered a pint. As his eyes adjusted to the dim light, he noticed two men seated at a table by the fireplace. One with thinning dark hair and rumpled clothing, the other fair-haired in a jacket and bright blue vest. They waved him over.

"Good afternoon Mr. Lewis and Professor Tolkien."

"Mr. Ogilvie," said Mr. Lewis, "back for another term, are you? Did you enjoy your holiday?"

"Aye, I did for the most part, sir, especially hunting up in Aberdeenshire. And some serious reading, *Spirits in Bondage* and *The Problem of Pain*." Then he turned his smile to the other man. "And delightful reading with *Leaf of Niggle* and *Farmer Giles of Ham*, Professor Tolkien. Och, and 'Sir Gawain and the Green Knight' for your lecture on the poem this term."

"I say, did you shoot any dragons on your hunt like Farmer Giles, Mr. Ogilvie?" A sly smile slipped across the professor's face like he could read Ollie's mind. He can't know about *my* personal dragon.

The professor rose. "Well, Jack, I must leave you. Until Tuesday at the Bird and Baby. I want to hear what you've done with this next Narnia book. About a voyage, is it?" Mr. Lewis nodded as his friend departed.

"Sit down Mr. Ogilvie. Tollers doesn't always approve of my more serious stuff since I'm not a trained cleric, and he thinks my Narnia tales perhaps too flippant. Roman Catholic, you know, they're sticklers for protocol." He chuckled. "Now the saga he's been penning for a decade strikes me like lightening out of a clear sky."

"Apparently an epic sequel of *The Hobbit*. I look forward to reading it. A story for adults, he says. May I fetch ye a pint, sir?"

"Thank you."

Ollie collected two pints, handing one to his Literature tutor.

"I was only twenty and just back from World War I, and an agnostic, when I wrote *Spirits in Bondage*. Combined with *The Problem of Pain*, makes me wonder if you're having difficulty putting your war experiences behind you?" Ollie looked down.

"You don't want to talk about it." Ollie nodded. "Oh, I do understand. Few, who have lived through war, want to remember, much less speak of it. I was engaged in the war for barely a year before being wounded and sent home. Tollers' enlistment was short due to his contracting trench fever. But he lived through the Battle of the Somme. You probably know that 20,000 of our men fell that first day."

"Aye, sir."

"But still our service was brief and our maladies mild. I still can't fathom why he and I were spared. You, on the other hand, must have lived a lifetime."

"Three years, sir."

"North Africa, Normandy, Germany, I understand. And, the Victoria Cross. I'm honored to know you, Mr. Ogilvie."

"Sir?" Ollie gaped. "How?" Heat rose up his neck to face and ears.

A curious smile bloomed on the don's face. "Does it matter? And, it is not sinning to be proud of that, my boy."

Ollie took a long pull on his ale. Who? Of course. Hornsworth. Just like a wumman, canna keep a secret. The next time I see Percy, I'll give him a pasting.

Mr. Lewis gazed down at his flagon. "That first 'modern' war slaughtered not only men but our innocence, faith, and our tradition of heroism. That war was supposed to be the war to end all wars, instead it devastated Europe, killing hope for a generation and laying the foundation for an even more disastrous war — yours.

"My memories of my six months in the trenches haunted my dreams for years." His keen eyes pierced Ollie's. "They will *ebb* in time, but now you feel like they are carved into your soul for eternity. Both Tollers and I lost most of our close friends in that war. Our battle experiences show up in our work in one form or another. You'll see that in Tollers' new *Hobbit*. So sad that too many writers of our generation have repudiated God and the Bible, permeating their works with guilt, sorrow, doubt, and disillusionment. Tollers and I aim to foster a vision of hope and we are of the opinion that fantasy is a splendid way to accomplish this."

"Fairy stories, sir?"

"Yes, as a matter of fact, Tollers gave a lecture in '39 exploring the nature of fantasy and the cultural role of fairy tales. He argued that there is no such thing as writing for children. I believe he has an essay on the subject somewhere. Ask him for it. You've read *The Hobbit* of course?"

"Oh, aye."

"You might revisit it and discern for yourself if it's just for children. Myths can open the heart's back door when the front door is locked. When the veil of the familiar is lifted in Fantasy it reveals a glimpse of underlying reality or truth. You're never too grown up for a good story, dear boy."

"Point taken, sir."

"Mr. Ogilvie, I don't wish to minimize your struggle. But you are not alone. You have a powerful ally to guide you through. In Tollers' new *Hobbit* there is a great deal of hand-to-hand combat. His heroes wield swords with mighty names and magical powers. But then don't we — as soldiers of Christ — battle one-on-one against powers and principalities? Yet, do we not wield the living powerful Sword of the Spirit — the Word of God?"

"Speaking of powerful arguments, Mr. Lewis. Thank you."

CHAPTER 39

GOODBYES

Parting is such sweet sorrow.
Romeo and Juliet, William Shakespeare

11 January
The Havens
Lily entered the breakfast room at half six.

Phila rose. "Lil, so glad you made it in time. I'm off to take Hughie for his flight." She gave her friend a big hug.

"Phil?" Tears gathered in her eyes.

"Yes?"

"I will never be able to thank you for being here for me." Lily clung to Phila. "I couldn't have managed without you and your parents."

"We love you."

"I know, and I'm so grateful for everything."

"It was nothing." Phila cast her eyes down.

"No, it was *everything*." Lily hugged her.

Phila beamed. "Euripides said that friends show their love in times of trouble, not in happiness."

"Who?" Lily's forehead creased.

"An ancient Greek playwright."

Of course. "Well, he was right." Lily stifled a sob. "I was so alone. And then when Uncle Gordy went back to Egypt, I thought I would die."

"Dash it all, Lil, it made me think of someone other than myself."

"But you missed so much of your term at university—to stay with me."

"St Hilda's managed without me boarding. There is no way I could have left you. I still met with my tutor and attended lectures." Her face lit up and she giggled. "Oh, I forgot to tell you about this bloke I've caught looking at me, quite often, actually."

"Reeeally? What's he like?"

"The biggest chap I've ever seen. Way taller than my brother and older like Hughie, red hair like mine, intriguing green eyes though and a shy smile, deep voice—Scottish burr, always sits in the back. He acted interested but has never said anything."

"I hope this term makes up for all you sacrificed. Will you see him?"

"I expect so in Professor Tolkien's and Mr. Lewis's lectures."

"O-o-o-o, a prospect." cooed Lily.

"A towering *red*head? Me?"

"What? He doesn't meet your specifications for Prince Charming?"

"Prince Charmings are *always* handsome, he's—"

"Petunia!" Hugh's harsh voice cut in. "I'm ready." He popped his head in. He sounded angry. What's that about?

But then his glare melted into a beaming smile. "Lily, my dear, come and say good-bye."

"*Good-bye.*" Fear squeezed her heart.

A real dryness loomed ahead—alone. She dashed into Hugh's arms, his embrace a welcome, comforting blanket.

He leaned back to look at her. "Goodness me, Lily, I'm not going to my death, only to America. I shall return."

She loosened her hold on him. "It's, it's just everything is so—different."

"Buck up, ole girl. Here I thought you were tendering your undying affection, and all you're doing is telling me I'm comfortable."

She looked up and thought for just a moment she saw hurt in his eyes, then resolve. He cupped her chin and gave her a peck on the forehead like always. Then, as though he had forgotten something, he kissed her gently on the mouth and studied her face briefly.

Odd. She flung her arms around his neck and gave him a big smack on the cheek.

"Will you look at this?" Phila bounded back into the room. "Shall I leave?"

"No need. Cheers, Lily." Hugh traipsed out.

"Lil promise you'll come soon to Oxford for a visit."

Then they were gone.

"*Now you're really on your own,*" Loneliness laughed.

※ ※ ※

Phila followed Hugh out. His shoulders were so taut, it unnerved her. Anger radiated, not explosive like last night, but frigid. She couldn't recall a time when she'd seen him so irate.

János brought his coup around and helped Phila in.

"Hughie, I am *so sorry*."

"Please, don't talk." He slipped in and stared forward, his face set, his jaw working.

After what seemed like an eternity, Phila couldn't stand it anymore. "I am so very sorry, really."

"You're always sorry." He still didn't look at her. "I will allow you to drive me to the airport if you keep still and let me talk. Or I will get out and call a taxi."

For several miles, Hugh looked straight ahead, not saying a word. Phila threaded the car through London traffic, almost hitting a lorry.

"Hang on, Petunia, I'd like to live a while longer. And this *is* my car."

"Sorry."

"Philomena, you've been told again and again that you have to learn to hold your tongue. Running off at the mouth can cause trouble for yourself and others."

Here we go—another lecture. "Uh huh."

"Have you no clue that your discussing me and my sentiments with the family and Lily's uncle causes me considerable embarrassment."

"I am so sor-ry."

"*Sorry* is a nice word, Petunia, but it's just a word. And words are your problem."

She concentrated on her driving. Of course, the proud Mr. Proper Pomposity would be mortified. His image was paramount to him. Resentment welled up inside her. And, of course, he couldn't bring himself to even say the word "feelings."

He remained quiet for a while. She dared not say a thing. She could hear him breathing. Finally, he took a long deep breath and let it out slowly.

"This is difficult for me to say—you're doing that caused me great discomfort."

"I hurt you?" Of course, he hadn't used the word *hurt*. But still.

"I would like to think that as my sister you love me enough to consider my sentiments—OK, my *feelings*—so as not to broadcast them. Can you do that in the future, please, Pet?"

She braked just in time to miss bumping the auto in front. He actually used *the word*. Suddenly she realized that he had invited her into his soul, to see and feel with him. What a new sensation.

She stopped at a signal. He looked down at her. Love had replaced the anger in his eyes, and he was smiling.

"Hughie, I do love you."

"I know." He put his hand on her shoulder.

It was then that she noticed how swollen it was. "Hughie, your hand!"

He withdrew it. "It's nothing. But can you concentrate on using that brilliant mind of yours to *think* before you open your sweet mouth in the future? Put your words in action?"

"I will try." He *was* right, of course.

The light changed. She pressed on the accelerator.

"This is important. Pet, please listen." He tugged on one of her curls. "Let me be the one to choose if I speak about my personal life, and if I want to tell you about my work, I will. Otherwise, keep your imagination to yourself and be discrete. Agreed?"

"Aye, aye, Commander."

"Good girl."

As Hugh waved good-bye, his parting words were, "Drive carefully."

The most exasperating, irritating, insufferable, beloved sibling a girl could have. And she *would* try harder, because she did love him.

As she pulled away from the curb she saw a couple kissing. Hugh had given Lily a peck on the forehead, then a kiss on the lips. If she were writing their story, she would have had Hugh pick up Lily and carry her off to America with him. It would be the Cinderella story—the future Earl of Wembley and the vicar's daughter.

And they all laugh at me for liking fiction. Why can't real life be more like make-believe?

No Cold War bombs. No tragic train crashes. No young people dying before their time. And, in her dreams, she would be beautiful like Lily. Real life wasn't fair.

She chafed at her friend. Here she has a bona fide Prince Charming who loves her, and she sends him away without any hope. And you?

Phila shook her head then braked hard, barely missing a car turning in front of her.

"I'm left with naught." Nary a ring from any of the men at the ball. She half expected Todd Thorndike might call. Both Jacquie and Tansy had stared murderously when he danced with her. She had gazed back at them triumphantly. For all the good it had done. Dash it all.

Speaking of naught, it was Naught Week at Oxford.

"What do you expect from *the other place* but a *nothing* week before term actually begins," Hugh often teased.

Maybe she would just show him. Maybe she would meet her Prince Charming this week before term began. And her supercilious sibling would be shamed. Plain, pudgy Phila would bring home a prince.

He would be taller than Hugh—though six-two was hard to beat—handsomer than Todd, the son of a duke like Percy Hornsworth, and a hero like her Uncle Lindy, but alive, of course. He would fall madly in love with her. And, they would marry and live happily ever after.

"Asking a lot, aren't you?"

No! she most certainly did not think so.

Impatient honking brought her back to reality. She thrust down on the accelerator and the coupe jumped. Right, shift. More honks. "Oh, put a sock in it!"

THE END
(for now?)

DISCUSSION QUESTIONS

What are the voices influencing *your* choices? Or should I say *who* are those voices?

Those voices have names. You've met them in this book. But are they *fiction*? You've heard from them just as my characters have, don't deny it.

That thought that flashed in your mind so vile you will never share it with another human being, even a priest in confession. Where did it come from? *Can you smell the sulfur?* Don't worry, you don't have to share that one.

"Oh, that's silly," you say. "You're just using the voices as a plot device." Am I?

Of course, you've never entertained Self-Pity's whining, have you, like dear Danny boy who was robbed of his dream by fate, or good looks like Phila? *Ah, the sorrowful strings of a violin.*

Or desired Recognition so much you could taste it like Hugh? *Is your mouth watering?*

Ridicule's sneers have never undermined your self-confidence like poor Ollie, right? *There go your dreams smashed against the rocks again?*

And who can fend off Sarcasm when she feels so right? *Hear the hiss of the snake?*

Does Guilt hound you like it does Ollie? *Do you feel the weight bearing down on your shoulders?*

Have you been beguiled by Ambition and Rebellion like Lily? Or puffed up by Pride? *Oh, those seventh heaven feelings.*

Does Spite and Envy tickle your brain and Desire drive you forward like Phila? *Is there a faint cackling in the background?*

※ ※ ※

These are just a few questions to get you thinking and recognizing the voices shouting at you from the father of lies.

Don't allow them to drown out the whispers from your Heavenly Father and the souls who love you.

The more you know about these conflicting inner voices inside your heads the better you will be able to discern where they're coming from and repel the malicious ones and welcome the heavenly ones.

For more on the subject go to **NanRinella.org**. Learn more about the voices from people who know how to defeat or welcome them. You'll have an opportunity to share your struggles and solutions. Let's start the discussion.

It's our choice, who will we listen to?

ACKNOWLEDGEMENTS

A writer once said writing a book is like birthing a baby. Of course, it had to have been a woman. But women do not bring new creations into being alone. For *Dreams in the Distance* to come to life, God planted a seed to grow in me. A few people shone light and warmth into it. Others rained their blessings and encouragement, and some nourished its creation with their help, contributions, and prayers. Gardeners pruned and weeded, and harvesters delivered this baby, then cleaned her up and wrapped her in a pretty package to present to the world.

A detailed account of these beautiful souls is found on my website: NanRinella.org. Also, a complete bibliography. A brief account here will suffice. Most of all I thank my muse, the Holy Spirit, for His inspiration & Jesus for being with me every step of the way, along with:

My favorite partner and military consultant:
Lieutenant Colonel Joseph Rinella, US Air Force, retired

Gardeners:
Editors Patti Townley-Covert & Karen Ball
Critique partners of the early years: Harry Haines, Stan Cosby, Diane Neal, Janda Raker, Bettie Haller, Linda Hill, Pam Kessler
British researcher & poetry contributor: Honor Clare Parkinson
Consultant & poetry contributor: Kirk Manton

Rain:
Sister-in-laws Karin Rinella & Cindy Rinella, & neighbor Tomi Lowe
The C. S. Lewis Foundation colleagues: President J. Stanley Mattson & Jean Mattson, V.P., Steven Elmore, Scott & Mary Key, Lancia E. Smith
Lewis scholars: Dr. Diana Pavlac Glyer, Dr. David C. Downing, Dr. Devin Brown, Dr. Louis Markos, Colin Duriez,
Dr. Robert L. Waggoner, Author of *Christianity or Humanism: Which Will You Choose?*
Lieutenant Colonel Bernie Ellrodt, USAF, retired, Fighter Pilot, Vietnam,
Lieutenant Colonel Pete Barnes, USAF, retired, Fighter Pilot, Vietnam

Sun:
Literary agent Steve Laube
Harvest House Editor Terry W. Glaspey

Nourishers:
Award-winning journalist Carolyn Curtis
Authors & novel workshop instructors Angela Hunt & DiAnn Mills

Harvesters:
Book cover designer Trif Paul of Twin Art Design
Book designer Jonathan Price of Jonathan Price Design

A heartfelt tribute to the WWII Scottish soldiers of the Seaforth Highlanders and British servicemen awarded the Victoria Cross.

ABOUT THE AUTHOR

Nan Rinella is a Hobbit in Narnia. Her research of all things C. S. Lewis and J. R. R. Tolkien has taken her to Narnia for seminars at C. S. Lewis's home, The Kilns, and to London, Oxford, and Cambridge. She's also met leprechauns in Ireland and angels in the Scottish Highlands. Well, she *did* kiss the Blarney Stone in Ireland, which endows the kisser with the gift of gab and eloquence, and a generous helping of blarney.

A writer, speaker, and journalist for the last 28 years, Nan is a regional representative for the C. S. Lewis Foundation, working alongside of other hobbits and elves. She's directed their Texas conferences and assisted with events such as their tri-annual "Oxbridge" Summer Institute at Oxford and Cambridge. In 2009 she introduced a writers workshop to their events.

Nan's written more than 200 articles for publications such as *Focus on the Family Magazine*, *Human Events*, *Consumer Research*, and *Daily Devotions for Writers*. A National Journalism Center senior fellow, who interned with *Human Events* in Washington, D.C., Nan's a graduate of Bible Study Fellowship and Christian Leaders, Authors & Speakers Services Seminar and Personality Training Workshop.

An aficionado of historical, suspense, and supernatural fiction, Nan revels in these subjects. Her favorite topics to write and speak about are writing, travel, networking, personalities, inspirational subjects, and C. S. Lewis and J. R. R. Tolkien. Her website "Nan Rinella: Listen for the ONE" (see NanRinella.org) focuses on the Voices that influence your Choices, as introduced in THE CHOICE. This dramatic series begins with Book I,

Dreams in the Distance and continues with soon-to-be released Book II, *Hope on the Horizon*. Her website also offers additional info on C. S. Lewis & J. R. R. Tolkien, and *The Turquoise Traveler: Tips & Tricks for Globe-Trotting Women* from her nonfiction book, *Smart Steps for Safe Travel*, written after 9/11.

On the board of directors of Panhandle Professional Writers, now Texas High Plains Writers, for fourteen years, Nan has directed many writers' conferences.

Born in Hollywood, California, Nan resided in Los Angeles for many years. A former flight attendant for United Airlines, she flew the Hawaii route. As a military wife and Military Airlift Command crewmember flying troops to and from Vietnam, Nan has a heart for US and UK servicemen and women, and WWII and Vietnam veterans. She and husband, Lt. Col. Joe Rinella, USAF, retired, were based in Hawaii for four years. Having traveled extensively, she especially enjoys exploring in Scotland, Ireland, London, Oxford, and Cambridge.

A civilian job for Joe moved the Rinellas to Amarillo, Texas in 1991. Now he is retired. Their son, Ryan and his wife live in Dallas with their 4-year-old daughter. Nan continues creating THE CHOICE series with such great enthusiasm that she can hardly wait to discover what happens next.

THE CHOICE
THE SERIES

Coming Soon

Keep your heart open to dreams.
For as long as there's a dream, there is hope,
and as long as there is hope,
there is joy in living.
— Unknown Author

"The Cloister" Oxford *Image by Jonathan Kirkpatrick*

HOPE ON THE HORIZON

BOOK TWO

NAN RINELLA

CPSIA information can be obtained
at www.ICGtesting.com
Printed in the USA
BVHW071420110319
542310BV00012B/1317/P